MW00585952

A CHILD ALONE
WITH STRANGERS

A CHILD ALONE
WITH STRANGERS

A NOVEL

PHILIP FRACASSI

TALOS PRESS

Talos Press books may be purchased in bulk at special discounts for sales promotion, corporate gifts, fund-raising, or educational purposes. Special editions can also be created to specifications. For details, contact the Special Sales Department, Talos Press, 307 West 36th Street, 11th Floor, New York, NY 10018 or info@skyhorsepublishing.com.

Talos Press is an imprint of Skyhorse Publishing, Inc.®, a Delaware corporation.

Visit our website at www.talospress.com.

10 9 8 7 6 5 4 3 2 1

Library of Congress Cataloging-in-Publication Data is available on file.

Cover design by Claudia Noble

Print ISBN: 978-1-945863-74-5
Ebook ISBN 978-1-945863-75-2

Printed in the United States of America

There were humans long before there was history.
                    —*Yuval Noah Harari*

The primitives and ancients evidently had relied greatly on the strange occur-
rences that would today be called psychic in forming their concepts of man,
his spiritual make-up, and his powers over nature.
                    —*J. B. Rhine*

And you can see the daisies in her footsteps . . .
Dandelions! Butterflies!
                    —*Ben Folds Five*

A CHILD ALONE
WITH STRANGERS

Prologue: The Dead Man

The dead man was collecting flies.

When the creature returned from gathering, it found the pupa wiggling weakly on the floor, covered in bits of tissue and blood. The man's hands and feet remained spread, stuck to the walls and dirt, but his teeth were spilled down his chin and chest, the matter from inside his head a sodden heap in his lap; his piss-stained clothes and chemical-tinged sweat filled the stale air, mixed with the stench of mud and saliva. His head had burst like a flower; the larva had grown too large and split his skull through the forehead. Now the body would rot before the child came, spoiling the meat that would have fed it in those first crucial days.

Hastily, the creature bundled up the exposed pupa and covered it with the armful of sodden leaves it had gathered, providing the unborn the first layers of a protective shell. As it worked it chittered, repeating the same pattern again and again, like a prayer, or an incantation.

The buzzing of flies ceased as they lifted from the corpse and flew up and out the open cellar door, into the dying day. After a few moments, the room was still and quiet.

Ceasing its patter, the dark sharp-angled figure, bone-thin and animated in the shadows of the dim root cellar, spat more of the fluid into its palms, coarse and grooved as tree bark. Slippery as spilled ink in the subterranean gray light, the creature pressed and patted more of the gelatinous saliva against the chrysalis of mud, leaves, and debris, the excretion bubbling momentarily before drying quickly into a tough gray paste.

The long, misshapen cocoon was tucked against the roughly mortared brick wall, high up and away from the room's puddle-ridden dirt floor. A moss-hued window let through enough sunlight to provide the unborn with the nutrients it needed while in embryo.

While the larva grew, it would hunt; prepare for the birth, its release from the crude shelter into a strange new world.

It would be hungry.

As she worked, the thin mouth beneath the creature's muddy yellow eyes stretched, creasing the leather-like texture of her face. A hitched, phlegmy cough came from her throat, emitting hot, sour air and a sound neither human nor animal.

A joyous sound.

The sound of a mother's love.

PART ONE: JACK CATCHES THE BUS

1

Sometimes good people did bad things.

Only nine years old, Henry Thorne hadn't yet learned this valuable life lesson. But he would. He would learn it on a mild summer day in 1995 in the most horrible way possible.

Henry waited patiently as his father Jack locked the front door of the apartment, a downgrade from the house in Lemon Grove. Henry hated that the apartment didn't have a backyard, but it was only the two of them now. Dad said their old place had too much space, had cost too much money.

His father lowered his hand for Henry to hold as they walked along the open-air balcony toward the stairs.

Henry studied the hand, thought of all the change he and his father had been through. All they'd lost. Even Blink hadn't made the trip to Grantville, which was, for Henry, even worse than the loss of the backyard. Dad had explained that the new apartment didn't allow kitties, dogs, or any other animals. The day they dropped off Blink—an orange male tabby with a bad paw and ten years under his neutered belt—at the shelter, his dad offered to get him a bird, or a turtle, from the pet store. Henry had declined, not seeing the point of it. Birds and turtles didn't purr, and they weren't furry, and they didn't sleep on your legs at night.

They had been in the apartment almost a year. Henry had been forced to transfer to a new elementary school, but he didn't mind. He didn't have many friends at his old school to begin with. Nothing lost, nothing gained. His teachers had loved him, though, mainly because he was smart. He was *advanced*. But kids didn't care about how smart you were. They wanted you to be funny and know about all the new video games, to play as good as they played at recess.

Henry sighed inwardly—an old man's hidden sigh of regret and loss, contained and handled with wisdom—and reached up to clutch his daddy's offered hand.

Fingers wedged into that warm palm, Henry looked up and smiled his best smile, tried to read his dad's face. But he looked straight ahead, a giant figurehead of safety, of love.

Together, wordlessly, they went down the flight of stairs to the sidewalk. Henry reached his other hand over, clutched a couple of his dad's thick fingers and gripped playfully, hoping to be lifted into the air, to be swung up and over the sidewalk. His daddy used to do that to him all the time, but maybe he was getting too big now. Too heavy. The kids at his old school called him chubby, and he hated it. But Henry was small for his age (despite a minor case of potbelly), and knew his dad could lift him as easily as raising his own arm. For a moment, Henry thought he felt a tug, and smiled in anticipation of being raised from the ground—to *fly*—to have his heart warmed, the way it always used to feel when they played together.

But the arm slackened, leaving Henry's feet on the pavement, and they continued to walk toward the street corner.

It didn't matter, Henry's mood could not be deterred. He was supposed to be in school today but was skipping to be with Dad. It was "Take Your Child to Work" at the office, and he'd be able to sit with him and watch him work, maybe even help. Dad was an accountant, someone who took care of folks' money for them, helped them with their taxes.

He had taken a bunch of time off when Mom died. Months. They'd sold the house, packed all their stuff, all the toys and things he'd collected over the years—his posters of outer space, his collection of action figures, his books . . . everything. Even his bed had been put onto a truck and taken to the new place. The apartment. The movers had put everything back like it had been in his old room, except some stuff didn't fit right, and his favorite lamp broke—the one with the horses—but Dad promised to buy him a new one. He never did, but Henry didn't say anything.

It was hard for his dad to be happy since Mom left them. He never laughed, hardly ever played. At one point he had gotten sick and Henry had stayed with his godfather, Uncle Dave, and his wife, Aunt Mary, for a while. They also lived in San Diego, but in a better part. Aunt Mary wasn't always nice, and her skin was different than his; more white. She was Asian, not black like Uncle Dave and Dad, Henry, and Mom. Henry didn't care about that, he just didn't think she was as fun as Dave, at least not all the time. Uncle Dave was cool, and always brought Henry a toy when he came over. Henry loved Uncle Dave. Not as much as his daddy or his mom, but he did love him. Uncle Dave would always come into his room without knocking and yell, "Where's that boy!" real loud, and Henry would always laugh and jump onto his bed, hide under a pillow, and wait for Uncle Dave to come get him, to pick him up and hug him.

Later, Uncle Dave would sit in the living room with his dad and say things like, "Okay, Jack, okay," and "I'm here to help, Jack. Let me help you, brother." One time Dad cried and Uncle Dave saw Henry watching, but didn't get mad, and didn't send him away. He just looked at him, his eyes sad, then waited for Henry's dad to stop crying so they could talk some more.

"Dad, we taking the bus, Dad?" Henry said, seeing the blue shelter on the sidewalk ahead.

"No, bud. No bus," he said. His voice was heavy, like sad but different.

"How are we getting to the office?"

"We're gonna walk. Just walk," his dad said, and Henry felt his father's fingers tighten against his own. Squeeze them.

As they walked past the blue bus stop, Henry studied the face of an old woman sitting on the bench, waiting. She smiled at Henry and he smiled back, raised one hand in a wave. Her eyes sparkled and Henry thought she was pretty. She also smelled like peanut butter, which made him hungry, and he tugged Dad's hand.

"Dad, can we eat when we get there? I'm still hungry."

His father didn't say anything, just kept walking. Walking faster now. Henry found himself skipping a bit to keep up.

"You're going too fast, Daddy," he said, but playfully, not really minding. "We're in a hurry, huh?"

"No hurry," he said, then stopped. He looked down at Henry. Not quite *at* him, though. He sort of looked ... *through* him, as if he were addressing Henry's shadow instead of Henry himself. "I don't have my job anymore, son. They took it away. You understand?"

Henry nodded, but something cold blossomed in his stomach. Adults needed their jobs, because it made them money. And money did everything. Without it, you'd be homeless and hungry.

His father shook his head, as if warding off a mosquito, then continued walking. Henry, still analyzing this new information, studying it like a strange object found in the woods, did his best to keep up. He was trying to figure how they were having "Take Your Child to Work" day if Dad didn't have a job anymore. He thought about asking, but was afraid it might upset him, or worse, make him realize their outing was a mistake and he'd take Henry straight to school instead. Henry would be late and Mrs. Foster would be annoyed. She got that way a lot when kids did stuff like mess up the workstations, or talk when they weren't supposed to, or get laughing fits. She got *annoyed*, and she'd be annoyed if Henry walked in late, that was certain. Henry kept his worries to himself.

They turned another street corner, and they were on the big road. Henry knew it was called Fletcher Avenue, because he'd memorized it. Cars were going by a lot faster, and Daddy kept walking. To another bus stop? To a new office? Henry turned the options over and over in his mind, trying to figure out where they were headed. The park? But that was the other way, down Sycamore where they lived, at the end of the street. He wondered if the lady who smelled like peanut butter had gotten onto her bus, then was distracted when a large truck roared by, the exhaust pluming into their faces. Henry put his free hand to his left ear, blocking the noise.

"It's loud, Daddy!" he yelled, tugging at his father's meaty hand.

His dad stopped walking, turned, and looked back the way they had come. He was watching something, Henry thought. Henry looked back as well, saw the bright blue bus coming around the corner a few blocks away.

"We getting on the bus?" he yelled, hearing the cries of seagulls over the noise of cars zooming past.

Jack Thorne let go of his son's hand, knelt, and looked into his eyes. Henry smiled and put one pudgy palm on his father's face.

"You won't remember this," Jack said. "You were small, barely walking. There was one time, well . . . you were reaching out for me. I was at my desk. I was tired, working. You kept reaching, reaching. I picked you up and, by accident, you knocked my drink onto my papers. A job I was doing."

Henry frowned, not remembering the incident but unhappy he'd done such a thing. "I'm sorry, Daddy."

"No!" his father said, so loud and sharp it scared him, made the skin on the back of his neck crawl. "No," he continued, stroking Henry's head. "The point is that I got mad, so mad, and I wasn't thinking. I reached out for the spill . . . you fell . . ."

Henry saw a tear slide down his dad's unshaven cheek, drip away off the cliff of his jaw. His eyes were dreamy, focused on the memory.

"I dropped you. You hit your head on the floor. You weren't hurt. Just scared, I think. We were all scared. Your mother was furious with me . . ."

Jack trailed off and he grimaced, almost a smile, at the memory. A smile filled with fresh pain, fresh doubt. "Anyway, I wanted to say I'm sorry about what I did. I'm sorry for dropping you that time. I love you, son."

"I love you too, Dad," Henry said, and his father embraced him tightly. In that moment, Henry didn't care where they were going, or the apartment, or about losing Blink or the backyard or the kids at school. Dad felt so strong and warm that Henry smiled and laid his face on the blue fabric of his work shirt, closed his eyes and smelled him. He wanted that hug to last forever, because it had been so long since he had been held just like *that*.

"I'll never leave you, son," he said.

Jack stood, Henry still wrapped firmly in his arms. Henry lifted his cheek to his dad's own, felt the smear of cold, wet tears. He started to say something back, to ask why he was crying, when they moved.

Henry opened his eyes and saw they had stepped into the street. He looked up, past his dad's shoulder, toward the vast blue sky beyond. The world spun as his father turned around, and Henry saw a blur of honking cars, the running colors of people pointing from a sidewalk, his father's rushed voice screaming into Henry's ear, "Don't watch!"

Henry's bladder emptied into his jeans and he screamed as he saw the bus bearing down on them, its horn blaring. He struggled for a split second against his father's viselike hold; instincts surged and he pushed hard as he could to get *away*. There was a mechanical roar and a crunching thud and then Henry was flying. He heard the seagulls scream or was it a woman's scream and he wanted to scream, too, but he had no breath in him.

Something large and heavy drove itself into his small body and the world went black.

2

Henry's mind woke, and sound poured in.

Voices. Some yelling. Scared. Crying. Someone was saying, "Oh my God, oh my God," over and over again. A woman's voice. Hysterical. A horn blared. More voices—rushed, commanding.

His dead body lifted, and the sensation of *rising* was strong, even though he felt nothing of his physical self. There was no pain. There was only *warmth*.

So wonderfully warm. Like his insides were heated with light. He *became* the warmth—lifting, lifting, higher and higher. The voices grew quiet. Distant.

He opened his eyes.

There was a flash of white light and then a busy street, a crowd of people. He was above them all, a low-flying bird. A fire truck, a giant red one. There was an ambulance and two police cars. The hot pinpricks of orange flares. Policemen yelling at cars as they went by on the road, waving at them. Henry saw the ocean, the white slivers of distant seagulls floating above.

He saw everything at the exact same time. Some part of him knew it was impossible, but it also felt *right*.

Then the world blurred to a hard white; nerve-scorching pain rushed through his body. He closed his eyes tight, wanted to cry out, to scream, but could not.

BANG!

Henry kept his eyes squeezed shut. He was scared, terribly scared. There was so much yelling. Hands tugged at his body, pulled at his limbs and he wanted to shout at them to *stop*!

BANG!

He was atop a rolling bed, the vibrations of the wheels against the floor humming into his back, his legs. He was moving fast as the wind—*flying, flying*—through chaos and noise. The pain had drifted away, somewhere far off, and he pushed it back even further, created barriers between its gnashing teeth and his flesh. He was afraid of the pain, terrified at what it was doing to his body, his mind. The pain was a beast, a *monster*, tearing away at the flimsy walls of his consciousness, desperate to reach him.

So scared get him away make him stop . . .

Then—when the pain was almost unbearable—his grateful mind flooded once more with that familiar, welcome warmth. That *peace*. He floated upward again and joy sang in his heart as everything fell away—the sounds muted, the sickening feeling of flying gone; the monster trapped in a place it could not reach him. He waited a long moment, made sure he wouldn't be locked back into that cage of chaos and pain, locked inside with the monster.

When he felt safe, felt *sure*, he slowly opened his eyes once more.

He was in a large, bright room.

His back was to the ceiling. He looked down from a high, distant corner.

Floating.

He saw people crowded around a small body. They were cutting away clothes, grabbing clumps of gauze and pressing it into bloody flesh. He moved without thinking—a *flicker*—and he was watching from over the shoulder of a large man with a hairy neck. The man wore white clothes and aggressively attached something to the body. A woman was still cutting—*snip snip snip*—then pulling off bloody pants, peeling away the rags of a blood-soaked shirt.

Henry rose higher, looked at the motionless body being jostled like a doll.

The face was his own.

He felt no alarm. No fear. No panic.

His naked figure looked frail and broken on the large bed. Tubes sprang from his arms and legs, a mask covered his face. He wanted to laugh at how silly he looked, naked in nothing but blue underpants, but he saw the fear in the grown-up faces. *Nurses and doctors*, he thought, and studied himself anew. His leg was bent strangely, and his chest, sunken above his small round belly, looked *wrong*. One man took a knife and cut into the skin covering his ribcage. A surge of blood pushed out, trailed down his skin to pool on the bed. Someone handed the man a fat tube; he slipped the end of it into the cut. Henry looked away.

"Henry!"

Flash.

A different part of the hospital. He saw his Uncle Dave and Aunt Mary. Aunt Mary was crying. Uncle Dave was yelling at a man in a suit. Why was he so angry? What was there to be angry about? Everything was so wonderful, so peaceful.

"Henry!"

The voice came again and Henry felt a renewed heat surge into his being, a *brightness*. He smiled, then laughed out loud.

He closed his eyes, overwhelmed with happiness.

Something . . . *brushed* him. It was like being touched by fire that did not burn—like having your innermost being, your *soul*, kissed and hugged, smothered by pure love. He opened his eyes.

His mother was there, waiting for him.

She was beautiful. His mind, his consciousness—his *spirit*—leapt for her and they joined, their beings twisted into each other, an embrace like no other he had ever experienced. He absorbed his mother's love—a stream of light pouring into his soul. It felt *glorious*.

"Momma," he said, and realized he was seeing her without eyes, for he no longer had eyes, or a body; no weight, no flesh hung upon him. There was no pain. No monster. Mother was a brilliant shining light filled with love. He saw her completely.

"Henry," she said, her voice a rush of warm wind. "Henry, I love you."

Then she was talking, telling him things, telling him secrets, but he didn't hear the words, only felt the vibrations of them, growing steadily, humming, shaking him. Henry's mind caught fire and he opened himself to her, to what lay *beyond* her. To what waited. His consciousness blazed like a struck match, ignited and burned to cinders, and he was wholly consumed by the power. He expanded, became part of the world that lay beyond.

A second presence. A familiar one. Comforting.

Daddy?

It slid into him like oil into blood, filled him. Henry reached for more, craved more . . .

Tug.

Something pulled at him. Like a fish nipping at food on a hook. He tried to will it away.

Tug.

Tug.

TUG.

The light was slipping, fading, and his essence contracted. His mother called to him, a goodbye. Her love frayed like ribbons, the bonds of light wrapped around his tiny spirit dissolved.

But that other thing, that *new* presence . . . it stayed. Settled somewhere deep inside, tucked itself into the crevices of his mind like a cat in a spot of sunshine.

The last of that binding light slipped free from him. Henry was let go, feeling as if he'd been dropped from a great height.

Consciousness hit him like a slap. Someone laughed. Hands tugged at his arms, legs, face. He pulled away, fought them. Hot hands, hateful hands. More laughing . . . then *pain.*

"Daddy!" There was fire, painful now, and he erupted with it and the tugging hands fell away and something grabbed his tummy and pulled him downward and his chest burned like he'd swallowed acid, his lungs *filled* with that hateful fire—

Flash.

Deep down inside, Henry screamed. Screamed because he now felt *everything.* Cold and dark. Impossibly heavy. His body, cut up and broken. *Oh no oh no oh please no!* It was too much, too much pain, too much *hurt.*

He wanted to open his mouth and wail, to reach out his arms and find his mother, find the light, but he couldn't move, couldn't breathe. His mind raced—his thoughts broke apart, shattered beneath the pain.

A distant sensation. Something slid around in his head like an eel through rocks beneath a dark stream, and then it was gone.

Hidden.

A soft finger raised one of his eyelids and he saw the world for a split second—a shadowy, blurred blast of yellows and browns. He smelled rot and decay, the stink of blood and death. So much hurt! Throbbing aches, stabbing pain. He wanted his mommy, wanted his daddy, but his body was ripped up; he was breathless and blind. Sharp points stabbed him. His mouth flexed open and something hard and cold forced itself inside, down his throat, further, further, snaking inside him. Skin was punctured and sliced. *Momma!* he cried, the plea caught in the echo chamber of his mind, *Momma, they're tearing me apart!*

The fuse box deep inside him sparked and went dead; his brain fizzled out like a snuffed candle.

He let go. Let go and fell backward, away from the pain, away from the light, backward into the dark.

It was eternal.

And then he thought no more.

3

Ten days after the accident, and less than twenty-four hours after he'd lost his job (his employer finding him culpable in the death of Jack Thorne by the combined rationale of gross negligence and the fact he was intoxicated at the time of the incident), forty-eight-year-old US BLUE bus driver Gus Rivera, single and childless, the son of Juanita and George Rivera, drove his gray Honda Civic to the Coronado Bridge just past midnight. He parked carelessly, wheels up on the pedestrian walkway. He left the engine running and stepped over the guardrail. His body fell 200 feet and struck the icy water of the San Diego Bay at approximately 70 miles per hour (18 miles per hour faster than the grill of his bus had struck Jack and Henry Thorne), the impact of which shattered his skull and broke his spine, killing him instantly.

US BLUE, wary of further negative press, and having received a potential damages estimate of ten million dollars from both their inhouse lawyers and their insurance company, quickly responded to Dave Thorne's demands with an offer of two million, along with a standard Confidential Release Agreement.

Dave accepted, and the matter, as far as US BLUE was concerned, was closed.

4

Dave was tired.

He looked down at the neat stacks of paper, each clipped and dissected with Post-It notes and marginalia decorated in his meticulous, neat writing. He wondered for the thousandth time over the last few months whether to bring a wrongful termination suit against his brother Jack's former employer, a franchised tax preparation and corporate accounting service company called Equator Financial. Now that the US BLUE suit had been settled (out of court, can you say hallelujah), Dave would have more time to possibly go after Equator. He honestly believed he had a case, and if he deposed a few of the current and former employees, including the local office manager—a fat, slippery fella named Trent Riventon—then he *knew* he'd have enough to prove Jack was let go for racially prejudicial reasons, not performance or fiscal ones, as they'd claimed at the time.

I'd like to sue Alexa Hastings while I'm at it, he thought sourly. *That racist witch.* Dave believed it was she who flicked over that first domino in the short chain of events that ultimately led to Jack's "accident." He figured the devil was warming up a nice cozy room in the absolute worst ghetto of hell for Alexa Hastings.

It was Hastings who had complained about Jack being assigned to her account, and it was she who had demanded a white accountant for her personal finances and her string of old-fashioned ice cream stores. Grandma's Habit had gone from one small store on a relatively barren corner of downtown's Gaslamp District to two, then there were three within a half-mile of each other, then four. After an infusion of cash from an angel investor, Alexa expanded Grandma's Habit to over ten locations in Southern California in the course of a few short years. All-natural ice cream made right there at the store; over one hundred toppings, mixers, syrups, and sauces. Dave himself had tried one of Grandma's classic waffle cones with pistachio, topped with slivered cashews and hot fudge, and could not argue the quality or, sadly, the massive caloric intake of each and every homemade bite. Grandma likely died a hundred pounds overweight and riddled with diabetes, based on how much sugar (all-natural or no) was packed into every loving spoonful.

What he could argue, however, was that the face behind the cherubic, smiling, pasty white visage of Grandma that hung on every storefront and blazoned every napkin was a skinny, twice-divorced former schoolteacher named Alexa Hastings. And old Alexa, schoolteacher or not, newly minted business mogul or not, was nothing more than a good old-fashioned, deep-South rooted, Confederate-flag-waving bigot.

A week after she complained to the firm about a Black man handling her enormous and incredibly complex tax burden, Jack was dismissed. That bastard Riventon had been more than happy to blame the dismissal on Jack's performance, citing that his "recent loss" had affected his job, that he wasn't able to properly perform the duties being asked of him. As if it wasn't enough for a man to lose his wife of twelve years to breast cancer, not enough to fire him because some rich racist bitch told him to or else, Riventon had to amp things up by leveraging the man's grief as his excuse; in case the poor bastard wasn't feeling horrible and guilty enough, he made him feel it was *his* fault for grieving, *his* fault for not sucking it up and doing the job he was so proud of. A job he had worked his ass off to get, finishing school while Olivia (God rest her soul) stayed home with their young son during the day and worked nights as a waitress to help make ends meet.

Yeah, Dave would love taking Alexa Hastings and Trent Riventon to court, all right. That would be sweeter than Grandma's pistachio-filled waffle cone. But for now he'd settle for attacking Equator Financial instead, along with their highly paid and prestigious New York law firm, just to see if he could squeeze a quick settlement out of them as he had with US BLUE.

Lord knew the boy would need it.

Dave pushed the papers aside, took off his reading glasses, and settled back into the stiff fabric of the hospital chair. He looked across the room at the monitors and machines, the blinking lights, the beeping sounds that he hoped meant everything was A-OK, steady as she goes. He looked at the boy lying there, so fragile and small, his body almost half the weight it had been three months ago when they'd first brought him in, his right leg and ribcage shattered, his skull cracked, his brain dangerously swollen.

But he made it, by God, he thought fiercely. He was a *fighter,* and he'd made it this far. He had lived through every surgery, every setback.

Dave watched him closely, saw his chest rising and falling. Saw the steady rhythm of his heart on the monitor, the multihued lines on another screen showing his brain activity, which was not dormant, despite the coma. In fact, it was "unusually active" according to the doctor. As if he were on the edge of a dream, about to wake up any moment.

But Henry hadn't woken up. Not yet. Not when they were burying his father. Not while Dave's firm had gone after US BLUE, claiming the driver had been negligent and getting a lightning-quick settlement, things being hastened by an unforeseen break when Dave got word the bus driver had failed a sobriety test, blowing three times the legal limit. The bastard even had a flask of vodka under the seat, literally drinking while driving.

And then he'd jumped off the Coronado Bridge.

Despite several eyewitnesses saying under oath that Jack had *willingly* placed himself—and his child—in front of the full-speed trajectory of the bus, and although US BLUE initially claimed the bus was breaking no speed or lane laws, the overwhelming evidence against the driver and the ensuing public drama that would play out over the months—potentially *years*—of a trial forced them to pony up a decent out-of-court settlement. Regardless of who did what, one thing clear to everyone was that the boy was most certainly a victim, and US BLUE had no interest in fighting a nine-year-old comatose boy in the court of public opinion. "Drunk driver versus young boy in a coma" was not a campaign they would win. So, after just two conference calls in as many weeks, they settled, and the amount had been fine with Dave, who knew he could have gotten more had he felt like drawing it out. It was a fight he knew he could win.

But all Dave wanted, for him and for Henry, was to move on.

So he agreed, asking only that the bus company also cover the funeral costs for Jack. That had legally closed the matter, and Dave would have felt victorious about the whole thing had his younger brother not been dead and were his nephew not breathing through a tube, his brain snared within in a web of deep unconsciousness.

No, it was a bad business, Dave thought, watching the same rhythms on the monitors he'd been watching for the nearly three weeks. *But sometimes good people do bad things, don't they?*

Dave looked down at his hands. He supposed he should be thankful Henry wasn't awake to see his father buried. Hadn't had to endure the questions he may have been asked had he been awake and alert during the negotiations with the bus company.

Thankful, yes . . . there was much to be thankful for.

Including the fact that he and Mary, despite all odds, now had a child of their own to raise. Mary hadn't been thrilled, still wasn't, but she'd get over it. Part of her hadn't wanted to let go of having her own biological child, despite knowing in her heart it was near impossible. He was sure she'd end up loving Henry as her own. This was his flesh and blood. This was his nephew, his godson, the only son of his only brother, dead now, struck down by grief, murdered by depression.

If only Dave could forgive that, forgive his brother for doing such a selfish thing. Forgive him for trying, inexplicably, to murder his own child in the process. If he could forgive, then perhaps, one day, he would allow some love for Jack back into his heart. But now . . . No, not now. He'd seen the boy's body. Seen the accident site. Studied the photos taken just after, and just before, the ambulance and life support units had heroically saved Henry's life. He had seen Jack's body—torn, broken—still stuck to the grill of the blue bus like a giant bug, bone shards puncturing skin, limbs loose and split, a long streak of blood trailing from underneath the bus ten yards or more, mingled with the black streaks of the tire's brake marks.

That had been one of the (numerous) points of evidence against US BLUE: that the skid marks didn't start until ten yards *past* the point of impact. Nearly three seconds. That fact alone had caused Dave to inquire about the driver's sobriety, the lack of which had been confirmed by San Diego PD, and had nailed the coffin on US BLUE pushing for a trial. During the calls with the bus company's lawyers, Dave had kept his mind cold and emotionless, thinking of the smear of blood and flesh in the street as nothing but the strokes of a painter's brush, a piece of evidence to be analyzed and utilized, nothing more. Because if he allowed himself to think, to *remember*, that the streak of red had once been his little brother Jack, who he had played baseball with, who he had bunked with for ten years of their childhood, who he'd stood next to, both of them stiff and smiling in their tuxedoes, on the day of his marriage ... if he'd thought all that, then he might have screamed. Screamed and run from the conference room, pulling at his hair and wailing, crying out with the horror and sadness of it all. The *tragedy*.

And worse, far worse, were the photos of Henry.

Jack's body had cushioned the point of impact *just* enough that Henry survived, but not before the boy was knocked out of his tiny sneakers, thrown like a stone twenty feet before finding the rear windshield of a parked BMW, his body resting limp over the bright red Beemer's trunk, one leg twisted at a disturbing angle, the shattered glass a terrible pillow beneath his head.

For that image alone, he could not forgive his brother. The memory of the boy's body stole forgiveness from his heart. The knowledge of what Jack did hurt him terribly, kept him up at night and scrubbed away his appetite. To forgive someone you love is to allow healing, but Dave feared his wounds would never heal, that he'd be forced to live with pain and regret and anger the rest of his life.

Sitting in that hospital room, listening to the familiar beeps and whirs of the machines keeping Henry alive, Dave planted his face in his hands, wanted to cry, wanted to scream, for the millionth time.

More than that, more than anything, he wanted Henry to *wake up*.

"Please," Dave said quietly, praying into his palms, as if begging forgiveness, for the release of his own painful grief. "Please, Henry ... please wake up."

God almighty, he thought, sniffling into his hands and wiping away the tears of exhaustion and suffering, *but I am so very, very tired*.

5

Dave washed his hands and stuck them under the bathroom's hot air dryer, waiting patiently as the water was whisked away from his skin. He was in no hurry to return to Henry's room, no hurry to go home or call the office, to check in on the increasingly long list of clients he'd neglected over the last few weeks.

No, Dave only stood there a bit, let his hands dry, and gave thanks that every day he came to the hospital was another day he was coming as a visitor and not a patient. He'd been there, done that. A bladder infection a few years back had made his prick burn like a fire hose pumping acid, and the two nights he'd stayed while they ran tests and flooded his system with antibiotics were two of the most miserable of his life. It was a stay he had no intention, or desire, to repeat.

He sighed and caught his own face in the mirror. He saw the bruised bags under bloodshot eyes, the tint of gray at his temples, the deep worry wrinkles in his brow. He thought his neck and cheeks looked fat, despite the fact that he exercised every day, without fail, for an hour in the morning before leaving the house. He was assured his heart and cholesterol were fine and dandy, sure, but that didn't keep him from looking like hell in a handbasket. Mary had always told him he looked like Sidney Poitier, and that might have been the case at one time, but even Poitier went gray. *Even the pretty ones get old*, he thought wearily, then laughed at himself.

"Old, vain asshole," he said, and laughed again, wondering if his lack of sleep, pressure from the lawsuits, and Henry's condition were finally making him crack. He thought probably so, leaving the bathroom convinced that tonight he would take a couple of Mary's melatonin capsules and see if that would allow him a few hours of—

His thoughts broke off at the sound of loud footsteps in the hall.

Someone was running.

Dave blinked, came back to himself. He pushed through the bathroom door and watched numbly as nurses ran down the hallway.

Toward Henry's room.

Why are they running? he thought, and felt his knees turn to water. *Oh God my God, why are they running?*

6

Henry had been wandering for lifetimes.

Blasted landscapes, skies that peeled from black to red to blue to white, often seemingly within minutes, often for what felt like millennia. He'd tasted the universe, heard the song of creation. He'd listened to desperate singing, sung desperate songs, screamed hymnals, prayed and worshipped and begged forgiveness for himself, for his father, for humanity.

He spent an infinity in the dark. The deep, warm dark. There were creatures there, demons that whispered, that fought to hurt him—that did, in many ways, hurt him badly, irrevocably, for stretches of time unfathomable. He'd been tortured, loved, held ... and then released.

His mind narrowed; his consciousness ground itself into the heavy crust of hard reality, folded itself up like the reverse blooming of a great mysterious flower, a vibrant mandala reduced to a pinprick.

Gradually, his physicality returned.

First hearing. Then smell. He winced at the sensations, hating them; disgusted by the sharp tingling in his muscles, the throbbing of his heart, the aching in his neck and back and leg. His heavy, bludgeoned head. The stink of death wafted off him, the stench of lethargy. Worse than the pain was the total sense of despair, consuming as a hungry black mist, devouring the light inside him. His soul felt heavier than the flesh awaiting its return.

As the pain grew he slowly woke, as if lulled from a dream by a melody that quickly became a siren, a blast of sound that *yanked* him abruptly from the mire, jerked him up and out of the mist. Shadows chased him as he was pulled upward. As he rose higher, colorful lights flickered through his mind, faster and faster ... then the flickering slowed to a steady rhythm.

The lights swelled and the strobe effect blurred and flattened until it became one uniform, impossibly white *light*.

The piercing glow burned against his closed eyelids, demanding entry. So he opened them.

Henry winced at the brightness of the room. He tried to speak, but could not. Something was in his mouth, filled his throat. He turned his head, tried to comprehend where he was, what was happening. Tubes in his arm. His fear spiked when he looked down at his exposed body—a tube protruded from his stomach, another from between his legs. His breath quickened. A steady beeping sound kept pace with his increasing heart rate.

What's happened to me?

The memories of the time away from his body tattered and tore, then disintegrated completely. This place was not for them, was not for timelessness and visions of the afterlife, the astral planes of the spirit world.

He tried to focus, caught the glimmer of something shiny resting on a table near the edge of where he lay. He willed his hand to reach for it—to touch it, study it. He wanted to understand this new world. There was more input coming, more sensations: memories, thoughts. But not his, no, not his.

Others.

Every second, more and more filled his head.

I'll never see that asshole again, I swear . . .

My mother hates me. If she was dying in this very hospital she'd demand to be . . .

I hate this. I hate the pain, the constant fucking pain. Please let me die . . .

Henry closed his eyes, tried to slow things down. Slow the sensory overload hitting him. Limit the input—the things he saw, the sounds of voices and footsteps and beeping instruments, the discomfort of his body, the *feelings* from all the souls around him. He willed his mind to be quiet, to stay within himself. He breathed in through his nose, let it out slow, and opened his eyes once more.

He pushed away the thoughts, the pain, the strange feelings, and focused on *one* thing. Grounding him. An anchor in this strange new existence. The shiny object on the table next to him, silver and spherical. That would be his first goal.

Focusing—with purpose now—he ordered his hand to *move*. To his amazement and delight, the small hand lifted off the white sheet and reached outward, past the safety bar at the side of the—*bed, it's a bed, Henry*—and pushed against the shiny metal bowl glinting at him, his fingers looming large and grotesque in its curved reflection. He pushed further, trying to feel it, to touch it . . . he pushed . . . and it slid away, vanished off the table . . .

. . . and fell with a loud *clang* to the floor.

The feeling of *alarm* broke into his mind.

But not his own.

The door to the room opened and Henry turned his head to the visitor. A woman was watching him. He could *hear see touch feel* the *colors images thoughts* flooding out of her. For a moment, he was terrified. He wanted to shut the woman out, desperately wanted to close his eyes, to go back to the quiet dark.

Instead, he opened his eyes—ALL of his eyes—wide.

He opened *everything* wide.

Wonderment. That's what came from the woman—*nurse she's called a nurse*—at the doorway. She stared at him in, yes, in wonderment, and then came a dominant thought, as vivid to Henry's mind as if the woman were a brightly lit neon sign:

He's awake! My God, the boy's awake!

Henry's fear vanished, buried beneath the nurse's overwhelming amazement and joy.

When she laughed out loud and put a trembling hand to her chin—and despite the plastic covering his mouth and the painful dryness of his lips—Henry couldn't help but smile.

7

A few days after Henry's endotracheal tube was being pulled free from his throat, Jim Cady, a mountainous man dressed in cross trainers, black Dickies cargo pants, and a bleach-clean white T-shirt that bulged at the shoulders and biceps, ordered two more shots of Jack Daniels. His hands were curled into fists that rested like the ends of a twenty-pound dumb-bell on top of the varnished mahogany bar. His hair was close-shaved. His downcast eyes matched his skin, the color of grave dirt.

But unlike most assholes who sat at a bar in the middle of the after-noon staring hard at a shot glass that keeps getting filled and going empty, again and again, Cady had actually found a job today. A job, and with it, a purpose.

Sure, he didn't have it yet. Not officially. But he would. He'd made sure of it.

He opened the cover of the edge-frayed red spiral notebook lying next to the drained shot glasses on the bar. The first few well-read pages were filled with underlined names partnered with phone numbers. There were neat notes under each entry, line by line, bullet point by bullet point. What he needed from them. What they could give him. Who was in. Who was out. Who was owed, and who owed Jim.

He had drawn hard lines through many of the names. Most of them, in fact.

These entries, these pages, were the substructure—the *foundation*—of his Plans.

And there were many Plans.

Some came to fruition but most, admittedly, did not. The success or failure of many were tied to fate. Within the pages of the worn notebook (and the many others like it) were quick-grabs—the kind of immediate

violence and short-term benefit that would land him back in prison for a
few years—high-risk, low-reward kinda deals. For desperate times. Other
plans were longer term. Years in development. Hands greased all over the
city, birds situated in key places that would chirp to him if *this* happened
or *that* happened. He had pages and pages of Plans—some good, some not
so good, some potentially great. Some were no more than sketches, ideas
to be fleshed out if the right opportunity came his way.

You could never have too many options.

Jim started his first notebook when he was a teenager. He'd lost count
of how many he'd filled since then—some were gone forever, burned to
protect the guilty; some he kept safe for future reference. As a young man,
he had sketched out all the different crimes he dreamed of committing,
designed and schemed while his father slept it off in the next room, not
caring, not daring to be a parent. Scared sack of shit that he was.

That kid—that younger version of Jim Cady—mapped out the details
of the dream scenarios and then, slowly, made those scenarios a reality.

Albeit with slight alterations.

The dream of a bank heist became a real robbery of the local flo-
rist; the fiction of assassinating the "top dog of the streets" became shots
fired at a local gang leader in the dead of night. Fighting his way toward
becoming a crime boss—the ultimate dream—became more real as he
began meeting and working closely with other like-minded people, both
criminal and legit (*paying 'em or slaying 'em* was a frequent motto), in order
to land the right job, shake the right hand, or remove the wrong ones, and
ultimately he put himself in a position to finalize the details of his many
complex *Plans*.

His first successful manipulation, when he was just nineteen (but
already big and broad as a man in his prime), secured him the position of
night manager at a nearby 24/7 supermarket. That job gave him access to
food, to booze. Things he could eat, drink, or sell. To start, he'd needed
to intimidate a few more-qualified candidates into walking away, turning

down the position. Then he'd laid five hundred bucks on the assistant day manager to recommend him, promising him a piece of the action, money the man needed to get his lady an abortion they couldn't afford. A fact he'd discovered from another of his birds. If the chump had turned down the money, then he would have been forced to hurt that lady, pregnant or no. Hurt her bad.

And so it went, through the many years since.

So many Plans. Pages and pages of ideas, of life—some left behind, some still being written.

When he eventually, inevitably, landed in prison, he had worked with other inmates to develop more ideas, more schemes. They all went in the notebooks. Every scheme, every detail, every potential route to success. The guards didn't care. Hell, he'd tipped most of them generously enough that a few were still in his debt to provide information from the inside, or do the occasional favor, if needed.

Flip.

His finger fell on a name. This one had been underlined. Twice. A cop who didn't owe him nothing, but who he'd been told would happily trade information for a couple hundred bucks and some dope.

In this case, some DUI results from an accident nobody gave a shit about.

Flip.

Another name. This one a maintenance guy with a taste for shitty cocaine who had promised to let Jim know if a certain kid ever woke from a coma. Jim closed his eyes, took in a deep breath, smelled the stale beer, the warm air carrying its own ash-tinged scent of streets and dead cigarettes. *Another dumb bird,* he thought, almost smiling. He imagined the information flowing over a wide, multi-threaded network, right to him. His own personal matrix, and he the spider at the center of its vast web.

Flip. Flip.

This was the page he wanted. The newspaper clipping was there, folded over and taped down. The sad story of a man and his boy who had been hit by a drunk asshole driving a touring bus. But the kid . . . the kid had lived. The kid had been in a coma, but had woken up. Had somehow, miraculously, *lived*. And as fate would have it, the kid had a hotshot lawyer uncle who surreptitiously sued the ass off the bus company. Everyone expected a big trial, but it all vanished quickly, which Cady had made careful note of. His eyes traveled across the article for the hundredth time until he came to those words, those magic words:

Settled out of court for an undisclosed amount.

Cady smiled because he knew the amount. Oh yeah, he did. Hells yeah, as they said in the joint. It was a doozy. A straight-up ballbuster. Over two million bucks, he'd been told. All that money to a little kid because his jerkoff piece of shit father had stepped in front of a bus driven by a drunk Chicano.

Under the clipping were more names. Some were contacts. Some were potential candidates he'd come up with. Others had been crossed out, rejected.

But the time had come to execute this plan, and he'd need help. Reliable help. He scanned the names, his mind doing quick calculations, routing destinations, creating the ways and means to a glorious end.

First things first. The Long Play. The long play needed to go into effect immediately. No time to waste. Not now. Once the first move was settled, he'd begin making calls, setting up meetings, gathering a team. He flipped the newsprint over, found another name. He put his finger on it.

Step one.

It would be easy. Like a chess game, he had all the moves mapped out in his head. A little personality adjustment, some forged papers, the right recommendations. And, most importantly, an opening. But compared to everything else, that was the easy part.

A little violence to grease the wheels. A little murder to get things moving.

Cady shook his head. God*damn* but folks were stupid.

He tapped his finger on the bar. More whiskey appeared, disappeared.

He stood up, closed the notebook, threw down twenty bucks. Probably owed more, but ain't like he was getting charged. The twenty was a tip.

"You out?" the long-haired, bottle-glasses-wearing white-ass gorilla said from behind the bar. Or, as those who drank here knew him, Adolf.

"Yeah. Gonna go upstairs, change, then head out. Got to see your cousin."

Adolf nodded, stood absently, and watched his one customer drift out the door and toward the stairs that led to the small apartment on the second floor. The one he knew better than to ever mention. To anyone. Ever.

"Good luck."

Cady nodded, let the door shut. The muggy San Diego heat barreled into him as he hit the sidewalk. He smiled tightly, knowing damn well luck would have nothing to do with it.

8

"Henry, can you hear me, son?"

Henry did hear him. His daddy's voice.

Daddy had come back.

His throat hurt and he was bone weary, but he was glad to have the tube out, glad to suck the cold ice chips they'd given him.

Soon after he'd woken, after many tests and many questions and many more tests, Henry had grown tired and fallen back to sleep. It was a different sleep this time, though. A *normal* sleep, with dreams that were only in his subconscious mind, dreams that did not affect his immortal soul.

"Henry?" his dad said again, but Henry, lost in one of those dreams, could not answer. The dream would not let go.

There was a dog running toward him from a long way away, and he badly wanted to pet it. As it got closer, he noticed the dog was drooling. Long strings of white, foamy saliva slipped from its open mouth like thin snakes. Its bared teeth weren't showing a playful smile, but a hungry snarl. A *mean* smile. Henry reached out his hand, knowing in his heart the dog would bite it, but still unable to stop himself.

Beyond the dog, Henry saw a horizon of green. Hundreds of trees. A forest.

And something else. Something that lurked in the shadows of those tall trees, something making the dog angry, making the dog want to *kill.* But still, Henry kept his hand stretched forward, fingers trembling with the anticipation of great pain. He heard laughter from the trees, the air around him swirled with it, and then the thing laughing from the shadows somehow *became* the dog, and when it did, it leapt.

Henry had time to see the dog had yellow eyes, then its teeth stretched and spiraled away from the dog's head, became branches that sprang at him through the air like gnarled roots. Long brown fingers coiled around Henry's hand, his arm, and although he pulled and pulled, he could not release himself. Ropy tendrils punched through skin, wrapped around bone, dug themselves into his neck and up his throat, punctured through the roof of his mouth, his tongue, his cheeks. He tried to scream—

"Henry?"

Henry opened his eyes.

He was in the hospital room. His daddy stood beside him.

"Daddy?" Henry said, and reached toward the familiar face at his bedside, put his palm against the stubbly cheek. Then he paused, fingertips frozen on the man's face as he slowly remembered.

Dad holding me tight, the roar of the bus, the honking cars, the screams, then flying . . .

The face beneath his small fingers transformed as his vision cleared, the blurriness of sleep dissolving into the sharp contrast of reality. Henry pulled his hand away, snatched it back as if from a hot fire. It wasn't his dad's face at all. It was Uncle Dave's. Uncle Dave was at his bedside because his daddy . . . his daddy . . .

"Where's my dad?" Henry asked, his voice a whispery croak, his throat still raw.

Uncle Dave turned to look at a woman sitting near the foot of the bed. Henry followed his gaze, recognized Aunt Mary. She tried to smile, to appear comforting, but Henry didn't think she was all that good at it.

"Henry, we have a lot to talk about," Uncle Dave said. "The good news is you're doing very well. The breathing tube is out, and you're getting stronger. Doctor says you're out of the woods, son. You've . . . you've been awake almost a week now, and you'll need to stay here for a good while longer, until you're healed and strong. But I think it's time we had a talk about what's been going on. How'd that be? Can we have a little talk?" Dave waited for a response, but Henry could only stare back at him, his bottom lip quivering.

Dave cleared his throat, continued. "A lot of what I have to say is going to be difficult for you, and we can go slow, okay?"

Henry thought a moment, felt goosebumps rise on his flesh. A cold ice pick stabbed his guts, then the chill spread outward, into his chest, arms and legs, up his neck. He squeezed his eyes shut, felt tears push from beneath his eyelids, roll down his temples.

Henry knew what Uncle Dave wanted to talk about. His daddy was gone, just like his mom. He kept his eyes closed tight, as if the dark would shield him from the pain, from the truth that he would be alone. He would have no one.

Poor kid. Poor, sweet child. Be calm. Be strong for the boy.

Henry didn't want to hear Uncle Dave, didn't want to hear his thoughts. In his mind he *saw* his sadness, his terrible sadness. The colors of his despair came off him in waves—pale gray-blues, deep dirty yellow—and Henry wanted the colors to go away, the feelings to go away. Uncle Dave was so sad, so sad.

Look at how sad you are, Uncle Dave. Please, please don't be sad.

Henry's eyes shot open, his misery momentarily replaced with a child's wonder, the elixir of a great distraction.

Without understanding how, or why, Henry understood—could put substance to—what had been happening to him the past week. The voices, the colors.

He could see what Uncle Dave was *thinking*.

Not just words, not mindreading . . . but *feelings*. Like the nurse who'd found him when he woke up, like the others who had visited, or were in the other rooms and halls of the hospital.

But this was stronger, much stronger.

Henry had thought himself crazy, or delirious; still sick from the accident, from his injuries. But now everything made sense—all the confusion of the last few days settled into a pattern, a puzzle in which he'd placed the last piece, and now the picture was clear. Suddenly he realized the truth of it.

But a mist of doubt crept into his thoughts, clouded his excitement. *What is this?* He felt more confused than frightened, unable to shake the feeling he was being bad, doing something he should not be doing. Something unnatural.

What's wrong with me?

He turned away from his uncle, put balled-up hands over his eyes, wanting to shut it all out, no longer wanting to see Uncle Dave, see the colors, all the things inside him. Henry didn't want to know what anyone was thinking—had not asked for it and hated it. Because right now, in this moment, he knew that what he could do was bad.

Very, *very* bad.

"Henry?" Uncle Dave slipped his hand onto the bed, gripped Henry's fingers in his own. Dave's skin was smooth and dry. Soft sandpaper.

Henry breathed heavily. He shook his head, spilling tears. He let out a sob, wanting to shut himself off, *needing* to shut himself off. To shut out everyone—Uncle Dave, the nurses, the other patients. Everyone and everything.

You can't hide, said a voice from inside his head. Foreign, yet familiar. *You better open yourself up and take it all in. You're not in the dark anymore, son. You're in the* light.

Henry resisted, shook his head once more. He sensed the unseeable world all around him—a battering kaleidoscope of colors, a mad chorus of thoughts—knocking at the door of his mind, begging to be let in.

Let it come, Henry. Life is pain, boy, but this is a gift. You know what you do with a gift, right? You open it, son.

Now . . . open.

With great caution, Henry did.

He opened himself up, and let the world come.

A knot came loose in his mind, and it was as if he'd opened a door and let it all rush into him. He could read them, feel them. Somehow, in a way he thought he might never understand, he could *see* them. Effortlessly, he understood the swirling emotions of the people surrounding him—patients and doctors and nurses and family members—could translate all of their pain or fear or hate or sadness into something comprehensible. But among all the swirling, bombarding emotions there was also love. So much love. And in his room, here at his bed, Uncle Dave and Aunt Mary were bursting with it.

It all rushed into his mind so fast! But Henry found that, with effort, he could compartmentalize the input. Like tuning a radio, leaving one station behind so another came in more clearly. Although it hurt his head a little at first, to focus in a way he'd never done before, he found that if he did it just *so* . . . he could control it.

Daring once more to open his eyes, to add another layer of input to what was already both overwhelming and somehow controllable, he slowly turned to Uncle Dave, half expecting the man's face to be a writhing mass of color.

But it was just his uncle's face, tired-looking and wearing a sad, knowing smile. It was the face of a man who Henry knew, without doubt, loved him very much.

Henry allowed himself to drink it in, absorbed the nourishing warmth and protection that exuded from his uncle, like a flower absorbed life from the sun.

That warmth—that love—reminded him of a distant, unattainable memory. A remembrance from when he'd been asleep. While in the coma. Something had happened to him there.

Something had come back with him.

Henry didn't reach for the memory. He didn't want to go back. Not ever.

So he forgot about it, squeezed his uncle's hand, managed a small smile of his own.

"What do you say, Henry? Can we talk?" Dave asked gently.

"Okay," Henry said.

His uncle let out a held breath and glanced toward his wife. Then he told his nephew, his godson, what he needed to know. That he'd been in a coma for almost three weeks. That a lot had happened in that time. That he was going to come live with Uncle Dave and Aunt Mary, and they would take care of him. He told Henry he'd never have to worry about money again. He'd be protected.

That his daddy was dead. That his daddy was buried in the ground.

And then together, for a while, they cried.

9

Wilson Tafferty was done with kids. Done with their condescending, disrespectful remarks, their long, snarky glares as they watched him work. Picking up their filth.

But mostly, done with their gum.

If he had to scrape one more petrified pink ball of Bubble Yum off a desk bottom he was gonna make one of them little cum-squirts swallow it.

They were nothing but a bunch of pack animals, shitting everywhere and on everything. Vandals, all of 'em. He knew it was Bill Hartnett, that little bastard, who broke the window outside Room 230. He *knew* it was him. He wanted to say something to the little punk, grab him by the collar of his windbreaker and shake the truth out of him. But no, he had done what he was supposed to do and told the main office. Of course, the main office only asked the kid, "Did you break that window?"

What's a boy gonna say?

Yeah, sure, it was me. What, did I forget to run over here and tell you all? I'm sorry, but yes, ma'am, yessir, that was me all right. Funniest thing, I threw a baseball at the sucker and I'll be goll-damned dipped in honey if that frackin' thing didn't crack like Charlotte's motherfuckin' web.

Nah, he just looked at the principal, Ms. Terry, a pretty little thing all the older boys got crushes on (and some of the teachers, to boot), and gave her big eyes and said, "Nooo ma'am, not me. I have no idea how it happened."

When the boy had left the office, Wilson had been right there waiting. Waiting to see the smug little bastard's face crunched up into tears, all red and humbled like the little shit-stain he was. But he hadn't been crying. He wasn't even worried. When he'd gone by Wilson, the boy *smiled* at him. Not a cruel smile, not even a mean smile. Just a *hey, what's up, ya old piece of shit* kinda smile. Like he didn't give a damn whether he was the floor janitor or a mutt waiting to be let outside. Wilson figured he was lucky Billy-boy didn't smack him on the rump as he went by, all friendly-like.

Yeah, yeah, he was sure sick of those kids. But soon it'd be summer, and Wilson would be cut back to part-time, and he'd go see his sister in Sacramento. Take the bus up most likely, make a vacation out of it. Stop in that garlic town, or do some wine tasting up there in Napa. Hell, maybe it was time he listened to Barbara and moved out there to live with her, Robert, and the kids. Sis was still young and healthy, a working girl, and Robert had more money than those kids could spend in a year of playing in the arcade or buying all them new clothes they were so proud of. They could take care of him, sure. Even had a room there for him, all done up like a mini-apartment.

He could *retire*.

Hell yeah, he liked the sound of that more and more. Yessir, *re-tire*. Sounded real nice.

But then he'd remember who he was, and how he was. About how, when he'd visit, he'd stay a week or so, and he'd get itchy. Cagey, like. Ready to move on, get to work, take care of things. He supposed that meant he wasn't ready to retire. Retire meant you could do nothing and not give a damn that you weren't doing nothing. But for Wilson, that kind of thing got old real quick. Plus, the school needed him. He'd been there twenty-three years. More than anyone but that wonderful old lesbian Ms. Auerbach, the English teacher. She'd been at Liberty since the 1950s and showed no sign of slowing down, no sir. He'd miss their coffee times if he retired. Miss seeing the other teachers, too, some of whom were friends. He'd miss the Spanish teacher, Ms. Hodge, and Ms. Terry, both of who were real kind, and easy on the eyes, yessir. Ms. Terry, that was.

But he sure as hell wouldn't be missing those kids. Hell no. And he sure as hell wouldn't be missing their gum, their nasty looks, and their even nastier graffiti. Not that. Not a scratch.

Wilson looked up, surprised to see he was almost back home. He'd walked to and from the school, a good mile, twice a day, every weekday, for every one of those twenty-three years. He knew the walk so well by now he was surprised he didn't look down and see a curved groove in the sidewalk from the path he'd trod, swore to heaven he could have done it blindfolded, without slowing a step or bumping a knee.

Well, it would be good to get home. It was Friday, and that meant sleeping in a bit tomorrow, at least until Fix woke him up wanting her breakfast. Damn cat knew how to open cupboards and windows, how to lift the toilet seat and do her business in a box the size of an Oxford dictionary, but the dummy couldn't feed herself if her life depended on it. For that reason, and that reason alone he was sure, old Fix kept Wilson around. Put up with him, as it were.

Wilson laughed to himself. By God, he was turning into a bitter old pill. And him still a few good years shy of seventy. *Too young to be so damned cranky*, he thought. Well, he'd take care of that old cat when he got home, and then he'd make himself a little something, nip a little more of the Amaretto he'd been given as a Christmas present from Ms. Hodge and savored and saved like it was heaven's own elixir, which in many ways he figured it was. It surely was.

He pulled the heavy ring of keys from his belt and unlocked the door to the lobby of the small twelve-unit building, almost as beaten-down and old as he was, and headed for the stairwell; still too proud, after all these years, to use the elevators for what a single flight of stairs would accomplish just as well. He thought of the warm liqueur waiting for him, and it brought a smile to his face. The faces of Bill Hartnett and all those other grimy little bastards faded away with each stair he climbed to his second story apartment, toward home.

As he rounded the stairwell and came up onto his floor, he paused. *Now that's funny*, he thought. *Why all them damned lights out?*

It was nearing seven o'clock, and the sun was settling into the Pacific, but the hallway window in Wilson's building faced east, so there was hardly any light coming through there. The fluorescents lining the hall were all—oddly—off. Wilson knew there was no switch for the lights. He also knew for a fact they were all on a timer, and the timer, all year-round, was set for 5 p.m. sharp. On at 5 p.m., off at 9 a.m. Been that way every day since he moved in. But now they were all, most certainly, for no good reason he could fathom, off.

He craned his neck up toward the third floor, saw the hall lights spilling onto the stairwell above. He looked down to the first floor, not trusting his own memory at the young age of sixty-seven, and saw that yes, those lights were going strong, too. So not a power outage. No, it was just *his* floor that was off. *His* floor, along with the three other folks and families living on this level, who had been left in the dark.

"Humph," he grunted, debating whether to go back downstairs and call the super. But it was getting late, and he'd had a long day, and he could all but taste that sweet, warm Amaretto on his dry tongue. Hell, if he could walk from Liberty Elementary School to his home blindfolded, through busy streets and around all them other obstacles, then he could surely make it the fifty paces to the end of the hallway and the door of Unit 8. Yes, yes, he liked the sound of that. The lights could wait. He'd tell the janitor part of his brain to shut the hell up, because the non-janitor part of him wanted to turn on the television, kick up his feet, pet his kitty, and have himself a little nip of the sweet stuff. Yessir, time to get home.

Wilson waved a hand casually, letting the universe know it could go on and fornicate with itself a good long while, and made his way down the shadowy hall to Unit 8.

A few feet from the door, he pulled out his massive ring of keys once more, extended the thick bunch of metal on the retractable string from the clip on his belt, and began feeling for the right key with the pads of his weathered fingers.

But God it's dark down here, he thought, and felt the hairs on the back of his neck come to half-mast. He scolded himself for getting the willies, but he'd never been fond of the dark, truth be told, and he didn't much like walking through—

Something creaked behind him.

He turned, his mouth hanging open, his eyes wide. The hairs on his neck were at full attention and saluting now, and the gooseflesh crawling up along his arms was marching right along to whatever bugle his frayed nerves were blowing.

"Probably that damn cat," he mumbled, referring to the Willoughbys' fat orange tabby, the one he and Fix didn't care for; no sir, not a bit. "Run on now," he said, trying to sound strong. To sound *in control.*

His voice sounded like a dead thing in the empty hall.

A window at the far end, past the stairs, showed the day outside turning the color of a plum, and now even the stairs themselves were nothing but a fuzzy penumbra at the end of a long dark tunnel. "This is bullshit, is what this is," he said, and turned for his door. Moving quickly now, he pulled the keys away from his belt once more, his fingers moist, and the heavy ring of metal got loose, slipped, and zipped back to slap his bony hip.

"God *DAMN,*" he said, more loudly than he'd intended, hearing the first jingles of fear in his ears, the first fingertips of dread walking up his spine, sharp nails at the end of strong fingers crawling like a spider onto the back of his neck.

Fumbling, he jerked the keys out again.

There! There was that noise again.

But this time Wilson didn't turn; he felt the right key in his fingers, like a magician pulling the trick card from a thick deck. He gripped the key and thrust it cleanly into the deadbolt, twisted it, then pulled it out and stuck it into the handle down below. With a turn of the handle and a shove, the door swung open and Wilson all but leapt inside, slamming the door shut behind him and springing the bolt.

Something grabbed his leg.

He kicked out, screaming. "Aaahh!" He twisted so violently he felt something tweak out of place in his back. He pushed his shoulder against the door and flipped on the light, praying *Oh god in heaven please let the lights come on.*

And they did.

"I'll be double-dipped damned, Fix!" he said as he stared down at what had reached out for his leg in the dark, his heart hammering in his thin chest. "Damn it, cat, you nearly killed me."

Fix, overly eager to see the man who brought her food, sat innocently on the linoleum of the kitchen floor, a few feet of safety between her and the human's boot, which had so rudely shoved her away. Fix licked attentively at one forepaw, eyes veiled, not giving two shits for the scare she'd put into good ol' Wilson.

Wilson felt blood pounding in his temples and realized he wasn't breathing. He let out the held breath, and it came with a *gush* sound. His chest relaxed, his heart slowed, and his body lost the tension.

He unclipped the key ring from his belt and dumped the thick wad of metal unceremoniously onto the kitchen counter. He bent down, stroked Fix's head. The Siamese, as if just now deigning to acknowledge the old man, looked up at him with her lovely blue eyes, meowed a few times, then upped and did some figure-eights through his legs. The universal sign that it was feeding time, and if the old man did what needed to get done, there'd be no problems.

"Okay, okay, my friend," Wilson said and moved into the kitchen to retrieve a can of tuna-turkey pâté for his kitty. "You first, then me. I see how it is," he said, smiling as he pulled open the cupboard.

When he turned back around, the smile fell from his face like an anvil slipping off the ledge of a high cliff.

A man stood in his kitchen.

He must have been in the bedroom, Wilson thought absently, his mind not yet catching up to the strangeness, the danger, of the situation.

But then it did.

"What!" he said, and dropped the can to the floor. He heard Fix hiss, but the big man between him and the front door never twitched. "What do you want!?" Wilson yelled, his voice shaking.

The man was wearing black jeans and a thick black jacket. He had a ski mask pulled over his head. *Just like in the movies,* Wilson thought. Then he noticed the large rusted pipe wrench the man was holding in one giant, black-gloved fist.

"I don't got no money, now!" Wilson stammered, wondering if he should be doing something, if he should be reaching for a knife from one of the drawers, or screaming for help, or fighting, or begging. But all he thought to say was, "I ain't got no damned money!"

"I know," the big man said, his voice low and muffled through the mask. "You ain't got shit. I looked."

Wilson thought about this a second. *He looked? And found nothing.* And yet he was still here, wasn't he? Waiting. Waiting for old, worthless Wilson to come home. Because it was Wilson he was looking for. Because old Wilson, for whatever reason there was, was what this man had come to take.

Wilson felt the fight go out of him, felt the fear seep away from his insides and spill harmlessly to the floor. He hung his head.

"Why you want to do this to me, son?" he said, shaking his head, his trembling hands feeling their way along the counter. "I ain't nothing," he said, his voice shaking. "I ain't nothing but a damned janitor."

The big man took a step closer. Fix hissed at the intruder again, fur standing straight, tail rigid as a railroad spike.

"I know," the big man said, almost apologetically. Then he sprang forward. Fix meowled and dashed from the room. Wilson lifted his arms in pathetic defense.

The big man swung the pipe wrench down in a shining black arc and crushed Wilson's forehead with a loud *smack*. Wilson's legs crumpled and he dropped like a sack of dead puppies to the linoleum floor. Fighting unconsciousness, he felt himself dragged away from where he'd fallen, laid flat on his back on the kitchen floor like a sacrifice. The big man stood over him, legs spread over the thin man's chest like he was fixing to take a piss onto Wilson's weathered, dented face.

Wilson moaned, realizing he could only see through one of his eyes. *Brain damage, most likely*, he thought for no good reason at all.

He heard purring and felt the warm fur of Fix beside his broken head. The cat had curled down next to his ear like they were getting ready for a good night's sleep, all tucked in and comfy in his sagging double-bed. *I'm so sorry, sis*, he thought, and rolled his working eye up toward the stranger.

"Nice cat," Cady said, then pulled up his mask, revealed the grinning, shining black face beneath. "I'll let the fucking thing live. How's that sound?"

Wilson thought that sounded pretty good, all in all, what with his bargaining position not being what it could be. He wanted to nod, to maybe shake the killer's hand? To tell him *yeah, yeah, we got us a deal, we surely do, we cooool.* But all rational thought went out of his mind when the big man lifted the massive wrench and once again brought it arcing down onto his skull.

He felt the blow, heard a pistol-shot, and saw a blast of blinding white light and then . . . nothing.

Luckily for Wilson, he didn't have to see the ugly remains of his bashed-in skull, nor the red pool of his blood and brains that covered half the grimy white linoleum of the kitchen floor.

After a day went by, Fix found a taste for the blood, hungry as she was. And old Wilson would have been mighty glad he didn't have to see that, either.

Yessir, mighty glad.

PART TWO: NIGHT VISITORS

1

As they entered the doctor's office, Dave sensed Mary's scrutiny.

It had been six months since they'd put Dr. Ryo Hamada in charge of Henry's psychiatric care, and the rewards for Henry had been extraordinary. He'd slowly reoriented himself with the world around him. His new world. And though Henry's issues were delicate, they'd noticed him making great strides since beginning his biweekly sessions with Hamada.

Since he'd come home to live with Dave and Mary (after two grueling months of inpatient rehab, during which Henry regained a majority of his physical capabilities, while also serving as a crash course on empathetic parenting), Henry's guardians discovered something . . . *unique* in the child. Identified and labeled a strange power inside the boy that the newly-minted parents could only guess at, giving it vague conference in the dark of their bed, whispered about in hushed tones while they explored the mystery Henry had become. They used words like "special" and "gifted" with no real understanding of what it all meant; what it signified for Henry, or for their family.

Dave knew Hamada had experience with all types of known brain anomalies. Had studied patients with both physical and chemical disorders—even those with violent, or murderous, histories. Dave didn't doubt that Hamada was well versed in patients who had gone through intense trauma, and also didn't doubt he'd at some point dabbled in some of the fringe sciences of the mind.

But what he *did* doubt—doubt highly, in fact—was that the good doctor had ever seen anything like Henry. And though Hamada had never spoken of Henry's "gift," Dave thought his silence on that matter would be broken today. He appreciated the doctor's caution, but he was eager to hear a professional take on what was happening inside the boy, hear a theory on the hidden ghost roaming the halls of Henry's mind, a ghost who had infiltrated Dave and Mary's thoughts, had haunted their home these past six months.

Hamada closed the office door as Dave and Mary sank into a large burlap couch across the room from the cold, clinical desk, backdropped by a wall littered with degrees.

"Mr. and Mrs. Thorne, delighted you could make it today," Hamada said, perching on the edge of a stiff leather chair adjacent the couch. His gray hair was short, his linen suit pressed but relaxed on his thin frame. "I thought it time to speak face-to-face about Henry's progress. Please know you are free to talk with Henry about anything we discuss today. It's vital your communication at home continues to be open and sharing. I think that's important for Henry's continued development."

Dave said nothing, eager to get to tacks, as his mother used to say. Mary picked invisible lint from her perfectly ironed skirt, her back rigid, her face unreadable.

Hamada continued. "We've made a lot of progress, and it's safe to say Henry is a special little boy. That said, I thought it prudent we discuss Henry's—" Hamada laughed nervously, shook his head. "Some things that make Henry unique. Things you may already be aware of, perhaps."

Dave felt Mary ready to jump in, and he hoped she'd keep it civil. Her concern for Henry—her motherly instinct to protect—had turned out to be savage. Dave loved her for it, though. She had become a wonderful mother, now she'd been given the chance. "I don't think we know anything, doctor," she said. "He's just a little boy. A child. We need to tread lightly. Don't you agree?"

"Of course, Mrs. Thorne," Hamada replied. "We all have Henry's best interests at heart. That's why I wanted to have this conversation, to discuss Henry's—"

The doctor fumbled for a moment.

"Let's call it a gift," he said finally, like he was passing a gallstone. "Anyway, it will make what I am about to show you much more palatable."

Dave looked up. "Show us?"

"Yes. If I may." Hamada stood and went around the coffee table to a large oak cabinet. He opened the doors to reveal a television, a VHS player, and a small stack of neatly labeled tapes. Hamada turned on the television, pushed a tape into the machine. He picked up a small remote control, pressed a button, and stood aside. The screen came to life with a flap of folded white light, then static. "It takes a second . . . ah, here we are."

Dave was looking at the same couch he sat on, except instead of him and Mary, the couch held only Henry. In the video, Hamada crossed the frame and sat, only the top corner of his head visible.

"Okay, Henry," the TV version of Dr. Hamada said. "Are you ready?"

★ ★ ★

Henry liked it here.

He liked having someone to talk to, someone who didn't think he was weird or a freak like some of the kids at school. He didn't mind being different, and he knew he was smart, that learning came easier to him than other kids his age. But at school, all being smart got you was made fun of. Cindy Wexler liked to point at him during recess, giggle with her friends and chant, "Look who's a smarty-party! Look who's a smarty-party!"

Henry only longed for one thing in life: acceptance. He wished there were more kids like *him*, who didn't care about sports or looking cool or dressing a certain way; kids who liked science and history, who actually enjoyed learning, enjoyed stretching the boundaries of what the world was, discovering the secrets and mysteries it held. The universe was a locked box in Henry's mind, a heavy door he wanted desperately to open. He hated that his curiosity, his intelligence, made him different. Hated that he was too small to stand up to bullies, too shy to make new friends. Too damaged, maybe, by his past.

Watching Hamada, he let his thoughts come back into focus. It would be the cards again. It was Tuesday, after all.

Tuesday meant tests.

While he waited for Hamada to start, he wiped his nose, lightly drummed his heels against the front of the couch. He was antsy, impatient. He knew how much these tests excited the doctor, but they bored Henry. It wasn't special to him. It was *easy*. He'd much prefer to talk about other stuff, like Uncle Dave and Aunt Mary, or the kids at school. About ways he could be more normal. More accepted.

"Okay Henry, are you ready?" Doctor Hamada asked, the cards stacked neatly in his lap, the notebook he always used laid open beside him, the camera on a tripod in the corner, red light unblinking.

Henry nodded.

"Good," said Hamada, "let's begin."

In Henry's imagination, he sensed the eye in his brain—the one that had sprouted there, *grown* there, while he'd been asleep—slowly open.

He could almost feel the thin gray lid peel upward, the darting black eyeball beneath. His chest tightened, but not uncomfortably so, as the doctor's mind spilled information—sounds, visions, thoughts.

Colors.

Henry let the black eye focus in on the strongest colors, the ones that held stories and thoughts, and let the rest become a soft static of dull browns and mild grays. He did this subconsciously now, without effort. While his physical eyes focused on the half-turned vertical blinds against the window, breaking the hard block of glowing daylight that pushed through from outside, his new eye stared, wide open, at the doctor.

Hamada lifted the card, held it poised before his chest. The side facing Henry was completely blank, the other stamped with the stark blue outline of a singular image. It was Henry's job to guess what that image was. He wasn't guessing, though; he saw it as clearly as if he were holding it himself.

"Star," Henry said, then let out a sigh, trying hard not to let his boredom show, lest the doctor think him rude.

Hamada silently lowered the card, brought up another.

"Circle," Henry said automatically.

Hamada shuffled the Circle card under, lifted a new card.

Henry studied Hamada with a renewed focus. *I haven't seen this one.* He wondered if the doctor was trying to make the test harder. Henry nearly giggled at the idea. *If he only knew how easy it was.* Henry reached for a description of the image.

"Squigglies?" Henry asked.

"Correct," Hamada replied, with only the slightest hesitation. "This is a new card I recently added." Henry nodded, allowed himself a small smile at Hamada's expense. "So, Henry, next time I use this card, will you please refer to it as waves? Just so we are both clear on which card it is."

"Okay," Henry said.

Hamada smiled gratefully and continued, holding up the cards, one by one, and Henry answered in a dull monotone, as if reciting prime numbers for the hundredth time.

"Rectangle. Circle. Plus sign. Circle. Circle. Uh, waves. Star. Circle. Star. Waves . . ."

As he responded, he stared at the window, at his kicking feet, at the ceiling. Only once did his eyes flick to Hamada, and then only long enough to see if there was pleasure, perhaps pride, on his face.

To Henry's delight, there was.

The video paused.

★ ★ ★

"The cards were sent to me from a colleague at Columbia," Hamada said, answering their unspoken question. "They're called Zener cards, named after Dr. Karl Zener, a very famous psychical researcher."

"I'm sorry, psychical?" Mary asked.

"The study of psychic science. You may know it better using terms such as ESP, or telepathy."

"What, like a psychic on late-night TV?" Mary huffed. "Are you saying Henry's coma gave him, what? Special powers? Is Henry a fortune teller now?"

"No, no, not like that, not at all," Hamada said, unruffled. "What you're referring to is clairvoyance. Clairvoyance is the ability to see things that cannot be seen with the human senses as we know them. Henry's ability, in my opinion, is something much closer to telepathy. Which means, in layman's terms, that he can see people's thoughts. The Zener cards, for example. Henry is not *seeing* the cards, necessarily, he's seeing *me* see the cards."

"Regardless, Doctor," Mary said, and Dave heard the tremble of emotion in her voice, "I understand your enthusiasm. But to be frank, we're not paying you to experiment on the child."

Hamada's eyes narrowed. He leaned forward, fingers curling into balls on his knees.

Easy doctor, Dave thought with a wry, internal smile, *you wanna go eeeaassy now.* He debated whether to intervene, offer Hamada a lifeline of confidence, because he *did* want to hear what the man had to say. He also knew Mary respected a man with conviction.

To a point.

"Mrs. Thorne, this treatment we are doing is of the utmost benefit," Hamada said, retaining his calm demeanor, much to Dave's relief. "It will help him understand things he is capable of that he does *not* currently understand; just as you don't understand it, even as I can barely comprehend. If Henry understands his abilities, he will become more comfortable with them. He will not perceive his gift as something that is *wrong* with him, which might frustrate him and, more severely, make him withdrawn. Perhaps even make him dislike himself, to some degree. He is unique, obviously, but we want him to embrace that uniqueness, not fear it."

Mary opened her mouth to retort, but Dave interjected. "Dr. Hamada, how rare, how *unique*, exactly, is Henry's gift? I mean, to Mary's point, a lot of people claim to have these kinds of abilities."

"True," Hamada said, "but only a small percentage of those people have been properly examined by a health professional under relatively scientific conditions."

"You mean tested," Mary said under her breath.

"Yes, that's what I mean." Hamada went to his desk, pulled a thin black ledger from a pile and handed it to Dave. "Please."

Confused, Dave opened the ledger to the first page. He saw Henry's name above a staggered series of dates in a left-hand column. The middle column was a neat vertical row of the number 25. Next to it, an exact duplicate row of 25s.

"What is this?" he asked.

"Those are the scores of every test I've given Henry using the Zener cards, along with some notes from a few other small, inconsequential experiments. Here, on the first page, you can see that he—"

"He got them all right," Mary said, looking over Dave's arm.

"Yes, twenty-five out of twenty-five, those first times. There is a point here, believe me. If you would please turn the pages."

Dave flipped through the pages. Months of tests. The dates were all different, but the columns remained the same.

All identical. All 25s. Dave let out a low whistle.

"Henry scored one hundred percent accuracy on every test I've ever given him. Dozens of tests to date, over a period of many weeks." Hamada leaned forward, lowered his voice. "The average historical score—and we're talking about tens of thousands of tests, tests that include even those subjects who are defined as being extremely gifted, on the best of days and using this exact system—is less than *ten percent.*"

Dave's eyes shot up, and even Mary seemed impressed.

"So, to answer your question, Mr. Thorne. Henry's gift, the strength and precision of it, is rare indeed. If not, to date at least, completely unheard of."

Dave looked at Mary, whose skepticism, he noticed, was on the ropes. *Good,* Dave thought, and felt himself relax. *If this is gonna work, we all need to believe.*

"Now, let me show you one last thing," Hamada said. He went to the cabinet and pushed a second tape into the VCR. "I don't normally share personal information about myself," he said quietly. "But today I'll make an exception."

"Personal?" Mary said.

With a sad smile, Hamada started the tape.

★ ★ ★

Henry didn't want to play this game anymore. He was tired, and bored.

Part of him, a sorta bad part of him he didn't much care for, wanted to cheat. Wanted to say the wrong answer to the cards, to say the wrong answers to *every* card! Then they'd never have to play the game again, and they could go back to talking about stuff Henry was thinking, and feeling, and not sit around looking at dumb shapes all day on the stupid—

"Henry," Hamada said, "are you ready?"

Henry's attention snapped back to the doctor. One more time, he'd said. One more time through the cards and then they would stop and talk some more. He'd promised.

Henry nodded.

"Very good. Here we go." Hamada held up a card.

A moment passed. Then another. Henry waited for the image to come, like it always did. But something was ... *blocking* it. Interfering. He couldn't see it. He looked at the doctor, increased his focus, let that inner eye open all the way ... but there was a wall of thought—of color—he couldn't get past. Dark green fog like pea soup shrouded Henry's vision, a dense cloud opaque as stone.

But there was something else, something deep, like a low-lit highway sign in a rich fog.

A name.

"Doctor Hamada," Henry asked. "Who's Franklin?"

Hamada lowered the card, swallowed hard. "Excuse me?"

"You're thinking about a man named Franklin. Really, really hard," Henry said, eyes wide in mock exasperation.

The doctor lowered the card, closed his eyes for a moment. When they opened, he looked away from Henry, toward the far wall, as if looking away might stop Henry from seeing.

Henry stood up and walked to the doctor. Yes, he saw it all. Mustard yellows, dark greens, tendrils of black despair tinted with flickers of astonished pink. Franklin was the man the doctor loved, and the man had left. There had been a fight.

"You're sad, huh?"

A thin tear ran down Hamada's cheek. His astonished eyes flicked back to Henry, and he nodded dumbly. Henry reached out a hand and lightly patted his knee, his young face radiant with a smile. Then he put his small arms around the astonished doctor's neck, and hugged him.

Hamada paused the tape.

★ ★ ★

With a flowering awareness, Dave realized what he had seen. What it meant. "Franklin?" he asked.

Hamada smiled sadly. "My partner of many years. We decided to end our relationship the night before my session with Henry. I wanted to give Henry the usual test, but my feelings . . . they must have overpowered my thoughts. I was looking at the cards, but my mind wasn't seeing them. To Henry, it might have been like trying to see the moon, but through heavy black clouds filling a night sky, blocking his vision."

"I'm not—" Mary started.

"I think," Hamada said, measuring his words, "that Henry *feels* what other people feel, and sees their thoughts. Imagine what the world must look like through his eyes. How heartbreaking. How overwhelming. How *complex*. His mind has been forced to adopt a means to translate these projections, to transform the raw data into something he can understand, that he can *see* in his mind. I've since learned he uses colors to translate this information—black for hate, red for anger, that sort of thing. It's fascinating how quickly the human mind can adapt or, in this case, evolve."

Dave looked at the image on the screen: Henry's wide eyes as he reached out to comfort this man. His innocent, loving smile. *Sweet Henry,* he thought, and felt another wave of love for the boy. "How do we help him, Doctor?" Dave asked, and felt Mary squeeze his hand. "How do we protect our son?"

Hamada sat back, opened his palms in a gesture of intellectual defeat.

"All we can do is support him, love him, and help him understand and accept who he is, what he is capable of." He leaned forward, rested his elbows on his knees, his brow furrowed. "Ultimately, Henry must learn to protect himself. In many ways, he'll be alone in this. But he's a smart boy, and if it helps, and if my theories about his gift are correct . . ."

"Yes?" Mary asked.

Hamada smiled at Mary, but his words were weighted. "Let's just say I think Henry is far from defenseless."

2

Fred shoved the rust-speckled hammer and battery-powered drill into his tool belt, opened the ten-foot ladder, and climbed up to the hanging gutter. He stopped on the second to last step, his tall frame allowing him to access the damaged gutter easily while also affording him a view of the gravel-strewn rooftop.

He saw the balls of duct tape, footprints, and equipment scrapes the roofing crew had left up top, but nothing that needed repair and nothing he'd have to alert the school about. Just minor wear and tear. The gutter was a different issue. The painting crew's scissor lift had been too close to the wall when being raised and one edge of the safety rail had clipped the gutter, knocking it off its mounting and all but ripping the metal in two. Ms. Terry was convinced he could fix the gutter without needing to replace it, so he'd stayed late—well after classes were over, the kids bused home, and all his other chores completed—in order to address the damage.

Now that he was up here, though, he thought the principal was dreaming. Either that or overestimating his abilities. The metal was ripped and the moorings had left nasty black holes in the side of the trim. He'd need weatherproof putty, would have to drill new support holes and see if he could bind the gutter so it could still hold water in a heavy rain. *Damn it all*, he thought, and was about to come down the ladder when the first rock pinged off the metal to his right.

His eyes narrowed a moment—*only a moment*—then went wide and scared. He turned his head and saw them. Jim Hawkes, Tyler Legge, and good old Tommy Patchen. Most of the kids called him Trailer Trash Tommy right to his face, and others (the smaller kids at least) behind his back. He was a tall kid, even for a seventh grader, and his lanky dark hair went past his shoulders, blending easily into whatever black T-shirt he was wearing that day. Today, Fred noticed, Tommy's T-shirt bore a pentagram, blood dripping from each white point, and the unreadable name of some metal band encircling the whole. Tommy looked like he had a few more rocks cupped in one of his grimy hands, and the two other boys were feverishly picking the ground like backpack-wearing hens in an attempt to supply themselves with more ammo.

"Tommy," Fred said, his tone sluggish and garbled, like his tongue couldn't get out of the way of the words coming from his mouth. "Tommy, d–d–don't be throwin' rocks, now. I—" he swallowed, working to get each word out. "I'll tell Ms. Terry if I have to. You boys shouldn't even be in here now, the c–c–campus is c–c–c–closed!"

Tommy's face lit up, his bushy eyebrows raised as his dull brown eyes widened in comic fear, pale chapped lips forming an O of mock concern. His normal squeal of a voice lowered into his best, nastiest Fred impression. "Der, well, I guess I better stop it, then, huh, fuh . . . fuh . . . Fred?"

Before Fred could mutter a response, Tommy let loose another rock, this one the size of a worn golf ball, that hit Fred squarely in the elbow, stinging skin and bone through the rough fabric of his blue coveralls. Fred grunted, turned his body reflexively away, and felt the ladder wobble beneath him.

"Damn it all," he muttered under his breath, then closed his eyes and took a deep breath.

"Hey retard!" Trailer Trash Tommy yelled, his squeaky voice now back in full force. "Look at the bright side. If you fall and hit your head, it won't matter, because you're already brain d–d–d–damaged!"

Tommy laughed his ass off at this, the sycophantic Jim and Tyler joining in with mocking guffaws. "Brain damaged!" Jim Hawkes squealed, laughing like Tommy had just channeled a racist, white-trash version of Lenny Bruce.

Ping! Pang!

Two more rocks hit the gutter to his right, and Fred pulled away, felt his balance begin to shift. He stood well over six feet tall and carried a solid 250-plus pounds of meat and muscle, and when that much weight went one way, even a few inches, it gained momentum quickly. One hand waved absently through the air, reaching for the top of the ladder, the other grasping blindly for the gutter. Another rock smacked the side of the ladder where his hand was reaching, catching the tip of his ring finger hard enough to send a jolt of pain through his hand and make him cry out. His left hand caught the gutter, saving him from falling ten feet to the hard concrete below and possibly doing some real damage. He shook out the sting in his right hand and whipped his head around to glare angrily at the boys.

To his pleasure (and slight concern), the three boys looked momentarily stunned. Even Tommy's smirk faltered and twitched. Jim Hawkes lowered one raised hand, a stone cupped tightly within, and put on an expression of a boy about to piss himself and cry. The expression of a child.

Easy now, Fred told himself, and let his face go slack.

"You boys best git," he said, taking a slow step down the ladder, "or I'll have to tell the puh ... puh ... principal on you."

Tommy turned and looked at his two friends. They all had stones now. *Each of them must have three or four balled-up in their sweaty little white fists*, Fred thought, moving slowly, not wanting to incite another barrage.

And when Tommy turned his acne-splattered weasel-face back around, Fred knew he was in trouble. That smile was back, and now the other two boys were smiling as well. Like a pack of prepubescent jackals.

Well, shit.

He rushed down the ladder as the first barrage hit, heard sharp *snaps and cracks* as the rocks hit the metal of the ladder and the stucco of the wall beside him. Something hard slapped the base of his smooth skull, an inch below his right ear, and a flash of white flickered in his head.

"You dumb black retard!" Tommy screamed, and Fred heard the real hate in his voice now, and behind it, that mad terror that all killers—present and future—had hiding inside them. When that dark passion released it scared you a little, yes it did, because you realized you were out of control, that something alive and hidden was uncoiling inside your guts, extending into your limbs and brain, taking over. It was even more terrifying when that *other* moment came. Not the moment you realized what was buried inside you, no, but the moment you realized that you *liked* it. Yeah, Fred recognized that dark voice, all right. Trailer Trash Tommy was a natural-born killer, you might say, which meant Fred, at the present moment, was in more than just a little bit of trouble.

"Get the fucker!" Tommy shrieked, and Fred felt more stones smack into him, into the ladder, into the wall, cracking one of the windows leading to the boys' locker room. He jumped off the last step and—tossing his pride aside and accepting the shame of a grown man's full retreat from three schoolboys—he ran.

The boys were on his heels, throwing more stones, some bouncing off the asphalt of the recreation area they ran through, some hitting him in the back. A particularly hot one smacked his ass so hard he hopped as he ran, wincing from the sting of it. His key ring jangled against his hip, giving him an idea for a safe destination. If he made it to the janitor's closet, he knew Manuel always left his walkie-talkie stashed there. He could lock himself in and call for help.

He had just turned a corner at full speed, making a little headway on the kids, when he nearly snapped an ankle trying to stop all his weight on a dime. Standing a few feet before him, directly in the middle of the open pathway, was Henry Thorne, staring up with wide-eyed fear at the giant man bearing down on him.

Fred shuffled his body mid-step to avoid ramming into the boy, and in doing so lost his footing and went down in a heap, knees and palms smacking hard into the concrete, his tool belt ripping and something—the mini-driver drill, most likely—crunching with what sounded like a death-knell.

"Jesus Christ!" Fred yelled, his voice loud and clear as he crashed to the ground. He flipped over onto his ass, scorched palms burning against the walkway, and stared at the stunned little boy.

Henry seemed to have moved past the shock of the near collision and now looked at Fred with more wonder than fear, as if he were a meteorite dropped from outer space that had smacked into the Earth, inconveniently blocking Henry's path. Fred noticed Henry was carrying a heavy textbook and wearing his black Carhartt backpack. *Boy must have been hiding out in the library again*, he thought.

"What you doing here, son!" Fred yelled.

"I forgot my science book, then Mr. James and I were working on my AP project," Henry said reasonably, his calm broken only by the sharp narrowing of his eyes, as if he was looking *into* Fred, rather than *at* him. "You're scared," he said. "And . . . *angry*."

Before he could say anything further, the three boys came tearing around the corner, all of them stumbling to a halt. If the devil's own spawn had a grin on him the day he got his first pitchfork, Fred thought maybe it would have looked something like the grin Tommy Patchen wore when he saw little Henry standing over the fallen Fred, hand already poised to hurl another stone.

"I'll be damned," Tommy said, almost in awe of the situation, "two dumbass niggers for the price of one."

Fred didn't care for the slur, but he almost chuckled to himself hearing ignorant, straight Ds and Fs Trailer Trash Tommy describe Henry Thorne as a "dumbass." Sure, maybe Fred Hastings, mentally handicapped janitor working at the school through a state system for the disabled, was easily labeled as such, but ten-year-old Henry was not only a straight-A student, he was already doing advanced-level classes and working off-hours with two of his teachers to lay the groundwork for future scholarship opportunities. Fred knew all this about Henry, and a bit more about him as well. He'd read some of the school psychologist reports, the ones that outlined certain special needs Henry had. Certain *issues* disclosed to the school when Henry returned after his time away—like the fact the boy was still very much traumatized by the incident with his father and ensuing coma. That he was *sensitive.* An *introvert.* He tended to *internalize emotions.* Fred thought maybe Henry was all those things, and something more to boot. Fred wondered if Henry's repressed despair and anger might pop out of him one day, like an arrow that's been pulled taut and held, the tension of the string building until it snaps free and the arrow flies. A rocket with a devil on its tail.

Yes, Fred had read *all* about Henry. Being a janitor, after all, had certain access privileges.

He'd also read about Trailer Trash Tommy. Knew his father was a former convict, his mother on state probation, that one more strike meant a new school for Tommy and a nice, state-funded home, the kind created for kids who are taken away from degenerate parents. He even knew about 123-B Hickory Lane, the address of the dumpy little trailer where Tommy, his ex-con father, and his whore of a mother lived. *Fred may be dumb, all right,* the big man thought. *But he sure as hell isn't stupid.*

"Ow!" Henry yelled, and Fred jerked free from his thoughts. His eyes darted to Henry, who was rubbing his arm, a tear running down one cheek. The boys were laughing again, and Fred saw them winding up for another volley. A stone flew, this one from the Legge boy, and Fred had only a moment to realize the stone—a large, jagged, fist-sized number— was headed straight for his forehead. A dark shape flickered out—Henry's science textbook—and blocked the stone's trajectory with a dull *thunk.*

Their eyes met, and there was a flicker of satisfaction in Henry's, one quickly replaced by fear. They were in deep shit, those eyes said, and Fred agreed.

This won't do, he thought.

He sprung to his feet and the boys' hands froze momentarily, rocks cocked and ready, all of them watching the giant janitor, waiting to see if he would run . . . or attack.

Fred spread his arms, took two quick steps toward the boys. "ROOOOOWWWWRRRR!" he bellowed, and thought for a gleeful moment that the Hawkes kid really would wet himself. Tyler Legge actually turned and ran, while Tommy simply took one hesitant step in retreat, throwing arm raised.

Fred turned, scooped up Henry like a man might lift a large sack of grain, and began to run.

"Get back here!" Tommy yelled, whether at Fred or his frightened sycophants he didn't know and didn't rightly care. He turned another corner and grabbed the jangle of keys in his free hand. His fingers quickly found the shape and heft of the one he was looking for as he slid to a stop before a blue metal door; a scratched, worn plate above reading MAINTE-NANCE. He stuck the key into the handle and, with a deft twist, turned the knob and yanked the door open.

He launched himself inside the room, set Henry down quickly—but gently—and closed the door behind them. Henry took a few steps deeper into the tight, darkened room while Fred pressed an ear to the door.

3

While the big janitor listened for their attackers, Henry tried to slow his breathing. After a few moments, he couldn't help but take in his surroundings. He'd never been in the maintenance closet, and he studied the shelves of bottles and brushes, boxes and bulbs. He turned around, felt compelled to study a small, caged window glowing with a square of late-afternoon light.

His head snapped back to the door just as running footsteps went by outside. Moments later, the frustrated cries of bullies from far off. Henry knew they would not push their luck getting caught while hunting for the handicapped janitor, and would bug out sooner rather than later.

Henry wasn't overly worried, himself. He knew all about bullies, had lived with them his entire life. Since starting at Liberty Elementary School, however, he had learned to deter the assaults by reading his antagonists. He knew, to a degree, when kids were angry, or depressed, or simply bored, and reacted accordingly. After learning to say the right thing or respond a certain way—boldly if it was a false threat, coyly if it was legitimate—the bullies of the school had left him alone. As if, after a few encounters, they *knew* something was off about him and were, just maybe, a little afraid of Henry. Afraid of the part of him that was *off.* People feared the unknown, after all. And an elementary school bully, for all his or her bluster, was still just a kid. And kids were, for the most part—no matter their size or the tenacity of their hate—easily frightened.

Waiting for this newest incident to pass, Henry studied Fred, or rather, Fred's back. He started to read him, but knew to be mindful of people's privacy, aware that just because he could do a thing, didn't mean he should do a thing. Still, Henry couldn't help reaching out, if only a little bit, to see if Fred was still scared—

Then Fred turned and looked down at Henry.

In that dark closet, with nowhere to run, and being so close to the looming giant before him, Henry's thought-feelers retreated quickly. *No one knows I'm here,* he realized. Hugging his science book to his chest like a shield, he took a step backward.

"I think we shook 'em," Fred said. "Your arm okay?"

Henry nodded, although his arm did tingle with pain and would surely bruise. Still, it wasn't the worst he'd been through. *No,* he thought, *not by a long shot.*

"I'm gonna open the door, and I'll watch for 'em. You head for the exit over the other side. Someone wuh . . . wuh . . . waiting for you?"

Henry nodded, despite it being a lie. He walked home alone every day, and as long as he was in the house before 4 p.m. Dave and Mary had no problem allowing him this freedom. It was nearly four o'clock now, Henry knew. But unless Mary made a stink about it and felt inclined to bother Uncle Dave at work—and Henry didn't think she would—it would be a good hour before anyone would think to come looking for him. If not longer.

"All right, then," Fred said. He opened the door a few inches, looked through the bright gap.

With a sting of panic, Henry suddenly wanted out of this closet. Wanted to be through that gap, out the school exit, down Wicker Drive, and back home, safe, at Dave and Mary's. It wasn't like him to panic, or be afraid, but there was something oppressive here, something dangerous. It tickled his brain and chilled his spine. He could almost see it . . . if he only reached out . . .

"Okay, go!" Fred said in a loud whisper and flung the door wide, standing well aside while his eyes darted around for the others.

All his curiosity flew away as Henry darted through the opening and out into the light. He gave one quick glance up at Fred, who lowered his eyes to Henry momentarily before looking out for the bullies once more. Without a word, Henry ran for the exit just past the cafeteria building.

He reached out as he ran, black eye darting furiously, but felt nothing around him, nothing in front of him. Wherever the boys were, they weren't between him and freedom.

Far behind him, he heard the door of the maintenance room close, the faint footsteps of the janitor as he hustled away.

Henry didn't turn back. He didn't reach out toward the janitor.

He didn't want to know what he'd feel.

4

The motel room was suffocating. The Arizona sun was up and running, hanging high in the sky, shining on the desert floor full blast, sparing nothing and no one from its blinding furnace heat. The Arizona sun wasn't like the regular sun at all, that life-giving beacon of warmth and joy most of the world saw it as, but more as if God himself were holding a magnifying glass the size of the Milky Way galaxy, focusing the rays of that far-off gaseous energy into a piercing dot of destructive heat—burning that Southwestern desert, and its living creatures, like a kid might try to burn up ants on a summer day.

Baking underneath that death ray on this particular stretch of the Red Devil state was nothing but a brown ribbon of old highway, the occasional clumps of barrel cactus, greasewood shrubs, weedy toadflax, and other sun-sturdy vegetation. Insects, lizards and other fauna who thrived in dry heat lay stagnant along flat outcroppings of sandstone or skittered fitfully along stretches of cracked, sandy earth.

Among all this prickly nature and scaly life sat one other thing: a dark, forgotten monument hunched at the side of the brown highway, decrepit and unloved as the headstone of a serial killer. A sign hung out front of this mortuary of hospitality, bearing the sandblasted words COPPER MOTEL, the weathered letters hanging on for dear life to the flaking, faded white paint. Beneath the moniker were some black tea leaf fragments that might or might not have once been the words NO VACANCY. The plank that had once covered up the NO (depending on the occupancy of the place at any given time) had long since blown to dust. In any event, they were words that, upon looking at the Copper Motel's current state, you would most likely consider rhetorical.

The Copper Motel offered twelve identical rooms, a cracked parking lot peppered with sprigs of gnarled weeds (the lot's only current patron being a beat-to-shit '74 Chevy Camaro—once black, now a sunbaked charcoal gray), a broken soda machine, an office containing a snoring, wire-thin old manager, and nothing more.

Of the twelve rooms available, eleven were empty.

Inside Room 7, the small air-conditioning unit clattered steadily, the dull lukewarm stream of air that escaped its dusty vents doing little to nothing to lower the suffocating temperature of the room's shadowed belly.

The naked, sweat-slicked bodies of a man and woman lay on a sunken queen-size mattress, the sheets and duvet kicked off the end, clumped on the dusty floor at the edge of the bed in misshapen heaps.

The woman breathed steadily, sprawled ass-up, arms and legs splayed wildly, short black hair matted to her neck, temples, and cheek. The man was curled into a fetal position, one leg twitching involuntarily, his lips feverishly speaking words that came out as no more than silent gusts of breath. His pupils roamed wildly behind his eyelids, his face contorted in pain, or misery.

In the dream, he was always running.

He's with Timothy, his boy a few weeks shy of ten years old, and they've been hiding out almost three months now at the abandoned mill on his father-in-law's farm north of Bega. He and his son are running along sandy flat rocks, playing a game. His wife is home, doing her best to try to make the caretaker's shed habitable, at least temporarily, for all of them. Timothy laughs and turns to look at his dad when three gunshots come quick and clustered. The reports echo cleanly across the dry expanse, echoing as far as the not-so-distant river his boy had played along that morning, trying to catch yabbies but only succeeding in splattering his feet, knees, and hands with river water and cool mud.

When the shots ring out, Liam stops the chase, stands ramrod straight, looks toward his son standing bare-chested in green trunks past a soft ridge, a confused look on his sun-drenched features. He turns, panicked, toward the mill. From here he can see the whitewashed walls of his makeshift home, the brown patches of rust on the gray tin roof. A broken windmill hovers behind, its wide gray blades stagnant in the breathless air of midday.

They've found me, *he thinks. Another blast and one of the rocks spits dust.*

"Timothy, RUN!" he screams, like he has screamed a thousand times in a thousand dreams before.

Timothy does. He runs as fast as his young legs can carry him.

And then he's gone.

Liam runs to the spot his boy had stood only moments before, sees a crack in the rocks three feet wide, endlessly deep. He drops to his belly and yells for his son. A hand reaches up through the darkness. Timothy is crying and the sounds of his misery echo flatly in the dark.

"I'm hurt, Dad!" he yells, and then there are footsteps coming up behind him fast and he reaches his own hand down, searching for the thin fingers of his child, when a heavy boot stomps onto his back.

He wants to explain that he needs to lower himself into the jagged-edged crevasse, where the creek runs into the hills and disappears underground, where it spreads and rushes into a river. Needs to be with his boy in the cold and damp of the dark.

In the dream, in every instance of this recurring nightmare, something inhuman reaches out from the dark and closes itself over his son's chest and face with slick black arms that curl like pythons. The thing pulls him deeper down, into the inky black, and Liam tries to scream out, to wiggle free of the heel digging into the small of his back and slip into the crevasse, into the dark, to save his child.

And that's when the roar of a shotgun blast crashes into his skull . . . and he wakes.

"Jesus, Liam, are you okay?" the girl asked, bleary-eyed, breath foul.

Liam sat up, heart pounding, air coming in gulps. *The fucking dream,* he thought, more angry than distressed. Angry that no matter how far he seemed to run his goddamned mind was always with him, hauling that dirty sack of old memories right along with it.

"I'm fine," he said sharply, pushing himself off the bed, alarmed at how terribly hot it was in the room.

It must be past noon, he thought, and looked around for his jeans.

"That musta been some crazy nightmare," the girl said.

Liam found his jeans, scooped them up, and stuck his legs through. He buckled his wide brown leather belt and gave the woman his attention for the first time since waking. His brain was muddled, still thick with the booze they'd drunk last night—and through the early morning. First at that shit bar back in Yuma, and then, when it closed, back here at the motel, the first one they'd found after taking his car north.

What the hell is her name again?

He shrugged, figured it didn't matter, and debated whether he should take off now or strip back down and get a shower first. While he was debating and trying to forget about the damned dream, and the memories that came with it, she also got out of bed, smiling slyly now. She slunk toward him, naked as a snake, and began fiddling with the buckle he'd just clasped.

"C'mon, Liam, let's get back in bed for a bit. What's the hurry?"

"Back in bed? It's got to be a hundred degrees in here." He thought a moment, debating. "I'm gonna take a shower, then I gotta hit the road."

The girl put her arms around him, pressed her breasts against his ribs, and he found himself responding despite the heat, the annoyance, and the dream.

"Well, that sounds good, too," she said. "Let's take a quickie shower, then you and me go to California, right?"

She giggled again and pressed him tightly, pushing her body against his in a way that suggested their respective ideas of a shower differed substantially. He screwed his eyes shut and thought for a moment, tried to remember when the hell—more importantly, *why* the hell—had he told her about California?

Dumb dumb dumb dumb dumb . . .

Then it came back to him. She worked at that bar, a barmaid. Near closing, she'd stolen the booze and he'd promised to take her to a motel. They'd slipped out the back easy as you please while the old man tending bar went to the shitter for what was going on ten minutes before they'd hauled ass out of there.

And yeah, he'd told her more, hadn't he? He'd told her about his past. About his running from Australia after . . . after what happened. Then falling in with some small-timers in London after he'd had time to settle and make some contacts. And . . . yeah, damn it . . . he'd told her about his ex, Kaaron, and about Timothy.

Liam, you may be smart as hell when you're sober but when you're drunk and squeezing a pretty girl you're dumber than a dingo.

He let out a breath, looked at the top of the girl's head. Wondered, somewhat sadly, if he'd told her too much. Told her stuff that could follow him to California, to Jim . . . *and to the job, dumbass.* Yeah, and that. He racked his brain, but he would never have said anything about *that . . .* would he?

He didn't want to hurt her, and he sure as hell didn't want to kill her. But she needed to be cut out, and fast, before she got any more bright ideas like coming with him anywhere, much less California.

"Listen, love," he said, trying to sound like the rough-edged Aussie she'd fallen for, and not the conniving criminal he was. "Why don't you go start the water, yeah? And I'll follow in a moment."

He pushed her away, kissed her on the lips, and when she slid her hands up to his cheeks and through his tossed black hair, he almost thought about erasing the lie, because suddenly a shower, her version, seemed like a damned fine idea. He broke the kiss, looked away from her, from her body, as if searching for something.

"I've got to make a quick call, okay? Go start the water."

She looked at him a moment, questioning, then smiled, turned, and walked slowly, ever so slowly, to the bathroom.

She is pretty, he thought, then closed his eyes tight. *Yeah, mate, but imagine what Jim would do to that pretty face if she showed up in California, asking questions, asking for sweet old Liam. It wouldn't be so pretty any more, not by a long shot.*

He picked up the receiver off the nightstand's pay-per-call phone and waited for the water to start. Once he heard it, he waited another few beats, heard the toilet flush, then the scrape of metal shower curtain rings dragging along a rod. He dropped the phone receiver onto the mussed bed, grabbed his T-shirt, threw it on. He searched the room for his duffel, panicked when it wasn't on the worn chair or underneath the heaps of bedding, then remembered he'd left it in the car, along with the loaded Glock handgun.

When he was sure he had everything—keys, wallet, and sunglasses pretty much covered his earthly belongings—he slipped quietly out the front door, careful not to rattle the safety chain, and closed it slowly behind him. He jogged to the car, got inside. The heat trapped in the car swallowed him like an oven turned to broil and he was forced to take a precious few seconds to roll down one window. He reversed onto the brown narrow highway, his eyes locked on the motel room door. If she came out, if she had even a small chance of seeing his plate, he'd have to use the Glock.

He prayed she stayed inside.

As he accelerated away (the old girl had lost her looks but the motor worked fine, thanks), he checked the rearview to be sure the girl wasn't coming after him, pissed off and dripping naked while running through the sweltering waves of afternoon heat. When he saw no sign of her, he let go of the tension that had tightened in his chest, let out a breath. After a few miles, he stopped to roll down all the windows, the AC having bugged out months ago.

Heading west, Liam thought about the nightmare, which wasn't technically a nightmare, because it *had* happened. Hadn't it? Yeah, all but the last part, because there were no creatures living in caves that grabbed little boys.

Were there?

No, but there was evil.

He had seen it. He had done it. *Monster.*

He sighed, knowing in his heart he wouldn't have been able to kill the girl, but still wished he hadn't told her about Kaaron, or more so, Timothy. Those were things he liked to think of as hidden. The parts of him no one else could see. He thought if he kept them—the *thoughts* of them—locked inside his mind, then they were less real, and he wouldn't have to miss them. Wouldn't feel the pain of missing his boy.

"What's done is done," he said out loud, reassured by his clean exit, being on the road, the solid sound of his own voice.

He smiled, pushed the dented Camaro to eighty, and figured he'd be calling Jim right on time, give or take a few minutes depending on traffic. Which was good, because in all the years he'd known Jim Cady, he'd discovered one major thing—a thing it was important to never forget, no matter how many jobs they did together, or how good a friend Liam might think Jim was—you should *never* piss off Jim. And Jim liked punctuality. He liked precision. And so far, those traits had paid off handsomely for Liam, who, if he thought about it, was Jim's number two. His right-hand man, so to speak.

Yeah, well, hands can be chopped off, can't they, old boy?

Liam's smile smoothed away, and he began thinking about the job. Started working through the bullet points, the plan. It was important he have everything down before he arrived, because it would be way past stupid to show up unprepared, and this particular job was more complicated than most. Everything would have to be perfect. Yeah, they'd done a smattering of tough gigs together, all over the world it seemed—bank heists, break-ins, even a little bounty hunting for a chatty witness for some wise guys in Chicago—but this one was different. Unexplored territory.

They'd never done a kidnapping.

5

The Thorne home, settled snugly in the moderately upscale suburban streets of northern San Diego, was a ranch with white siding, an iron-work railing around a small but clean front porch, and a roof metaphorically sagging from the second mortgage they'd obtained after the death of Dave's brother. The mortgage was a necessary evil, a short-term (or so Dave prayed) loan to pay for Henry's medical bills. More specifically, the months of both inpatient and outpatient physical therapy sessions, not to mention the ensuing therapist visits that followed upon his waking, a necessity their insurance company wasn't inclined to cover.

At least Dave and Mary had the small comfort of knowing they would recoup some of those expenses once Henry was of age and the trust released, but there was nearly a decade of life between now and then. They had both agreed as part of the settlement to put every cent gained from the suit (minus a small amount to cover Henry's extended hospital stay) into a trust in order to quickly wrap things up and move on, knowing in their deepest hearts they would struggle, but also knowing that they would make it. They'd have to. What other choice was there?

When Henry came to live with them, there had been other sacrifices to make as well, all of which were done happily and without regret. The most immediate being that Dave's home office, where he worked on his cases at night, during weekends, and often over holidays, was moved into their already too-small living room, so that Henry would have a bedroom to call his own.

To make ends meet, and catch up on neglected clients, Dave was working longer hours (even more so than usual) at the office. Mary had been forced to adjust the hours she worked at the local branch of the State Farm Insurance office, where she shared an agent desk with a trim, tidy man named Leopold Gantry, who, being an angel from heaven, had understood Mary's plight and had been happy to shift his own hours to accommodate her new schedule.

Still, despite the shifted schedules, extended hours, and financial stresses, the Thornes had never been happier. They were a *family*, and there was no price tag to put on that, especially given the impossibility they had come to live with since Mary's ectopic pregnancy and subsequent pelvic disease that fused her fallopian tubes together forever, a sealed door that would never open again, no matter how many of Dave's eager fellas came knocking. Yes, a family, and Mary saw to it they damned well acted like one, despite the horrific circumstances that brought them together. With her adjusted hours, she was able to make meals nearly every night, and it was a given that the three of them, despite any scheduling issues, work emergencies, or any other of life's little annoyances, ate dinner together every evening. To talk. To share their lives with one another.

Normally, these meals were filled with Henry's silly jokes, and Dave's sillier reactions, the ones that made Henry laugh and forget his painful past, forget the bad in the world.

But on this night, there was a palpable unease, a tension neither Dave nor Mary could put their finger on. Mary supposed it might be because of their visit with Hamada, and about them wanting to talk to Henry about his gift. The two of them had discussed bringing it up with him. Had *strategized*. But now, seeing Henry sitting at the table, looking sullen, both of them had pulled back, wondering if this was indeed a good time to broach the subject.

Dave coughed lightly. He and Mary exchanged a meaningful glance.

Henry, for his part, was hardly paying attention to either of them, content to simply pick at the meatloaf with his fork, not feeling the slightest bit hungry.

"Henry?" Mary finally said, in an overtly sweet tone that meant she was getting ready to talk about something personal. Something about his brain or the doctor or what a teacher said at school. "We saw Dr. Hamada today."

Henry put down the fork, one of the big shiny ones he hated because it made him feel like a baby when holding it, his fisted grip needing to choke up on it, near the tines, in order to balance it right. He sighed heavily, put his hands in his lap, slumped his shoulders, and shifted his eyes warily to Dave and Mary. They had been staring at him the whole meal, he realized, waiting to engage him in this conversation. But he'd been immersed in his own thoughts, thinking about those kids that chased him, about the way the janitor had locked them both in that closet, about the hateful slur. He didn't want to talk about anything right now, and certainly not Dr. Hamada.

His eyes darted from one face to the other. Uncle Dave was smiling, but he looked nervous. Aunt Mary was also smiling, but there was steel in it, and Henry knew he couldn't get out of this one.

"Okay," he said quietly, the inflection giving away nothing.

"He told us about the—" She paused, then, "the games you've been playing. With the cards? You're very good at it."

"You mean the Zener cards," he said, knowing where this was headed. "I know, I get them all right."

"It's a good thing, Henry," Dave blurted out, putting down his own fork. "We just wanted to understand more about you; Dr. Hamada, and us, want to help you understand, help you be happy."

"I am happy," Henry said, and meant it. He tried to convey his earnestness to Dave and Mary, wasn't sure if it stuck. Dave looked nervous again, and Mary looked worried, like Henry had shouted "I hate you!" instead of what he had actually said.

"That's good, Henry," she said, "and that's the most important thing. We just—"

"Do you want to know if I can read your minds?" he said abruptly. "Read anyone's mind I want?" Dave froze mid-chew, and Mary sat back straight, as if he'd pulled a snake from his pocket. "Because I can," he said. "I don't, because it isn't polite, but if I wanted to, it'd be easy. Like picking up a book and reading it. Or watching a TV that's been left on."

There was a moment of silence while Dave and Mary recovered from the frankness of Henry's statement. The three of them had never talked so directly about these things, about his strange abilities. Henry figured that Dave and Mary hadn't wanted to know. Hadn't wanted to know, for sure, know the extent of what he could do.

It was like the time Aunt Mary asked him about whispering to his dad at night, and he'd told her the truth, that he'd been talking to his daddy. That had scared her. And when Uncle Dave found out, he seemed more than scared, he seemed angry. Like Henry had been doing something bad or playing with someone he wasn't supposed to be playing with. And once they knew, it didn't make things better, not at all!

So he started to talk to his daddy only on the inside. At least he tried to. He forgot sometimes and whispered or spoke out loud, but knew if he did that around them they'd be scared and angry all over again. And even though they were trying to be nice, and wanted to help him, he knew they couldn't.

He'd only frighten them, like he was frightening them right now.

Henry felt incredibly tired. He dropped his chin, his eyes staring at the cold meatloaf and mashed potatoes on his plate, the heavy fork forgotten on the tablecloth.

"May I be excused, please?" he said.

Dave and Mary exchanged a look.

"You didn't eat much," Mary said.

"Not hungry," he mumbled, and slid out of his chair. "Sorry, Aunt Mary," he said, and didn't know if he was apologizing for not eating the dinner she'd made, or not making them feel like they'd helped him. Or, more accurately, making *them* feel okay with who he was, instead of frightened and helpless, which is exactly how they were feeling.

He could *see* it.

"Henry," Mary started, but Dave put a hand gently on her forearm.

"It's okay, Henry," Dave said. "Why don't you go lie down. We'll save your food for you and if you're hungry later we can heat it up, okay?"

"Okay, thanks." Henry took a few steps toward the hallway, then turned back to them, watched them looking at each other, holding hands, the concern clear on their faces.

"I love you," he said.

Mary went to him, then kneeled and hugged him hard, kissed his forehead and his cheeks. He smiled, and the cold that had settled in his heart began to warm up.

"We love you, too, Henry," she said, stroking his face, his head. "You go lie down and I'll check in on you in a bit."

"Okay, Mary," Henry said, and went to his bedroom, closed the door behind him. The dying light coming through his single window bathed the room in hazy crimson sunset, the corners pooled with shadow. He crawled onto his bed, thinking he'd just lie down a few minutes. His stomach growled and he considered getting up and finishing his dinner. While he considered, he wrapped his arms around one soft pillow and closed his eyes.

6

When he opened them again, it was dark.

He was warm, sweaty. He was tucked under his covers and still fully clothed—wearing the same sweatpants and T-shirt he'd worn to school. His mouth was dry. He rolled onto his side, looked at the glowing digits of his baseball-shaped bedside clock.

12:34

He sat up, rubbed his eyelids. A little confused, out of sorts.

At some point he'd drifted off to sleep. Someone had tucked him in, left the door open. Henry smiled at that, his love for Dave and Mary helping to smooth the hard lines of his difficult day, disperse the fog of his temporary disorientation.

He liked having the bedroom door open because the nightlight in the hallway made his middle-of-the-night bathroom trips more manageable (and less scary), his bedroom having only one moon-soaked window that filled the room with silver-tinted shapes and shadows, a world of hiding places for a child's imaginary monsters.

Henry realized, with an internal moan, that what woke him was indeed that all-too-familiar need, the pressure on his bladder, the slight cramping pain in his privates. But when he pushed the blanket off his hot legs and swung them over the edge of the bed, he paused, his sleep-fogged brain rapidly catching up to some new, and relevant, data.

The nightlight in the hallway was off.

A vertical murkiness filled the space between his cracked-open door and the frame. The darkness gathered in the hallway oozed into his room through the opening spread along the floors and walls, coated the ceiling.

He studied that vertical black bar, wondered if he could withstand the building pressure in his bladder enough to fall back asleep. He also wondered, along with the first glowing embers of slow-building fear, why that soft, lemon-colored nightlight wasn't turned on.

There's nothing to be afraid of, a voice whispered from behind his ear.

Henry's breath caught.

Daddy?

He'd been hearing the voice for a while now, ever since he'd woken from the coma, but sometimes it still caught him off guard. Plus, he wanted to be sure. Was it his dad, or was it only in his mind? Sometimes he couldn't tell if the voice inside his head was real, or if it was nothing more than part of his subconscious doing its best copycat impression, a sly mimic of the voice, of the man he had known so well, who he had loved so much.

"Daddy?" Aloud this time. He waited.

The voice came back to him—so *close*—and it wasn't that copycat from his subconscious. It was the real deal. The straight poop, as Dave liked to say, usually to make Henry giggle.

I'm telling you, son, the voice said in a humoring tone, *you can go out there. I checked it for you, man. Ain't nothing but family pictures out there. You'll see. Go on.*

Henry shook his head, still not liking the prospect of walking through the dark.

"No," Henry whispered, but his bladder pinched painfully. He couldn't hold it all night. "Don't wanna." He pushed himself back against the pine headboard, knees to chest, away from the open door and the dark hallway beyond.

Hey now, tell you what, the silky voice said, moving from his ear to behind him, then to somewhere right in front, as if the thing speaking to him was only inches away. *I'll go look for you again, okay? Then I'll come back and tell you if the coast is clear.*

Henry considered this deal for a moment, saw the logic of it, and nodded.

All right, all right, we got us a deal, the voice said, obviously pleased with itself. *I'll be right back.*

The shadows next to Henry's bed vibrated, then slid into each other like puddles of black mercury. The dense black coalesced and rose, as if standing. The shade rose to full height—a tall, skinny figure—and walked away from Henry toward the door.

Henry watched as it slipped into the hallway, the black form barely visible in the darkness, as if outlined in silver, as if the shadow was backlit and haloed. It looked one way, and then the other, then turned back to Henry, hunched its dark shoulders in a mild shrug.

Nothing, the shadow said. *Now come on over here and turn on the light. I'll stay with you.*

Slowly, still wary, Henry slid from his bed and padded over to the doorway. As the shadow figure watched, Henry leaned down so he was eye-to-eye with the night light. *Go on, son. I'm standing guard.* Henry nodded, reached a finger toward the light and flipped the tiny plastic switch into the ON position. The narrow bulb, shaped like a candle flame behind a plastic seashell, came alive, and yellow filled his vision, dusted the hallway with soft light. Henry smiled in relief, and gratitude.

His smile faltered, however, when he caught movement at the end of the hallway, where a door had just clicked shut.

Uncle Dave stood there in boxer shorts and a white T-shirt. He was staring, wide-eyed. Not at Henry, but past him.

At the shadow man.

Henry twisted to look behind him and saw nothing but an empty hallway. He straightened, turned back to Dave, and smiled.

"Hi Dave," he said, rubbing his eyes, as if still half-asleep.

Dave's eyes flicked from Henry, to the air behind him, then back. His face softened, and he gave his head a little shake before giving a tired, hesitant smile in return. "What are you doing?"

"Gotta wee," Henry said.

Dave opened his mouth to respond, but Henry crossed briskly to the bathroom and shut the door behind him.

When Henry came out, Dave wasn't there. He walked to his bedroom, eager to return to sleep, but found his uncle sitting at the foot of his bed, waiting in the gloomy dark.

"Henry, you okay?" Dave said, sounding tired and, possibly, a little scared.

"Uh-huh," Henry said, and ran to the bed and jumped in, his feet knocking softly against Dave's arm.

Dave laughed, stood, and tucked the covers up to Henry's chin.

"Not too much, it's hot," Henry said.

"You want me to crack the window?" Dave asked. "I can, but you'll hear those garbage trucks early in the morning, banging cans around."

"No, just the sheet, though."

Dave nodded and neatly folded the comforter down past Henry's feet, then smoothed the sheet up over him. "How's that?"

"Good," Henry said. "Actually, window too, please. Just halfway. I don't mind the trucks."

"All right," Dave said and went to the window.

After the bright light of the bathroom, Henry's eyes were once again adjusting to the dark, made easier now by the soft luminescence filtering in from the hallway nightlight.

He could see Dave clearly as he spread open the curtains beyond the foot of the bed. Moonlight spilled in, bathing him in cool blue.

As Dave lifted the window, Henry could see the dark figure standing behind him, watching. The shadow man stepped into the moonlight, and Henry saw the face more clearly, duotone features glowing in the shapes of a nose, cheekbones, lips, and chin. Silver-penny eyes.

A cool breeze crept into the room. Dave sat down once more at the end of Henry's bed. "I heard you talking, son. Was it—" He paused, then pushed on. "Was it your daddy? Is your daddy here again?"

Henry looked at his uncle but didn't reply. He saw his father's shad-owed form approach. Saw a dark hand reach out toward Dave's shoulder.

Henry closed his eyes tight. *Daddy,* don't!

When he opened them, the dark figure was gone, and Henry sighed in relief, thankful his father had returned inside, where he belonged. Uncle Dave watched him curiously.

"No, Uncle Dave," Henry said and shrugged. "Having a weird dream, I guess."

Dave noticeably relaxed, a built-up tension slipping from his shoulders. He blew out a breath and smiled. "Okay, then. You get some sleep now."

Dave stood and went to the door, then turned. The nightlight filled the space behind him, making him the shadow now. "You know, Henry, your daddy loved you. And if he's with you, that's a good thing, because it means he's still alive in your heart. You know that, right?"

Henry saw the dark shape of his father standing in the hall behind his uncle, leaning back against the opposite wall, arms folded across his chest. A grin curved beneath those twinkling silver eyes.

"I know," Henry said quietly, and turned away from the door to find sleep.

7

In a different part of Liberty, a part that lay closer to the fringes of the town, where junkyards proliferated along with sewage and energy plants, where telephone poles tended to lean and businesses were primarily of the "closed door" variety (plumber offices and glass makers, small clothing factories, cage-faced liquor stores, and metal-working shops), there was a strip of industrialism that wore a rough cluster of trailer homes on its back, like barnacles on a tortoise's shell. If one were inclined to count, they'd reach a sum of fifty homes staggered in rows of ten, with odd standalone units here and there, latecomers finding a free patch of dirt, rooting as haphazardly as wild daisies.

The park was identified at the entrance by a curved metal archway of words that spanned from the top of one deteriorating brick wall to another, a potholed drive coming through beneath. It was under this archway that each of the trailers, at one time or another, had passed in hopes of finding a patch of earth to call their own, to slump down tiredly onto a designated rectangle of dirt (with three years paid in advance, of course) and sleep.

WINDOW TO THE SEA, the sign proclaimed. Each letter formed from a hard metal long since rusted by elements, tarnished by time. The name was deceptive in that the sea, although a mere six miles away, was impossible to locate unless one had a helicopter. The only thing visible through the figurative "window" of the trailer park was the view of a few square miles of brush land, a sloping mountain more brown than green most months, and, at the far end of this delusive vista, the southwest corner of a Walmart parking lot.

One of these rogue trailers was butted against the edge of the park's trash center, or what the residents called "the bins," an assortment of large metal dumpsters lined up along a low concrete wall. The dumpsters, once vibrantly multicolored, had long since gained uniformity and were now a murder of huddled black crows, stained to a grayish-black by years of harsh treatment by man, gods, and beast alike, having survived a generation's worth of soiled trash, exposure to every form of weather, and an uncountable chorus of dog's lifted legs to piss on their rusted steel wheels.

This trailer, a throwback that looked like a desert-beige Lego block dropped into mud, was the home of Tommy "Trailer Trash" Patchen, recent rock-thrower and common, everyday bully.

Inside, Tommy's parents watched *The Tonight Show* and split a fifth of Evan Williams Kentucky Bourbon. Tommy lay in his bedroom, the one all the way to the rear of the trailer, closest to the bins, reading an old, well-thumbed issue of *Heavy Metal* magazine his buddy Grayson had given him, and deciding whether to jerk off to the naked cartoon chick riding the white leopard or finish the comic strip about the space mutants who were enslaving the women of Earth. He was flipping the pages back to the image of the busty woman on the white leopard when something, or someone, knocked three times—*rap rap rap*—against the small window of his bedroom.

Tommy jumped a bit, startled, and looked up at the window, which was small and built to slide open horizontally, the pane blurred by the same distorted, semi-opaque privacy glass you might find in the bathroom of a roadside motel. It was high but not so high it couldn't be reached, even by a sperm-spit of a seventh grader like Tommy. Hunched against the wall beneath the window sat a milk crate filled with the debris of an average preteen—comics, baseball cards, an unused piggy bank—that served as a step-up. In the dirt outside, a second crate was pushed far beneath the raised trailer, accessible as needed for a boost. Tommy had long ago mastered the milk crate trick when needing to sneak back into his room in the middle of the night (or the early morning) after he had snuck out to meet the guys for beers at the shitty gas station. Or, on rare occasions, to meet Bets, his mildly not-gross-looking fourteen-year-old neighbor (who used to babysit him, for chrissakes) for a make-out session and a game of stinky finger at said gas station whenever she could sneak out of her own trailer from the other side of the park.

Tommy had no plans to sneak out tonight. And since none of the guys had planned to either, that left Betty "Bets" McKillen, babysitter extraordinaire, as the sole candidate for his unsolicited late-night visitor. Tommy raised himself off one sleeping elbow, already salivating at the idea it was indeed Bets, who was *this* close to giving him his first BJ if he could convince her—and Lord knows he'd been trying to convince her—that it wasn't a sin against God.

"Bets?" he said in a hushed tone, not wanting to alert his parents.

There was no response, and he was about to go back to his magazine, having now firmly decided on the jerk-off option and *then* the comic strip, when the knocks came again. Slower. Determined. He actually saw the hand through the semi-opaque glass this time. A blurred fist, visible only as a black smudge against the indigo night beyond.

Rap. Rap. RAP.

Tommy rolled out of bed and checked the narrow hallway leading to the living room. He saw the television and half of Jay Leno, wearing a stupid white wig as he did some lame-ass skit, and knew his folks were crunched back into the couch sipping their shit whiskey and likely smoking a fat one. He closed the door softly, letting it latch, then locked it for good measure. They wouldn't bother him—they never did—but if it was locked, they knew not to try to come in. They'd go to bed, fuck loudly, and pass out.

Horny from the magazine and thinking more and more that maybe tonight would be the night Bets finally gave in, Tommy threw on a black sweatshirt, checked his hair in the mirror, and went to investigate.

He stepped atop the bowed, hard red plastic of the milk crate and slid the window open.

"Bets?"

No answer.

Thinking more with his libido and less with his brain, Tommy stuck his head out the window in an attempt to see who, exactly, had come for him.

A massive hand snatched him by the hair, fingers so long they nearly encompassed his entire head. The hand yanked and he started to scream out in pain—in fear—when a second brute hand clamped over his face.

With the ease and speed of pulling a loose wine cork, Tommy was yanked through the window by his head and snatched out into the night.

He dropped and hit the ground hard, the breath knocked out of him. Before he could react, a massive pressure pushed into his stomach and a quick succession of punches pounded into his ribs with the force of a sledgehammer. Tommy heard something *snap* in his chest and he couldn't breathe, couldn't speak. Couldn't scream. The pain was so overwhelming it numbed him, and his mouth opened and closed like a fish thrown to the dirt from a river.

He opened his eyes and, for a split second, saw the face of his attacker. Terror and realization stabbed through him with such severity that he lost all rational thought. He stuttered a few words that might have been "mom" or "help." Or, perhaps, "I'm sorry."

Tommy was flipped onto his stomach. Dirt clouded into his mouth and eyes, and the piercing pain from the broken bone in his chest flared like a knife stab. A flashbulb popped in his brain. Impossibly large hands gripped the sides of his head and a jagged boulder of pressure drilled into his lower spine. As his head was yanked off the dirt, spine bending, Tommy knew it was a massive knee fixing him to the ground, as if he were a bug stuck to the wall with a pin.

Tommy thought about the girl in the magazine, and her white leopard ... or was it a tiger? He imagined riding on the tiger with her, holding her naked waist as they fled far, far ...

The giant hands squeezed, then twisted with a quick, savage ease. Tommy's neck snapped like a dried-out chicken bone.

The boy went limp. The attacker stood a moment, catching a breath, then lifted the boy's body and carried it to the bins, only a few yards away, where it was unceremoniously dumped in with the garbage of the entire trailer park. In the morning, the body would be taken away by a truck to the landfill where it would be buried in the earth, to lie forever amid the detritus of the park's inhabitants.

From inside the trailer, the sounds of *The Tonight Show* filtered out into the chilled night air. The audience howled with laughter.

8

As dumpster rats nibbled at the fingertips and earlobes of young Tommy's cooling flesh, another would-be victim ran to save his own needle-pricked skin, albeit from a predator of an altogether different nature.

Thankfully, the meth Richie had smoked an hour ago gave his ill-used muscles ample chemical adrenaline to propel him through the dark forest with enough speed to outrace whatever was pacing him. Strings of saliva hung in shimmering moonlit lines from his lower lip to the chest of his ratty T-shirt. Tears poured from his eyes as he whimpered, the moisture mixing with the sweat that beaded like oil on his forehead, temples, and cheeks. He'd lost a shoe along the way, and his feet now beat heavily through the moist soil with an asymmetrical *thump-splat, thump-splat,* as he ran from the monster, for that's what it was.

He had seen it up close.

When he'd staggered from the weak barrel-fire to shit in the trees like an animal, he had gone too far, gotten turned around, and found himself lost. He didn't much care; there was nothing at the camp, anyway. The small amount of powder they'd divvied up among the group was long gone, and he didn't feel like another night of being pawed at by that fat fuck Jerry, who he put up with only because it was his whore wife who had blown the dealer for the meager quarter-gram they'd all smoked away so voraciously. Instead, he'd wandered carelessly, eventually letting himself fall to the ground beneath the canopy of a vanilla-scented ponderosa pine, where he'd laughed at nothing and dreamed of cracked stars spilling diamonds.

He'd come to minutes later, when something hard poked his arm.

Then his chest.

Then rapped his head like a rubber mallet.

He sprang upward, ready to fight off whoever was testing him—coiled with the immediate readiness for violence one learns after years of hard-living on the streets—and found himself staring into large yellow eyes. Heavy lids squinted, as if the thing were studying him. It rose from a crouch, black limbs parting a slick outer shell that clung like soft, rounded plates to its body, hooded its gnarled head.

He'd screamed, and when the thing reached for him, he'd stumbled back, cried out once more, babbling nonsense in his panic. After a few failed attempts, he was finally able to find his feet. He turned toward the dark and ran.

The creature pursued.

Sometimes he'd hear it closing in, sometimes from the left, sometimes from the right. It hadn't occurred to him that the thing might be toying with him, herding him toward a destination. A nest. A killing cave where the bones of a hundred victims lay dense and brittle.

He dared a look back, searching, but his shaky, drug-addled vision showed him nothing but an army of silver-tinged trees.

There was no sign of whoever, or whatever, was following.

Richie spun his head back around, face forward, in time to see a low-hanging branch, thick as a full-grown anaconda, leap for his eyes. There was a split second of awareness, the complex pattern of the bark filling his vision, and then his head erupted in white light; a heavy *crunch* as the bridge of his nose slammed into the branch and his running legs swung upward, sending him horizontal before he crashed down onto his back. He moaned and blinked. When he brought a hand to his face he felt his nose move loosely, the tip skewed to one side. Broken. The internal grating of shifting gristle coincided with a deeper, piercing pain that jabbed into his head, soaked his already impaired brain with the thick syrup of concussion.

A twig snapped behind him, and adrenalized fear surged through his body once more, cleared the runway for his muddled brain long enough to emergency-land appropriate commands for his weak, shaking limbs: *Move, goddammit! MOVE YOUR ASS RICHIE!*

Richie moved. He scrambled to his knees, pushed himself forward, panting like a dog, his twisted nose sealed tight, his head pounding like a bass drum.

He pushed through branches, dipped below others, and sprinted into a small clearing. Surrounded by trees, he saw no clear pathway, no neon sign marked EXIT. He dared a glance at the moon, the night sky's great eye bulging in glee as it watched poor, homeless, meth-addicted Richie run for his life. *What the fuck does it want?* He felt the heat of tears, the twitching of his lips that foretold full-on blubbering. He swallowed the emotion, searched for resolve. *It's not gonna get me*, his mind whimpered. *It's not gonna get Richie!* He kicked his way through another patch of underbrush high as his waist and dense as briar. A broken twig stabbed into his bared foot, pierced sock and skin. Hot lightning shot up his leg. Richie went down again, howling.

Snap.

His head jerked back to search the surrounding trees. "Leave me alone, you bastard!" His screams were a prayer—what he was cursing was not something he could reason with or frighten away. He took a few deep breaths and tried to stand. The signals of pain from his foot were bad, but he could limp on it. As he hobbled onward he noticed, despite his panic, that the ground felt altered. He looked down, saw he was working his way through a strip of cleared forest, the dirt packed and smooth.

Holy shit! his brain screamed in furious hope. *A fucking road!*

Richie hobbled a few more yards and the trees in front of him thinned, the road bent, and he saw his salvation. A shadowed monument in the near distance. A stubborn prick of humanity stuck among the sprawling god-forsaken nature of the forest.

A house.

"Hey! Help me!" he tried to yell, but his face was so damaged and his fear so all-consuming that what escaped his torn lips was a mucus-dulled "Eh! El may!"

Richie covered the stretch of ground separating the tree line and the house in a dead, albeit hitching, sprint. Behind him he heard more movement. Closer. Faster. That *thing* was closing in—

Forcing himself not to think, not to turn back, he leapt the three steps to a hooded porch, let the propulsion of his body slam into the house. He raised a fist, pounded the door.

"Hey!" he screamed, his throat choked with blood, gagging him. He bent over, spat a glob of red mucus onto the porch, wiped at strings of saliva with a bare forearm. He coughed, pushed his cheek against the door, and wheezed a squeaky "Please . . ." into the moldy wood.

Had he retained the ability to smell, Richie would have taken in the odors of decay. Of neglect.

Slowly, the puzzle pieces connected in his mind. He took a step back, stared in horror at the door. He turned his head, saw the boarded-up windows staggered along the front of the house, the flaked paint of the siding. He stared at the door more closely, panic chilling to a deep fear, and realized it was secured shut with a rusted padlock and a sagging staple hasp affixed between the door and the frame.

"Abandoned," he said quietly, a hint of resignation blossoming in his chest. For the first time in many years, Richie felt totally and completely clearheaded.

A rustle of tree limbs.

He turned. Unfiltered terror seeped through his bones.

There were birds everywhere.

Crows, he thought. Or ravens. He never really knew the fucking difference. The ground was littered with them like black shavings. They hopped and cawed and flapped their wings at him.

In the near distance, just beyond the army of birds, a silhouette broke free from the dark trees, the thick curtain of black leaves. Had he not known better, he might have mistaken it for a woman wearing a robe. But had it close up for the monstrous, impossible thing it really was, and seeing it gave him a resigned knowledge.

Here, at the end, understanding came. Clear and chilling.

He tapped the rusted padlock securing the door of the abandoned farmhouse with a finger, and knew he'd done exactly what it had wanted him to do. As he watched the thing moving toward him through the sea of birds, the horrid fowl dividing like the red sea to allow her passage, he could have sworn it seemed content. Maybe even pleased. The way one might feel after a hard day's work; when the satisfying crack of opening a cold beer and a porch-view sunset was as fine and gratifying as the afterglow of the best sex in the universe.

'Cept that thing ain't gonna crack a beer, Richie thought, moving slowly back down the porch, birds cawing and flapping out of his path with hostility. The creature followed him with its gold-hued eyes, but otherwise went still, halting her progress ten feet away. Content to watch.

No no no, Richie thought, beginning to shuffle along the front of the house, ready to bolt around its corner if the thing gave him that kind of time, that kind of lead. *No, all that fucking thing wants to crack open is* me. Hysteria bubbled in the back of his mind because some part of him knew it to be true. Knew he was about to die.

NO! NO! NO!

A long-forgotten part of Richie's mind screamed out in rebellion, a part he'd thought had long since been smoked away in a meth haze. A part that still carried a will to *survive*. It screamed, and that long-forgotten scream gave him strength he didn't know existed.

LIVE! That voice shrieked. *SURVIVE!*

Richie spared a glance to his right, saw the corner of the house in spitting distance.

"Stay away!" he yelled, then ran for his life.

He turned the corner like a hoodlum clutching an old lady's purse with a cop in hot pursuit. A flapping, screaming crowd of black birds filled the air around him, blinding him. The toes of his bare, injured foot crunched into a rough lip of concrete. The jammed toenail ripped free and the bone of his big toe snapped. He cried out and thumped to the earth for what felt like the hundredth time that night.

Sweating and breathing heavily, heart racing, he sat up and clutched at the damaged foot, begging for a moment's respite, unsure if he could go on.

Two things forced him back into action. The first was the slanted double doors of a cellar that rose a foot from the ground, the thing he had tripped over when making his escape. The second, much more alarming, was the speed with which the creature was moving toward him across the moon-bleached, weed-sprung meadow. The birds, having sensed the end, all rose as one into the air, blocking out the moonlight, giving the creature a clear path to poor, fucked-up Richie.

It is *messing with me*, he thought absently, realizing this once he saw the true grace and power of the lithe thing; knowing damn well it could have overtaken him at any point.

"Please," he cried petulantly, every part of his body seemingly broken or bloodied. He debated giving up, but his drug-poisoned organs surged with one last push of adrenaline. "Fuck you!" he sobbed (it came out "Uck ew!") and crawled madly for the cellar.

He heaved one door open, saw only dark, and without hesitation threw his body down into it, letting the door slam shut behind him as his body bounced like a busted doll down a series of rock-and-mortar stairs before landing in a heap at the bottom. Cold dirt pressed into his face, and as he mumbled choked prayers his lips and tongue became coated with it.

He didn't hear the cellar doors open behind him, but he didn't need to. He dragged himself forward, turning back only once.

Above him, the creature stood black against the backdrop of blue night, the wide silver eye of the moon watching from over its shoulder as it descended. Richie crawled on his elbows, only going as far as the nearest wall, where he pushed himself into a sitting position, his back resting against cracked, coarse concrete. His wet breathing hitched and hiccupped as those yellow eyes approached.

He didn't beg. He just wanted it to be over.

The creature crouched at his feet. A slobbery, chittering sound came from its shadowed face. It crawled onto his legs, and Richie found himself with enough brain power to register—for something so skinny—how *heavy* it was. A long black limb slid out between two shifting plates, bent at a hard angle.

Without warning, the limb snapped downward in a fast, efficient stroke. Richie's left kneecap shattered.

He screamed, and the thing raised and dropped the bent limb again, smashing the bone cap of the other knee with a *crack* that seemed to fill the dark earthen chamber like a firecracker. Richie might have passed out from the pain had the meth pumping his heart and rushing through his brain not kept him awake and alert for each terrible, torturous moment. The creature crawled onto his lap, over legs now bent and broken. It clutched one of his hands and spat something warm—then burning hot—onto the skin of his outer wrist. He screeched as the flesh of his hand began melting, as if the creature had spat acid onto his skin. It pressed the wrist to the wall, where the flesh stuck, glued by an inhuman epoxy and the sticky residue of his own skin. It repeated this with the other hand, leaving Richie's arms spread like wings as his head dangled on his neck, cracked sobs erupting from deep inside him, ripped from his chest to fill his mouth with blood and phlegm.

The creature lifted itself off his legs. The long, oval shell covering the front of it separated like curtains while it let out a high-pitched keening sound. Dark eyelids fluttered over the yellow eyes in a sort of ecstasy. It grabbed Richie's hair and pinned his head to the wall, his broken face and dull eyes staring straight ahead. The creature thrust itself forward. Something hard and thick pushed into Richie's mouth.

And kept pushing.

Richie's eyes widened as the bones in his extending jaw snapped, his mouth lengthening impossibly as the creature's appendage pushed deeper down his throat, choking him. He could no longer scream, no longer breathe. He could do nothing but convulse when the thick muscle of the creature spasmed and a rush of burning fluid flowed like a hot, infested sea down his throat.

When finished, the creature pulled itself out, then settled back gently to watch, mustard eyes glowing with contentment in the dark cellar.

In the end, it was unclear whether Richie died from drowning, asphyxiation, or shock. But he did die, and luckily so. He did not have to feel the larva—a new organism infesting his still-warm flesh—swell like a fattening leech as it fed deep inside him. The new life devoured blood and fresh organs before it slid slowly upward, pushing past guts, then between lungs and heart. Up, up through the neck, and finally into the base of the brain, where it settled.

The creature cooed something maternal and, crossing the low-ceilinged room, went up the stairs, into the cool night, to gather what was needed.

Outside, the birds of the forest came alive with predawn song, and the old, weathered face of the farmhouse caught the dull orange of a new day, uncaring of the monsters that lay deep in its belly, unaware of the others who would soon arrive to join them.

PART THREE: THE JANITOR

1

The early-morning sky was the same shade as the smoke-colored Camaro that passed beneath the large green sign like an aging shark. The sign's reflective white letters flickered at the edge of the car's turning headlights: LONG TERM PARKING.

Liam pulled into the lot, a ten-level, low-security structure hunkered at the fringe of the San Diego International Airport, lit from within by musty yellow sodium lights. The automated kiosk at the entrance spat out a ticket. The security cameras would record the license plate (one of several rattling around in the car's trunk), and the police would eventually track the plate to a red Honda from the parking lot of a Joshua Tree motel he'd passed through on his way to the coast. But by then the job would be done, and he'd be drinking mezcal in Puerto Escondido.

On the top deck of the garage he spotted the van he'd been told to look for. He drove past it without slowing, made a long turn, and went down two levels before finding a spot to dump the Camaro.

Ten minutes later he pulled the white van alongside an automated parking kiosk almost identical to the one he'd used upon entering. He inserted the ticket he'd taken when he entered and the barrier lifted smoothly.

There was no charge.

A half mile outside the airport, Liam used a pay phone bolted to the white brick wall of an ARCO gas station. A few feet away a restroom door bore the white cutout of a man, the figure partially covered with a faded Mello Yello sticker. The door yawned open as the other end of the line began to ring.

Liam turned his back as an old homeless guy stepped out and brushed past him, leaving him with the sickly-sweet aromatic combination of soap, sweat, and urine. As the man shuffled away, Liam lowered his gaze to the cracked pavement.

"Right on time, brother," a rumbling voice said. The warm plastic pressed to Liam's ear conveyed the weight and raw closeness of Jim's mild approval.

"Of course. All well?"

"Yeah, man. We're good. You just getting in?"

Liam wiped sweat from his forehead. He stared at the brightening horizon and wondered how far he was from the ocean. He badly wanted to see it. "Yep, just got in and dying for some sleep. Been driving all night."

"Yeah, well, beggars and choosers, my brother. Timing is tight, understood?"

Liam nodded, turned away from the horizon. "Yes. What time?"

There was a momentary pause, and Liam wondered if Jim was scowling, smiling, or no longer listening.

"Quarter to nine. Where we discussed. Pick up Greg on the way. You know where he'll be waiting."

"The park."

"Yeah. If he's not there, keep going. Don't wait, don't call. Got it?"

"I got it."

A heavy sigh came from the other end, seeming part relief, part tension. "Okay, cool," he said. "Don't fuck it up." The line went dead.

"Cheers," Liam said limply to the irritating buzz coming from the handset. He set it back on the cradle and wondered if he could park somewhere, grab a couple hours of sleep. He momentarily debated finding a bar instead. Then he recalled Jim's rumbling voice.

Don't fuck it up.

Liam sighed and walked to the van. He got in, stared out the windshield to the ever-lightening sky. Seagulls circled like windblown ash in the distance.

He searched his guts for a bad feeling, listened for the distant flapping of any red flags in his subconscious, the tingling of a sixth sense.

This was bad business, after all. A *messy* business.

The taking of a child.

Things could get nasty.

But Liam's guts felt fine, and no red flags were evident, his sixth sense subdued and sleepy as he was. His stomach, however, rumbled with something other than imminent warning. He rolled down a window, took a moment to smell the salt on the air.

The ocean was close.

He smiled ruefully and started the van. He decided to go east, find a place to eat. After, he'd park, try to grab a quick nap before he had to pick up Greg, before . . .

. . . *before grabbing the kid.*

Liam frowned, looked down at the duffel bag resting on the floor between the two front seats. He thought of the loaded gun wrapped in oilcloth. He wondered absently if he would have killed that girl at the motel if she'd run after him.

He rubbed his eyes, suddenly overcome with exhaustion.

Moments later, the van pulled out of the ARCO, and Liam began to search for a decent café where he could get a pot of coffee and a big breakfast.

After all, today was a big day.

2

Henry stabbed the yellow eyes staring back at him from the plate. He watched them burst and run over the whites, spill into the hash browns, reach for the bacon with cooling tentacles.

"Looks like a yellow octopus."

Mary sat down across from him and he felt her displeasure. He decided to keep his eyes on the plate. He pushed some yolk into the crispy hash browns and forked it into his mouth. Chewing, he dared a look, hoping to have dodged a rebuke. He'd been told countless times not to play with his food, but he found the idea of tearing apart slabs of meatloaf (then dive-bombing them into a mountain of mashed potatoes) or twisting spaghetti onto his fork until he had a twine of noodle fatter than a baseball (or nearly so) or, in this case, pretending to poke the eyes out of sunny-side-up eggs too enticing to pass up.

Mary looked like she might be changing her mind on reminding him of this forbidden act—her colors were bright and red, like a fire truck—when Dave strode into the kitchen, pulling his jacket on and all but lunging toward the steaming mug sitting patiently next to the still-percolating coffee pot.

"Have an early deposition," he said, stealing a piece of toast from Mary's plate, biting it savagely between sips of hot coffee.

"And you wonder why you have indigestion," she scolded, moving the crosshairs from Henry to her husband, for which he was eternally grateful. They continued to chat as Henry focused on finishing his breakfast, but his appetite waned, and he found the broken-egg eyes suddenly disconcerting rather than humorous.

Something whispered in his ear that the face he saw on his plate was not far from the truth, and the truth was not too far from him.

What truth? he asked, hoping the voice wouldn't answer. Wouldn't even hear the question.

The response, instead, was a sensation of great pain, the most bottomless sorrow. The face on the plate—that broken face, those burst eyes—suddenly formed into another face. A *real* face. Someone he knew—a child—someone whose eyes were also being bitten, eaten, and were running not yellow, but red—

"Henry? Are you with us?"

Henry realized he was holding a large breath and released it with an audible sigh, the kind you loosed when breaking free from the pool after holding your body's inlets shut tight for as long as you could, creating that *pwah!* sound that popped from your guts and allowed breath to come in once more, feeding the blood with life.

"Huh?"

Dave and Mary both studied him strangely, with a peculiar concern; a concern which might not have been a protective one—say the one a parent gives a child who develops a wet, nasty cough—but more the defensive type. One you might have when your child is reading your mind, listening in to your thoughts and feelings, sucking at them like a sponge absorbing a spilled bottle of fluorescent ink.

"I'm okay," he said as a follow-up, and tried for a smile.

"You're sweating," Mary said.

"You look gray as a ghost, bud," Dave added.

Despite himself, Henry reached out. Gently. Just enough to tap the outer surfaces of their feelings.

Vibrant colors, swimming like fish in a pond, spun and circled within them. Flashes of other colors—bright reds and streaks of black, colors not known to him—perhaps not to anyone but God himself—flapped like flags, screaming feelings that his mind translated into words he understood.

Fragile, he heard.

Sick.

Worried.

Damaged.

Broken.

Lost.

Poor boy . . . oh, poor boy . . . can he hear me?

Is he reading my thoughts right now?

Henry stood abruptly, grabbed his pack from the floor by a shoulder strap. He slung it up and over his back. "I'm good. Gotta go."

Dave and Mary seemed momentarily frozen, faces blank . . . then they were moving once more. As if time had been stuck fast by a magic watch, and some higher power had spun the dial, rewound the motor, and let it loose.

"I'll take you, hon," Mary said, looking for her keys.

"I got him. I'm leaving anyway," Dave said, and kissed Mary on the cheek.

But Henry was already at the door. No hugs today. No rides, thank you. Sometimes alone is better, even when you're sad. Or when you really are lost. Or, perhaps, you really are broken after all. Because who loves a broken doll?

No one.

"Gonna walk," he said, trying again for that elusive smile. He pushed through the door. "Love you!" he yelled back and was down the steps, stomping quickly through the grass of the front yard.

He heard the door open behind him, could sense them both there. Watching.

"Henry," Mary called out, but Henry didn't turn back.

He lifted a hand instead. "Gonna cut through the park!" he yelled, and a tear rolled down one cheek.

Mary watched Henry march across the street. *At least he looked both ways*, she thought, and let herself feel, as parents, they'd done *something* right at least.

He was so small. The trees in the park towered over him, the blue sky a monstrous canvas and he nothing but a thumbprint smudge at its bottom. She had the irrational thought the world might, at any moment and without warning, swallow Henry whole. Gobble him up. He would disappear, and not even the birds in the trees or the bugs in the dirt would notice.

She felt Dave's hands on her shoulders, knew he was also watching the child.

Mary was surprised to find her hands balled into tight fists, and made her fingers relax before saying goodbye to her husband. As she kissed him on the lips, she thought to herself that if the world so much as laid a finger on that boy's head, it would feel the full strength and might of her fury.

And woe to those who would stand against a mother's wrath.

Fred stepped out the maintenance door of the school's warehouse annex and started to walk across the large, paved recess court. He spotted the principal, Ms. Terry, heading for the administration offices. Her eyes fell on him and she diverted her path in his direction, a broad smile on her face. He turned his head to catch a fleeting glance of a pale-faced Jim Hawkes scamper out of the cafeteria and head toward the south hallway.

Fred stopped walking, feigning confusion. He made a show of patting his pockets, as if they held lost keys, a misplaced wallet, or excuses.

"Hello, Fred," the principal said brightly, and her smile allayed his tension. "Lose something?"

"Hello, Ms. T-t-terry," he stammered, and smiled back crookedly, keeping his eyes on the bridge of her nose, away from the body he studied so vigorously when she wasn't paying attention. "No ma'am, just forgetful. You off to morning announcements?"

"Yes," she replied, and glanced at a sheaf of yellow papers in her hand. "Bell's about to ring, so I should probably hustle."

Fred nodded and let his lips hang open, scratched at his cheek.

Ms. Terry started away, then stopped, gave him a distracted glance. "Everything okay at the annex?"

Fred's face grew hot, and he turned around to look toward the loading dock area from which he'd come, more to avoid her eyes than anything. That area was for ADMINISTRATION ONLY and was always locked, used exclusively for maintenance access to the storage building, cafeteria deliveries, and garbage pickup.

"Yes, ma'am. Checking the dumpsters. Mr. Farrow said he'd seen a rat back there, so I thought I'd check it out fuh . . . fuh . . . first thing."

"Well, don't forget we have assembly first period," Ms. Terry said, stern but not unkind. "I hope those bleachers are pulled out."

Wanda Terry liked Fred. It had been a dark day at the school when poor Mr. Tafferty had been discovered dead in his apartment, murdered by a home invader. She had thought of him as a sort of father figure, and he'd been her confidant when she first took over the school's administration, giving her the scoop on the quirky personalities of different faculty members who predated her arrival. But Fred had been a blessing, and she was delighted to work with the disabled veterans program to bring in someone like him, an able-bodied younger man who could do twice the work of the aging Mr. Tafferty (God rest his soul). Fred would have been hard-pressed to find work anywhere else given his mental disability, the result of a head wound from serving their great country. In many ways, he was a silver lining.

But.

There was *something* about the man. A feeling she couldn't place, or find good reason for even having.

You know damn well what it is, Wanda. This big brute gives you the willies and then some. He could crush a child's head in one of those massive hands of his, or worse. And who knows what thoughts flow through that idle mind? You know, the one pretty much glued to neutral in the old brain's gear shift.

"Don't worry, I'll get them pulled out in time," Fred said, a dim smile on his face.

Wanda returned the smile and did her best to brush away the worries, her mind focused once more on the morning announcements, her favorite part of the day. "Well, let me know if you find anything. We certainly don't want an infestation. The parents would not be pleased."

"Yes, ma'am," Fred said, then turned and walked off.

Wanda watched him go for a moment, then pulled the janitor from her mind like a piece of hard gum from beneath a table and tossed it away.

The first bell shrilled across the campus, giving her only five minutes to get to her office and gather her thoughts.

In her rush, she didn't notice the police officer standing by the doors of the administration building, awaiting her arrival. Nor did she notice the school's assistant principal, Mr. Worthy, standing next to him, his face ashen.

★ ★ ★

The loud buzz of the morning bell shattered the half-empty halls, tingling Henry's teeth with its abrasive shrill. *It's not a bell at all, it's a big buzzer, like the one you get when you screw up in Operation and the guy's nose turns red.*

Henry yanked out his history book and slammed the locker shut. He gave a quick side-to-side glance down the long hallway, the floor polished to a reflective shine, the hundreds of lockers rigid along the sides like soldiers at attention. He saw no sign of Tommy or his buddies, and prayed their vengeance would somehow pass over him. He remembered a distant Sunday school lesson, and the image of smearing sheep's blood above his locker flashed through his mind as he trotted toward homeroom.

He pushed through the door just as Ms. Johnson was writing the first lesson on the chalk board. He rushed to his desk, his bottom touching the cool plastic mold of the chair as the second—and final—bell shrilled through the room.

Henry was sweating and his heart raced in his chest. He hated being tardy but the walk to school had taken longer than normal, given he was constantly on guard for a bully to leap out from behind every tree, every parked car, and smash him in the face with a tight white fist. He wondered absently how he would handle such an altercation. Would he turtle and take it? Or would he fight back? He liked to think he'd give as good as he got, but a thin voice in the back of his mind whispered another, more likely scenario. *You'd run like a chicken,* the voice said. And Henry, thinking of being hit in the ass with one of the rocks hurled by the bullies, was inclined to agree.

"Open your books, please," Ms. Johnson said without turning from her chalk scratchings on the big green board.

Henry sighed, tried to let go of his fear and anxiety, slow the thrumming of his tiny heart. He flipped open the book.

The classroom door opened.

Reflexively, Henry looked up. And froze.

Jim Hawkes, he of the rock-throwing hall of fame, esteemed colleague of one Mr. Tommy "Trailer Trash" Patchen, stood inside the open doorway, sweating and pale.

He was looking straight at Henry.

"Jim?"

Jim turned as if slapped, eyes wide, and gawped stupidly at the approaching form of Ms. Johnson, as if confused why she'd even be here.

Ms. Johnson held out her hand, and Jim wordlessly handed her a folded pink paper. All the kids shifted in their seats. They all knew Jim was this semester's office aide, which meant they also knew what the delivery of said pink paper prophesied for one lucky, or possibly *un*lucky, student.

She took the paper from Jim carelessly, then turned to the class. Henry watched her unfold it, then glance back to Jim, who had locked steely eyes on Henry once more.

Is he smiling? Henry had time to think, and was about to reach out and see what exactly was in Jim's head, when he heard his name.

"Henry," Ms. Johnson said.

Henry turned his attention back to the teacher, an unexplainable fear pinching his guts. As Ms. Johnson walked toward him between the row of desks, his peripheral vision saw the classroom door close. But he forgot all about Jim and his strange feral eyes, his half-smile, when Ms. Johnson calmly dropped the paper onto his desk.

He stared at it dumbly as she asked Beth Danchisko, a skinny redhead with enough freckles to match a star-filled sky, to read out loud from the top of page 126 of their textbook.

Beth's monotone recounting of the infamous Civil War battle of Shiloh was like a light, distant buzzing in Henry's ears as he unfolded the paper. Inside, the boldly printed words APPOINTMENT PASS ran along the top of a box, below which were the preprinted categories of REQUESTING TEACHER, STUDENT, CLASSROOM, and TIME. It seemed his English teacher, Mr. Godinez, wanted to speak with him at 8:45 in Room 14, where Henry normally went during fourth period.

Henry glanced at the clock: 8:40.

As Henry slowly, almost hypnotically, gathered his things in preparation to leave the classroom, the beating of his tireless little heart began to speed back up again.

Despite all his gifts, he could think of no reason why he should be nervous.

Or, more to the point . . . *afraid*.

4

An unmarked white industrial van slowed on Gossamer Street, showed the steady red beat of a turn signal, then accelerated into a gentle right onto Harker Lane, a quiet strip of suburban street that ran behind Liberty Elementary. No houses settled on Harker Lane's stunted stretch, since it was bordered by the school on one side and a dense copse of city-owned, undeveloped trees on the other. The narrow lane ended in a tight curl that took you back onto Gossamer, making the street nothing more than a scantly driven detour used almost exclusively by schoolteachers, garbage trucks, and delivery vans—not unlike the one currently cruising down its cracked, leaf-strewn pavement toward the school.

Instead of proceeding to the school's main parking lot, where a delivery driver would normally check in at the office before gaining access to the property, this particular van stopped at the gated-off entrance of the narrow, almost hidden entrance of a blacktop driveway that led into a shadowed alcove of the school most people never had occasion, or reason, to see.

A man in nondescript blue coveralls opened the van's passenger door, went to the gate, and slipped the unclasped extended shackle of the weathered Master Lock free of the latch that secured the entryway. He pushed, and the gate floated smoothly inward, allowing the van admittance to the area between the school's storage annex and cafeteria loading dock, the access route terminating at a brick wall that separated the alley from the school's large concrete recess pad. On a fall day, the screams and laughter of children would echo in the dark alcove, the wall acting as a protective barrier between the contrary worlds of joy and shadow.

The man walked through the opening and the van backed in carefully behind him. Once it was through, the man closed the gate and pushed the padlock through the latch once more. He did not lock it, leaving it, for the moment, unsecured.

The van stopped next to two brown dumpsters huddled in the morning shade the annex building provided. The man in coveralls slipped back into the passenger's seat, said something to the driver, and quietly shut the door. The driver nodded and looked at his watch.

It was exactly 8:45 a.m.

5

"Mr. Godinez?"

Henry entered Room 14, not sure what to expect. The hallways had been empty on his walk from homeroom. Almost every kid was in class and would continue to be for another twenty minutes or so, until the bell rang and the halls erupted in commotion and voices and the repetitive metal clang of slamming locker doors. He wasn't sure why Mr. Godinez wanted to see him, and so urgently, but he figured it either had something to do with the essay he'd turned in earlier that week or, perhaps, something to do with Tommy Patchen and the others. Maybe he'd heard about Henry being chased. Maybe he'd *seen* something and only realized, later on, that Henry had been in danger.

Or maybe it was something else altogether.

But what Henry was not expecting, especially not after being summoned in the middle of homeroom with one of the infamous pink passes, was an empty classroom.

The lights were on, and the single door leading in and out of the room was not locked, but there was no Mr. Godinez. More strangely, there were no signs of him having even been there. No half-empty coffee cup on the desk, and no leather bookbag slung over his chair, the one that always carried two or three books he was reading and would occasionally share with the students, proud and excited to show off whatever novel or dog-eared volume of science or philosophy he might be currently blazing through.

Henry stood silently by the teacher's desk, debating whether to wait a few more minutes or return to Ms. Johnson's class, when he heard a strange sound from the hallway, a repetitive echo from the other side of the classroom wall.

Squee . . . squee . . . squee . . . squee . . . squee . . .

Henry traced the sound with his eyes as it moved down the hallway, studied the wall that separated the classroom from the source of it—past the first few rows of seats, then past the large bulletin board that read TOP OF THE HEAP! along the top, the area below filled with pinned student essays, a culmination of the best grades from all three English classes Mr. Godinez taught at the school. Henry had a moment to wonder if the essay he'd turned in a few days ago would be on the TOP OF THE HEAP! board, but then quickly forgot all about such matters when the sound he'd been tracking—that strange, repetitive *squee-squee-squee* sound—suddenly stopped.

Directly outside the classroom door.

Henry took a step away from the desk, fighting the sudden urge to hide from whatever was in the hallway, the strange-sounding thing that stood on the other side of the heavy brown door with its tiny portal window, crisscrossed with black thread for reasons beyond Henry's knowledge, or care. At that moment, he wished—wished fervently—that the bell would ring, and the sound of kids would pour into the halls, creating the welcome clamor of normalcy and companionship.

Henry thought maybe there was a monster outside that door . . . a creature that wanted his brain, his blood . . . or was it simply Mr. Godinez (the more likely scenario, Henry admitted) late for his appointment with Henry? All smiles and apologies.

The door opened, and Henry, who realized he was holding a breath, forced himself to let it out when he saw it wasn't a monster coming into the classroom after all.

Nor was it Mr. Godinez.

It was a large, rusted metal *cart* that entered through the doorway. Henry blinked. And then he almost laughed.

It was the janitor's cart. He recognized the large gray Brute garbage can, the yellow tool smock draping down the side, the broom and dustpan protruding upward from the middle section like a bristled antenna.

The cart pushed slowly into the classroom, and Henry now understood what the *squee* sound had been: the rusted wheels of the old metal cart. He'd heard it a million times before but for some reason hadn't made the connection. Now, seeing the cart and hearing the familiar squeak, he felt like the biggest baby on the face of the earth. Of all the dumb things to be frightened of, a garbage can on wheels.

Then he saw Fred. Smiling as he pushed his way into the classroom, cart ahead of him, big eyes on Henry. As if he knew he'd find him here, standing dumbly by the desk, waiting for him to arrive.

Whatever relief Henry had been feeling evaporated, and a strange tension climbed his shoulders and clenched his neck. Oddly, even though he knew Fred, even though they'd been through "the shit" together the day prior (as Henry thought of it—somewhat hysterically—at that moment), he still felt a crawling tension enter his body at the sight of the big man as he stood there in his gray coverall, smiling wide, his eyes locked on Henry's own, that goddamn wheel crying *squee-squee-squee* as he pushed the cart further and further into the classroom.

The door closed with a soft *click* behind Fred, and Henry suddenly felt—for no good reason he could come up with—*trapped*.

"Well, hey there, Henry," Fred said, and Henry found himself taking an involuntary step behind the desk, as if it were a shield to protect him from whatever danger might be lurking on the squeaky-wheeled janitor cart.

Or from the janitor himself.

"Hey, Fred," Henry replied. Then added, "I'm supposed to meet Mr. Godinez, but he's not here."

Fred nodded, then pulled a set of keys from his pocket. As Henry watched, stunned into silence, Fred turned, pushed a key into the lock above the door's handle, and *turned* it.

Henry could actually hear the light *clack* of the deadbolt sliding into place.

"Why are you doing that?" Henry whispered, the words exhaled along with a release of hot breath. A subtle disassociation with reality spread through him, as if a rush of ice water had surged through his veins and into his brain, freezing his survival functions, his quick-thinking mechanism, his flight response.

"You don't know this," Fred said casually, as he reached into one of the many pockets of the dirty yellow smock that hung at the side of his cart, the kind of pouches that typically held cleaning sprays, brushes, and small hand tools. "But at this time of day, there ain't no class in Rooms 12 through 16. This whole end of the hallway?" Fred shrugged. "Pretty much empty."

A part of Henry's brain (slowly coming back online, as if downed switches were methodically being flicked back into the ON position, one by one) noticed something different in Fred's voice. His usual cadence was gone. That slowed-down, stuttering, poor *aw-shucks* dumb-guy voice had been replaced with something else. A voice far more assured. A voice far more sly and dangerous.

Shit, Henry thought, and now all the switches had been flipped back on, or at least most of them, and Henry was no longer thinking about Mr. Godinez stepping in to save him, eager to sit him down and discuss his essay on *The Outsiders.* That big black steam engine of Henry's thoughts was ready to chug-a-lug down an entirely new train track, boys and girls, and the big paper ticket punched by the conductor was stamped in big bold letters with one destination and one destination only:

ESCAPE.

Fred walked slowly toward Henry, strategically blocking the exit path toward the door. Henry noticed how the desks he passed looked like small toys compared with the man's height and girth, toys he could easily cast aside if Henry made a dash for it, along the wall toward the door, beneath the wall of essays and the bold purple letters now seeming to shout at Henry like a warning: TOP OF THE HEAP, HENRY! BETTER MOVE YOUR ASS OR YOU'LL BE *UNDER* THE HEAP, MY BOY!

Fred was at the first row of desks, and Henry could now see what he'd pulled from the pouch of the janitor cart's yellow smock.

It's a needle, he realized, and had a split-second flashback to a doctor's office visit for a tetanus shot (only nine years old at the time and, given his past, wanting nothing to do with doctors or needles *EVER*, had made for a wholly unpleasant experience. Even worse, when Uncle Dave subsequently explained what the shot was for, giving it a name as if that might soothe the boy's terrified mind, Henry had heard that he was being given a *tennis* shot. Despite being repeatedly corrected in the days that followed, he still—to this very day—got a sour stomach whenever he happened to see a tennis racket). And now the sight of the plastic plunger with the sharp pin at the end gave Henry that same stomach-swelling nausea. There was no longer any question what was happening here, and what he needed to do about it. There was no option left but to run for it.

But first I want to know what you're thinking.

"I'll scream," he said, using the threat as a distraction as he *reached* out toward the janitor with his mind, the inner black eye wide and eager.

Fred laughed, and as he did Henry's mind connected, flooded with the man's thoughts: Dark, horrible, deceptive thoughts.

Dangerous thoughts.

The colors that flew at his mind were black as a grave, but somehow vibrant, somehow energized and alive. *Vicious*, Henry's mind translated. Then added, perhaps more accurately: *Deadly.*

RUN.

Henry burst from behind the desk, sprinted toward the locked door. He screamed as he ran but could still hear desks being knocked into other desks, tossed carelessly aside by the angry giant's sweeping hand.

That same hand caught Henry's shirt and yanked him backward. It moved like a large spider to cover his mouth as he screamed, loud as he could, into the large, hot palm smothering his face from chin to cheekbone.

STOP! his mind ordered. and for a split second the hand covering his face relented a smidge, as if suddenly unsure, as if suddenly afraid. Henry twisted his head violently.

"You little shit," the man said in a voice Henry didn't recognize, one that wasn't Fred the janitor at all, but somebody Henry was just now meeting for the first time.

Then the long, strong fingers squeezed his cheeks tight, and something hard and sharp stabbed into his neck, and the colors in his mind burst apart into wisps, indistinguishable remnants of lost emotions and broken thoughts.

Henry's eyes glazed over. The door to the classroom blurred, and his brain grew thick, his body numb.

A hot breath in his ear whispered, "Easy now."

Henry felt his body comply. *Easy now,* he repeated to himself distantly, a radio transmission from a distant star. Then the world darkened, white static filled his ears, and colors blasted through his vision, electrified the gray screens of his closed eyelids . . . then extinguished. He slumped into the janitor's arms and, in a faraway sense, could feel himself being lifted into the air.

The white noise cut off as if by a switch. His body emptied itself of feelings and sensations. He floated through dead, muted space.

Dad, he thought. A shallow, weakened plea. A cry for comfort, for help.

There was no reply.

The veil of consciousness was torn away, and he was falling.

Floating into the dark, the heavy silence, through the infinite abyss of inner space.

6

Fred pushed the cart through the wooden double doors separating the cool tiled hallway and the growing heat of the concrete schoolyard. The gray rubber garbage can shook and rattled against the rust-specked metal halo that kept it contained. If one were to find the urge to pull the top of the can free and look inside, they would see a black plastic liner and an oddly large pile of dirty rags. If this same inquisitive passerby were to lift the rags away, they would be surprised to see the top of a boy's head. Beneath that, arms and legs curled into a fetal position. This passerby might think how very small the boy looked, curled up in the garbage can that way. *Just a child*, they might say, and find Fred's dark, soulless eyes and consider offering a rebuke, a warning, a plea. *Just a baby*, they might add, before replacing the lid and walking away. Perhaps clicking their tongue in disgust. Perhaps shaking their heads at the horror of it all.

As the cart squeaked its way across the empty courtyard, heading straight for the door leading to the storage annex (*fifty feet away*, he thought . . . *forty-five* . . . *forty* . . .), no such passerby entered the scene. To the janitor's bemusement (and inner shouts of joy), there wasn't a soul anywhere in sight. The children and teachers were tucked neatly into the classrooms. The principal (that nosy bitch) and the other administrative staff were completely occupied by the morning duties and the presence of several police officers and a detective, who were quietly, and with great care, relaying the information of a student's horrific murder the previous night. The detective, a woman in her mid-forties named White, was explaining how the body had been found only hours ago in a dumpster near the boy's home, his neck snapped.

(When Ms. Terry heard this word, she imagined the sound of a bone, broken like a dead branch over a knee, and had an unconscious flash of the giant janitor she had run into only that morning. *Remember, Wanda? The one who gives you the willies? The one whose massive hands could crush a child's head?* But the flimsy thought was gone as quickly as it came, discarded as frivolous and unfair, overrun by the despair of knowing one of her own had been slaughtered. And, along with the despair, an overwhelming rush of failure, a feeling that would soon increase—within the next handful of hours—a hundredfold.)

The janitor stopped the cart, forcing himself not to look around for anyone who might have stepped from a door, or might be peering out a window. He didn't want to look guilty. Didn't want to look anything but what he was. *Just the dumb janitor taking out the trash. Nothing to see here, folks. Nothing at all.*

Fred pushed the annex door open wide. The inside was dark and cool, the air tinted with scents of fertilizer, the clotted oil of machinery, and woodchips. He pulled the cart through, gave a quick glance toward the open courtyard and the staggered eyes of classroom windows beyond, saw no one, and smiled.

7

There was a clatter as the metal rollup door lifted.

Liam and Greg exchanged the briefest of glances, then Greg hopped out and moved to the rear of the van.

Liam watched as Jim pushed the janitor cart out onto the loading dock's raised pad. Greg popped open the van's rear doors. Moments later, Jim grunted as he lifted the garbage can off the cart and into the van's cargo area. The van rocked gently with the sag of new weight as rubber slid along thin carpet.

Liam turned to watch as the can was gently tipped onto its side. Jim held the can's bottom, the sunshine split along his arms, as Greg crawled into the van, reached into the can's black mouth, and birthed first a heap of rags, then a small, thin body, black plastic liner slipping out with him like inky amniotic fluid.

Liam turned away, gripped the wheel tight.

"Jesus," he said quietly, then immediately stiffened, praying Jim didn't overhear.

There was more noise from the rear of the van: the can being pulled away, the doors snapping shut, Greg adjusting the body. Liam started the van and checked his mirror. He saw Jim pulling open the gate, waiting.

"Gonna stay back here with him," Greg said quietly. "He's gonna need another shot soon."

Liam slid the van smoothly forward. As he pulled into the street, he glanced through the window as Jim unhurriedly closed the gate, locking it securely once more. Then the big man turned and made his way slowly, almost casually, toward the now-empty garbage can and his waiting cart.

Back on the quiet suburban street, canopied by the arching branches of hundred-year-old Chinese elms, Liam accelerated, hands still tight on the wheel. From behind him came the soft whisper of Greg unspooling rope and tying it to wrists and ankles. Liam's eyes darted to the mirrors, looking for someone following, for police. He saw only empty road and a line of gray-barked trees.

Minutes later, as he pulled onto the freeway heading north, he finally forced his hands to loosen on the wheel. The large breath stuck in his chest eased out between his lips. He turned the air-conditioning up a notch, wanting to keep the temperature of the van comfortable for everyone. He almost felt the Southern California sun pressing against the thin metal roof and sides, seeping inward like a curse.

Gonna be a hot one, he thought.

Then he stopped thinking, and drove for the forest.

PART FOUR: THE HOUSE IN THE WOODS

1

Henry is flying.

Hurtling through the air.

And the air is full of colors.

His limbs are bound and powerless, clenched tightly to his torso as his body whistles like a projectile through long, twisting strands of vibrant colors the consistency of smoke. He's frightened. He knows the end is near and his flight will soon be rudely and abruptly interrupted by the windshield of a parked car that will crack his head and spill his blood and break his bones.

And then the colors will slip into me. Through my broken head they'll slide through like eels, frenzied and hungry. All the colors in the world will push into my mind and when I open my eyes I'll see what they see, I'll see the colors that stir inside people, the vibrancies that tell me things, show me their thoughts, their feelings.

At first, I'll think: Stop.

Then I'll think: More.

Henry realizes only now—as the air flutters by his face and the brightly dyed strands of wispy tethers brush his cheeks and forehead, cling to his hair like powder, the colors whipping past him like flags—that his eyes are closed.

And so, ready to join reality, he opens them.

The real world is revealed as a flat, dull vista; an empty, blurred white. Empty and formless. There are no answers there.

So he closes his eyes once more, looks with his mind instead.

He senses two people. Very near. Their colors vary between light and dark, bright reds and shadowy blues. Fear. Anxiety. Hate. Confusion. Pity. Shame.

"Hey, I think the kid's awake."

Henry flies once more. But the colors no longer dissolve around him, but slide into his ears, his mouth, his nose, his eyes. The colors rush into him and it *hurts* and he wants to cry out but a rough hand squeezes his arm tightly; a sharp pain in his bicep. A sting.

He feels the collision of his body smashing into the car. There's an explosion in his mind as the colors all flare brilliantly—as if they've caught fire—and burn bright white.

This is followed, almost instantaneously, by complete darkness.

A black so dense he feels buried beneath it.

2

Dave tries not to panic.

He continuously checks the speedometer to make sure he's going the speed limit, not wanting to be reckless. No need for that.

Get home and sort it out, he'd thought, pulling out of the law office parking lot. *Mary's overreacting, nothing's wrong. It's a misunderstanding. A lack of Henry communicating. We'll discuss it with the boy, that's all. We'll all sit down and have a chat about communication, about not making us worried.*

Panicked.

"Gonna have a nice chat with Henry. A learning moment is what this is," he says out loud as he pulls off the highway at Exit 14, like he does every workday.

Nice and normal.

Routine.

"Nothing to worry about here," he adds to his prior soliloquy, letting the words roll around in the car's interior, soothing him, bringing the energy to a steady pace. Anxiety has a speed limit as well, and Dave checks all the gauges as he drives, the car's and his own. Keeps everything steady.

Mary's call to the office had started the same way: Steady as she goes.

But as she kept speaking—kept *explaining*—she'd ramped it up, her emotions taking control of the ship's engine for a while, and by the time he'd hung up she was hysterical, and it was he who needed to keep things under control. Keep his emotions from taking over the ship.

"The school called, and Henry's missing," she'd said, her words calm but fringed with a tickle of hysteria.

"Missing how? When?" Dave asked, not understanding his own questions, but unsure how else to ask.

"They don't know," she said, beginning to fray. "He never showed up for his second period class. And he's not *anywhere*, they've looked, and I came home and he's not here and, I don't know, maybe he's playing hooky but never once *not one time* has he ever done that! David . . ."

Dave had looked at the clock on his desk. It showed 4:35. School had been out for an hour and a half, and if Henry was missing since second period, that would have been—

"He's been missing since nine and no one thought to tell us?" he asked, calm and assured, (albeit with a tinge of accusation). Shame had kicked in seconds later and he quickly went on. "I mean, Mary, when did they call you? I'm sorry, but—"

"About twenty minutes ago. I thought I'd get home and check first, before calling you—his homeroom teacher said he'd been excused, and the other teachers just assumed he was absent and didn't think—oh, God, where is he, David?"

He's been missing nearly eight hours, Dave thought.

"I'll be right home," he said, sounding calmer than he felt. "Mary, you should call the police."

A pause. Then, "I already have. They're on their way here." She was crying quietly. "Please, David . . . please come home."

Within minutes, he left the office to do just that.

Dave slows at the last stop sign between his work and his house, the one with the weathered KGB radio station sticker partly peeled off at the edge, the same damned sign he's seen nearly every weekday for the last twelve years; the same sign that keeps the intersection of Parker and Graham safe for families and vehicles alike, halting traffic for playing kids, stroller-pushing mothers, or hand-holding couples out for an evening stroll.

He turns his head to look east down Graham Avenue, toward his home, like he always does. *Nice and normal, baby. Steady as she*—

"Oh, sweet Jesus," Dave says, seeing the cluster of vehicles on the street, his voice pitched an octave higher than normal. He's a bit surprised to find his teeth pressing into his knuckles, his fingers clenched tight to the top of the leather steering wheel. He begins to cry, right there by the stop sign at the corner of Parker and Graham. "Oh, please God, no," he prays and he cries and he stares at his beautiful home and the police cars now parked in front of it—blocking the driveway, lining the curb. One of them, he notes through his despair, is a black sedan with no markings.

Detectives, he thinks. *Look at them. Oh, Lord, look at them all.*

Dave sniffs and stiffens, sits up and wipes his eyes, composes himself. He hears his father's voice telling him to get his *shit together*, to *get right*, to *man up*.

"He's right, he's right," Dave mumbles, and for a brief moment he wonders if all this talking to himself is a good thing.

His brain tells him that maybe it's something to nip in the bud. *What do you say, Chief? Maybe we get right and keep that talking to ourselves bullshit tucked away, neat and tidy, in a small box with no keyhole. How's that sound?*

Dave pulls a few leftover In-N-Out napkins from the glovebox, blows his nose, and wipes his face. He checks his eyes in the mirror, sees some red but no panic. No anguish.

"That's good," he says, already forgetting his brain's instructions. "That's fine."

He forces himself to take a deep breath, lets it out, and then makes a right turn onto good old Graham Avenue, toward home.

He parks farther from his house than he would have preferred, but given the police presence, he has little choice.

Uniforms fill the small house. Strange men and women in his living room, kitchen, and dining room, all wearing crisp blues or well-worn suits. *And that doesn't include the armed cop at the front door, the one who ushered me into my own damn home.* The officer at the door was imposing, and part of him almost didn't want to approach the man, whose face had been set and grim, chest bulky with the bulletproof vest worn beneath his uniform.

"I'm David Thorne, this is my house?" he'd said, like a question offered in the hopes the officer could confirm what he knew, only a few hours ago, to be an absolute truth.

Inside, it's a place he hardly recognizes. Most of the officers are larger than life in their family's tightknit, domesticated world. Dave spots Mary right away, hunched on the couch like a child among a group of adults. *Like a child with stomach pains*, he thinks. She sits bent over at the waist, clenched into herself, her hands tight fists, her feet tapping anxiously. A woman in a suit sits next to her, asking her questions. Sitting in the adjacent chair is a large man, also in a suit, taking notes. Some of the officers look at Dave as he passes among them—some with sympathy, some with hostility—before returning to their business, whatever that is. From what Dave can tell they're all talking to each other or listening to the detectives, one takes photos of the house for some reason Dave can't fathom, while another sits at the kitchen table, leafing through Mary's address book like he's reading a damned Dickens novel. Two officers walk out from the hallway that leads to the bedrooms. He notices they wear latex gloves. Another officer, leaning against the kitchen sink, speaks rapidly into a microphone clipped to his shoulder.

Dave approaches Mary cautiously. His ears feel plugged and the room appears fuzzy, as if he is walking in a dream. His mind is slow, and it's at this moment Dave realizes he's terrified.

Truly, horribly terrified.

So this is what it feels like, he thinks dazedly, *to be so filled with fear that your body numbs you from the brunt of it. Knocks you out a little bit. Stuffs some wool into those portals of the brain that would probably short-circuit from the rush of poisoned adrenaline, blow those chugging pistons in your head like an overheated engine. POP, crackle, sizzle. End game.*

Mary looks up at Dave and wails. He runs to her, pushing aside an officer who walks absently in his way, no longer caring about their guns or their uniforms or their presence in his house.

"Oh, Mary, what's happened?" Dave says, and he holds her tight as she cries into his shoulder. Suddenly, he's free from his haze, suddenly he's talking and thinking a million miles an hour because now it's real. Now he needs to *do* something.

He comforts his wife and tries to unsee what he saw in her face as she reached for him. The absolute horror of it all.

Hard, grim reality washes over them both like a cold wave and suddenly all the fear is there, stark and high-definition, loud as thunder and deadlier than lightning, and all they can do in this moment is to hold on to each other. Hold on, and not let go.

3

Later.

The darkness covering his mind frays like a black veil turned brittle by age. When he wakes the second time there is no dream fantasy, no reliving of a tragedy. This time he's aware. He remembers the janitor, his attempted escape, the hot pinch in his neck, the slide into unconsciousness.

As Henry becomes slowly more alert, the first command his mind gives the body is to keep the eyes closed, the breathing steady, the muscles still.

Pretend.

Gather information.

Reach out with the mind but also listen, smell. Collect and assemble the pieces of data his body is sending.

He's moving; lying against something hard and cold. His wrists and ankles are bound. His arms tingle, his back is stiff. There's pain in his neck and arm, a distant throbbing where he's been stabbed with something sharp. *A needle.* But his mind feels clear. The drug has dissolved, left him alone for now. So he listens, and he reaches.

Henry hears the engine, but no other sounds—no traffic, no honking horns or the rumble of big trucks, no other cars at all.

He still senses the colors, but they're dampened now. The anxiety has lessened. There's a rhythmic pulsing coming from the two men; an anticipation, perhaps. Also, a tiredness. The mustard yellow of strain.

The vehicle seems to be going slow; the road it travels on is rough, jarring.

It's cold. His skin feels chilled as his body rocks lifelessly with each bump of the road. Crisp fingers slide along the side of the vehicle, scrape the thin metal . . .

Trees.

A pang of fear stabs Henry's guts, and his eyes—against his brain's specific instructions—spring open.

"Hey," a man says.

Henry ignores this and sits up straight, his breath coming in quick pants.

"Hey, hold on!" the man says. Louder. Alarmed.

Hands grip Henry's shoulders and pull him back.

"Where are you taking me?" Henry yells, feeling true terror for the first time.

Something about being in the *woods*, the disparate loneliness of a forest clashing harshly with his idea of home, of school, of the streets he had grown accustomed to; the familiar world. It hit him head-on, surged to the front of his awareness with each slow, rolling bump and dive of the pitted road beneath them; each soft, scratchy scrape of branches along the side of the . . . *van!*

It's a van!

"You okay back there?" Another voice. The driver. Henry can't see him, he only sees the dim backs of the van doors, windowless and shadowed. The driver sounds big. Tough. He has an accent—

"Fine, fine. Kid's freaking out. You think . . ."

"No, don't bother. We're almost there. Let him scream if he wants to."

The hands on his shoulders dig in hard and Henry's body is twisted so that he's face-to-face with the first man he'd heard. "Don't you fucking do it," the man says, and Henry winces at how bad his breath is. Like old onions.

He's ugly, Henry realizes. His face is lumpy and red in spots. His eyebrows and beard thick with coarse black hair, his eyes a dull brown.

"I won't, sir," Henry says in a soft croak, and the man noticeably softens. The fingers digging into his shoulders relax.

"All right, fine," he says. "Smart."

Henry turns his neck a bit more, looks toward the front of the van. He can see the back of the other man's head, and beyond it the windshield.

Headlights reflect against a rolling projection of crowding ghost-white trees, beyond them nothing but a blanket of black sky.

"Can I get some water?" he asks.

The ugly man looks at Henry a moment, then shakes his head.

"Almost there, kid," the driver says in his strange accent.

Henry sighs and lets himself slump back to the floor of the van. He tucks his bound wrists into his stomach and turns onto his side, his back to the ugly man with onion breath, the one who hasn't taken his stupid dull brown eyes off him, as if he's waiting for Henry to do something bad, something that would allow the man to hurt Henry again.

Henry closes his eyes, tries not to cry. He forces his thoughts to turn their gaze inward, focus on the data he's receiving from all his different sensory ports. He reaches out to the man next to him, feels the wariness, the underlying deep red ocean of hate, of violence.

"Daddy . . . Momma . . ." he whispers. "Uncle Dave . . . Aunt Mary . . ."

He says the names quietly, so the man won't hear him. He says the names to make himself feel better, to calm his fear, his anxiousness. He says the names like a prayer and hopes that someone might answer.

There is a sudden deep dip and the van bottoms out so badly Henry's body momentarily goes airborne before it's slammed down, knocking his teeth together.

"Ow!" Henry cries.

"Jesus," says the ugly man.

There's a grunt from the driver. Henry rolls onto his stomach, wrists pressed hard into his belly, legs stiff and bound.

The driver turns the wheel hard one way, then another. A bushy branch comes at the windshield fast and the driver hits the brakes so hard the ugly man falls onto his side and rolls through the vacant interior before thumping against the rear of the driver's seat, neck bent, hands pushed against the metal floor.

"Christ, Liam!" he screams. *Anger and hot crimson, spears of dark violet.*

The large branch settles against the windshield, leaves pressed flat to the glass like children staring through the storefront of a candy shop.

The driver—*Liam, his name is Liam*—puts the van into park, lets out a breath, then straightens to get a better look out the windshield. After a moment, he turns the key and the engine shuts down; pushes a knob and the headlights dissolve. Darkness swallows them whole.

Sweat drips off Henry's face, slides down the back of his neck. The quiet is so thick, the dark so total, he feels submerged in water black as night.

A trace of silver highlights Liam's face as he turns toward the rear of the van. The man's thoughts are a blur of slow-moving colors, churning and reckless. Aimless. Henry can make no sense of him.

"We walk from here," Liam says.

"Walk?" the other man says, angry. "Why?"

The driver doesn't answer, only stares out the windshield.

"Liam! Answer me. Why are we—" he says, then gets to his knees to study the scene outside the windshield. After a moment, he settles back to the floor, convinced. "Jenny made it," he says, almost pouting.

Liam opens the driver's side door and starts to step out. "Jenny wasn't driving a cargo van," he says, and disappears into the night. The door slams shut behind him, and Henry hears footsteps move alongside the van toward the rear.

The ugly man scrambles to the rear doors and pulls up a lock. He throws one door open, then the other. The man, Liam, stands there waiting, a dark outline propped against the surrounding night.

Henry feels hands on his ankles, and he's pulled toward the open doors. As he slides helplessly into the maw of strangers, he has never been more afraid in his life.

4

The forest is dark, and the night complete. The trees are so hungry, what will they eat?

Henry thinks of this rhyme the second his feet hit the dirt road they've been traveling on. It's from a book his mother read to him when he was kindergarten age, and although the pictures in the book were bright and cheerful—the trees smiling toothy grins as a row of children walked between them toward a house in the woods—the words have always stuck with him in a more ominous way, like a clown who seems gentle and funny at first, but later appears in your dreams as something much more sinister. That's how he'd thought of those trees in that story book: sinister. Even though they appeared to be happy trees when illustrated on the pages, with their black eyes and wooden teeth, he saw them as something vicious, possibly evil.

And now, here in the forest, even when standing within arm's reach of these strange, violent men, Henry glances left and right, staring wide-eyed at the giant trees surrounding him, crowding in from all sides—the arching, knobby branches, the rough bark of fat trunks, the swarm of leaves blanketing the branching nest of arches like the wild hair of a mad scientist. The trees appear as dim figures, sunk into the heavy fabric of black night; the ones nearest the van bathed in the blood red of the taillights, the eerie glow lending them an even more menacing appearance. To Henry, it seems as if the whole night is underwater, a dark lake where trees bob just below the surface, and whatever lies deeper is unknown and dangerous.

Deadly.

"Hey," the man says, and snaps his fingers an inch from Henry's nose.

Henry pulls his gaze away from the trees, looks up into the shadowed face of the driver.

"My name is Liam. But I think you know that. You're a smart one, I understand."

Henry says nothing, finds his eyes once again searching the red light smearing across the trees. *I'm underwater.*

"You need to pee?" the man asks, his voice sounding somehow close and distant at the same time.

Henry considers the question, focuses his mind inward on his body rather than his surroundings, leaving alone for now the minds of the men, and realizes, with a sudden stab of discomfort, that he does indeed have to pee, and badly. As the drug wears off and Henry's mind slowly clears (the skin-prickling chilled air of the forest doing wonders to help in that regard), he begins to clue into a great many things, the most primary being that his body (the still-recovering muscles of which stiffened at the best of times) *hurts*—his ankles and wrists sore, his back and neck stiff. And yes, now that things are clearing up in the attic, it's wildly apparent that the plumbing down below is indeed backing up, and to a dangerous extent.

Henry reflexively tightens the muscles of his stomach and fights not to cross his legs and grab his junk in a comical exhibition of how badly he really *does* need to urinate, now that the man has mentioned it. Not trusting himself to speak, and because some part of him holds dearly to his pride, he simply nods, albeit vigorously.

Liam nods in return, then sticks a hand in his pocket and unfolds a large, shiny hunter's knife.

Despite himself, Henry twitches defensively at the sight of the blade.

"Don't worry, kid," Liam says. "I'm just gonna cut your hands and feet loose. Lift your wrists . . . right, thank you."

Henry watches blankly as Liam slices through the white ropes twisted around his wrists. As Henry shakes his hands in an attempt to get the blood moving back to the fingers, Liam kneels and begins to cut the ropes binding his ankles.

"You think that's a good idea?" the other man, as yet unnamed, says from the bumper of the van's open rear end.

Liam doesn't respond, and a moment later Henry's feet are liberated. Before Henry can take so much as a step, Liam folds the knife and returns it to his front pocket, then casually reaches behind him and tugs something free from his belt.

Henry's eyes go wide when he sees the slick black metal of a gun—a *real* gun—slip from behind Liam's back and dangle carelessly at his side. Henry has time to think that if the man points that gun at him, there is no doubt in his mind his bladder will let go with a vengeance and his jeans will quickly be soaked, crotch to ankles, in warm piss.

But he doesn't point the gun at Henry. He lets it hang at his hip, his fingers wrapped around the metal like a pitcher might grip a fastball before release.

"You see this," Liam says, giving the gun a little shake, but leaving the barrel aimed at the dirt. "You try to run from me, Henry, and I won't yell," he says calmly, coldly serious. "I won't call out your name or tell you to stop or run after you or any of that other bullshit. I'm not a cop, I won't tell you to freeze. Do you understand?"

Liam drops to a knee and his bright eyes bore into Henry's own, the van's taillights causing his face to glow deep red. *Like the trees*, Henry thinks. *Like the devil.*

But Henry meets his eyes and does his best to hold the man's stare. After a moment, Liam's eyes soften, and Henry sees the slightest hints of a smile play at the ends of his lips, and he almost wants to smile back, because—for better or worse—children like Henry will always want to believe in the best of people.

And then Liam speaks.

"If you run from me I will shoot you in the back," he says, cool and methodical. Emotionless. "If by some miracle you're not dead, I will shoot you again, most likely in the back of the head, while you lie face down in the fucking dirt." Henry tries to look away, but Liam gently tucks a finger against his cheek and brings his eyes back until they are connected once more. "I will not think twice about doing this. I am not shitting you. This is not something I want to do, but it is—absolutely and without a doubt— something that I *will* do, and without hesitation." Liam rests his free hand on Henry's shoulder, as if he's relaying to him one of life's great lessons. "I need you to believe me, Henry. For both our sakes, okay?"

Liam waits and Henry's mouth hangs open, his full bladder as forgotten as the homework he might have due the following morning. Henry thinks about the man's words, and his eyes shift to the silvery glint of metal in his clenched fist. He considers trying to read Liam's mind but is too tired, too frightened—his brain feels shriveled and weak, his nerves fried, his thoughts sunken and sluggish. With every moment that passes in the cold woods, with these men, his resolve, his courage, weakens and the intensity of his current situation seeps like blood through the veil of disassociation and becomes more tangible, more terrifying. More *real*.

Terror shrivels his spine and he physically slumps. Speechless. Thoughtless. He makes a last half-hearted effort to reach out to Liam's mind but sees nothing but stray silky strands of black, of danger. A vague, cold emptiness.

Henry can't concentrate well enough to see much more, but he's seen enough to know the truth in the man's words.

He isn't lying.

"Nod once if you believe me," Liam says, the words almost a whisper in his grating, accented voice.

Henry nods.

Liam holds his eyes for another moment, then, seemingly satisfied, stands and points to the nearest tree. "Good, then go piss. That tree right there. Walk, don't run. Stay where I can see you." And then, as an afterthought: "Please don't make me kill you, mate."

As if in a dream, Henry slowly turns and walks toward the nearest tree, the one Liam indicated. He can almost feel the deadly power of the gun behind him, sense the light tingle between his shoulder blades where the barrel might be aimed, waiting for him to do something stupid. To run.

Henry reaches the trees and wonders for a moment why he can't unzip his pants. He notices, without much emotion, that his hands are shaking violently. He steadies them against the rough cold bark of the crimson-lit tree.

He has no intention of running.

5

Once the van is turned around (not an easy feat on the narrow road), Greg watches Liam and the kid grow smaller in the rearview mirror. As the glow from the van's taillights gets further away, the two figures—Liam almost father-like, his hand resting on the shoulder of the small boy—fade into the dark, and Greg focuses his attention on the darkened dirt road ahead.

After twenty minutes of cautious driving, he clears the deepest part of the forest, the roughest patch of the fire road, and decides he's okay to speed up. He's got shit to do and it won't do to be late. *God forbid*, he thinks as a needle of fear twists into the back of his brain; fear at what Jim would do to him if he screwed up any of the big man's well-laid plans.

He pulls out of the forest's narrow fire road and onto the private (and currently unoccupied) two-lane that will connect him with the 76 toward Hell Canyon, then toward Escondido, where he'll meet the 15. After that, it's a four-hour drive north to a rented garage where he'll switch vehicles before making the same four-hour drive back to meet Jim.

Caution is the name of this game, Jim had said when detailing this loop of the plan. *Maybe they're looking for that van, maybe not. But I want it the hell out of the county that night and locked up tight.*

Greg bats his fingers on the steering wheel and fights off the urge to stare at his rearview for red and blue lights. He highly doubts an APB has been put out on a generic white cargo van with California plates, but if it has they'll be looking for a needle in a haystack.

"I'm Mr. Nobody," he says, and drums the wheel more vigorously.

He considers the stereo, and as he reaches for the knob his eyes flick to the manila envelope sealed inside a plastic baggie on the passenger seat, and he tries not to think about that either.

Not yet.

An hour later, while Ronnie Van Zant croons about being a Free Bird through the van's blown-out speakers, Greg pulls off at the agreed-upon exit and into the suburban nest of homes near Riverside. The post office box is a few blocks off the highway, and he finds it without a problem; secluded from windows of neighboring houses and far from any main roads, it's the perfect drop point.

Humming to himself, Greg exits the van with the baggie and strolls to the mailbox. *Cool as you please, your honor,* he thinks, and then gives a quick glance around for dogwalkers, joggers, or some other dumb shit that will force him to ditch Plan A and drive even further off his path to Plan B.

Seeing no one, he pulls the latex gloves out of his pocket, puts them on, and pulls the envelope from the baggie. He opens the mouth of the rusted blue post office box.

"Bombs away," he says, and drops the thick envelope inside.

The job done, he sighs in relief and walks quickly back to the van. With the headlights off it's nothing more than a moon-tinted shadow on the darkened street. "Okay, okay . . . let's go, asshole."

Inside the van, he stuffs the baggie and the latex gloves into his pocket, studies the surrounding homes and sidewalks one more time—*please no dog walkers and please God no joggers*—then puts the van in drive and accelerates smoothly and silently out of the suburb.

As he approaches the main road leading to the 215, with "Free Bird" entering the guitar-soloing crescendo, he yanks the headlight knob and speeds up toward the entrance ramp. He still has a lot of driving ahead of him, and Jim wants him at the bar first thing in the morning. Greg figures if all goes well he'll be completing his round trip in just over eight hours, getting him back to the city outskirts by sunrise, and to the meeting place shortly thereafter.

He and Jim will hole up for a day, then together they'll drive to the farmhouse the following afternoon, after Jim wraps up his janitor shtick.

If I simply vanish, everyone knows, right? I gotta stick it out a day until the weekend, then we go. By the time Monday rolls around this whole thing is almost over.

Greg's happy to not be returning to the farmhouse right away because—all things being equal—that house gives him the willies. *Like a horror movie, that place*, he thinks, pressing down on the gas as the tinny-sounding stereo blasts San Diego's most popular classic rock station (having blended seamlessly from "Free Bird" to the Stones' "Paint It Black"). His palms batter the wheel to Charlie Watts's hellacious beat, and he feels some of the day's tension and anxiety melt away. He's making good time, and his schedule should work out perfectly, which eases his mind considerably.

With the calm comes a sudden rush of elation, of pride. *We actually did it!* he finally allows himself to think, and laughs out loud as he settles the van to a respectable—and legal—65 miles per hour. *No need to speed, man. Take it nice and easy. I ain't in no rush, baby.*

He wonders absently how Jenny's holding up, feels a twinge of guilt and worry knowing she's stuck there with Pete and Liam. But, hell, she's a big girl and if anyone knows how to take care of herself, it's his dear sister.

Feeling better, enjoying the elation and momentary freedom, Greg turns the radio up another notch and begins to belt it out along with Jagger, letting himself blow off some tension after a tough day and—for the moment anyway—forgetting about having to go back to the woods, to the farmhouse. Something about that place has got him jumping and jiving without a doubt, but at least he'll be going back with Jim, and the big man wasn't afraid of anything. Which is good, because although he would never admit it—especially to old Jim—the absolute *last* thing Greg wants is to have to walk alone through those creepy-ass woods at night.

Jagger starts screaming about painting the world black, and Greg stops singing along, the ragged beat beginning to infiltrate his calm, his good vibes.

He reaches out and spins the radio knob to off, hoping the silence will calm him down as he turns his focus back to the job at hand. The hum of wheels against pavement creates a sonorous backdrop to the night, as he keeps one eye on the rearview mirror, the other on the dim gray highway stretching endlessly ahead.

6

Liam trails a few feet behind Henry as they walk along the narrow dirt road. He can't get over how fucking *small* the kid is. Even for his age, he's skinny and short, and certainly no athlete. The boy would trip over his shoelaces if they weren't tied. He feels a sliver of shame at the memory of tying the kid up. *As if he was going anywhere.* But it was the correct thing to do and they couldn't afford any mistakes—not then, not now.

He takes his attention off Henry for a moment, studies the surroundings. Trees black as pitch, the stars hidden by a shadowed canopy high above. Liam spits and ignores the chill tickling the back of his neck. He never liked the woods. Couldn't abide all the natural hiding spots, the blind spots where anyone (or anything) could be lying in wait. Unseen. Watching.

And that's interesting, isn't it? Because he *does* feel watched. Ever since they'd left the van, a part of him—the part that has saved his neck more than once, that tingly sixth sense all bad men seem to have—has been telling him exactly that.

Something's out there, that sixth sense whispers, holding court just behind the eardrum. Perhaps nudging against the pink Jell-O of his brain, murmuring slyly, like a ghost that lives inside him. *Yes yes yes . . . something is most certainly out there*, that sly voice says, *and it's watching you. Keeping an eye on things, I think. And you know what's really strange, mate? I don't think it's* human. *How weird is that? Not an animal, no . . . but not a human, either. And it's afraid, but maybe not afraid enough. Of course, it could be far away, too far to do any real harm.*

Or maybe it's above you. In the trees, yes, or maybe—and I'm just spitballin' here, mate—but maybe it's about to slip out from that dark shadow right in front of—

"Oh man, gross!" Henry cries, waving his arms around his head like he's beating off bats. Liam instinctively grabs him by the arm and tugs him backward. "Ow!" the kid yelps, as if he's mistakenly broken the boy's arm.

"Take it easy, Henry," he says, trying to calm him. "Bloody hell, what's going on?"

Henry looks away from him, brushes the arm of his sweater, feels around his neck and hair like he's got ants crawling on him. "Spiderweb," he says, his tone suddenly calm and cool.

Tough little bastard, Liam thinks. He knows most kids would be bawling their eyes out right about now, crying for Mommy and Daddy, begging to be taken home, bitching about being hungry or tired or scared or whatever else they could think of to complain about.

But not Henry. Boy hasn't said a word since Greg left with the van, not until he walked straight into a motherfucker of a spiderweb. Liam waves a hand through the air himself, making sure there aren't any strands left crossing through the air over the road.

"Yeah, okay," he says, and pats the boy down a bit. "I don't see any bloody spiders on you."

"Of course not, it's dark," he says, and Liam can't help it. He laughs. The kid mumbles how it ain't funny, and he laughs a little more. The boy starts walking forward again, not waiting for Liam to prompt him. Not dragging his feet, just walking. Like a man determined to get to the gallows before sunset.

"I hate when that happens," he says, an offering, but Henry doesn't respond. Liam smiles in the dark. *Yeah, okay, tough guy. I get you. Respect.*

But even as he thinks it, Liam's smile falters, his appreciation for the boy twisting into something else. Caution.

Unconsciously, he reaches around his back and touches the grip of the Glock, making sure it's within quick reach. Yeah, the kid is brave, and they already know he's smart, but Liam worries the brave part might start having a negative effect on the smart part.

That would not do.

"Keep walking, kid," Liam says, feeling stupid for saying it, for feeling the need to retain control of a ninety-five-pound fourth grader.

"Duh," Henry says back, and doesn't slow.

★ ★ ★

Henry hates Liam. Hates them all. But he knows—as of right now—there is nothing he can do. If he runs, the man will shoot him and that will be that. Henry has no doubt this would be the case. So long as the dude has a gun and is close as he is, there's no point in doing anything but to just keep moving. *Don't get him angry, don't give him a reason to hurt you,* Henry thinks, and watches the dark road as best he can for rocks and divots. He's already tripped twice, once falling to his knees; and while it didn't hurt him physically it hurt his pride a lot, hurt him big-time to trip in front of Captain Asshole behind him. Mr. Big Shot with a Gun. Yeah, Henry hates him, and he promises himself he will not fall again.

The spiderweb scared him, though. Oh hell yes. Much more than he'd let on. He can still feel the tickling legs of a big old nasty, black, hairy spider crawling on his neck, in his hair, down his back. But he won't give Liam the pleasure of seeing him search and destroy imaginary sensations. The logical part of his brain knows the spider is long gone, and he knows his imagination is just getting away from him, but it still takes all his effort to keep his hands curled into tight fists at his side.

"You should have brought a flashlight," he says, willing his teeth not to chatter in the cold night, not turning around, watching for pitfalls. *And spiderwebs, don't forget that.*

Liam says nothing for a few seconds, and Henry doesn't care whether he responds or not. He likes to talk out loud every now and then, helps him feel *real.* Grounded. Because if this is *real,* then it sweeps away all the horrible ideas created by his imagination. All the things that can happen to a little boy in the dark woods. To kidnapped children. If it's real, then it's *normal.* And in the normal course of a boy's life, they aren't tortured and killed and cut to pieces. They're lost, and then they're found. Taken, then returned. And life goes on.

Life goes on.

"No lights," is all the man says, and suddenly it clicks: the accent.

Australian, Henry thinks, relieved and delighted to figure out a problem to a particularly nagging question. For a moment, he considers sharing his realization, but a warning bell dings in his brain, and he closes his mouth before the words spill out.

No point in him thinking you know jack-diddly-squat about him or where he's from or, for that matter, about where you think he might have taken you or any other damned thing. You keep all that locked up tight, son, his father's voice says, so clear and close that Henry would swear he was right next to him, bending down by his ear so he can whisper directly into it. *Your advantage, Henry,* his father says, *is in knowing more than they think you know. Then, when the time is right, you use that knowledge to help yourself. Your time will come, but until then, be patient, and most of all . . .* zip it.

Henry giggles at this last part, remembering the funny face his father would use when he pinched his fingers and pulled them across his lips, his eyes wide and comical. Henry always laughed crazily at this, and it was likely the reason his father said it so often. To make his boy laugh.

"Glad you're enjoying this," the man says, but it doesn't sound cruel. It sounds . . . *uncertain.* Henry, despite his fear and tiredness, lets his mind wander, tries once more to feel what Liam is thinking, feeling. There's the usual cold black nothing, but now there's something else as well. Something pinkish and flighty woven into those strands of black.

Humor. Or perhaps—

"There," Liam says, and Henry's mind snaps back into place like a rubber band. Up ahead, just off the thin road (which is now more of a path than anything), rests a massive hulk of murky threat. A hunched giant sleeping in the middle of a clearing, its blocky silhouette obstructing the field of hazy stars sprayed like glitter across the midnight-blue sky behind it.

As they walk closer, the moist brush dampening Henry's socks and pant legs, he perceives the shape in more detail—his eyes have adjusted to the dark, and even deep within the trees, with a dull moon perched somewhere high and out of sight overhead, Henry can make out the dull white exterior of a building. A bone-colored heap of wood with a blackened rooftop that swallows the sky, a cancerous bump on the earth dug into the surrounding foliage, a pale blister on the forest's thick green skin.

It's a house, Henry thinks, and his skin prickles with a chill of deep fear even colder than the night. Henry knows, knows immediately and with no uncertainty, that the house is the absolute last place in the world he wants to be.

"Welcome home, kid," the man says, and Henry has to swallow the sob of terror stuck at the base of his throat.

Yes, welcome home, Henry, the house says. *Come right on in. We'll have a grand old time.*

"Dad?" Henry whispers, the word escaping his lips before he can catch it.

From behind him, he hears a sigh, as if he has somehow disappointed the man dragging him to hell.

7

Henry has been missing for twelve hours.

"What's next?" Dave had asked the detective, a woman named Knopp, or Knott, he couldn't recall. It was past nine, and not enough was being done. He studied the large man in the gray rumpled suit, who sipped his coffee and intently studied his notepad. His name was Davis. "Detectives?"

They'd stayed—*all* of them—throughout the late afternoon and early evening. Dave thought maybe a couple cops had left, but more than a few came to replace them. They photographed the house, photographed Henry's bedroom, *their* bedroom, the garage, the kitchen, the backyard, and the porch. They'd been knocking on doors all over the neighborhood. Dave and Mary had offered them all the names and numbers they could think to offer—friends, acquaintances, schoolmates, teachers.

"This is the boy who got hit by the bus last year," Davis stated in reply to Dave's query, not looking up from his notes, just adding the fact to the clumsy, crisscrossed pile of information that had been tossed back and forth all evening between the four of them. A banal, useless game of pick-up sticks.

"Yes, that's right," Dave had said, thinking nothing of it, thinking the cops had seen a headline, or heard about it in the breakroom between shifts. But when he saw the detectives meet eyes, alert and aware, he knew it meant something more.

And then it clicked for him too, and his stomach plummeted.

"The money," Dave said, his voice shaking.

Mary stared at him, a hand covering her mouth, as if he'd said something awful. Something poisonous. The truth *could* be poison sometimes. It could act like a nasty virus, contaminating all those who heard it with inevitable conclusions, with the horror of an infected reality.

"Oh my dear God," he said, his mind racing, understanding fully now all the possibilities in play, all the potential for danger. Somewhere, deep in the back of his mind, he had been waiting—hoping—for the rational outcome.

Henry had fallen into a well.

He had run away.

He was at a friend's house and inexplicably didn't tell anyone (oh, yes, and during school, because anything is possible, right? Right?).

And then there were the other reasons. The reasons hiding in dark closets. The ones that lay quietly under the bed, smiling in the night; the ones hiding in shadow that leapt at you with sharp teeth and hooked claws when you least expected it, when you tried so hard to make yourself believe they didn't really exist.

Just like monsters didn't really exist. Or pure evil.

"The settlement," Dave said, slowly and surely, as if testing the words, the idea of it. The *implications* of it. He looked straight into the concerned eyes of Knopp (*yes, definitely Knopp*, he recalls). "They think there's money."

"Who's *they*?" Mary said sharply, not yet catching on. Not wanting to even consider the possibility.

Davis leaned forward, set his notepad down, and studied Mary, then Dave, an inquisitive and not necessarily kind look on his face. "Well ... isn't there?"

"No! I mean, yes, of course. But that's Henry's money. It's in trust. Mary and I, as his guardians, we get a stipend from the bank for Henry's care. It was all part of the settlement," Dave said, a strange pleading in his voice, hoping he didn't sound defensive, or overexplaining the facts. "We didn't want it to seem like the money would in any way benefit us, so we agreed for the bank ... the one that controls the fund ... to serve as trustee. But you have to understand, it's not like we can just ask for the whole settlement—" Dave laughed and looked to Mary with a fractured smile, trying to expound upon the absolute ridiculousness of the situation, the *impossibility* of what they were pondering. "This can't be relevant. Are you thinking somebody ... for the money ... I don't ... that can't be it. It's impossible. Isn't it?" Dave's hands fell into his lap, and he slouched back into the couch.

It wasn't until Mary was hugging him that he realized he'd been crying. "Did we do something wrong?" he asked as she held him, and if the cops heard him they didn't pursue it.

Three hours since that conversation, and suddenly the realities had altered.

Perspectives had changed.

The four of them had moved from the living room to the kitchen table, making space for a recording station to be attached to the house phone. As they sat looking at each other, Dave thought it akin to a penny-poker game where, at some point in the night, the stakes had grown increasingly higher, and now instead of a friendly game of cards, they were all wary of losing, of each other—all jagged nerves and paranoid thoughts.

Panicked.

Henry was gone. Missing.

Taken.

Yes, possibly. Taken.

Twelve hours now. Twelve hours means new stakes. Higher ante. Blood sport.

Knopp is speaking. "We've notified CART, which is a department of the FBI who will step in if ... no other information comes to light. We've put out an APB and activated the EAS system. If twenty-four hours go by and we have no leads, the FBI will step in and work with us on the investigation. We will also be assigning you a permanent liaison from the San Diego PD who will work closely with you and the FBI during the—until Henry is found."

"Wait," Mary says, a small fire back in her eyes. "What about you two? You're just gonna hand this off?"

"Mary," Knopp says, soothingly, "there are detectives who specialize in child disappearances. It's possible Detective Davis and I will be your liaison, but that's not up to us. We just happened to be first on scene. But now . . . now that things have begun to take shape—"

"Take shape?" Mary asks, her voice clipped and bitter. A mother's wrath.

"Yes, as far as the seriousness of what we may be dealing with," Knopp continues, calm and cool. "It's important you have someone with the experience of handling these types of situations with some regularity."

Dave wrestles with his hands and Mary's eyes return to their blank state, the small fire extinguished. He momentarily ignores the police standing around the house, the detectives sitting at their kitchen table, the absence of the boy they were supposed to protect. *What kind of father am I? What kind of protector?*

"Okay, fine," Mary says, and her voice strengthens, and Dave loves her for that strength. "So what do we do *now*, what do we do right this *moment* to help find our boy?"

"Now we wait, and not lose hope," Knopp says, and tries on her most compassionate smile. Dave thinks it strained, that she looks tired. Worn out. "If nothing changes by morning, we'll contact the FBI and assign . . ."

She looks like a woman holding onto bad news like it's your luggage, knowing that soon it will be time for us to carry the bags, Dave thinks, studying the lines under her eyes, the tightness of her smile, no longer hearing her voice, her useless words.

And oh, won't they be heavy? Don't let them be too heavy, Lord.

Dave grips Mary's hand from across the smooth, cool surface of the marble tabletop, the one where they've eaten dinner every night, hearing about Henry's day, his life, his jokes, and his endless laughter. *Don't forget his strange powers, Dave. Except you never talked about those too much, did you? Not what you'd call a dinner topic.*

Dave shakes his head. The detectives continue to talk, and he is pretty sure Mary is listening. He lets his mind wander for a moment, stares intently at the front door of their home. He wonders if he'll ever see Henry walk through it again.

I'm begging you, Lord, he silently prays, staring at the closed door. *Please . . .*

Not too heavy.

8

For Jenny, it had been a shitty day, so the cards were a nice comedown from a godawful morning followed by a grueling, stressful afternoon.

Meeting Pete at the storage unit before the sun came up was bad enough; having to put up with his slimy body-rub stares while they loaded the Pinto with tools, boxes of food, blankets, lanterns, flashlights, stinking cans of kerosene, and an ice-filled cooler packed with even more food, was just plain depressing.

She'd already packed sleeping bags and clothes for her and Greg, thinking at the time it might even be a little fun to get out of the city for a few days, have a sleepover in a spooky old house in the middle of the woods. Just like old times. But after humping the third can of kerosene and literally shoving the last of the supplies into the rear of the small wagon, she'd begun to think she might have been fantasizing a bit. Okay, a lot.

The drive in, also, had sucked hot balls. It took them over an hour to find the damned entrance to the unused fire road, and the Pinto was not exactly an off-road vehicle. It was barely an on-road vehicle, when the terrain was flat and paved. Bumping over potholed dirt and beneath reaching branches and through creeping brambles was a nightmare scenario.

The house was even worse. A real turd on a stick, to borrow one of Greg's favorite aphorisms from their childhood. Even worse, Jenny quickly discovered that the only thing worse than being alone in a shitty car with Pete was being alone in a shitty house with Pete.

Trying to keep busy so she wouldn't have to actually *talk* to the creepy son of a bitch, they spent the afternoon prepping for the others. After bolt-cutting the front door's flimsy lock and getting everything unloaded and inside, they'd begun the process of covering windows with the assortment of Goodwill-bought sheets and blankets. To his credit, Pete had taken over the labor of installing two brand-new door bolts—one on the front door and one (this one heavy-duty) on the only room upstairs suitable for the kid (the other three rooms either having no doors at all or, in one case, no floor)—while Jenny had put the car in the shed and done a quick search of the house, the perimeter, and a creepy-ass cellar you could access from a squeaky-hinged door in the kitchen.

Bottom line? The place is a shithole. And the idea of spending nearly a week in said shithole with company the likes of Pete Scalera is enough to make her want to scream. Still, the money's good, and a job is a job. With their cut, she and Greg can start over, get out of the game and retire on a beach somewhere. Not bad for a few days' work.

Assuming nothing goes wrong, of course.

Sighing heavily and doing her best to push the negative bullshit out of her mind, Jenny clutches the down jacket tighter to her body. The wool blanket across her thighs keeps her legs warm, but her feet are nearly numb with cold and the chill seems to run deep inside her, spreading from her frozen toes up through her legs, belly, chest, and head. She looks at her cards in the dim light, and the three queens warm her a touch. The knowledge that she's going to beat skinny-and-shitty at a hand of poker is like dropping a hunk of coal into a dying furnace.

She contemplates taking a swig from their shared bottle of Jack before raising the bet, but worries he'd see it as a "tell," an unconscious note of confidence. Not that she thinks Pete is all that perceptive; to him she's "blonde, tits, alone" and not much else. She would add "armed" to that little list of his, and maybe before the night's over she'll scratch it onto his chest with the needle-sharp eight-inch ice pick she keeps sheathed beneath her jeans, snug in a leather holster hidden at her hip.

But for now she's just happy to kick his macho ass at cards.

"Come on, Jen, pay or play," he says, and he does reach for the bottle (now half-empty) and takes a long swallow. *Maybe you're the one showing too much confidence*, she thinks, and that decides her.

She throws a twenty-dollar bill onto the healthy stack of fives and singles, gets a thrill at seeing his eyes widen, like a brainless shark darting for chummed waters. *Come and get it, motherfucker.*

"Tasty," he says, and takes a moment to study her. Wondering if she can back it up.

"Come on, *Pedro*, pay or play," she says, and gives him her most winning—and distracting—smile.

"You're lucky you're pretty and have a nice ass," he says, now studying his own cards, the oil lantern on the table providing barely enough light to make out whether you're staring at diamonds or hearts. "I don't normally let people call me by my birth moniker."

Jenny raises her eyebrows, keeps the smile. "Big words. I'm impressed."

"You just wait," he says, and begins fondling the bills stacked on the table in front of him. "My words aren't the only things that are big, sweetheart." He smiles large and she nearly flinches at the upper row of gold teeth that glisten treacherously in the lamplight.

"Aaaand I'm no longer impressed. Talking about your dick size immediately lowers you back to ape-level intelligent. What an amazing turnaround." She forces her voice to come out even and assured, but deep down she knows better than to push it with this one. Pedro "Pete" Scalera, at his roots, is nothing more than a gang-banging rapist who happened to be incarcerated at the same time her brother was. To her brother, at least, he has proven himself able, and loyal. But none of that changes the person he is—the violent, sexist, mean motherfucker from Oakland who would be all kinds of comfortable (morally and ethically) slicing a woman into ribbons for badmouthing him or, even worse (and potentially fatal), questioning his manhood.

For now, though, Pete only gives her a cold look, his dark eyes flickering shadows in the poorly-lit kitchen. *If that's indeed what this room used to be. This place has lost all defined order. It's nothing but rooms now. Shitty, moldy, rat-infested rooms.*

Jenny watches with interest as Pete calls her twenty-dollar bet. "You're not gonna raise, *big* guy?"

"Yeah, okay, enough," he says, and she can almost feel the anger rising inside him. His words are clipped and sharp. He doesn't like indecision, she realizes. He also doesn't like being flustered, and certainly not by a woman.

Besides, there's probably a hundred bucks in that pot, that's gotta sting a little.
"Touchy, touchy."

"Call," he says, and lays down his cards. "Beat a straight, bitch."

Jenny holds her breath and looks at her hand one last time. At the three queens, and the lovely two jacks beside them. She lays her hand on the table with the gentle touch of a mother settling her baby into a crib. "The house, I'm afraid, is full. Oh, and look at that—ladies on top."

Pete stares at her flat cards with a look that bounces between shock, anger, and confusion. Possibly a flicker of hate, to boot. When she scoops the money into her pile her eyes never leave his, and this has the effect of getting his blood up a few more notches.

"Jesus, you act like you took my life savings," he says, and she senses he's calming down, getting his swagger back. "We're gonna be stuck in this hole for a few days, I'll win it back."

"Ya think?" she says, and begins organizing the cash into neat piles.

He smiles that gold-toothed smile again, playing the only card he has left: the Great and Powerful Male. "Tell you what, I'll double whatever's in that pot for some of that sweet ass of yours. What you think, baby?"

"Wow, I didn't know my ass was worth so much," she says, and slips a hand nonchalantly beneath her shirt, rests her fingers on the grooved wooden handle resting at her hip.

Pete pushes the whiskey bottle toward her. "C'mon, Jenny. You won some money, now you can win some more. Let's party, baby. I'm cold and this place is a shithole."

Jenny snaps the buckle off the end of the sheath and draws out the pick. The eight-inch, fixed-handle shaft of shining steel would punch in and out of Pedro's torso as if he were made of pudding. As she rests it in her lap and continues to stack her money, she laughs at the thought of his dying face, the stupid shocked look when he realized he'd been stabbed in the groin, guts, and heart before his brain even registered the pinch of the first cut.

Pete's smile falls away. "Something funny?"

"No, man. It's all good," she says, not wanting to do this here, knowing it would piss Jim off royally, but also feeling it might be sort of fun to rid the world of one more swinging dick. "Let's just play cards, huh? No hard feelings."

Pete stares at her a moment, debating. Then the smile is back, and right behind it a boisterous, honest, deep-throated laugh. She watches, amazed and amused, as he tilts his head back and makes a real show of it. The pit bull head tattooed across his neck seems to bark and snarl with every twitch and bob of his Adam's apple. She has to admit, it is mesmerizing.

"Should I deal, or—" she says, and his laughter slows, then stops.

He looks at her with the look of someone who has decided they're going to kill you and, upon further introspection, that they're going to enjoy doing it.

Huh, is all she thinks as she grips the handle resting on her thigh. *Well, I guess that makes two of us.*

"Not now, *puta*," he says, still smiling that smile. "I know who you are. I know who I'm messing with. We're good." He leans forward across the cheap card table, his ugly features made even more gruesome by the light from the flickering oil lantern, the dancing shadows. Somewhere along the line his smile disappeared again. "Now put that famous ice pick away before you stick yourself with it."

They stare at each other a beat, debating.

There's a loud pounding on the front door of the house. The noise shatters the silence, fills the air with demand and consequence. Pete and Jenny scramble to their feet, their feud and their cards forgotten. Pete pulls a pistol from a deep pocket of his Dickies. "Name!"

"It's Liam. I've got the kid. Open it."

Pete stashes the gun as Jenny slides her weapon back into the hidden holster. He goes to the door, pushes away the metal bar of the new bolt, and turns the rusted knob to let the door swing inward. He peeks around the edge and into the night like a half-naked woman might do for a mail-man bringing her an unexpected package.

The Australian pushes the door open and shoves his way through. Pete takes a few quick steps back, not ready for the violence of the intrusion. The man—Liam—pushes a little black kid in front of him. The kid stares wide-eyed around the house before his eyes fall on Jenny, linger a beat, then move on.

"That him?" she asks.

Liam looks at her like she's an idiot, and she doesn't blame him. Pete closes the door, bolts it. "Yo man, take it easy."

Liam spins and sticks a finger at the pit bull tattoo at Pete's throat. Jenny doesn't even realize she's taken a step backward. "Shut your fucking mouth, Pedro, or I will knock those gold chiclets down your throat then stick you down a hole until you've shit them out, you got me?"

Pete nods stupidly, like a child would at a raging father. "Yeah, man, Jesus."

Liam pushes the kid roughly into the kitchen. For a fleeting second, Jenny thinks to tell him to take it easy, after all the kid's no bigger than a third grader, and skinny. But she swallows that thought, and the accompanying words.

Guy's been here six seconds and he owns the place, she thinks, feeling a stir of heat in her belly. *Better him than me, I guess.*

"Greg okay?" she asks, using the voice she uses with men she's afraid of. That one she hates more than anything. That subservient tone she thought she'd lost years ago, with the two thrusts of her trusty ice pick.

Liam looks at her a beat, eyes fire, mouth tense. Then he moves his gaze around the room, dismissing her as a non-threat, or at least not a competing alpha he has to put into place. "Your brother's fine," he says. "Doing his thing."

"Cool," she says lamely.

"Where are the other lanterns? Is the room set up?"

Pete emerges from the shadow, no longer the bad man, but the follower. Mr. Fucking Helpful. "Yeah, man, it's all done. I put the lock on myself. Window boarded. I covered over most of the windows in the house, but not some of the floor-level ones. Figured we'd want some light, you know?"

Liam walks to the table, pulling the kid by the collar, but not roughly. The boy seems resigned to the whole thing, and Jenny is a little impressed. *Least he ain't a crybaby. Thank God for that.* Liam picks up the whiskey and takes two, three deep swallows. He hands it to the boy, who pulls away.

To her surprise, Liam seems to almost go easy on the kid. Gentle, even.

"Henry, I want you to take a sip of this. Not too much. It'll warm you up a bit and calm your nerves."

Henry, she thinks, knowing full well his name, the names of his guardians, his school, his home address. But seeing him now and hearing the name out loud brings a rush of substance to the entire plan. *This is the boy. This is Henry.*

"No, thank you," Henry says, and Jenny doesn't know whether to laugh, hug him, or slap the little bastard.

"Have a sip of this or I'll give you another stick with the needle. Your choice. Make it now."

Henry grabs the bottle without thinking about it. Liam tips it and she watches in amusement as the kid swallows the whiskey. She waits for him to sputter it up, to gag, to spit and curse.

He winces, and his eyes are watering, but he keeps his mouth shut, impressing her for the second time in as many minutes.

"Give me that lantern," Liam snaps, and her attention jerks back to him, away from the boy. "Light a couple more. We need more light in here. Put blankets over the windows that aren't boarded."

Jenny hands over the lantern. He puts the whiskey back on the card table and wraps a hand around the kid's neck.

"Where are we going?" the kid asks, and Jenny feels a wash of relief as he and Liam exit the kitchen, leaving her in the dark. She hears their steps climbing the rotted stairs.

"Your room," Liam says. "No more questions."

Jenny waits until she hears the creak of footsteps on the second floor before she digs the lighter from her pocket, starts hunting for the additional lanterns.

Pete walks into the kitchen, but even in the dark she can tell he's no longer a threat. Not anymore. Not with Liam around.

"Nice kid," he says, and laughs a little under his breath. "Like a pot of gold with legs."

"Yeah, sure," she says, lifting the glass of the old lantern and lighting the wick, crowding the room with flickering shadows. "I'm sure we're all gonna be great friends."

9

Upon entering the house, Henry doesn't hesitate to reach out and try to get an understanding of the people waiting to greet him and Liam. He's feeling better now, stronger. Something he attributes to being out of the biting cold of the forest and into a shelter—albeit a decrepit one—and to the drug they'd given him finally wearing off. His mind feels free again, and he launches it like a white net into the spacious dark of the house's interior.

He does not like what he finds.

The skinny Latino man is bad. He flows with a cape of black and dark purple, deep reds of raw violence and careless hate, dirty gold tendrils of sly cruelty. Henry thinks the man with the gold teeth is the type of person who would cut your throat in your sleep for the wallet in your pocket. *Like a pirate,* Henry thinks, and not kindly. *Like a nasty old pirate.* There are other colors, other thoughts in the man's head—thoughts about the woman, and about other women. There's even a slimy train of thought about Henry himself that he dares not explore further, and one particular strain of feelings about Liam that's raw and throbbing as a wet, pus-filled boil.

The woman is worse.

Henry recalls a conversation he once had with Uncle Dave about a man who'd killed lots of people. A man named Dahmer who was recently murdered while in prison. And though Uncle Dave wasn't happy about Henry knowing about such a thing, he figured giving Henry some context would be helpful.

"That man had a psychotic personality, Henry," Dave had told him. "Likely a sociopath."

"Socialpath?" Henry had asked, alarmed and excited at this fresh vein of adult information.

"So*cio*path," Dave reiterated. "It means he doesn't feel things like we do. Doing bad things to people doesn't bother him. He has no conscience. That makes him dangerous."

Dave's definition sparked another memory in Henry, from when he was very young.

He'd gone to a matinee of the movie *Pinocchio* with his dad. In the movie, there was a funny cricket with a top hat who had been Pinocchio's conscience. His teller of *right* and *wrong*.

Seeing the woman's mind, Henry realizes that she has no top-hatted cricket. No conscience. Where the cricket would normally live, there is nothing but an empty cage. Where feelings and emotions should spew colors and feelings . . . there is only a void. A blank space.

Socialpath.

Cute kid, she thought when she first saw him, but the words didn't come wrapped in any emotion. She might as well have been describing a book, or an insect, or the color of a dress. She scares Henry on a level different than Liam or the other man. She scares Henry because she would hurt him without debate, without reluctance, without guilt. In some ways Liam was like this; Henry had sensed that from the beginning. But with Liam, he thinks it's something he'd *trained* to do, something he'd worked hard on, built up over time like tall walls around his mind, like a fortress.

For the woman, it's natural as breathing.

As for the house itself, it is nothing to Henry. An empty husk. The house is like a cracked egg with its gooey contents leaked into the dirt, the remaining shell dried up and brittle—yeah, it smells bad and the wood is rotten, the walls mildewed, but it's still just a house.

No ghosts here, Henry thinks.

And then, like a light breeze caressing his face, Henry *does* sense something.

Something *else*.

And just as quickly, it's gone.

He reaches out, tries to grasp it once more, but can't locate it, can't navigate back to whatever it was.

There's something else here.

Before he explores further, Liam is yelling and bossing people around. He makes Henry drink whiskey and it's horrible, bitter and burning. It hurts his throat and makes his stomach instantly queasy. He doesn't feel warmer, just sicker.

Liam pushes him deeper into the house, toward a staircase, decayed wood steps.

"Where are we going?" he asks.

"Your room," he replies. "No more questions."

The upstairs is weird. A narrow hallway overlooks the rickety banister down to the main foyer beneath. They have to walk around a hole in the floor filled with heavy darkness, like a liquid pool of black ink. Henry figures it drops through to the first floor and would likely do some damage to an ankle or leg if anyone accidentally slipped through. He steps around cautiously, actually puts a hand on Liam's wrist, the one gripping his neck.

"Up on the right, go through there," Liam says, and Henry sees the pitch-black rectangle embedded in the dirty gray wall.

He knows instinctively, with a rush of horror, where that blackness leads.

His room.

As he passes through, the light from Liam's lantern catches something shiny on the door and he quickly studies it. A new, thick bolt lock has been mounted to a massive, heavy-looking plate screwed into the wall next to the door. It gleams silver against the dingy wood, the peeling paint that might have once been white but is now a time-aged yellow-brown, the color of disease.

Liam stands at the door holding the lantern high, and Henry is filled with a thick, cold dread. It rides on his shoulders like a sack of black worms, writhing and heavy. His body wants to let go, drop to its knees, lie

down on the floor and wait for it all to be over. He sighs heavily, feels the
physical slumping of his shoulders and wills his body to straighten, to be
alert instead of beaten, to be thoughtful instead of terrified.

"You got an old man sigh," Liam says, and Henry doesn't respond.
Instead, he studies his prison.

There is a rusted iron-framed bed in the corner, a thin mattress resting
on top of it. There are no pillows, but there is a heap of folded wool blankets. Henry's so cold that he looks at them longingly before moving on to
the rest of the dim room, the corners thick with gloom.

There isn't much else to take stock of. A bucket in the corner opposite
the bed. A kerosene heater against a wall. A window that is shiny and black
like the eye of a shark. Henry walks to it, looks out, curious why he can't
see the stars.

"That's boarded from the outside," Liam says, hanging back at the
door, as if not wanting any part of the room. Henry wonders if it's fear or
shame that keeps Liam at the door and goes with the latter. He doubts the
big Australian man is afraid of much, if anything.

There are some moldy boxes strewn against a far wall, soiled and torn
apart. Empty.

"I'm hungry," Henry says, his surveying complete for now. He'll wait
to do a more thorough pass in the light of day. "And cold."

Liam comes in finally, sets the lantern on the floor, and goes to the
kerosene heater. He pulls a box of matches from his pocket, turns a knob
so that the heater hisses like a snake. He sticks the match into a small, open
door and there's a soft *whoomp*. A few moments later, the heater's small
window is glowing a dull red, like a demon's eye that's been awakened.
"There's your heat," he says, and goes back to the door, scooping up the
lantern as he goes. "As for food, you'll be fed in the morning. If you don't
give me any shit I'll bring you a bottle of water in a bit. Or you can go to
sleep. Matters not to me."

Henry looks at him, wide-eyed at the thought of not eating until morning. His stomach is clenched tight with hunger and he wonders how long it's been since he's had food. *Since breakfast*, he realizes, and remembers stabbing the eggs and worrying Mary would scold him.

A wave of self-pity and despair washes over him, and he suddenly misses Dave and Mary more than he's ever missed anything or anyone in his life, including his own mother and father. He wants badly to cry, but refuses. For now. He'll wait until the man leaves, when the man goes away and lets him be.

Henry steps to the bed, begins unfolding the blankets.

"Hey Henry," the man says, but Henry refuses to turn around, and can tell Liam couldn't give a shit about his weak defiance. "Let me tell you something, all right? Outside this house, about twenty feet away, is an old shed. Think it was a garage at one point, maybe held horses or pigs, dunno. I bet it's just as drafty and filthy as you can imagine. And here's what I'm gonna tell you . . . you listening, Henry?"

Henry continues to unfold the blankets, but he nods. Not wanting to upset him, knowing that would be a mistake.

"Good. Well, here's the deal, mate. You be quiet and not try any bull-shit, yeah? No running for the stairs or messing with the window, and you can stay here in your cozy room with your nice heater and mattress and warm blankets. All the comforts of a civil home, right?"

Liam takes a couple steps into the room. Henry can hear the boards creak beneath his weight. "But you fuck with me, and I'll tie your hands and legs and carry you out to that shed and drop you in the dirt and lock you in tight. No bed. No blankets. No heat. Even worse," he continues, "no protection."

Henry can't help himself. He turns his head and looks back at Liam, an ugly black shadow holding dirty orange fire, the flickering light of the dull flame, muted by soot-smeared glass, painted against his flesh like an infection. "That's right. You think I'm bad? You don't even want to know what's prowling these woods at night. They'd snuggle up to you and have a nice breakfast, they would. These forest creatures. The rats and the vermin and the insects. They'd nibble at you while you screamed. They'd eat your guts while your heart pumped more and more blood into their giddy, waiting mouths."

Henry feels a sharp pain in his bladder and stops himself before the piss runs out of him. But the fear stays and he does start crying now, tiny hiccups with tears, and he can't hold it back no matter how hard he tries and the shame of it swallows him and it's all he can do to keep breathing, breathing deep and holding back the *big* tears, the unfiltered sobbing and wailing press against the back of his eyes, creep up his throat, fill his chest.

"So I'd keep nice and quiet if I were you," Liam says, and steps back into the hallway. "Good boys live to tell the tale, Henry."

Liam grabs the handle of the door and shuts it. The light filling the room vanishes as if a switch has been flipped.

Henry hears the bolt snap into place. He doesn't move for a few heartbeats, waits for his eyes to adjust. He's alone now. Alone for the first time since they took him.

He turns and begins to unfold the blankets once more. His hands are shaking and he's talking to himself but doesn't know what he's saying. The words are like trapped steam that his mind lets flow to diffuse the pressure, to fill the air with something other than the soft hiss of the heater, the smell of kerosene and rot.

Henry pulls himself onto the bed, lets his feet dangle off the side, and wraps himself up in the blankets.

"Daddy?" he says. The word, hardly more than a whisper, fills the room.

I'm here, son, comes the familiar voice. It sounds strained and sad and helpless. *I'm here, and I'm so, so sorry.*

10

Faster!

The creature—lithe and short enough to skip roots, skim between trunks, and duck low branches—sprints after its prey like a dancing shadow in the moonlight. With a guttural snarl and a final leap it catches the small deer mid-stride and they tumble into the sodden earth.

Sharp claws dig deep into the fawn's throat, punch through the thick hide and into muscle. She whispers into a twitching ear—rasping sounds of comfort. The deer stops kicking, slows its struggle. As it goes limp, she grips the slick cords of its neck and rips them free. Bright blood pumps out of the torn artery and into the soil. After a minute, its heart stops.

The creature lifts its face to the night sky and lets out a choked howl. A killing cry.

It guts the fawn, pulls a shred of raw meat and feeds itself. What remains will be taken to the unborn. A tribute of a successful hunt.

From the shadows, a sleek bobcat, gold-toned and muscular, stalks closer to the kill, and the killer. Its ears are pricked, its eyes silver discs in the dim moonlight. It shows a mouth of teeth and a low growl rumbles from its throat. The creature turns its yellow eyes on the beast and makes a few quick, soft clicking sounds, then goes back to pulling the meat from the deer, unconcerned.

The bobcat ceases its warning growl, puts away its fangs. It pads in a small circle, moving a few feet away, and obediently sits and watches from the short distance, waiting until it's released to finish what the strange creature does not take.

The cat's eyes droop, half-lidded. It purrs serenely as the sounds and smells of ripping flesh continue, the stink of raw meat flooding the crisp air.

PART FIVE: MIND GAMES

1

A shit-brown Duster rolls into a narrow alley still smothered in the dusty purple shadows of predawn. The car's body is dented, but it's been recently painted; the taillights, turn signals, and headlights work as well as a new Cadillac fresh off the line, and it sports brand-new, heavy-tread tires.

Greg pulls the car into one of three spots reserved behind the building for bar employees and tenants of the second-story apartment. He looks up through the windshield, surprised to see the windows dark.

He was expected, after all.

Making sure both doors are locked, he tucks the keys into his pocket and knocks on the door separating the upstairs unit's stairwell from the alleyway. A moment passes and Greg starts feeling what he calls the "twitches"—a jittery, nervous electricity that flickers deep inside the sinews of his muscles, tingles along the surface of his skin. The feeling of something being *wrong*.

"Fuck me," he mumbles, his breath a white plume in the early-morning December air. He shakes off a chill that climbs into his gut through the heavy jacket.

He knocks again, a bit louder this time, but knowing he shouldn't have to knock at all, that Jim should have been looking out the damned window for his car to pull in. Being late wasn't like Jim. Wasn't in the man's nature.

Greg spins, looks at the car, begins to debate his options. *Do I run? Go grab Sis and what, head to Mexico? With what money, dipshit?*

"Damn damn damn," he mutters, and is about to walk around the front of the building for some sign of *something*, when the service door of the bar clanks, then swings open into the alley.

Jim stands in the shadows, and not only does Greg not feel relief at seeing the man (alive and well and unhandcuffed, thank God), but for some reason he's even more frightened than he was before. His body nearly spasms as the twitches erupt in his back and shoulders, sizzle his nerves like bacon on a hot skillet.

I just need some sleep, that's all. One good night's sleep to whisk away the willies.

"You gonna come in or what?" Jim says.

"I thought you'd be upstairs?" Greg says weakly, defensively.

Jim shrugs. "Shit changes," he says, then turns and disappears inside the dark interior of the bar, leaving the open maw of dark doorway behind him.

After a momentary hesitation, Greg shrugs and follows.

Once inside, he turns and reaches for the warped handle of the metal service door. He takes a last, longing glance toward the car, the alley, and the brightening blue air as dawn breaks over the city. He has the irrational thought that it might be the last time he sees a sunrise, then smirks at himself for being a complete and total pussy, and yanks the heavy door shut, sealing himself inside the sour dark.

"Sit down, brother," Jim says, sliding gracefully into the torn red faux leather of a booth.

Having never been inside the bar, Greg takes a moment to inventory the exits, windows, and blind spots, a habit he developed many years ago when he was on the wrong end of some large-ass debts to guys who liked to collect interest in the form of broken bones and sliced skin. Jim had been one of the reasons he'd gotten out from under that debt, and Greg had been part of his crew ever since; even did time for the big man when things went south on the fucked robbery of a pawnshop in Bakersfield. Jim had been able to get away with the jewelry stash he'd coveted (something he could turn quickly for fifty thousand clean), but Greg had been caught at the heel by a damned guard who was *supposed* to have been

drugged into a lethargic stupor—so as alarms wailed and Greg fought off
a somewhat dizzy security guard, Jim had seen the writing on the wall and
vamoosed with the stash and the car.

Greg didn't blame him. It was an unspoken rule that the first priority
was to secure the stash. If someone had to do time, his piece would be
waiting for him when he got out, sometimes with interest.

Greg did his time, kept his mouth shut on his accomplice, stayed
out of trouble, and was back out again in eighteen months. The cops
could only get him for a misdemeanor burglary charge since the jewelry
they'd stolen was hot before they'd ever touched it, and Jim knew it. All
the apoplectic shop owner could do was tell the cops the burglary had
been "attempted," otherwise known as breaking and entering (a point the
defense lawyer repeated ad nauseam), thereby letting Greg get off with a
greatly reduced sentence.

While in prison he'd bunked with a sketchy Hispanic kid named
Pete Scalera, who he'd hated with a passion right up until the time Pete
saved his ass when Greg was jumped by "friends of enemies" while folding bleached sheets in the laundry room. After that, they'd started talking
more civilly, discovering many similarities between their upbringing and
outlook on the world as a whole—how it was like an oyster that needed
only to be cracked open to reveal the dirty pearl tucked inside.

Once they were out, Pete was introduced to Jim, and after a couple
small jobs the team had a nice rhythm.

On *this* one, however, the windup had been much more serious.
Months of planning, of setup. They'd needed two more bodies for the
crew—Greg had pulled in the only other person in the world he trusted,
his sister Jenny, and Jim had brought in one of his former partners. The
Aussie.

Greg didn't mind Liam, but he also didn't trust him. Not completely.
Greg thought maybe Jim had a soft spot for the guy. Maybe that was jealousy talking, but something about Liam bothers Greg a little. *Nags* at him.

Frustratingly, it's nothing he can put his finger on. At first, he'd thought the Aussie a bit soft, but he'd since come around on that. Sly, maybe, but not soft. Not after working with him on grabbing the kid. No, he figures it's probably nerves. Or, hell, maybe he's just jealous. *He* was Jim's right-hand man, after all, and now he's . . . what? A driver.

Regardless, he made a point to keep an eye on Liam throughout the job. Greg figured maybe he'd finally get a handle on what bugs him so much—what he doesn't all the way *trust*—even if it's something Jim himself is blind to.

"Everything worked out, I assume," Jim is saying, and Greg snaps his attention back to the boss, already nodding.

The place is silent as the grave and dim as a cave. Except for a few lights behind the bar and the multicolored glow of a nearby jukebox, there is no illumination whatsoever. There are no windows except for the glass diamond stamped into the locked front door, which is steadily brightening from dull-blue to milky-white as the sunlight strengthens.

"All good," Greg says. "Dropped the package at the house, hit the mailbox we discussed—the first option—switched the cars no problem. Squeaky-clean, boss."

Jim nods. Greg notices he's wearing his janitor uniform and realizes he doesn't have long before he needs to be back at the school, most likely answering some questions. Something he expects and is prepared for.

"Wish I could say the same," Jim says. "The man who runs this place got cheeky, wanted in, et cetera. Threatened me, can you believe that shit?"

Jim actually laughs and Greg laughs nervously along with him. He wonders where the guy's corpse is now, and decides not to speculate.

"Between that and . . . another issue I had to address—" Jim shrugs, wipes a massive hand smoothly across the dry, black-lacquered tabletop. "Anyway, I felt things were getting tight, understood? But now, we're good. We're fine."

"Sure, sure," Greg says, still nodding. "We leave tonight, yeah? Same plan?"

"Always," Jim says, and looks at his watch. "I gotta go. There's some food in the freezer, use the kitchen all you want. Keep the lights off, though. This shit's closed today. Already got a sign on the door. I'll be back around four, then we head out."

"And hello winter break," Greg says, smiling.

"Hell yes," Jim agrees, sliding out of the booth slowly. "Dumb old Fred taking some time off. Gonna see some family."

"That sounds nice," Greg says, and yawns.

"It sure does. Get your ass some sleep, but not upstairs. We done in that apartment."

"No problem," Greg says, confident of *exactly* what he'd find in the small second-floor apartment where Fred the janitor has been living these last few months. "You be careful today."

Jim gathers a few things off the bar. "Ain't no worries. I just hope we're all good at the house, you know? I don't like not being there."

"What could go wrong?" Greg asks, already headed for the kitchen and praying there's a frozen steak or two he can start thawing out. "I mean, come on, he's a little kid." Jim grunts and disappears into the shadows. Greg hears the service door open, then shut with a bang, startling him. As if shaken loose by the sound, Greg realizes, in a flash, what it is that bothers him about Liam:

The guy is completely unpredictable.

Fretting, he opens the large freezer in search of a grilling steak and feels those damn twitches again. *Ain't nothing worse on a job than a man who's unpredictable*, he thinks, then dismisses the thought—and the twitches—when he spots a fat T-bone wrapped in clear cellophane.

"Breakfast of champions," he quips and for the moment forgets all about Liam, the twitches, and whatever—or *whoever*—Jim's got stashed in the apartment upstairs.

2

Henry.

Henry, do you feel *that? Can you feel it, Henry? I don't think we're alone, son.*

Damn it, Henry, wake up. It worries me.

Henry? Henry . . . darn it, son, I said WAKE UP!

Henry opens his eyes . . .

. . . and finds himself staring directly at the bucket in the corner of the room.

A hot rush of shame sears his mind at the memory of having to use the bucket in the middle of the night, finding his way toward it by the dull red glow of the stinking heater. He'd cried as he peed into it, hated being treated like a prisoner. Like an *animal*.

And now he has to go again.

This time, however, it's not so bad. It isn't dark, for one thing, and the slivers of daylight coming through the boarded-up window make the room less sinister, his predicament less surreal. Last night it felt like he was stuck in a nightmare—shivering and weeping as he peed into the metal container, the walls of the room swallowed by darkness, the glassed-in heater flame not revealing what might have hunkered along the base-boards, or been perched up in the high corners, watching and waiting.

It's still dehumanizing, he thinks, allowing himself a weak smile of pride for conjuring the word. *FUCKING DEHUMANIZING!* he screams in his head, and almost giggles at the secret swear. His brain continues to screech and rant as he finishes his business, his mind enjoying the freedom of the *inside*, of the secret place where only he is allowed. *FUCK FUCK FUCKITY-FUCK LIKE A DUCK DUCK DUCKITY-DUCK!* Henry zips up his jeans and almost laughs out loud at his brain's tired, rebellious antics.

Henry!

Henry spins around but sees nothing but beaten white walls, dusty angles of determined daylight. He walks to his bed, pulls a blanket over his lap, and closes his eyes.

Dad?

I'm here, son. I'm here.

Henry opens his eyes. A gray figure stands amid the morning shadows in the farthest corner of the room, just past the locked white door.

"Can you help me?" Henry asks, unsure if what he's seeing is real but too weak and scared to care.

I don't know . . . I don't think so. Oh damn. Henry . . .

"What is it?"

Hush. He's here.

Henry's eyes leave the shadowed corner and move to the door. A second later, there's a loud *snap!* as the lock is slid aside.

Quickly, Henry throws himself flat onto the mattress and yanks the blanket up over his chest. A second later the door opens, and Liam steps inside.

★ ★ ★

Liam rushes with the lock, not liking what he hears from the other side of the door. It's not Pete or Jenny in there, he knows, having just left the two of them in the kitchen, struggling to fire up the gas-powered hotplate so they could boil water for coffee—something all three of them badly needed.

He flips the thick-gauge bolt out of the way and pushes into the room, not knowing what to expect but immediately relieved to see Henry lying down in the bed, the blanket pulled up to his chin . . . and no one else.

Kid must have been talking in his sleep.

On instinct, Liam glances behind the door, but sees nothing.

Of course. There's no one in here, man. Get a grip on your shit.

Relaxing his hold on the cool plastic of the SunnyD bottle he'd brought the kid, he steps deeper into the room and frowns.

It's cold. *Too* cold. Having the kid get pneumonia would be *plan-adverse*, as Jim liked to say. It was an idiom he pulled out whenever Liam would offer a somewhat-stupid suggestion to one of their setups. "That would be plan-adverse, my man," Jim would say, and Liam would grind his teeth, not appreciating the dismissive tone the big man used in those instances. *Just say it's a dumb fucking idea,* he'd think. *I'm a grown man, I can take it. What I can't take is the condescending parental tone, you two-ton murderous mad-bull son-of-a-bitch.*

It also smells like piss, which bothers him. There is no need for the kid to have to breathe his own waste. He makes a note to walk the kid like a dog during the rest of their stay, let him shit and piss outside like the rest of them. The boy isn't gonna run or make trouble, and if he does, that will be the end of the walks, and the brat can smell his own shit all day and all night long for all Liam cares.

"Kid," Liam says, beginning to get the feeling Henry might be faking it under all that heavy breathing bullshit. "Henry!" he barks, too loudly.

The boy springs up, eyes wide.

Scared, Liam thinks. *Good.* "I brought you breakfast."

Liam goes to the cot and hands Henry the bottle of SunnyD and a six-pack of chocolate-covered Dolly Madison mini-donuts. He almost laughs when Henry's eyes go wide as saucers, then feels a pang of guilt for not feeding the kid sooner. *He must be starved,* he thinks, then shakes it off. This isn't daycare, after all.

"I'm not supposed to drink that," Henry says, but Liam can all but feel the kid's hunger snarling from the depths of his potbelly stomach. "It's got too much sugar in it."

Liam squints his eyes at the label, and this time he does laugh. "So? You allergic?"

Henry shakes his head. "Nope. Mary says it makes me hyper."

Liam sits on the cot at Henry's feet, curious to see how long the kid can hold out before ripping that red plastic cap free and downing the juice. He figures the donuts won't last long either. "Don't worry about that. It ain't gonna hurt you and you need something in your stomach. Go ahead, I won't tell. Promise."

Henry holds out another half second, then twists open the juice like a man who's been lost in the desert and takes three or four large swallows. When he lowers the bottle, he lets out a held breath, followed immediately by an equally large and rather wet belch.

"Excuse me," Henry mumbles, then tucks the juice bottle between his thighs and rips open the bag of donuts.

"Don't eat too fast," Liam says and stands to leave. "I'll be back in a bit."

He's at the door when he stops, half-turns back toward Henry. "Hey, if you need to go to the bathroom again, just bang on this door. I'll hear you fine, and it's okay if you do that. I'll come get you and you can do your business outside. No need for you to—you know—"

Liam pauses, feeling momentarily displaced. The situation feels suddenly ethereal, like a dream, or a memory. He has the strong, impulsive, irrational urge to walk out of that cold, stinking bedroom, down the stairs, out the front door, and straight to the airport. Then he'd fly the hell back to Australia and forget all this. Maybe have some sort of life again. *Kaaron . . . Timothy . . . oh my boy . . .*

Liam wipes a hand across his mouth, dashes the thoughts from his mind, and lets the old numbing black smoke fill him up once more—the smoke that keeps away the past, hides the pain. Erases the damned regrets. He clears his throat.

"—just knock, like I said. Got me?"

The boy says nothing, and Liam turns his attention back to see him chewing on a donut, his eyes locked on Liam as if the kid's trying to memorize every inch of him. And those eyes don't look like little-kid eyes, no sir, not at the moment, anyway.

They look *wise*. The eyes of someone who knows something important about you that you do not know. Old-man eyes to go with his ridiculous old-man sigh.

Still, the look Henry fixes him with makes Liam's skin bust out in a goosebump parade; to be stared at like that—to be *scrutinized*—is not a comfortable feeling, and it's certainly not a feeling he cares for, not one bit. It makes him feel . . . *uncertain*. And feeling uncertain? Well, that just pisses him off.

"Okay, Henry?"

Henry nods and swallows, his eyes still focused—raptly so—on Liam.

"What? Why the fuck are you looking at me?" Liam says, feeling more creeped out by the second.

"Nothing," Henry says, shrugging slightly. "I just . . ."

Liam takes a step back toward the bed, and not in a friendly way. "What?"

Henry looks up at him again, that dissecting glare gone now, those old-man eyes replaced with the sad, pouty eyes of a child.

Liam almost sighs in relief.

"We both want to go home, huh?" Henry says, and Liam feels an ice-cold vibration scurry up his spine and spread out across the back of his neck. *Red flag, mate. And it's a big motherfucker, too.*

"How—" Liam starts, but then looks deeper into the boy's frightened doe eyes, sees him chomping down another chocolate donut, and realizes how incredibly stupid he's being. He laughs once—a quick, harsh bark—then shakes his head and walks through the open door. As he starts to close it, he gives Henry a last hard look, lets the comfortable feelings of reproach and scorn and hate fill his mind once more. He suddenly wants to hurt the little bastard, to see him cry, to make those creepy old-man eyes of his take a long walk down a short dock. "You're a weird fucking kid, you know that, Henry? What's wrong with you, anyway?"

But the boy doesn't cry, or whimper, or even seem to be taken aback. He just shrugs and lets out that heavy, drawn-out sigh of his, stares lamely at the half-eaten donut in his small hand.

"Oh gosh," he says, shoulders slumping. "All sorts of things."

Frowning, Liam closes the door and secures the lock. He heads back toward the stairs, praying those two idiots have finally made the coffee.

3

Henry finishes his donuts and sucks down the last of the SunnyD. His mouth feels pasty, his tongue coated and lips sticky from the overly sweet breakfast. Despite his fear of the man, he actually hopes Liam will come back soon so he can ask for a big glass of clean—and sugar-free—water. And maybe a toothbrush.

After wiping his hands on the corner of an extra blanket, he jumps down from the bed and crosses the room. He gently pulls one of the moldy cardboard boxes from the small pile that sits mildewing against the wall and, straightening it as best he can, sets it down in the corner. He puts his empty plastic bottle and the chocolate-smeared donut packaging inside.

"There," he says, enjoying the small victory of control, of cleanliness. Of humanity.

Henry glances cautiously into the other boxes stacked there and is thankful not to see any bugs or other nasty stuff lurking inside—no skittering cockroaches, no slippery little snakes. All he finds is a dirty sock in one and some old newspapers in the other, gray and soiled. He leaves them as they are but, grimacing in disgust, pushes the empty boxes as far away from his bed and the heater as he can, shoving them along the coarse wooden floor with his foot into the dark confines of what must have once been a closet, although now it seems like nothing more than a large hole in a deteriorating wall; a dark portal, perhaps. From what he can tell in the growing daylight, it's less a portal to another dimension (like in Dave's science fiction books) than a portal to rotting drywall and exposed wooden beams.

Probably a nest of mice or rats hidden away in these walls, Henry imagines, and then quickly tries to *un*-imagine it. It wouldn't do to be thinking about such things when nighttime comes again and he has nothing but the muted crimson eye of the kerosene heater to keep him company, to push away the monsters born of fear and shadow, to illuminate the blackened corners of his cell (for that's how he thinks of it, and rightly so) and shed light on any imaginary—or otherwise—skittering sounds he may hear in the dark.

Unsure what else to do with himself, Henry goes to the window, tries to see the outdoors through the light-filled slats between the boards nailed across the other side of the grimy glass. Even standing on tiptoes, however, all he can make out is the mulchy green of distant trees and, much closer, some gray shingles of the roof as it extends outward.

He thinks on that for a moment, interested in the fact that just outside his window is not a twenty-foot drop, but an angled section of rooftop he figures must cover the rest of the living area he hasn't yet seen.

I get though the boards, I can climb out of here. Find a way down. Run my ass home.

He raps the glass gently with his knuckles, then remembers what Liam said about the shed, about locking him in there at night, tying him up and letting the bugs and varmints do whatever they pleased while he froze on the hard dirt.

Shivering as if a black goose has stomped across his grave, Henry lowers his hand from the glass.

That's just information, Henry. File that away, now. Keep it tight. *Remember what I said, son: ZIP IT!*

Henry mimics his father's motion: runs pinched fingertips sideways along his closed lips. He doesn't smile, however, but instead turns from the window, walks back to the bed, and sits down. He's bored, scared, tired, and anxious. He badly wants to go *home*.

Not knowing what else to do, he lies back down, closes his eyes, and tries to relax. His stomach is gurgling uncomfortably, and he worries for a moment he's gonna need to go big bathroom—and *fast*—before a squeaker of gas slips out and things in the ship's cargo hold settle down a bit.

Let's see what's what, son. Let's check things out a bit. I got a bad feeling.

Henry takes a deep breath, lets it out. He thinks about Doctor Hamada and the Zener cards; he thinks about Dave and Mary taking him to the ocean, holding his hands as they walked down the Mission Beach boardwalk, laughing at the strange people while Henry begs to go to Tiki Town for a round of mini-golf.

He thinks about holding his daddy's hand, moments before they stepped into the street. Into the path of that big blue bus.

Now now, son. Let's not dwell on that. Let's focus.

Henry tries to steady his breathing. He feels that familiar presence nearby and wonders, if he opens his eyes, will he see his father's shape standing over him? Will he look up into those silver-penny eyes and see them shining back?

"Waves," Henry says quietly, willing his mind to quiet. To *focus*. "Plus sign. Star. Circle. Waves. Plus sign. Star. Circle . . ."

Slowly, the inner eye yawns open, and the slick black pupil in Henry's mind begins to dart left and right, up and down. All around. It wants badly to *see*, as if it's hungry. Or scared. Threatened, perhaps, Henry thinks, focusing harder on that black eye. He opens it wider and wider, reaches out to everything all around him.

He pushes out even further, opens that inner eye as wide as it will go. Henry sees the colors of the kidnappers close by, bright and complex. He studies their glow, their strings of light, their mood, their emotions, their innermost feelings, their *thoughts*.

Henry is ready to dig deeper, to listen in, to go against all he has trained himself so hard *not* to do—not to pry, not to invade another person's privacy, not to be weird or different or strange; not to instill fear, or worry, but to ask for and deserve love. Just love.

But this is different, and he knows it. The voice inside him knows it as well. This is life and death, that's the reality. This is him doing whatever he can to stay alive, to keep in charge of things, to gather information.

To find a crack.

An opening.

An escape.

So Henry reaches.

Guy needs to relax. He's beginning to piss me off. I bet blondie loves that accent, though, oh hell yeah. Crazy bitch.

This place is a dump. Greg, get your ass here already. God I'm hungry.

Don't know what Jim sees in these mutts. Pete's dangerous, and I don't trust Jenny. Will keep an eye on her, and that hidden needle of hers. Need to calm these two down or it might get ugly. The kid will need a break soon. Freaky little bastard.

Snatches of conversation—meaningless.

Colors weak but vibrant—*anticipation*.

And then—

There is something else.

Henry's calm face tightens. He frowns. His brow furrows. He grunts uncomfortably, not aware he is doing it, not even aware he's shaking his head, that his fingers are twitching, his toes curling up inside his sneakers.

There's something down below*, Henry. My god, can you* feel it?

Henry's eyes shoot open and he's suddenly gasping at the air as his mind clutches hungrily at the reality of his room, the growing light of the day, the cobweb in one high corner, long abandoned.

Breathing heavily, he sits up clutching his stomach—not in pain, but in worry. Something he does when anxious, when frightened.

Henry shakes his head at no one. He's never been so afraid.

"Uncle Dave, come get me come get me come get me, *please.*" Henry whispers the prayers to the empty room, to the piss-filled can in the corner and the darkened portal of the weathered closet. He is alone, and yet it feels like a crowd is pushing in on him, swarming his thoughts with naked need. Even with the connection broken, his mind feels the pressure of that voice, that unknown presence, that *other* thing he sensed so clearly.

Where is it? Not downstairs, not with the kidnappers. But . . . *below.* Beneath the ground. Something primal and wild and *strong.* Innocent and *hungry*. Like a blind bird wanting a worm. Like a child wanting its mother. Wanting to feed.

Henry thinks maybe it's an animal, but he's never been able to connect with an animal before. He's tried with dogs or cats, but their minds are blanks to him. Empty pages.

So what is it?

Whatever it is, he doesn't think Liam and the others know about it. No, they don't know, because if they did they would have killed it by now, and their colors would be bright neon reds, lightning-bright streaks of orange.

The colors of fear.

Because as afraid as he is of the kidnappers—the ones who have taken him away, who want to hurt him—Henry is much more afraid of the *other*.

And if the people downstairs were smart, as smarty-party as they thought they were?

They'd be afraid, too.

4

Sali Espinoza was almost positive this was an inside job.

And his shoes agreed.

As he approached the Thorne home from his unmarked black sedan, he took in the immediate surroundings of the neighborhood.

Three squad cars. One posted at the end of the block doing minor surveillance. Press van—just local (for now). They'll have to wait. Geez, not even a mic stab for the FBI guy? What's that about? Unmarked detective vehicle. Single white male neighbor on a porch. Send a blue down there—get that guy's info. What's he doing home, anyway? It's a Friday afternoon. Interesting. Old couple looking out the window from next door. Don't care. Or do I? Yard looks nice, house looks nice. Reminder: check out the back yard. Okay, let's meet the parents. Detective . . . shit. Knopp. That's it. And the ball-buster with her is Davis. Let's cut him loose. What the . . . is he smoking on the fucking porch? Jesus. Okay, that's okay, we'll get rid of that goon. God, he gives me the heebie-jeebies, he's probably driving the parents crazy. Fuck it, smile, Sali.

"Detective Knopp, Detective Davis, I'm Salvador Espinoza from the FBI." Sali flips his ID but the dicks don't bother. Knopp shakes his hand and Davis sticks his cancer lollipop between his teeth and does the same. "Parents inside?"

★ ★ ★

The interior of the house is as he'd hoped. Homey and pleasant, clean for the most part, or as clean as it could be with a dozen blues walking around and techs monitoring phone calls from the damned kitchen.

"Mr. Thorne, Mrs. Thorne," Sali says, shaking hands with the couple who look like they've been dragged through hell a few miles—*his grip is strong, but he's the emotional one; she's tough, but won't be as forthcoming. Untrusting.*

That's okay. Focus on Pops, make sure Mom's tied into any decision-making. Easy-peasy. "I'm Special Agent Salvador Espinoza, FBI. You can call me Sali, which is what I answer to unless I'm in the shower or got a mouthful of food." He smiles and shows them the badge, and they glance at it with hollow, tired eyes. He doesn't mind the joke falling flat, it wasn't meant to charm, but to soften. Put a pin into that fat balloon of worry and tension, get everybody breathing again. Sure, they only have two days—realistically and statistically speaking—to find the boy, but these people don't need to know that, and he doesn't mind bearing the burden of statistics for these poor souls. "Mr. and Mrs. Thorne, is there somewhere we could sit comfortably and talk alone? Maybe a guest room, or your bedroom?"

Mr. Thorne stands up and nods. "Bedroom, I guess. And Agent? I'm Dave, and this is my wife, Mary."

Sali nods acceptance of these labels as Mrs. Thorne—Mary—stands. Her eyes level out right around his tie clip, but he has the insane urge to take a step back from this woman regardless. "And our son's name is Henry, and we're gonna get him back. Safe and sound, am I right?"

"Yes ma'am," Sali says. "That's why I'm here."

★ ★ ★

The Thornes sit together at the foot of their bed, and Sali closes the door, shutting out the murmured voices of officers, the stress and worry of the last twenty-four hours. He drags a small dressing chair over from a corner to sit near them. He notices they're holding hands, and that's a good thing—a *great* thing. He hopes they'll still be there for each other if things go bad.

"Okay, so I know you guys have been through the wringer here and I can't tell you how sorry I am about that. But my job is to fix this. I'm very good at what I do, and what I do is specialize in abductions."

Mary leans forward. "We heard about another boy, from the school. It's hard to believe."

Sali looks her in the eye. "The Patchen boy. We know."

"So you don't think—"

"No ma'am, no way," Sali says, shaking his head, looking at both grieving faces with what he hopes is reassurance. "That boy's murder has nothing to do with this. A horrible coincidence. That's all. I read up on the Patchen case last night, and that boy had a lot of trouble in his life. Bad parents, bad friends. Lots of small run-ins with the law. Almost expelled from school last year. This is not a good kid, and my hunch is he got in over his head with some thug and, sadly, was killed for it. There were signs of a struggle at his residence, and it doesn't fit with what we're going through here with Henry. No, Henry is a good kid. I've done my reading here as well. Straight A's, quiet, well liked by teachers. Good home." He says this purposefully, making sure they know he's on their side, that he *likes* them, that he *trusts* them. "So no. We believe Henry was abducted, that his kidnapper or kidnappers will be seeking ransom. We know about the lawsuit settlement, and about what happened with Henry's father; your brother, Mr. Thorne. We have a lot to support this. A vehicle was seen leaving the school yesterday morning—an unmarked white van. Henry was called out of homeroom and that was the last time he was seen, which means the boy who brought the note to Henry's class may know something, the teachers may know something. We're almost positive this was an inside job, folks. It was somebody *at the school* who did this."

"My God," Dave says, and Mary puts a hand to her mouth, stunned. "A teacher?"

"Maybe," Sali says cautiously. "Could be a faculty member, but more likely it's a parent of another student, or someone who had access to the school, someone who wouldn't cause suspicion. They were able to spring Henry from class, which means they had access to administrative supplies. I mean, look, there's a lot there. And that's where I'm headed the second I leave here today. Straight to the school. My associate is there now setting up interviews for me, and we're gonna get to the bottom of this."

He sees the hope in their eyes, a trickle of the stuff falling like a light rain on their faces, wetting their eyelids. "I'll tell you guys a secret. When I shine my shoes every morning they give me a sign, okay? Think of it as my own crystal ball. It's strange, I know. I can be a quirky guy. But my shoes tell me Henry's okay, and that we're on the right track."

They look at him like he expected them to. Like he's crazy. But Sali only smiles.

"I'm gonna get your boy back. There are a thousand police officers in Southern California who have seen Henry's photo and are looking for him right now. The FBI has a unit called CART, the Computer Analysis Response Team, that is powering through tens of thousands of criminal profiles *as we speak* to see what kind of matches we get for former criminals in the area who might be involved—or know someone involved—in something like this. Later, I'm going to get with the NCIC and run checks on every parent, guardian, teacher, substitute teacher, janitor, and student at Henry's school. If we get a red flag on anyone, we'll move in like lightning. Now look, here's the big thing: In the next day, we're gonna likely see a ransom note. An officer or one of the detectives will retrieve this and get it to me. This will bring us another massive pile of information about who might have done this, and get us that much closer to catching up with them. Everything is in motion here, and we're moving quickly to end all of this. Now, do you have any questions before I head to the school? I should be back here to speak with you in a few hours, and I'll update you on what I find out. I'm not gonna leave you on an island. We're all in this together."

Dave and Mary look at each other, but Mary only shakes her head. Dave looks back at Sali, a questioning look on his face.

That's the one he wears when he cross-examines a witness. I like it.

"Just one, Agent Espinoza."

"Sali, please. We'll need the shorthand, trust me on this."

"Why did you tell us about your shoes? It's . . . weird, and you don't seem weird to me. You seem very calculated, in fact."

Because you guys need to open your minds. You need to keep thinking, keep believing, keep coming up with ideas or scraps of information or just plain dumb old hope. Because I can't have you shutting down on me. Not when I'll need you so badly.

And besides, it's true!

"No reason. Just a quirk. Now, here's my card. My pager number is on there. You call me day or night, twenty-four-seven, with any little thing—no matter how strange, how dumb, or how insignificant you think it might be. Never hesitate. Hell, even if you want to talk things through, you page me and I'll call you back quick as darts. Okay?"

Mary sinks into Dave's shoulder, exhausted with worry and despair. "No matter what happens, he'll never be the same," she says. "I keep thinking, not about what *might* happen, but what *is* happening to that sweet little boy."

Sali puts a hand on Dave's shoulder. "I have to go. You guys should get some rest. Maybe one of you can sleep while the other stays up, whatever you want to do. But get some sleep, please. You have a dozen police officers in your home, your phone is tapped, your neighborhood is under surveillance, and the best personnel of the San Diego PD and the FBI are working full-steam on this. You can take a nap, it's okay. And Mary?"

She looks up at him, eyes bruised from lack of sleep, tear-streaked cheeks shining.

"Kids are resilient, and I promise you one thing: The last thing these kidnappers want to do is to hurt Henry. Contain, yes. Hurt? No. They want the money, which, by the way, the FBI is getting together as we speak. So try not to let your imagination go wild, okay? Chances are he's sitting in a locked bedroom somewhere, waiting to come home. Besides, from what I've read about your son, he seems like he's got his act together, and he's smart. I'd bet he's pretty capable as well. Am I right?"

"He's capable, all right," Dave says, and Sali is the smallest bit surprised to see the two guardians share a knowing, unspoken look. "I don't think those bastards have the slightest idea how capable Henry really is."

5

It's like they're camping.

Henry sits on the floor of the kitchen, his wrist handcuffed to an exposed pipe in one of the walls. At his eye level are ten legs—three kidnappers and a card table. He's taken the last several minutes of his new situation to study the surroundings. In the daylight—makeshift as it is through moth-eaten blankets hung over the windows, the rest boarded up and dark—he has a new perspective on the people that have taken him.

He sees the two large coolers against a wall of the kitchen. The card table and two more kerosene heaters, identical to the one in his room. There are also cardboard boxes—new ones—filled with groceries. He sees bread and peanut butter, granola bars and potato chips. Paper plates, plastic forks and spoons, a can opener tossed on the weathered countertop (with a snaggle-toothed hole where the sink should be). He figures the coolers are packed with sodas and waters, milk and juice. *They probably filled them with beers*, he thinks sourly, after spotting another box on the floor filled with bottles of liquor. He knows enough of the world to know what a bottle of whiskey looks like, and there are a bunch of them in that box.

Next to a closed, rotted door are two big metal cans, rusted along the edges and on top where there is a handle and a screw cap. The cans are a little bigger than the gasoline can Uncle Dave keeps in the garage, and they are cylindrical versus square like Dave's. Also, these aren't red, they're white and blue, the word KEROSENE blazed across the curved face. Henry figures it's what they use to keep the heaters going, but he can smell the chemicals inside from where he sits and crinkles his nose in disgust.

He didn't get a chance to look around into the house's other rooms, the larger rooms on the other side of the stairway, for instance, but he glanced that way quickly when Liam walked him down and saw sleeping bags and a couple of old-style lanterns, like the ones they have in cowboy movies, except these looked new, shiny red with green bottoms.

It *is* like they're camping, he realizes. Like they've gathered a bunch of stuff you'd take for a weekend in the woods. Henry has never been camping, not with his mom or dad, and never with Dave and Mary, but he knows what it's about and knows you take food with you and sleep in sleeping bags and tents. Henry smiles a bit at the idea of Mary camping; he doesn't think she'd like it much. She likes things neat and tidy. Orderly. And nature isn't like that. The real world, he knows, isn't like that. It's *messy*. There's dirt and bugs and bad people everywhere. Yeah, it's super-messy, all right. Messy and dangerous. Sometimes deadly. Henry knows that better than any other ten-year-old on the planet, perhaps. Or, if not the planet, certainly in the small sliver of North American coastline named San Diego, California.

"You gonna deal or what?" the man with the gold teeth asks, and then snickers like an idiot. Pete, that's his name. But his real name is Pedro. Henry can see that plain as day when he reaches into his mind and looks around. Pete also has a lot of violent, sex-filled thoughts, but Henry isn't as afraid of him as he would have been if he hadn't been able to read him so easily. He doesn't think Pete is a killer, even though he acts like one, and talks like one. But he is mean, all right. And Henry doesn't like him much. He thinks Pete is pretty gross.

"Okay, I'm dealing," Liam says, and flips the cards out to Pete and the girl. *Jenny.*

Henry *is* scared of her. Her mind is quiet, but not in a relaxed way, in that sociopathic way he'd thought about last night. Henry doesn't worry about her getting mad at him, or doing anything weird, but he thinks maybe she'll kill him if she's told to. He doesn't think it would bother her much. If at all.

And now they're all playing poker, and, despite himself, Henry sorta wishes he could play, too. But that would be awkward, and the cops might think *he* was a kidnapper. And then, for the first time since he was taken,

Henry wonders what the hell these crazy people expect to get in return for him. Dave and Mary are not wealthy, and Henry thinks it's almost funny, and strange, that they'd targeted him at all.

And the *janitor*. Fred. Where was he in all this?

Not able to play cards and tired of trying to figure out all the rationale and personalities behind his abduction, he instead settles in to read the paperback Liam had pulled from his backpack, the one he was reading for school: *Lord of the Flies*. He doesn't like the book that much, but given his options, he'll take what he can get. It is certainly better than watching a dumb poker game from the floor and worrying sick about Dave and Mary.

I wonder if I could reach them from here, Henry thinks, and a bright surge of hope and excitement flows through him, and he decides to try. He begins to clear his mind, to open it as wide as he can.

A warped, beaten door next to him gives a little *creak* and opens.

A waft of odor hits him, so foul, so nasty that he puts a hand over his mouth and nose to avoid breathing it in. "Ugh," Henry says into his palm.

Liam stiffens, sniffs, then twists in his seat to glare down at Henry. He has a funny, disgusted look on his face, and Henry scowls right back at him. "Ain't me," Henry says loudly. "It's coming from the door."

"Jesus," Liam says, and his head snaps around to Pete. "What's down there?"

"Nothing," Pete replies, focused on his cards. "It's a fucking root cellar or some shit. It's empty and filthy and wet. You want to go check it out, be my guest."

Liam's tone goes hard, and his face no longer looks comically scrunched up to Henry. It looks mean. "Does it go under the whole house?"

Pete shrugs, but Jenny, Henry notices, looks nervous. "Partly, I think," she says. "It's just an old root cellar, man. No entrance, no exit. It's clear, I swear. We were both down there. Whole place is nothing but dirt and old bricks, Liam."

Pete's eyes twitch up at Jenny, maybe not liking the way she said Liam's name so casually, as if they're friends now. Henry tries to tune in to Pete's thoughts, but that *smell*—

And then he remembers.

The *other* thing.

Henry takes a deep breath, ignoring the stench, and his eyes lose their focus, and he lets his mind reach out, drift down the stairs, into the space beneath.

And it's there.

Henry gasps audibly enough that Liam hears and looks at him with a confused stare, but Henry doesn't respond, he couldn't if he wanted to—the *thing*, whatever is down there, is so *strong*. It gives off wave after wave of pure darkness, and Henry finds himself swallowed by it, as if lost in a fog, searching for an island in a black ocean, seeing nothing but gray clouds, hearing nothing but the soft lapping of unseen water. He focuses harder, tries to breach the waves of mist the creature gives off, and he sees a *light*, like a candle fluttering alone on a dark plain—the spark of life, of first awareness, of new consciousness.

Hungry. Alone. Scared.

Henry feels all these things, not as colors, but as something more physical. As arrows, as spears of need piercing his brain, entering him as much as he enters *it*.

It can see me, Henry realizes, and a cold fear settles in his belly.

Holy crap the thing can see me.

Desperate, Henry tries to communicate. *I'm* scared, he thinks, frantic, desperate. *Can you help me?*

But the candle flares and a heavy wave of darkness sweeps over Henry's mind. The sudden wave is so dense, so vast, that he is swallowed by it and his inner vision goes completely blank, as if whatever he's connected with has blown out the candle of Henry's brain, shut down Henry's individual receptors—feelings, awareness.

Fully immersed in the creature, he feels the incipient heart beating in its chest. Arms and legs unformed, pulled tight to its body. Its skin, near translucent, absorbs what it needs from the fluid gathered around it. Its mind is fully formed, but weak.

Henry can only feel the most base impulses. It's like, for him, what it would be to go back into the womb, waiting to emerge into the world of light, waiting for—

MOTHER.

Henry feels a rush of joy, of desire, of need.

MOTHER IS COMING!

He feels it . . . feels her. She's coming back, coming back to him.

Henry's mind opens even wider, forced open by the thing he's inhabiting, by the mind he's invaded and been snared by. And now he touches—only briefly— her mind.

The vast darkness of the creature's subconscious ensnares him, holds him like a spider's web holds a fly. Henry struggles to be free, to escape.

"Let me go!" he screams. What he feels when he brushes against this creature's mind is too much to bear.

THERE ARE MULTITUDES!

Henry's eyes roll up into his head; the heels of his feet begin pounding the floorboards, his fists clenched, knuckles taut. His lips pull back from his teeth in a rictus as his body stiffens and convulses.

"Henry!"

Henry hears his name but cannot respond. Cannot *think.*

"Jesus, maybe he's got what I got. Hey, put your fingers in his mouth! You gotta grab his tongue or he'll choke on the fucking thing! I got Klonopin, man, hold on!"

Hands are on him. Two rough fingers shove their way into his mouth, cold palms push hard on his cheeks. More hands clamp onto his legs, hold him. Henry gags and pushes the hand out of his mouth, shakes his head and wants to spit the taste of dirty flesh out but swallows it instead, feels a wave of nausea.

"I'm fine!" Henry yells, but his voice sounds a hundred miles away to his own ears. He clears his throat and the dark lifts like a windblown mist. "I'm okay," he says, and forces his eyes to focus on Liam's face, on the girl who holds his ankles. He almost laughs at how worried they look since he knows they'd probably kill him if they had to. If they wanted to.

"Here, here," Pete says, running back into the kitchen. "These are my pills but I have plenty. I get 'em too sometimes, the seizures. Once in a blue moon, but still."

Henry looks up at Pete holding a bottle of prescription pills, then back to Liam. "I'm fine. It just smells bad . . . can I have some water?"

"Get him some water," Liam says, his eyes never leaving Henry's. Pete goes for one of the coolers. "You sure you're okay?"

"Yeah," Henry says, and even tries to smile a little. "Maybe close the door?"

Liam studies him another moment. "We'll close the door. Nail the fucking thing shut, okay?"

There is something else Henry knows. Something his kidnappers are not aware of. Something they have missed. There is more to the cellar, and that's where the *thing* is. And Henry thinks that's where the smell is coming from as well.

Something's rotting down there, and they don't know it. It's hidden *somehow.*

"Henry? Jesus, you're spacey." Liam glares at him, that quizzical look Henry doesn't like much. The look that says: *I'm gonna figure you out, kid. And when I do, that's gonna be bad news for you. Like, the ALL CAPS HEADLINE kinda bad news.*

"I'm okay," Henry says quickly, and Pete hands him the bottle of water. Henry takes a swig, relishing the cool rush of hydration cleansing his mouth, filling his belly with cool comfort. He stares up at Liam, eyes wide and innocent. "But . . ."

"But what?"

Henry tries a weak smile, then rubs it away and chooses his best cute kid face instead. "Can I watch you guys play?"

Liam looks at the kid for a moment, wondering what the hell the boy is up to, if anything. But he doesn't like this kid—doesn't *get* him. Can't figure him out, or understand why he's doing all the goofy shit he's been doing. Acting tough on the way out, sure. But he's scared shitless and Liam knows it. Still, he kept his act together and that was respectable. But it still feels like the kid's playing him.

And what about all that talking to himself?

Yeah, that was weird. Because the thing is, in Liam's mind, the kid *wasn't* talking to himself. He'd been talking to someone else. A third party. Maybe an imaginary friend?

Maybe. But this kid doesn't seem the type. It's something else.

And now the seizures, and his immediate response, after all but swallowing his own tongue, was he wants to watch them play poker? Liam doesn't like this one bit. Sure, the kid is okay as far as it goes, but he's hard to predict, and Liam doesn't want any surprises, no thanks. Three, four days they'll be cooped up here, tops. And all he has to do, him and the other grown-ups that is, is keep the kid alive and secure.

Seizures and bizarre conversations with empty rooms are not a good start.

"No," he says, too loudly, like he's giving a goddamn order or something. *Jackass.* Still, he waits for the kid's chubby cheeks to sag into some pouty bullshit face. But the kid just looks back at him, like he's interested in something written across his forehead. Like he's curious. "I mean, I don't care what you do," he says, resisting the urge to wipe a hand across his forehead to make sure he hasn't grown horns in the last few minutes. "But your wrist ain't leaving those cuffs, and the cuffs ain't leaving the pipe. Clear?"

The boy looks at Liam some more in the way that makes him nuts, then he turns to study the pipe, then he *stands*, watching carefully as the cuff slides up the length of the pipe.

"Is it okay if—"

"Yeah, fine, fine. Jesus, kid, it's just cards. Stand if you want to. Jump up and down for all I care. Just don't make any noise, and don't piss me off."

"Bet you wish you had your Nintendo right about now, huh Henry?" Pete says from the table, having reclaimed his seat after the excitement, then laughs like a jackal. "Tough shit, kid."

"I don't have Nintendo. Dave and Mary don't allow video games in the house."

"Geesh, and I thought *we* were supposed to be the assholes," Pete says, and Liam turns on him, happy to see the grin slide off his skinny rat face.

"Enough talking, let's play cards." Liam closes the door leading to the cellar hard and holds it. "Pete, let's wedge this thing with something. Maybe stick some rags beneath to keep the smell out."

"Yeah, sure. No problem," he says, as Jenny deals out the cards.

Henry stands and watches the three kidnappers play poker.

Liam has his back to him, so he can see his cards, which is fun. Or at least distracting. Pete is on the other side of the table, facing him, and Jenny in between.

After a few hands, Henry starts to feel bored and antsy. He's tired of standing and his wrist hurts from the metal cuff rubbing against his skin.

"Can I have a chair?"

"No, now be quiet," Liam says without turning around, and Pete laughs that stupid laugh again. Henry watches the dog tattooed on his throat when he does it, his Adam's apple making the dog look like it's barking when it bobs up and down. It's almost funny, but only in the way seeing a person trip and fall might be funny—it tickles for a second, but then you feel sick for thinking in first place.

Liam loses the next hand, and the next. Pete is really letting him have it, laughing and mocking him. Jenny just smiles and sails along, mostly calling and folding. Henry knows she's enjoying this, seeing Liam lose to Pete. She likes seeing him . . . *taken down a notch.* That's what she thinks. Henry thinks she's being a jerk, and that it's Pete who needs to be taken down a notch.

Maybe a whole bunch of notches.

In the next hand Liam has three queens, which Henry knows is hard to beat. He slips into Pete's mind as easily as putting a hand into a bucket of water and "looks" at Pete's cards.

"Well, I've been doing pretty good, so I won't be stingy with my bets. I'm a good sport like that," Pete says, and pushes some bills into the pot. "Raising a hundred."

"Jesus, Pete, it's a game," Liam says. "That much will clean me out."

"Then don't call, no big deal. No skin off my nose."

"I'm out," Jenny says, and tosses down her cards.

Henry studies Liam, pushes past the colors of anxiety and doubt and reads his thoughts.

He's not gonna do it.

Henry smiles a little. "Do it, Liam. It's okay."

Pete's smile drops like a mask with a broken string. Liam lays his cards facedown, but not *all* the way down, and turns to look at Henry.

"Oh yeah? You think so, huh?"

"You can beat him," Henry says.

Liam smiles, and Henry thinks it might even be genuine. "I appreciate the confidence, Henry, but that's a lot of money in there."

"I know, but he doesn't have diddly-squat."

Liam laughs out loud at this, and even Pete manages a sneer. "Sure, kid, and how the hell would you know?" Pete turns his head around, studies the blank wall behind him. "I don't see no mirrors behind me. Maybe you should sit your ass back down."

Henry says nothing, but looks back to Liam, who is still turned toward him, a look of amused perplexity on his face.

"You think I should call, huh? You think he's got garbage over there?" Liam looks to Pete, who's smiling now, but his eyes don't smile. They flick between Liam and Henry with nervous energy, like a trapped rat. "What did you call it? Diddly-squat."

Henry nods and lowers his voice to a whisper: "All his cards are different colors, and the numbers aren't in order. I don't know much about poker, but I know you've got to have stuff that matches, or goes in a row. He has none of that."

Liam laughs again, and Pete's face stiffens as if frozen. He looks to Liam. "Whatever, man. Believe the kid if you want, all good with me. Let's do this. Come on, bitch, show me the money. Let's go."

Henry sees the hot reds now, the swirling black. Pete's *angry*, and he's getting angrier with every passing second. *And he's nervous*, Henry thinks. It's a lot of money for him, too. A whole lot.

Liam's laughter dies out, and he's now studying Pete instead of Henry. "Sure, what the hell. We're all gonna be rich in a few days anyway, right?"

Liam pushes all his money into the middle of the table, then pulls a clip from his pocket and peels off two more bills as Jenny hoots and claps. Pete looks ready to throw up.

"All right, there you go. Hundred bucks. Let's see what you've got. Me? A ménage à trois with three *gorgeous* ladies."

Pete stares at the three queens, then his eyes—blazing and dark now—dance to Liam, then to Henry. He slams his hand onto the table and stands so fast his chair falls to the floor. Henry, ready to laugh along with Liam (who is laughing quite hard), realizes a moment too late that he might have made a mistake. He tries to shrink back into the wall as Pete, flaring all the colors of rage and violence, strides around the table toward him.

"Hey now, go easy, Pete. I'm serious," Liam says, but despite his warning he looks nothing but interested as Pete steps in front of Henry.

"How did you know, huh? How the fuck did you know what I had?" Pete spins, studies the room from Henry's perspective, looking for reflections, but there's nothing.

"I didn't," Henry says weakly, scared now. "I was just messing around."

"Oh yeah?" Pete says, and throws his hand of cards into Henry's face. "Then how the *FUCK* DID YOU KNOW THEY WERE ALL DIFFERENT, HENRY? TELL ME!"

Pete grabs Henry by the collar and shakes him. Henry can't help it, he starts to cry. "I'm sorry, I don't know! I was being funny—"

"*Bullshit!*" Pete screams into Henry's face, his own face red and shiny with sweat, neck veins bulging, distorting the tattoo of the pit bull. "You know what, little *ese*? I think I'll add a hundred bucks to the ransom tab your parents are gonna pay us, what do you think about that? Huh? Of course, that's if I don't slit your fucking throat first, you *pedazo de mierca*. You hear me? You don't *ever* fuck with me, kid! You got that?"

Henry nods, crying harder, not able to stop, to control himself. An adult has never yelled at him, never threatened him physically.

Before he can say anything further, Pete whips out a hand and slaps Henry hard across the face. There's a sharp *smack* that fills Henry's head. He howls and drops to his knees. When he does, Pete pulls back one cowboy-booted foot and kicks Henry in the hip, kicks him so hard that Henry screams, grabbing the hip with his free hand, hoping to protect himself. He huddles into the wall, more terrified than he's ever been in his life.

"OW! OW!" Henry cries, sobbing through the words.

Pete leans down over him, sticks a finger in his face. "*Ever!*" he screams once more, and then he's gone, stomping off into the other room, where Henry hears something crash.

"What a sore loser," Jenny says, already organizing the cards neatly back into the box they came from.

Henry curls into a ball, unable to control his sobbing. Everything that's happened, all the horror of what's been done to him, comes pouring out. He can't stop it, can't do anything but let it flow through him.

Fear.

Despair.

Exhaustion.

Hunger.

Terror.

Liam pushes his chair back from the table, and Henry looks up at him through tear-filled eyes.

"Thanks for the tip, kid," he says, shoving a folded wad of bills into the front pocket of his jeans. "Now do me a favor and shut the fuck up, will ya? Or I'll kick you next."

Liam walks out of the kitchen, and Henry brings his knees to his chest, closes his eyes, and sobs. He doesn't feel strong, he doesn't feel in control. He feels weak and alone.

He feels like a child.

6

Sali isn't happy.

He'd thought the school was a sure thing; thought he'd storm in here and sit down across from a few nervous teachers, flash the badge, strategically pull aside the suit coat to show the butt end of his Browning 9 mm, and some guy or gal would spill the beans. Easy-peasy.

Didn't happen that way.

His first interview was with the principal. A tightly wound and intensely concerned woman named Ms. Terry. He liked her, and thought she'd get along great with a certain Mary Thorne, but her accusatory gaze made him a smidge nervous.

She doesn't know whether she's angry that two of her students have been either killed or abducted in the last forty-eight hours, or because I've just shown up to accuse her staff of being complicit in one, or both, *of those crimes. If it helps, lady, I ain't too tickled myself.*

"If you want to interrogate the teachers, Agent Espinoza, today is your day to do it," she'd said, sitting across from him in her office, shielded by the desk overstuffed with stacks of paperwork, the bulletin board behind her heavily decorated with photos of her students, greeting cards from a recent birthday and past holidays signed in shaky print by CHARLES or AMAYA or JULIUS. There was even an art project—a collage of photos from an entire graduating class on a piece of bright yellow poster board, each photo with a message written specifically to her.

Shit, when I was a kid we hated *the principal. Times are changing, though. These new kids, they're better than us,* he'd thought, then brought his attention back to the blazing (and pained) eyes of Ms. Terry.

"I understand," he replied.

"Because we are going on winter break for three weeks, starting Monday."

"I know, I realize. I'm sorry for the inconvenience."

She nodded, softened, the hurt in her eyes temporarily overriding her anger and frustration. He leaned in from his chair, trying hard not to feel like a teenager who'd been caught cheating on his geometry test. "My associate, Agent Grimley, he tells me you've pulled the files of all hires from the last year, is that right?"

She handed him two thin file folders. "We've only had two new hires this past year, for the current school year, that is. Which is not unusual. I'm no detective, but I doubt these men could be involved. One is our new math teacher—first and second graders mostly—and the other is a janitor."

Sali's ears perked up. "Janitor?"

His enthusiastic reply must have shown, because Ms. Terry shook her head and sighed. "Yes, but he's . . . what the heck is the politically correct word these days? He's special."

Sali's enthusiasm leaked away, out of his gut, down his legs, and into the quagmire of ignorance that lay all around him. "Special?"

Ms. Terry eyeballed the closed office door a moment, then came back to him. "We hired him as part of a program. For disabled veterans."

"Disabled? I'm sorry, you're losing me, Ms. Terry," Sali interrupted. "What kind of program?"

She'd sighed again, a little heavily this time, the concern and fear and anxiety of the last couple days wearing her down as much as all the others caught up in this nightmare. "He's mentally handicapped, Agent."

"What . . . you mean he's retarded?" Sali said, indignant at this new—and damning—information.

Ms. Terry nodded wearily. "I believe the correct terminology is 'mentally challenged,' due to a war injury," she said, sitting back and staring blankly at her hands clasped atop the cluttered desk. Sali thought maybe she was jonesing for a cigarette. "But yeah, as far as what you're looking for? Yes, the man's retarded. Or might as well be."

That was when his stomach had dropped, and hope had leaked away.

So now here he is with the geekiest math teacher in the history of geeky math teachers, who looks less like the cat who swallowed the canary and more like a Poindexter who was late for his mystery book club meeting. His hair is mussed, his glasses oily, his knit tie crooked and stained at the end where it had likely dusted the man's breakfast.

If this guy is a kidnapping mastermind, I'm the Queen of England.

"Thanks for sitting with me, Mr. Pollack. You mind if I record our chat?"

Pollack looks at Sali sheepishly, eyeballs the tape recorder on the table, and shakes his head.

Other than a desk shoved into a corner (bearing the weight of a phone, an empty wire basket, and a broken-tipped pencil), the office is bereft of clutter—or furniture. Totally abandoned. "Tax cuts have left you with some interrogation room options," the principal had told him, and she'd been right. Sali had grabbed two metal folding chairs from the cafeteria—the word LIBERTY neatly stenciled in yellow along their bottoms—and placed them in the middle of the browning linoleum floor of Room 21. All in all, he thought the room was pretty damn similar to an interrogation room at the local police station: grill work shading the window, dirty gray walls . . . *yeah, this would do.* That said, it wouldn't matter if he was asking questions in the filthiest cell of Alcatraz. It wasn't going to change the facts of what he already, instinctively, knew about Mr. Pollack:

That the guy had nothing to do with it.

No tells, no defensiveness, no nervous tics, and based on what Sali knows about liars (and he knows a hell of a lot), and the more Pollack politely and thoroughly answers Sali's questions, the more it's apparent the fella's telling the truth about not knowing what has happened to Henry, or the Patchen kid for that matter.

"All right, Mr. Pollack, thanks for your time," Sali says after wrapping it up more quickly than he'd envisioned. He hands the teacher a business card. "You plan on traveling over the break?"

"Oh, me? Oh, no. No, I'm afraid not. I have my birds to worry about, and Churchill—that's my cat—he'd go nuts if I left him alone or, God forbid, boarded him. Plus, when Church gets alone with Perry and Smoke—those are my parrots—he gets a nasty look in his—"

"All right, that's fine," Sali says, ushering the man to the door. "Just give me a ring if you leave the city, okay?"

Sali's pager buzzes as he closes the door. It's the office, but he's gonna hold off calling them back. The brain-damaged janitor is waiting in the hallway, sitting in a small plastic chair made for a child, as peaceful and calm as an apple on a tree. Sali had the contents of both files copied and faxed to the office, and he knows they're running background checks, but it can wait. If the janitor—who looks to run a bit north of six feet and 250 pounds—has any red flags he'll just bring him back in. But he's certain this is another dead end, and he's antsy to get it done and over with so he can follow up on secondary leads, all of whom are associated with Liberty Elementary in some way. He just knows someone at the school is involved. They had to be. *Right?*

Unfortunately, his star witness—a troublemaking kid named Jim Hawkes who, it turns out, was good buddies with the deceased Thomas Patchen—had vanished. Never made it home last night. His mother (the father was living in San Francisco with a new girlfriend and hadn't been in touch with his son for weeks) didn't bother contacting authorities because, as she stated early that morning, "He was always running off doing some stupid shit or other."

So now the San Diego PD is on the lookout for *two* kids—Henry Thorne and Jim Hawkes. But without knowing who had put Jim up to passing the note, there isn't a whole hell of a lot to go on.

Sali frowns, feeling the morning coffee returning to the world as a slick squirt of acid climbing the back of his throat. Things are getting muddier right when he desperately needs them to get clearer. The clock is ticking, and ticking *loud*. Despite what he's told the Thornes, he knows damn well Henry is in great and perilous danger. After thirty-six hours, that probability of recovery index sank right off the bottom of the chart.

And the odds of getting Henry Thorne back alive after missing for three days?

Next to nil.

"Mr. Hinnom?" Sali says, and takes an involuntary step backward as the janitor, wrapped in a blue jumpsuit like a convict, stands up to greet him. *This guy's a house,* Sali thinks, but this doesn't worry him. If anything, it makes the acid working its way through his intestines wash out a tiny bit. It's replaced with a flood—albeit a *mild* flood—of adrenaline.

This guy could snap one of these kids in half without breaking a sweat, he thinks—not in fear, but in a bizarre sort of joy. A feeling of . . . perhaps.

The feeling doubles when Fred Hinnom takes Agent Espinoza's hand, the fingers wrapping clean around Sali's own, the grip viselike, the muscles in his exposed forearms rippling as he shakes. His smile, although seemingly genuine, looks somehow empty to Sali.

But his eyes don't look empty at all.

They look alive, Sali thinks, and does his best to match the casual smile of the giant as he prays the janitor won't get it in his broken head to squeeze. Sali has a feeling his fingerbones would snap like toothpicks.

"Can you come in a moment? Answer one or two questions?"

"Sh . . . sh . . . sure I can," the janitor says, and Sali finds himself analyzing the stutter. "Ms. Terry said it was okay."

"Great, great," Sali says, and steps aside as the hulking man slips into the office. He's already forgotten about the math teacher, and about the page from his office. Right now all his energy is focused on the interrogation at hand, because his guts are boiling with something other than the shitty coffee; the same something that makes him very good at what he does for a living. It is what any good agent has—that proverbial, cliché, but all-so-true gut instinct.

And right now, his gut is telling him something is *off* about the janitor.

Yes indeed, now. Yes indeed. The voice in his gut is definitely chatty. It's telling him—quite excitedly—that things might not be as muddy as they seem, and when Sali sits down across from Fred Hinnom—who looks from the tape recorder to Sali, his broad, unreadable face emotionless and serene, his smile gone but his eyes alive—Sali isn't surprised to find himself grinning ear-to-ear.

Like a man who'd been lost in the dark and just spotted a distant light, bright and white, and growing bigger.

7

RAGE.

That's exactly what Henry feels, and he doesn't care *doesn't care doesn't care DOESN'T CARE* what the others are thinking, or feeling, or what disgusting, dumb horrible things are going through their minds.

Rage, yes. But also *pain*.

He'd nearly forgotten how much pain he'd had following his accident, the months of physical therapy leaving him so achy and sore he'd often cry himself to sleep, but after the beating from Pete, it's as if his body is replaying the greatest hits: his chest aches, his hip stiff and sore to the touch, and he feels a twinge of pain at every step. But what really hurts, what's turning that pain into a simmering fury, is his young man's pride. He's ashamed—ashamed at having cried like a baby when Pete yelled and hit him and kicked him.

He's nothing but a bully, Henry thinks. *And I know all about bullies, don't I? Yes I* do.

Henry can't wait to get back at that man, to get into his mind and find the perfect opportunity to hurt him.

And then there is Liam. The traitor. Who walks beside him right now, watching him, waiting for him to run or hide or try to escape. Henry thinks it's pathetic. If this man had ever seen him run he'd stop worrying so damn much. Whatever middling athlete Henry Thorne might have been was erased when he was thrown into a parked BMW after being smacked by a bus that squished his father like an old grape and sent Henry flying. Superman without a cape.

Ever since the accident he's had headaches, sometimes his chest hurts for no reason at all, and he has a slight limp when he walks (something he'd have his whole life, according to the doctors). He compensates for the limp as best he can, but *he* knows it's there, knew it when he went out to the school track one day and tried to run all the way around. A quarter mile is all it was.

He made it halfway.

Not because he was tired, or out of shape. But because his leg hurt. It *ached*. That same leg that got broken into pieces and bent sideways when his father . . . when his father . . .

Okay son, okay. I hear you. Relax, Henry. Try to relax.

Henry takes a deep breath, watches the tree line come closer.

And now I gotta shit, and this white man's walking me out to the trees like a dog, Henry thinks, and if he is surprised at his sudden hate, he pushes that surprise away, into a box at the back of his mind, because he doesn't care about being good right now. Doesn't care about being nice. He wants to hurt these people.

Hurt them bad.

"That's far enough, I think," Liam says, and Henry turns.

"You want me to squat right here in view of everything? No way." Henry feels comfortable talking back to Liam, because he can see the man's restless feelings. The dull blues of distress, the muddy orange of confusion, the crimson flickers of shame. He plays the tough man—and Henry knows he isn't a *good* man, not really—but deep down Henry thinks most of it is a front. Yeah, maybe he'd kill Henry if it came to that, but since the incident that morning Liam's guard has slipped; that dull, dark blank slate of his mind is *leaking*, and suddenly Henry can read him like a Zener card. *Plus sign. Circle. Star. Waves.*

Doubt.

"Well, if you think you're jogging into those woods, you're wrong. Remember our chat from last night?"

"Yes, I'll go to the first tree, okay? That one right there."

"Fine, fine," Liam says. "Take this." He holds out a roll of toilet paper.

"What about a little shovel? To bury it?"

Liam looks at the horizon, his hand still extending to roll. "Why, so you can stab me in the gut with it? No thanks. Now go."

Henry takes the offered roll of TP and slips behind a tree. He pulls his pants down and squats over a patch of black dirt. "I hope I don't get poison ivy on my butt," Henry says, and Liam snorts.

As Henry waits for nature to take its course, Liam paces, stubbing his toe into tufts of grass. "While we're waiting, can I give you some advice, Henry?"

"If you want," Henry says, and is relieved when the train finally leaves the station.

"For the next few days, while you're with us . . ." There's a pause, then: "We're not good people, Henry, that should be obvious. You're smart, you know the kind of people we are."

Henry doesn't respond, but stands and wipes. He drops everything into the same spot, then pulls up his pants. He starts kicking loose dirt over the pile, like a cat.

"So my advice is this," Liam continues. "Don't piss anyone off. Especially—"

Liam pauses, and Henry looks back toward the house. From here he can see the side of the house, a part of the house's exterior he hasn't been able to check out yet. Something blue catches his eye, lying dormant in the tall weeds. Curious, he reaches out, immediately feels that presence again.

The foreign one. The alien one.

The stranger among the strangers.

But he doesn't let his mind drift too close. Not this time. He stays distant, on the far side of the veil; away from the light, from that flickering candle of alien consciousness. Whatever it is, Henry doesn't want the thing to see him again. He just wants to know it's *there*. Right there. Under the house, near that glimpse of blue in the tall grass.

That's where it is, and that's how you get to it.

"You understand what I'm saying, kid?"

Henry walks out from behind the tree. "Yes, I understand. I was trying to help you."

Liam says nothing, but holds out his hand for the roll of toilet paper.

"I need to wash my hands," Henry says, but Liam only shakes his head.

"Sorry, no running water here. No soap. No showers, no baths, no handwashing. It's gross, I know, but it's temporary."

"Then how do I clean my hands?"

Liam looks around, then points to a clump of weeds. "Just . . . wipe them in the grass there."

Henry studies Liam, then looks at the grass. "That's horrible," he says. "That's not cleaning my hands, it's just wiping stuff around."

Liam shrugs. "Sorry, kid. Like I said, it's temporary."

"It's totally gross. When we get inside I'm using a bottle of water and some soap. I don't want to get diseases."

Liam takes Henry by the shoulder—gently—and guides him toward the house. "We'll see. Maybe there's something in there we can use, okay?"

Henry doesn't answer. He forces himself not to limp.

"Tell me something," Liam says casually, but Henry can sense the seriousness in his tone, the deep desire to *know*. He stops walking and turns to face Henry, who also stops. Liam is a dark silhouette, the risen sun in the sky behind him filling his hair and ears with light, the sky beyond a hazy pastel lemon that offers little heat. "How did you know about Pete's cards? No bullshit. And don't give me that 'I was just playing' nonsense. I don't buy it. I don't think Pete did, either. That's why he got angry, you know. Because of the money, yeah, but also because I think you scared him a little. And, frankly, you're freaking me out a bit as well. So spill it, mate. How'd you pull that trick?"

Henry studies Liam's dark profile. It reminds him of his father.

The idea brings no comfort.

He shrugs. "I read his mind. I could see what he was seeing. It's harder, sometimes, with people like Pete, because he's dumb, like an animal, and that makes it more difficult for me to see. But if I concentrate, it's not so bad. Especially if it's a visual thing, instead of something they're, you know, only thinking about."

Liam says nothing for a moment, then he puts a hand on Henry's back and they keep walking toward the house. After a few steps, he stops again and kneels, looks into Henry's eyes. "Tell me something else," Liam says, studying Henry's face closely, as if looking for lies on his skin. "Do you have brain damage or something? I mean, seriously. Are you screwed up? I know about the accident, and about your shrink. We know all sorts of things about you, son."

Liam smiles, and Henry sees the colors swirling in his mind. Hot red. Streaks of dark violet. Bully colors. Mean colors. "I knew you were a strange kid," he says, a mocking tone creeping into his voice. "But man, the more I hang out with you . . . it's like you're not right in the head. You know?"

Liam looks ready to laugh but Henry doesn't react. He matches Liam's stare, looks deep into his mind, behind the façade, behind the sarcasm and the cruelty. *He's let his guard down*, Henry thinks, and revels in plundering the man's brain. *And he's scared.*

Henry hears his father's voice chime in. *Tell him what we were talking about earlier, Henry. But not too much gas, Henry. Nice and easy . . . just get him thinking a little. Can you do that?*

Henry could.

"I have a question for you," he says, and Liam laughs with what sounds like—to Henry's ears, anyway—forced humor.

"Sure, go ahead," he says. "Hit me."

"Since you brought up brain damage," Henry starts, picking his words carefully, seeing the flutter of worry already brewing in Liam's mind. "And it was Fred, who's nothing but a big faker, who helped you get me—"

"Uh-huh," Liam says, the smile dimming, his eyes hardening.

"What I want to know is why you're so afraid of him. I mean, if I didn't know any better, I'd say you were his little bitch."

Liam's eyes flick down to Henry, the muscles of his jaw clenching.

"Just like Pete is *your* little bitch," Henry continues, undaunted. "So, when Fred comes here, what happens then? Do you get kicked down to number two? When your master comes home, do you stop being the alpha and go back to being the coward you know you are? When you don't have a gun, I mean? Or, you know, bullying a little kid?"

That's enough gas, boy. Go easy now, Henry. Eaa-ssy now . . .

Henry shuts his mouth, but his eyes don't leave Liam's, not even when he sees the hot red spikes of rage popping through the black canopy of his thoughts like fireworks in hell.

Liam stands up, and Henry watches with a sort of fascination as his feelings boil like a tempest. The violence and rage so acute, so powerful, it's like watching a volcano about to erupt, but you're so close that you know running will do no good, so you do nothing but watch and wait, fascinated at the sheer power of the thing's ability to destroy.

And then, from one second to the next, the colors bursting from Liam change so suddenly, so drastically, that Henry almost gasps out loud. Mushroom clouds of white and pink and bright royal blues erupt like geysers, and then the man is *laughing*. Laughing as hard as Henry has ever heard anyone laugh.

He's busting a gut, all right, isn't he, son?

Henry agrees. Yeah, sure, he *is* busting a gut, isn't he? Henry watches, still in fascination but now without fear, because there is no violence in these colors. No hate, no murderous rage. It is *pure*. That's the only word Henry can conjure. Pure.

It's almost joy, Henry thinks. *Almost.*

Finally, after Liam is able to control himself, to slow his laughter, his sky-wracking guffaws, he wipes his eyes, takes a few deep breaths, and pats Henry firmly on the shoulder. "Okay, Henry," he says. "Okay."

Henry nods, stupefied. *What is this man?*

Liam lowers his hand, and Henry—surprising himself—reaches up to take it. "I think you better go to your room for a while," Liam says.

"That's fine," Henry says quietly, feeling like a nap might be exactly what he needs.

As they walk back toward the house, he thinks about all the things he has learned about Liam, all the things he *saw*. But the one thing that sticks out the most, more than the laughter or the bursting colors of all those emotions, is one small sliver of information. Of truth. A truth that Henry, despite all his bluster and insult, had hit square on the head.

Liam isn't just afraid of Jim, or Fred, or whatever his dumb name is.

He's *terrified* of him.

"So, Mr. Hinnom, or can I call you Fred?" Sali begins, nudging the tape recorder a few inches closer to the giant sitting across from him.

"Fuh . . . Fuh . . . Fred is fuh . . . is okay," the big man answers, and Sali's smile falters a touch. *He's either an insanely good actor, or he really is driving the car with a broken engine.*

"Okay, Fred, thank you. I'm Salvador, but you can call me Sali, or Agent Espinoza, whatever you prefer. Okay? Okay." Sali flips open the file on his lap (which he's already meticulously read through twice) and studies the school photograph, the same one that dangles from the ID badge clipped to the chest pocket of the janitor's coveralls. "It's a good photo, looks just like you," Sali says, and forces himself to laugh.

Fred smiles, but says nothing. The smile doesn't last.

"You don't have a driver's license?"

"No, sir, I can't—"

"But you have a state ID."

"I have to, for the program. Can't get a job . . ."

"Can you tell me where you were yesterday morning between 8:30 and 9 a.m.?"

Fred's eyes narrow a moment, as if in thought, and he replies: "At the school here."

No shit, dummy. Okay, okay, but how much of a dummy are you, really? Let's find out, huh?

"Ms. Terry says you were in the rear parking lot around that time. Which she also says is not your usual routine. Why were you back there, Fred?" Sali watches the man's face closely, looks for a sign of concern, or fear, or even to see if the man was plain old thinking too hard.

"One of the teachers said they was rats by the dumpsters."

"Rats? Or a rat? Singular. I mean, were there *many* rats, or just one ugly fucker you had to put down?"

Come on, big guy. Get mad.

But Fred only looks momentarily confused, and then, as if recalling the title of a movie you've been picking at a while, like sirloin between your teeth, his face opens and relaxes. "Just one, sir. Agent, sir. Just one."

"Which teacher mentioned this?"

There! There it was!

A pause.

Not an "I'm trying to remember" pause, but an honest to God "oh shit" pause. *Because you knew we'd ask, didn't you? Hell yes. That cover story may have flown with the principal, but this is the FBI, motherfucker, and we're a different kind of lie detector.*

"I'm sorry . . . I don't remember," he says, and drops his eyes.

Liar.

"I guess I'm nuh . . . nuh . . . nervous is all."

"Sure, sure. There's been a lot going on, right? First one kid is killed, then another goes missing . . . that's a lot of bad shit in one place, you know what I'm saying? I'd be nervous, too, if I were you. I mean, you're not a teacher, right? And you haven't been here that long. In a way, it sort of makes you our number one suspect right now. Hell man, I'd be shitting my blue jumper if I were you."

Fred says nothing in response, but Sali sees those eyes darken. It's only a smidge, but it's there. Anger, perhaps?

Let's hope so.

"I didn't do anything to the kids," Fred says slowly. "I would never hurt a child. I . . ."

"You . . . what, Fred?"

"I don't like you saying that, sir. No offense."

Now Sali is the one given pause. *Okay, so maybe underneath the fuh-fuh-fuhs and the first-gear intelligence the guy has feelings, Sali. Retarded—sorry, "mentally challenged"—folks have emotions, too, right?*

So let's try something else.

"I'm sorry, I really am. But these are the facts. Okay, moving on. You went and checked out some rats for teacher unknown, and then what? You saw Ms. Terry, right?"

"Yes, yes. I saw her after I was back there. But I didn't see a rat, sir. I looked under and behind but saw no rats, no droppings either. So I don't know if I even need to get the traps."

Sali closes the folder, leans in close. "What did you do after you saw Ms. Terry?"

"I, uh . . . I pulled out the bleachers in the gym. There are assemblies on Thursdays . . . and then . . . I did my normal routine, sir. Trash pickup before lunch. Then I eat, before the kids. Then I clean the cafeteria, then other odd things that need doing. At three o'clock I clean the locker rooms, unless there's a practice for basketball or soccer, those are the sports we have here at the school. In that case, I do it in the morning . . ."

"Okay, okay," Sali says, feeling an insane desire to hear a conversation between Mr. Pollack and Fred Hinnom. Pollack can start with the parrots and Fred can hit him right back with the locker room cleaning protocols. They'd likely entertain the hell out of each other. "So, you didn't see Henry Thorne?"

"No, I didn't see him yesterday. But I saw him earlier in the week. He and I were together because some kids were throwing rocks at me . . . and then him. He protected me. He's a good boy. I hope he is okay, sir."

"Who were these kids? The ones throwing rocks?"

"Oh, that's easy," Fred says, and a smile breaks his features. It's not pleasant. "Tommy Patchen, he's the leader, I think. Jim Hawkes, and, uh . . . shoot, what's that boy . . . oh! Tyler Legge. Those three are always causing trouble. But you know what they say, what goes around comes around."

Well, two of them aren't gonna be going around anymore, I imagine. Something tells me Jim Hawkes isn't missing like Henry. Something tells me Jim Hawkes is dead. Like his buddy Tommy, whose eyes and earlobes and fingers were gnawed away by rats, much like the ones you were looking for—supposedly. Yeah, the Hawkes kid played a part, all right. Might not have known he was in over his head until it was too late, I'd guess. But that's a loose end, now tightly tied up.

Sali flips open the folder again, turns a few pages over, lets the silence build for a few moments. "Is this your current address, Fred?"

Fred leans forward, and Sali can't help but feel threatened by the man's proximity, his massive bulk casting a shadow over the pages like a storm cloud. "Yes sir, that's an apartment I rent."

"How did you get hurt, Fred? I have no information on your deployment record, but you were given this job as part of a disabled veterans program, correct?"

"Yes, I . . ."

"But I've requested to see your military records. I should have them by the end of the day, they're being faxed to my office now. I'll be interested to look at them."

Fred hesitates a moment, as if not sure how to proceed. "I don't understand. What's the question? I'm sorry, I get confused."

"Sure, sure. How did you hurt that big head of yours? I'm assuming Vietnam, right? You're a little old to have fought in Desert Storm."

"Yes sir, that's correct. I was just eighteen when I went over there. Six months in I got shot—went through my helmet and into my brain. I was flown out and they saved my life, but the damage messed me up a bit. Clouded my thinking, makes it hard to talk sometimes. I have bad balance, for another. It was hard. But it was a long time ago, sir."

"I'm sorry to hear that. Where, specifically, were you when you were shot? I mean, that's horrible, it is. But see, here's the weird thing, Fred. I *also* fought in Vietnam. Weird, right? Shit, man, we're about the same age, right? Late forties. Hell, you and me might have been in the same place at the same time."

Fred's face is unreadable, his mouth slack, his eyes dark. His hands tighten slightly on his knees, but not enough to raise a red flag in Sali's mind. Not yet.

"So," Sali says, his voice no longer cheerful, no longer friendly. "Where were you?"

Fred says nothing a moment. He turns still as a statue. And then, slowly, as if chewing on the words before releasing them into the air, he says: "Dong Ha. Quang Tri Province. I was shot when the NVA overran Lang Vei Camp. Sir."

"What division was that?"

"Third Recon. Sir. Under C Company."

Sali sits back, studies Fred's face, his eyes. *He looks good and pissed off, all right. And maybe for good reason. Shit shit shit. I don't got him. I don't got him, and all I'm doing is being a grade-A dickhead to a combat veteran who got his brain scrambled by an NVA bullet. Fuck!*

"Okay, okay, Mr. Hinnom," Sali says, trying to keep the defeat from his voice. "I think that's all I need to know for now. And there's nothing else you might tell me? About the kids who threw rocks at you and Henry? About something you might have seen yesterday morning? Something that seemed strange to you?"

"No, sir. But you should talk to the Legge boy, he knows the other two, the ones killed."

Sali freezes.

He waits, holds his breath, unmoving; his fingers clutch the folder in his lap, his eyes focus on a mystery spot on the linoleum floor that a distant part of his brain prays isn't black mold. But it's a faraway thought, background conversation at a cocktail party, because right now all of his attention is focused on one thing and one thing only:

The ones killed.

Sali smiles again. He looks up to meet Fred's eyes.

Do you know? Do you know I know? Do you realize the slip, mother- fucker? Are you in full-blown panic mode *right now, or do you already have your comeback lined up for my question? Yeah, you're ready for it, aren't you? You know what's coming, big fella.*

Because why would you say both boys were killed?

Jim's just missing, that's all. And now that we're talking about it, how would you even know that? You're the fucking janitor. There's nearly three hundred kids in this elementary school—and yet you not only know Jim Hawkes is missing—hell, brother, you think he's dead. *Well well well . . . but you know what I think? I think this ruse has played out.*

Let's go to Phase Two, how about it?

"We'll be sure to do that, Mr. Hinnom," Sali says calmly, all smiles. "Now, I'll let you get back to work. I've got a lot to do and many more people to speak with."

"All right, sir," Fred says, and stands.

Sali stands as well. "Because I *will* find Henry," he says, his eyes hard steel above a mirthless smile. "I'll find him safe and sound and return him to his parents, and I will make sure the people who took that boy go to a very dark place and never see the light again. And if—I hate to even think it—but let's say for a moment the boy is *hurt.* Well then, I'll make sure to *personally* oversee that dark place, and make sure that where those animals go—because they *are* animals, am I right—is the absolute lowest pit of hell. The worst-case scenario anyone could imagine to live out their remaining, pathetic days of life. How's that sound?"

Fred's back is to Sali, his hand on the doorknob.

Is that tension in your tree trunk neck, Fred? Is that rage . . . or fear? Sometimes it's hard for me to know the difference, causing so much of both as I often do. Nasty habit of mine.

"I hope so, sir," Fred says, and opens the door.

Sali watches him walk away down the hall for a few seconds, waiting to see if the guy wants to risk a look back or not, and then decides to give the big fella one more poke:

"Oh, hey, Fred?"

Fred pauses, turns his head back. Not all the way, but some.

"Don't leave town, huh?"

"No, sir," Fred replies. "Wha-wha-where would I even go, sir?"

Sali smiles and waves. He goes inside once more, closing—and locking —the door to the abandoned office. He picks up the phone and dials 9, then the number to the field office.

Nora McCallister picks up, and he can't talk fast enough.

"Nora, it's Sali. I need you to run an ID through NCIC. Yeah, one of the faculty at Liberty ... guy's name is Fred Hinnom—H–I–N–N–O–M, should be in the files ... You got him? It's in the ... yeah, thanks. Right, the janitor. Check the social out. No driver's license, but check his ID. I want records pulled on his lease, his phone bill, his electric bill, I want to know who his family is and where they live. I want to talk to his mother, his father, and his priest. If he's using an alias, let's find it. This guy stinks, I know it. He's ..."

Like a rat in a dumpster.

"... dirty."

Sali's eyes find the floor, his mind spinning with what will need to happen over the next several hours. He stares at the black spot he'd seen earlier, thinks maybe it looks a little bit bigger than it had just minutes ago.

You better be right, Salvador. You've got to be.

"And Nora? I'm gonna need a warrant for surveillance and a search of the residence. Soon as possible. The address ... right, you got it. Tell them we need it in the next hour, or sooner. Now would be good. I'll call the PD detectives myself, give them a heads up. I'm going back to the Thorne home. Buzz me when you know something. Thanks, I agree. This is the lead we needed, and it might be our best shot."

And if we play him right, he'll lead us straight to the boy.

I'm coming, Henry. Hang in there.

I'm coming.

9

Greg debates whether to pour himself a third beer from the tap. He doesn't need it and frankly doesn't want it, but goddamn the temptation is almost too much to resist. *I mean, come on, people, when does a man get left alone in a bar, where all the booze is free and the kegs are cold and the grill is hot? It's like heaven with a hangover.*

He'd already stolen a roll of quarters from the register and emptied the entire roll into the jukebox right after Jim had taken off. It had been a steady dose of 1960s rock and roll ever since, a regular catalog of an era's greatest smackeroos, everything from Steppenwolf to Booker T. and the M.G.s to the Animals to the greatest of them all (in his humble opinion), those brothers from across the pond, the Kinks.

And now, while "Lola" tinkles and strums in the background, he's behind the bar, pacing before a line of beer taps as if he was a beauty pageant judge contemplating a row of slick-skinned, tan-bodied swimsuit contestants. He's finally decided to go ahead and taste the Rapture spelt saison Cesare—*a little squirt won't hurt,* he reasons—when the black rotary phone stuck against the wall (jammed beneath the broken black-and-white RCA and hung next to a sun-faded, autographed headshot of Loni Anderson of all people—who Greg thought was all hair and teeth and creepy brown eyes, tits or no tits) starts to shrill loud enough to make him jump out of his skin.

Shit.

Greg slams the glass down onto the worn mahogany bar and skitters across the drymats to the phone, plucking it clean midway through the third ear-splitting ring. As he picks up, ready to play bartender for a few minutes, he realizes with a dull thud and a stunned sort of panic that he has no fucking idea what the bar he's holed up in is actually *called.*

Desperate, he looks around at the walls, counters, and windows, hoping to see a branded matchbook, a sign, a check pad for the love of all things holy. Nothing. So he does the only thing he can do: he clears his throat, puts the phone to his ear, and bullshits.

"Bar," he says in a gruff voice, wondering if that's even what the dead schmuck rotting in the upstairs apartment sounds like.

"Greg?"

"Yeah. Jim?"

"Did you say 'bar'?"

Greg winces. "Uh, what's up? I thought you'd only call if—"

"Shut the fuck up."

Greg's mouth closes so fast and tight there's an audible *click* when his teeth come together.

"Listen, we have a problem. Things didn't go as I'd hoped. I won't get into details, you understand? So don't ask. This phone call may not be just the two of us."

The feds, Greg thinks. And damned if he isn't spot on.

"Here it is. I want you to grab the large duffel bag in the office. Shut everything down, lock every door, and get the fuck out of there. Look at your watch."

Greg looks. "Yeah, okay."

"You got fifteen minutes. Then a bomb goes off, understood?"

"Yeah, yeah, I'll be long gone, trust me."

"Cool. You know where to rendezvous. We planned for this contingency, right? Tell me you know."

"I know, man. I know," he says, and he does. There's a Vons grocery store a half mile from the school with a nice busy parking lot and a robust number of exits, and that's where Jim would be. *Hope he ditches the blue jumpsuit first,* Greg thinks, wondering how bad it really is. *It can't be good, that's for damn sure.*

"Okay, good. I'll see you there in twenty minutes. Stay cool, but move your ass. And if you *don't* see me, don't stop."

"I got it, I'll see you soon."

"Don't dawdle."

"I know, Jesus. Fifteen minutes, then KA-BLAM."

"Now it's fourteen."

The other end of the connection *clicks* and Jim's voice is replaced by the cool shimmering hum of an empty line, followed by the familiar monotone voice of Ma Bell.

If you'd like to make a call, please hang up . . .

Greg hangs up, then gives himself a count of ten to slow his heart, bring the power knob on his brain all the way up, and take care of business. Things have been moved up, that's all. They always knew this was a possibility. Still, it gives him goosebumps and makes his stomach cartwheel to know the game is finally *on*.

There's no looking back now. Nothing back there but a dead end. It's time to move forward, to play it out, to follow through on everything they'd planned out so meticulously.

Greg goes to the jukebox and yanks the power cord from the wall, effectively killing "Summertime Blues" mid-chorus. He needs to think.

No mistakes.

He walks to the office, grabs the large duffel, hoists it over his shoulder. His wallet and keys, sunglasses and Yankees cap all sit in a neat pile where he left them at the corner booth—everything together and ready to go. He pulls on his jacket, dons the cap and glasses, pockets the wallet and keys, and gives the booth a quick dummy-check; but he knows this is all he brought in, and it's all he needs to go out.

He doublechecks the lock on the front door, kills all the lights, and makes his way down the dark rear corridor toward the service door, the alley, and the shit-brown Duster.

Hang on boys and girls, because things are about to get interesting.

At the car, he tosses the duffel in the backseat, gets inside, gives a quick glance toward the end of the alleyway for a black sedan or a blue-and-white, then plugs in the key and twists. The Duster's engine rumbles with clean, loud life, and despite his anxiety, Greg feels a rush of pure adrenaline that gives him a little shot of the good stuff, the endorphin kick that comes during a job, the one that makes him feel a little bit high.

Hey-ho, let's go. Greg's ready to start the show.

It's time to rumble. It's time to hustle.

It's time to run.

10

Henry hates going back to the room, but he figures it's better than being locked to a pipe on the floor of the kitchen and getting the stuffing kicked out of him.

Liam stands at the door while Henry shuffles to the bed, morose and annoyed. He pulls one of the itchy green blankets over his lap and stares at the far wall. His stomach growls but he ignores it. He just wants to sleep until this is all over.

"Henry," Liam says.

Henry looks at him, offers no response. Liam is complicated, but Henry hates him no matter who he is, or *what* he is. Henry thinks Liam is a lot like tropical weather he studied last semester in Earth Sciences—rainy one second, hot the next, and then, when you least expect it, a crazy-ass hurricane.

"This will be over soon."

"Yeah, okay," he says, and lies down on the sprung mattress, the rusty wire cot squeaking its annoyance with his every movement.

"Hey, Henry."

"What?" Henry moans, wanting to be left alone, wanting more than anything in the world to be away from this place, these people.

"What number am I thinking of?" Liam says, and Henry can't resist. He knows Liam's just making fun of him, but it's like someone tossing a ball at your gut, you just lift your hands and catch it. Instinct.

"Twelve," he mumbles into the pillow, then winces.

Henry! What did I tell you? Don't let them know your secrets, son! You gotta find out their secrets, not the other way around!

But Henry is tired, and he's scared. He doesn't like feeling alone, abandoned. And if giving Liam a little glimpse into his world makes him like him more, or maybe not want to *kill* him when this is all over, that can't be a bad thing. Can it?

"Holy shit," Liam says, the words escaping in a shocked breath.

"Now ten, now forty-two, one-hundred-eighteen, now nine, twenty-seven, forty, two thousand—"

"Stop! Jesus!"

"Then stop thinking of all the numbers!" Henry yells back, knowing he is asking for trouble but not caring. "You told me—"

"Okay, okay. But give it a rest a second. I mean . . . how? How, Henry?" Liam half steps, half stumbles into the room, closes the door behind him, then lowers himself against the wall, knees bent, hands folded in front of him, as if praying. "Let me think for a second."

Easy, son. That's enough. He's impressed, we can see that. But let's not give him the whole show, okay?

"Okay," Henry says, knowing Liam will think he's answering him and not the voice. He waits for Liam to gather himself, but he never stops reading his mind, his thoughts, his feelings: *What the fuck is going on? Who is this kid? Damn, maybe I am nuts. Make him prove it again, think of something impossible. Something no one knows.*

"How are you doing this, Henry?" he says, finally. "No bullshit."

Henry says nothing for a moment, then: "I just do."

Liam starts to respond, and Henry knows he's going to ask for more parlor tricks. More Zener cards.

What am I thinking?

What am I thinking?

What am I thinking?

Henry doesn't understand what the big deal is. Why people get so excited. Thoughts are like seeing what's in someone's desk drawers, or stuck in a shoebox buried in their closet, or the color of their underwear. It is invasive and meaningless. Seeing people's feelings is all well and good,

but if Henry is *really* special, he'd be able to tell what someone was thinking or feeling *without* seeing all the colors surrounding them. Uncle Dave
once said that when he was in a courtroom, he could tell just by looking at
their faces which jurors were with him, and which ones were against him.

"It's in the set of their mouths, the tightness of their eyes," he told
Henry once, giddy after winning a case. "The way they're holding their
hands. Their posture. It all paints a picture, one I can use as I continue to
convince them of my position. Reading people isn't hard, Henry, not if
you know how to look."

Henry thinks that's true, but he also thinks some people are harder to
read than others. Men who look gentle can be serial killers, and ladies who
look nice may be cold as ice inside. Children who act kind may, behind the
mask, want to hurt you. Strangers are especially difficult, because you're
only seeing them for the first time, and their smiles can mean *anything*.
Anything at all.

But before Liam can follow up his question, or Henry can think about
Uncle Dave some more, they both hear it.

The sound of a car engine.

Henry sits up fast, and his feet are on the floor before he realizes it.
Liam seems as surprised as Henry to hear the approaching car—his jaw
hangs open and his body tenses. For a brief moment he and Henry lock
eyes, each thinking the same thing:

Someone's found us.

Without thought, without debate, Henry sprints toward the unlocked
door. Liam, taken off guard by the pudgy little kid's burst of speed, stands
to grab him but his ankle twists as he raises himself and he drops to a knee.

"Henry, stop!" he roars as Henry yanks open the door and rushes past.

Henry hits the hallway at a hitching sprint, already breathing hard.
He jumps the hole in the floor, surprised as anyone at his sudden burst of
speed and agility.

Funny how having your life threatened makes you move your butt! he thinks, somewhat hysterically, and then he's screaming, screaming at the top of his lungs, yelling "*HELP!*" as loud as he can, yelling it over and over. He turns the corner at the flimsy banister and begins to sprint down the stairs. Liam bellows from somewhere close—but not too close—behind.

Henry flies down the stairs toward the front door of the house.

It's directly ahead.

PART SIX: THE BODY IN THE CELLAR

1

"Aw, hell."

Sali backs out of the bedroom, a hand over his mouth. He isn't going to be sick, this is not the worst he's seen by a long shot, but the lack of ceremony is unnerving.

The man's body has been tossed onto the bed, facedown, his head bludgeoned badly enough to show jagged shards of skull and splatters of brain.

The boy is crumpled on the floor at the foot of the bed, twisted in a broken heap as if he'd been kicked there, cast down as carelessly as a child might toss a broken toy, frustrated at its inability to animate.

It appears at first glance that the boy has been strangled, and Sali doesn't have to overwork his adrenalized brain to know it is Jim Hawkes, the infamous note-passer who aided in getting Henry out of the classroom and alone, where the janitor (allegedly) could grab him.

Three uniforms in riot gear stand a foot inside the door, guns drawn. Normally Sali would have put a Kevlar vest over his dress shirt, but he'd opted for the sport coat. It isn't a macho thing, it's an instinctual thing. Part of him knew what they'd find here, and it wasn't a hail of bullets.

"All clear," Sali says, trying to sound casual but still fighting down the fright and horror of finding the bodies. "You can put those away," he says, motioning toward the weapons. *Don't need any of you boys shooting me in the ass.*

Detective Knopp, who breached the apartment with him, pushes past him into the bedroom as he backs out. He has to give her props for being able to handle the stink—the bodies aren't decomposing quite yet, but the sealed room, the heat and the open wounds of the guy who had his skull smashed-in combine to thicken the air with the warm, coppery taste of death and rot.

"Would one of you please secure this entrance?" he says to a random uniform near the stairs. "This is a murder scene. We'll need to tape off the perimeter, downstairs as well, seal everything. No one in or out until forensics arrives. And notify the coroner."

Knopp steps out of the bedroom. "I'll get an APB going on Hinnom," she says. "Obviously he's in the wind, along with whoever he was with. It's too bad, and bad news for the kid."

"Yeah," Sali agrees. He knows this had been their best chance to find a real lead to Henry. Still, it isn't a total bust. They've fingered the man—or at least one of the men—responsible for the kidnapping, and Sali knows in his guts that the man was both the brains and the brawn behind the abduction of Henry Thorne.

The fucking janitor.

After leaving the school that morning, Sali had returned to the Thorne home and told them as much, and as little, as possible. He admitted that he still believed someone with access to the elementary school had, at the very least, assisted in Henry's abduction. He let them know they had not found any trace of the white van spotted near the school at the time of their boy's disappearance. Knowing he had to give them something positive, something to keep them motivated and energized as the ordeal dragged on, he broke protocol and informed them—albeit vaguely—of his intentions regarding Fred Hinnom.

"That all said, I do have a lead I'm interested in. We are getting a warrant right now to look into an individual's residence who we feel might have played a part in all this. But honestly, it's only a hunch. Meanwhile, we still have one big trump card coming our way—at some point these bastards are going to have to contact you. Historically speaking, these letters, phone calls, whatever they might be, are always a strong piece of evidence we can work up, and they often hold the key to finding the parties responsible, and the child."

The Thornes had nodded dully and clutched hands, wanting to believe but not able to shake that feeling all parents get when a kidnapping occurs—that overwhelming rush of helplessness, the guilt of letting the child down, of failing as parents, of not protecting the most important thing in their lives. He'd seen it often, on a lot of faces, and the only thing he could do for them was to keep digging, keep attacking the leads, find them some goddamn *hope*.

The warrant had finally been issued right before noon, only a few hours after he wrapped up his interview with Fred Hinnom. Sali had requested surveillance on the property almost immediately, and Detective Davis along with another detective had been watching any comings and goings ever since. But without the warrant they could do no more than watch—no enhanced audio equipment, no entering of the residence. Sali needed everything to be one-hundred-percent by the book, just in case they found some significant evidence in the surveillance or search of the janitor's residence (and the bar that operated beneath it), wanting to be sure it wouldn't be thrown out of court on some technicality, or a breach in protocol. Once the warrant came through, Sali got a debrief from Davis: They hadn't seen any activity since their arrival. No one in, no one out.

Sali cringed internally at the news, knowing that if Fred was their guy, he had given him the slimmest of windows to clear the place out. Needing only one more reassurance he was on the right trail, Sali called the school and asked to speak with the janitor, who he'd been told never left the school grounds until 5 p.m.

As he sat on hold at the Thorne home, the minutes ticking by, Sali knew the worst-case scenario had likely occurred, and cursed himself for it.

The bastard's running.

He handed the phone to a uniform, told her to page him if they located Hinnom—*fat chance*, he thought—and headed for the front door. Dave Thorne popped up from a kitchen chair, apparently seeing something in the agent's face he didn't like. "What is it?"

"Nothing, Mr. Thorne, but I have to leave. I have to check something out." He swiveled his head around and spotted Detective Knopp on the far side of the living room, staring at her notepad as if it held secret messages if she could only decode the bitching things. "Detective," he said, loudly but not loudly enough to cause alarm. She looked up at him, eyes wide and alert. She slapped her notepad shut and headed straight toward the front door to meet him. She read his face easily, because she'd likely been thinking the exact same thing: *We're running out of time.*

They had to breach.

They had to take a shot.

"I'm sorry, Mr. Thorne. I promise I will be back later and give you a full debrief. But right now I really have to go."

A strong hand gripped Sali's forearm and he looked back, startled, into the wild, desperate eyes of a man on the brink of losing everything. "Take me with you," Dave said. "Let me go with you. Please, I need—I need to do *something*. If I sit here for one more minute—"

"Mr. Thorne . . . Dave . . . listen to me. I can't do that. It's not possible. So please, stay here, take care of Mary. I need you here in case they call, you understand? They could be calling any minute, it would fit the profile. I need you here for that, to talk to them."

Dave held Sali's arm tight a moment longer, then squeezed, then let it go. Sali could almost visibly see the man shrink in front of him, like an inflated doll that suddenly lost a few pounds of air. "Stay strong, Dave, I'll be back," Sali said, and left the man to his pain.

During the twenty-minute drive from the Thorne home to Hinnom's apartment, Sali ordered a three-block perimeter surrounding the building, monitoring every road, street, and alley going in or out. Officers had been told to look for a white van, or a driver or passenger matching Hinnom's description. An FBI SWAT team, along with two additional field agents, had been deployed to the scene, and a cranky, weathered police captain heading a team of officers in full riot gear also waited for Sali and Knopp's arrival. Sali received a debrief from Davis and the other officers on the surveillance, then consulted with the SWAT team on the best ways into the first and second story access points of the structure. Dixon Avenue, the street running north/south, had been blocked off from foot traffic and cars, as had Fourth Street, which crossed Dixon running east/west; the brick structure of the bar and Hinnom's apartment sat right on the southwest corner, dead as night and lifeless as a corpse.

"He's either there and knows we're here, and he's just waiting for us," the captain overseeing the armored officers stated, "or he's long gone and we're twiddling our dicks out here."

"Let SWAT take position," Sali had said, and they all continued to wait, tension building, as the area was properly secured.

In the end, it had been Sali's call to breach.

The pair of FBI agents, along with half the shielded officers, entered through the bar's front door with the assistance of a ram. Davis and a second team went in through the service entrance (shockingly left unlocked) from the alley while Sali, Knopp, and three officers smashed through the doorway of the second-story apartment using nothing more than the heel of Agent Espinoza's wing-tipped shoe. SWAT monitored windows and doorways from adjacent rooftops but left the brute groundwork to the adrenalized officers of the San Diego PD, a gesture of respect for their brothers in blue.

The entire first floor was discovered empty, and had been quickly sealed off from any additional traffic until forensics could arrive to pull fingerprints which, in a public place like that, was like asking for the brownest blade in a field of dead grass.

The apartment had been a much different, and grimmer, revelation.

★ ★ ★

"The guy wearing his brains like a hat is Adolf Politzcki," Knopp informs Sali as they sit on the cooling hood of his black sedan, twenty minutes after finding the bodies. "He's the owner of the building and the business on the first floor—well, I should say his *mother* owns the property, but she's been holed up in St. Mary's retirement facility out in Arroya Vista going on seven years, so I doubt she's been keeping tabs on the place, or her son. Oh, and guess what? Adolf's cousin, a Mister"—she consults her notebook briefly—"Frank Politzcki, is a steel worker who also happens to do volunteer work for the US Disabled Veterans Group of Southern California."

"Never heard of it," Sali says, confused.

"That's because it's legit as Ivan Boesky. We think the school job came through him. The whole Politzcki clan had a hand in this, certainly as accessories. Frank, sadly, is in the wind. Likely interstate, so good luck."

Sali nods. "That explains the Fred Hinnom conundrum."

Knopp raises an eyebrow.

"Deceased. Or, not officially. Officially, the guy disappeared a few years ago. No criminal file, but he did serve in the military. Navy Reserve, if you can believe it. Regardless, an easy identity to take on, especially with the right rubber stamps."

"Well hell, there you go," Knopp says, nodding. "Anyway, to greener pastures. The dead juvenile in there, as I'm sure you've surmised, is the missing Jim Hawkes. Coroner says he'd been strangled with enough force that, in addition to the busted windpipe, he's got three broken bones in his neck. I'm sorry, Agent, none of this is good news."

Sali spits onto the pavement. It is the worst possible news, because it means the kidnappers aren't just a few hoodlums looking for an easy score. He isn't dealing with small-time crooks who have recently moved up a notch on the crime ladder to attempt a bigger, more dangerous job. They're dealing with a cold-blooded murderer. Someone who has no qualms killing to suit his end game. Which means Henry's odds of survival just dropped from infinitesimal to sub-zero, and they all know it.

What the hell do I tell the Thornes?

"There is some good news, if you want to call it that."

"Please, because my shoes can't take much more of this," he says, studying the scuffed toes of his wingtips. "They've assured me Henry will survive, and I never doubt them."

Knopp ignores most of this and flips the page of her notebook. "Well your shoes need a timer. Seems we missed the accomplice by about three hours. He left a steak thawing on the grill and a half pint of warm beer on the bar."

Sali curses under his breath, thinks about that poor dead kid crumpled on the floor in the apartment, and knows in his heart the boy found in the dumpster is also, most assuredly, part of this guy's trail of bloodshed. What had he said during the interview?

You know what they say, what goes around comes around.

Sali makes a mental note to get the Legge boy into protective custody, although now that the perp has split, the boy is probably out of danger. Still, the last thing anyone needs is another dead kid.

"Anyway, on the bright side," Knopp continues, "I just got off the radio with my lead investigator, and we've got a positive ID on the janitor."

Sali stands up straight, nerves blazing. "Jesus, you're kinda burying the lead, detective. Tell me."

Knopp reads from her notes. "Guy's real name is Jim Cady, last known residence Oakland, California. Mother and father are dead, no siblings, but we got a hit on his photo that had been sent to all the state prisons, and Folsom came back with bingo. We were able to match fingerprints with the ones the school had on file. Same guy."

"Okay, okay," Sali says, the despair washing off him like dust in a hot shower. He feels rejuvenated, excited, and—there's that word again—*hopeful.* If the guy is an ex-con, it means he has known associates, and that means they've gone from one lead—now dried up—to what could potentially, and very quickly, become several leads. "So he has a record ..." he murmurs, already thinking of the follow-up he needs to do.

"Longer than the *White Album*," Knopp says dryly, and hands Sali the folder she has tucked under her arm. "Known associates, aliases, prior residences. It's all there, sir. The thing now is, if he's running, it means we've sped up his plan. Our window, already closing fast, is about to slam shut."

Sali takes the folder, flips it open, and is immediately struck by the mug shot of Jim Cady, aka Fred Hinnom. Despite all he now knows, it's still a shock to see the cold eyes of a killer staring out of a man's face who, only that morning, had looked into his own eyes with the dull, helpless gaze of an old hound dog.

This guy ain't no hound dog—this dude's a mean, rabid pit bull motherfucker. I'm dealing with Cujo here. Even worse? Now I've most likely, almost certainly, really pissed *him off.*

Great.

"I'll take a look at this," Sali mutters, feeling impatient to chase the leads held in his hands. "In the meantime, let's see what we can find here that might help us figure out who's helping this guy. If we can get a bead on his crew, maybe we can start mapping out where they took the kid."

Knopp nods and starts to leave. After two steps, she turns back, lowers her voice. "You think the vic's alive, then?"

"He ain't a vic yet," Sali says quickly, defensively. "I think Cady is a murderer, but he's also methodical. This is a long-play setup. We're talking what? Over six months to plan this thing, working at that school all that time? Can you imagine? Guy's committed, I gotta give him that. We may have cramped his style a bit, but my gut tells me he knew we'd be onto him. It might not have been his best-case scenario, but I doubt it was his worst. Look how fast he was able to move—this guy's not going to panic. He's gonna play the game out, and that means he needs Henry alive and well until he gets the money. No doubt about it."

"And then?" Knopp says, digging into her sport coat for a pack of Marlboro.

"Then nothing, because it ain't gonna get that far."

Knopp sticks the unlit cigarette in her mouth, one eyebrow raised.

"I'm gonna find him first. I just need a little time. Meanwhile"—Sali pulls a cheap Bic from his pocket, lights the detective's smoke—"we gotta hope Henry has enough sense to stay out of Cady's way. If he behaves and does what they want, he might make it out of this thing alive."

2

Henry leaps from the third step and hits the floor with both feet. He spares a glance to his right, toward the kitchen, and sees the surprised faces of Pete and Jenny, both of them sitting at the table. Pete jumps to his feet but Henry doesn't wait around to see what Jenny does. He can hear Liam stomping down the stairs behind him and he knows he's out of time. He'll never outrun them, but if that car out there is a Good Guy, Henry might have a fighting chance.

He grabs the handle of the door—a small part of his mind stunned the idiots hadn't locked it, obviously underestimating his desire to get the hell away from them—and yanks.

Bright daylight stabs his eyes, slathers the porch in blazing white. But before Henry can look up to find the car he heard from the bedroom, a great shade erases the sun, an eclipse so sudden and terrifying that it stops him in his tracks. He stares up into the shadow's face and his jackhammering heart skips a beat. His harsh breathing catches in his throat like a lump of stuck meat.

"Hiya, Henry," Fred says, and a massive hand grips Henry's shoulder hard enough to make his legs buckle.

"Owww," Henry whines, hating himself, but the hand is like a tightening vise, the strong fingers pressing into the tissue and muscle below his shoulder bone—*grinding, kneading*—until Henry wants nothing more than to drop to his knees.

But he won't do that.

The others come up behind him, panting and heavy-footed. Pete speaks first.

"Jim," he says, sounding to Henry's ears like a man who is very afraid. "You're early."

"A good thing, too," the big man says.

Jim, that's his real name. Not Fred at all. And he's not talking like Fred, not acting like Fred. He doesn't even really look *like Fred.* Henry's vision has adjusted to the shadow, and now he can make out the features of the man he'd known as nothing more than his school janitor the last few months of his brief life.

"Now," Jim says. "Someone want to tell me what the fuck is going on?"

Henry is twisted around like a doll beneath Jim's cement-fingered grip. He winces but keeps his mouth shut as he's guided firmly back inside the house.

Wouldn't have mattered, he thinks. *It wasn't the good guys, anyway.*

"Jim, I'm—" Liam doesn't sound scared to Henry, but he's lost that cool-guy swagger his voice usually has, that deep-toned Australian man-ly-man sound. Henry thinks his voice is also a little higher than usual. He takes a peek up at him, sees muddy yellows, dark, fragmented greens—his mind flustered and embarrassed.

Good. I hope he kills you for messing up. I hope he kills you all.

"—shit, man. I'm sorry. I would've caught the little bastard . . . another few seconds . . ."

"Uh-huh," Jim says, and pushes Henry toward Liam without cere-mony. Greg, following behind Jim, slips into the house without a word, wanting no part of whatever fuckery was happening at the entryway.

Liam grabs Henry hard around the neck—not as hard as Jim but hard enough to make him know he'll have bruises.

"He heard the car and bolted. Listen . . ."

Jim puts up a giant paw and shakes his head. "Whatever. It's all good. Go lock his ass up and then come back down here. We gotta talk."

"Right," Liam says.

Before Liam can push him toward the stairs, Henry makes a point to get a good look at the entire group one last time.

Pete looks pissed off but scared, like a kid whose brother has tattled on him and now he's gonna get a beating. Jenny is holding the hand of the guy who'd been in the van when they took him. He and Jenny are smiling at each other and Henry wonders if they're married. He also figures this guy, who has messy black hair and a stupid-looking moustache, is not all that smart, and probably handles easy stuff. Like a foot soldier.

Jim looks angry, giant fans of crimson and black pouring off him like a swirling, smoky robe, and he stares daggers at Henry as he makes his quick evaluation of the room.

"Hold up," Jim says, and Liam stops pushing Henry toward the stairs, holds him firmly, looking straight ahead, squarely at Jim.

Henry drops his eyes, but Jim kneels down in front of him. A hard finger presses underneath his chin and forces his gaze back up, his eyes forced to look directly into Jim's.

"You think you know me, but you don't," Jim says slowly, in a voice Henry does not recognize. "All that shit with fuh-fuh-Fred? That's all bullshit, my brother."

Henry's eyes widen as Jim's face actually does transform—for a split second of time—into that of Fred the janitor, the one who Henry had been locked into a maintenance closet with, the one he'd saved from getting hit in the head with a rock.

"That's right," Jim says, and grins, showing two rows of strong, white teeth. "All that was just for *you*, Henry. For this *moment*. Me and these guys, we're all here for *you*. Hell, man, you should be flattered. That was a lot of work I put in." Jim's face hardens slightly. "A lot of *time*. You know what I'm saying?"

Henry nods, feeling that now is probably a good time to go along with things, to calm everyone down, to keep himself alive.

"So if you go running around like you just did, trying to get away, and become a *problem* for me? Shit, man, I'll have to kill you, and I don't want to do that."

Henry swallows, makes sure to keep his eyes locked on Jim's, calm as you please. "I know this speech. Liam already gave it to me. You guys don't need to threaten me every five seconds."

Jim studies Henry mutely for a moment, looks up over the boy's shoulder at Liam, then stands up, doing that eclipse thing again. "All right, so I guess we're all on the same page. But let me elaborate one point, son," Jim says, and Henry lets his eyes fall again. He's shaking in fear and knows Liam can feel it. The hand tightens on his neck, but not painfully. *A warning?* "If you run again, I'll break one of your legs. I don't need to return you unharmed, Henry, to get what I want. All I need to do is keep you breathing. Broken leg?" Jim shrugs. "Keeps you from giving me trouble. I won't lose a dime."

Henry says nothing.

"Did Liam give you that speech, too?" Jim asks. "I don't think he did. Liam's more of a shoot-first, ask-questions-later kinda guy. Me? I like to use my hands." As if to demonstrate, Jim puts his hands on each of Henry's biceps and squeezes. Henry doesn't scream, or cry out, but a tear streams down his cheek as the pain flashes through his muscles like fire.

Then, from one moment to the next, Henry is released, and Jim is turning away, walking toward the kitchen while the others follow. Henry spares them a glance—Pete is smiling, Jenny looks bored, the other one—Greg?—confused. Henry figures that's his default state.

Then he's turned and pushed roughly toward the stairs.

"Move it," Liam says.

Henry moves it.

★ ★ ★

Liam can't believe his bad luck. Of all the moments for the kid to give him trouble, it's the very *minute* Jim arrives. Well, the little shit has been too coddled, that much is apparent. Liam doesn't care if he can read minds or do a standing backflip, from now on there will be no more screw-ups, no more taking it easy.

No more Mr. Nice Guy.

He shoves Henry hard as they enter the room, and the boy stumbles and falls to the floor. "Big man," he mumbles as he stands up, brushes off his jeans.

"What was that?" Liam says, his neck burning with oncoming rage.

But Henry ignores him and walks straight to the cot, lies down with his back to Liam. "You guys are making a mistake," Henry says quietly, looking to the wall, his small body sunken into the thin mattress.

Liam steps further into the room. "And why's that, Henry? Because the cops are going to get us? I don't think so, mate. I think you need to realize how deep in shit you are right now. This isn't a game, and if you keep pushing things, I guarantee you, whatever you think of me, that man downstairs will—"

Henry turns over, looks numbly at Liam, his eyes empty, his face slack. Waiting.

"He'll do what he says he'll do, Henry. He will break your bones if he has to. He will kill you if it comes to that. You need to smarten up and keep your head down."

Henry stares at him, his eyes half-closed, but concentrating. Liam can almost feel his little fingers picking at his mind, inspecting his thoughts.

"We're not alone here, you know," Henry says, and Liam feels a chill run up his spine. "There's something else. Something you don't even know about."

Liam stares at Henry, breathing hard and fast through his nose, trying to control his boiling anger. He refuses to be baited by the boy, but he also—for reasons he can't fathom—believes him.

Henry sits up on the cot, almost smiling now. "And it's dangerous, I think. More dangerous than you, or that asshole Jim, or dumb Greg, or scary Jenny, or freaky-ass Pete. I think it could hurt you, hurt *all* of you."

"I don't know what the fuck you're talking about, Henry, and I don't care. Keep your mouth shut and maybe I'll bring you dinner."

Liam turns and stalks to the door. Henry speaks up from behind him.

"Who's Timothy?" Henry says. His voice begins to rise, pleading. "Is that your son? Did you leave him? Did you leave him because you're nothing but a goddamned criminal?"

Liam spins and covers the distance between him and Henry in three large strides. The boy, a look of childish terror on his face, throws up his palms.

"Wait! I'm sorry!" Henry wails.

Too late, fucker.

He grabs the edge of the cot and flips it onto its side as Henry screams, his body slamming hard into the wall, then the floor. Liam grabs his arm and yanks him up out of the mess of metal and blankets. He feels something in the kid's shoulder give as he tugs, and Henry shrieks in pain.

"Shut up!" Liam screams into the boy's face. Henry's eyes go wide with terror, tears stream down his cheeks, but the boy's fear and despair only fuel the flooding rush of anger.

Liam lifts a hand and slaps Henry so hard the boy crumples down on his side. Terrified, he turtles, tries to hide between the tossed bedframe and the wall. He blubbers incoherently.

"Shut up! Shut up! Shut the *FUCK UP!*" Liam screams, kicking the turned metal bedframe into the cowering boy over and over again.

After a few moments he's able to gain control of himself. He wipes his mouth, smooths back his hair. Ignoring the sobs, the cries of terror, he kicks the bed weakly one last time and leaves the room, locking the door behind him.

As he enters the hallway, he can still hear Henry screaming through the closed door, but he keeps his face stoic, his mouth tight. *Enough is enough*, he thinks, and he starts down the stairs to meet up with the others.

In all his anger, in his sudden burst of violence, he has momentarily forgotten all about what Henry said about them not being alone, about there being something else there with them.

Something dangerous.

3

Dave knows it's late because the bedroom windows have long gone dark.

Agent Espinoza has come, and Agent Espinoza has gone.

In the end, there hadn't been much left to say.

The man, the one who worked at the school, had slipped past the FBI, the police.

The man who has their boy, who has taken their Henry, is long gone.

Mary groans and Dave twists to watch her restless sleep. She's taken a mild sleeping pill, of course. Something for her nerves. It seems to be working. For the most part, anyway.

Dave, on the other hand, is awake. He sits slumped on the edge of the bed in boxers and a clean gray T-shirt. He stares out the windows, at the dark, and he wonders if Henry is also somewhere, looking out a window at the black night.

Waiting for rescue. For salvation.

Waiting for those who were supposed to protect him to come and *find* him.

Bring him home.

Dave hears the muted conversations of the officers stationed in the kitchen and living room. The night shift had shown up . . . at some point. He can't recall the time. The day was a blur, a nightmare of questions and events he can't piece together, even when he tries to think about all the things that have happened, all the people who have come and gone, the information that has been shared with him and Mary.

What do they know? What do they really know?

Nothing.

Just this: Henry is gone.

Henry has been taken.

Henry is in great danger.

And he's scared. And he's alone. And he's just a boy, a little boy.

Dave buries his face in his hands, wondering if now is the time he'll finally be able to cry, to weep for Henry, for the pain he must be suffering, for the fear he must be feeling. This is their second night without him, and Dave can't help doing the math.

Taken at 9 a.m. Thursday. It's . . . well . . . He looks at his watch, sees he isn't wearing it, and turns to look at the digital clock on his nightstand— just past eleven.

My God. It's been more than thirty-six hours. What are the statistics? Thirty-six hours is "the window." After thirty-six hours, most victims of kidnapping are not recovered alive. Oh yes, the percentages really plummet after thirty-six hours, all right. So, I suppose he's dead for sure, then, most certainly. The God of Statistics says so. It has been decreed—no one shall live after being taken for thirty-six hours. NO ONE SHALL LIVE.

"Dead," Dave says as part of an exhale, as if his life force is spilling into the air. Henry's death becoming a solid thing lodged in his chest. Expanding painfully. "Oh, Henry, oh my boy!"

Dave finally finds his anguish, his despair, and his tears.

He sobs into his hands while sitting, pathetically, in his underwear, while his wife sleeps a drugged, restless sleep, and the officers murmur and mumble and monitor the phones, and his child is somewhere in a cold ditch, in the dirt, strangled or beaten to death or shot or stabbed in the heart, his neck cut open, his young life snuffed out.

"I'm sorry, Henry. I'm sorry, son," Dave says as he cries. "I'm so, so sorry. And I'm sorry, Jack!" he wails, his voice rising, hating the knowledge that he couldn't protect his brother's son, his only child. "I'm sorry, little brother!"

The voices from the other room have stopped, and Dave guesses they can all hear him just fine. He doesn't care. He doesn't care about anything but getting his boy home safe; alive, unhurt, and unscarred. "If they've touched him!" he roars suddenly, and Mary shifts in the sheets behind him. "If they've touched my son!"

"Ssshhh, baby," Mary says, and wraps her arms around him while he shakes and cries and rages. "Dave, it's okay, please ..."

"If they've touched my son, I'll *kill them*!" he yells, and beats his fists into his bony bare knees. "I'll kill them," he says again, but more quietly now, the sobs overwhelming the anger, dampening it like a wet cloth as his wife holds him tight and cries into the curve of his back, rocking him.

He tries to stand, to vent his outrage, but she holds him too tightly and he simply sinks back down and then, just like that ...

... it's gone.

The rage, the fire, the defiance. *Gone.*

He's empty. An empty man, hollowed out. He feels so light, so devoid of strength and life he's surprised he doesn't simply crumble to dust in her arms, turned to mud by his tears.

He sinks into her and they cry together while the dark night stands passively outside their windows, unaware and uncaring, unbeholden to the problems of man.

4

The same dark night stands sentinel outside the abandoned farmhouse, a fragmented backdrop seen only through thin cracks between the boards pressed against Henry's lone window.

He has righted his bed, slid the mattress and blankets back on top of the sagging, rusted springs. He has a cut on his forehead from where the metal of the frame caught him after one of Liam's kicks, and his arm pulses with a dull throbbing pain just above the elbow. He doesn't think it's broken but something—a muscle or tendon—has torn or been badly strained. He can't bend the arm too well but, all in all, he figures he got off lucky. Upsetting men like Jim or Liam, or *any* of them, was stupid. Henry didn't understand why he antagonized them, why he didn't just nod and keep his mouth shut.

Maybe it's because he's scared—badly scared—and this is how his mind copes with fright. Or maybe it's because he's hungry, and tired. One of his teachers once joked about how she needed a bagel in the morning or she'd be cranky until lunch. Saying she had hypoglycemia and needed sugar *all* the time or she'd get crazy. Henry had been fascinated with this and even researched the word in the library. It reminded him of the story about Jekyll and Hyde, and he wonders if Dr. Jekyll had hypoglycemia as well.

And this makes him think of Jim. The man with two personalities. One false, one real. One kind and childlike, the other brutal and murderous. Evil.

Henry sighs and sinks into his blankets. The heater emits a warm stench and he'd used the bucket, so the room stinks, but he doesn't care anymore, and despite what Liam said yesterday he isn't about to draw any more attention and ask to be walked outside like a dumb dog. *They'd say no anyway, then maybe hurt me again.*

Maybe next time they'd kill me.

Fresh fear rushes through Henry at this thought. The *reality* of his situation sinking in deeper. He's been drugged and beaten. He's being held prisoner by a man he knows, without a doubt, has murdered people. He couldn't see it before, when the man was faking, but he saw it downstairs when he looked into his dark brown eyes. He saw all the people he'd killed. Old men, women . . . children. He'd stabbed them, strangled them, beat them to death.

I like to use my hands, he'd said, and gripped Henry so tight he wanted to scream.

I have to escape, he thought, shaken. *Or I'll be dead, too. I need to get away.* He closes his eyes, concentrates.

Dad? he thinks, beckoning. *Dad, please . . .*

But his father is silent inside him. As if he has taken a vacation, or gone to sleep, or simply stopped paying attention.

Or maybe he's gone forever. Really gone.

Feeling desperate and alone, not knowing what else to do, where else to seek help, Henry reaches again, but not inward. He reaches *out*. Not to his father, and not to spy on the feelings and thoughts of the kidnappers.

To the thing in the cellar, and to the Other—the one it longs for, the one it needs.

MOTHER.

Henry takes a deep, steadying breath. Nervously, he opens that internal black eye wider, lets himself tumble into the Other's mind like a stone kicked off a cliff into darkness.

He immediately recognizes the creature's vague, innocent, primal thoughts, but this time he waits; he absorbs the feelings of the Other, just as the Other, he knows, is absorbing his. Henry tries to shield himself, throws up imaginary walls between his mind—his feelings—and the Other.

To a small extent, it works.

He has more control this time. He's neither aggressor nor victim. It's a mutual sharing, and Henry is relieved he's been able to create an equilibrium of sorts.

Now . . . he thinks. *Show me Mommy.*

A wave of ancient, instinctual *love* floods into Henry, and he gasps with the power of it. This thing, this Other, is only a baby, an unborn child, but it still knows love the same way it knows hunger; recognizes and pursues a desire for life.

Henry's mind slips down a new, unexplored channel. A tunnel that he glides through seamlessly, black and silver and twisting, leading him to a new perception: the Other's internal perception of the surrounding world.

It sees much as Henry sees, using a psychic power buried deep within, but the creature has little to no comprehension. The world is a blight of muted colors, dull and lifeless to the unborn mind. But then . . .

There.

Henry sees her.

A blinding white flame amid the gloom of the surrounding world, so bright and welcoming as to blind anything other than *her*. She is the source of every need, every desire; the source of his love, his *want*.

And she is close.

No, Henry thinks.

She is here.

Pushing himself further, experimenting in ways he's never done before, he tries to join the bridge between them, a strong psychic bond Henry joins with effortlessly. To Henry it feels alien, but welcoming. There is no hate, or violence, although he is aware of her scrutiny. He is not hidden here; she can see him as vibrantly as he sees her.

She sees all of them. She *smells* all of them.

Henry cannot hold the connection much longer, but he wants to stay, to be part of this strange bond, this immediate familiarity.

Come back, Henry!

Henry hears his father's voice but ignores it, glides further into the psychic slipstream. He wants to communicate with her, discover who and what she is.

Henry, NO! Come BACK!

There's a tug, and the feeling of being sucked backward through a slippery, slim funnel. Henry carries the image of being pulled from the gravity of a black hole.

He gasps, and his eyes open to darkness. There's a soft hiss and clink of the heater beside his bed, the rough fabric of the blankets, the wet chill of the air, the throbbing pain in his arm and forehead.

It's like waking from the coma all over again, he thinks.

Exhausted, he closes his eyes once more, but this time to rest.

A shadow in the form of a man stands at the foot of his bed, watching him as he passes into sleep.

★ ★ ★

She sits high in a tree, sniffs the air, golden eyes reflective amid dark branches. She watches the house, studies a high, darkened window, as if in contemplation. She makes a succession of small sounds—*tucktucktuck-tuck*—that sounds like a woodpecker at work, then a slow, soft whine pours from deep in her throat.

Raw strips of fresh meat are hung on a nearby branch, the blood slowly dripping to the ground below. The dirt absorbs what it can.

5

The hard, pale light of dawn shines through the cracks in the blankets and boards covering the windows of the house's first floor, giving the dingy walls a gray tint and revealing every defect of the chipped, ancient floor. The air is filled with dust motes and—were it not for the view—Pete would have woken up miserable and depressed to have found himself stuck, yet again, inside such a shithole.

Instead Pete watches Jenny breathing, oblivious to the flaws that surround him.

The girl and her brother are camped on the far side of what he assumes used to be a living room. Both of them are still asleep, having taken that previous night's late shift.

After the kid slipped past Liam, Jim was taking no more chances. From now on it was around-the-clock sentry duty until this thing was over. Pete had settled down far from the weird siblings—*he's probably fucking her,* he thought, both disgusted and aroused—because he knew the dyke hated him and there was no point in getting things more tense than they were. When they were in prison together, Greg spoke often of his twin sister, like most guys talked about their wives or their girlfriends, right up until the week before he was released—only a few months before Pete's own sentence for breaking and entering would be running out.

"She's mean, like you," Greg liked to say, always laughing. A few days before his release, he'd told Pete: "She'll be the one waiting for me when they buzz the big gate, her and no one else. Because there is no one else."

Pete hadn't asked anything further, because he frankly didn't give a rat's ass about Greg's family. But he liked the dude and he trusted the dude, and they'd made plans to regroup once Pete was sprung.

"There's a guy you need to meet. Jim Cady. Biggest, meanest, smartest son-of-a-gun you'll ever come across. He's always looking for a crew. The guy never sleeps, never stops. He's a machine. You'll love him."

Eighteen months later, here they all were. Best pals and shit. Kidnapping a little kid—the worst kind of crime, the one even criminals thought was beneath the black line of common decency. Pete doesn't give a shit. And he doesn't give a shit about Greg's stupid sister, either. Fuck her and fuck him.

But.

He still wants to keep them both in sight, and within earshot. That goes double for Jim and Liam, who he trusts (to a point) but also fears. Pete doesn't think those guys would double-cross him, no more than Greg would, but Pedro Scalera is still alive because the only person he trusts in this shitty old world is himself, and a healthy dose of skepticism is plain old good medicine, as his *abuela* used to say.

"Trust no one, Pedro, and no one can ever deceive you," the old lady would croak, sitting out on the dusty front porch of the run-down Oakland tract house they shared with another family of immigrants—all of them carving out their personal space where they could. Bedrooms were reserved for the parents, his *abuela*, and the other family's parents. The rest of them—four boys and two girls (two of the boys his own brothers)—slept on cots in the mostly bare living room area, a sheet strung between the genders for privacy, which was a joke, but there was a respect among the savages, the young castoffs, that kept the home civil.

Pete stayed bundled in that room with the rest of them until he turned fifteen, and then he made the mistake of thinking it would be a good idea to have his own space, him being the oldest of all the kids. One morning, without preamble, he moved his cot and few personal belongings into a makeshift shed he'd built in the tiny dirt backyard using three sheets of burn-blackened plywood (that he'd pulled off a deserted storefront in the middle of the night) and a blue plastic tarp.

Moving into his new space that first afternoon made him feel like a king. He laid his thin mattress on top of a five-foot by three-foot metal Coca-Cola sign he'd stolen from a junkyard. The thing was so rusted there were jagged brown holes where you could see dirt and dead grass.

That first *night*, though, was when he realized he'd made a horrible mistake.

With the curse of rushed miscalculation so prevalent in teenagers, Pete had unwittingly set up his shanty atop a massive ant colony—bright red fire ants the size of full-grown termites. And while he slept, they swarmed. Over and through the sign, over the cot and under his blankets. Into his clothes. When he scratched at the tickling of their legs at his calf, they began to *bite*.

He'd shot up in the middle of the night, panicked and howling in pain, slapping at his legs. Then his arms caught fire, his back, his neck, his scalp.

They were all over him.

He'd run from the shanty, knocking one flimsily nailed wall to the ground, ripping through the blue plastic tarp, bolting through the back door and into the house, screaming and slapping at his skin. His father came out of his bedroom holding a pistol and fired at him, barely missing his own son and taking out a chunk of the kitchen's porcelain countertop.

"Pedro!" he yelled when he realized who it was. Once the older man had caught his breath and discovered what was happening, he dragged the boy out back, turned on the garden hose, and sprayed him down as Pete stripped off his shirt, sweats, and underwear.

That night was also the first time Pete had a seizure, although he hadn't known it until he woke up in the emergency room. His father said his eyes had rolled up in his head and he'd began talking gibberish before falling down, unconscious.

He was taken to the ER where, at the age of fifteen, he was first diagnosed with having epilepsy. The doctor had prescribed Klonopin to use "as needed," and from that day forward he was never far from his medication. Just in case.

For months he'd had recurring nightmares that would trigger the disease in his brain, send him into that comatose state, sometimes throwing his body into fits, sometimes causing him to black out. Now, though, it happened only once every couple years. He'd become better at managing stress and anxiety. He found that rage and anger helped, gave him strength. Still, the fits could kill a person, and he watched for them like a man watching the shadows for an unwelcome visitor, one with every intention of doing harm.

A year after the incident with the ants, Pete finally moved away for good—out of that child's life, out from behind those parental walls. There was no shortage of gangs willing to recruit someone like himself—desperate, hungry, mean. With the Border Brothers he found a new home, a new family. He didn't care about that race shit, he just wanted to belong somewhere, to feel like he meant something.

But regardless of the years that had passed, or the full-grown strength of his righteous, badass anger, Pete still hated sleeping on floors. Especially in some nasty-ass crack house in the middle of a forest. Further, he'd never completely gotten over his fear of insects, another reason he wasn't fond of being on the ground.

But you cannot argue with that view, he thinks, his gold teeth casting a dull glow within the stretched hollow of his grin.

From his vantage point, he can see how Jenny's sleeping bag had loosened over the course of the night, exposing her down to the ribs. Of course, she was no fool and kept her tank top on (but no bra, mis amigos!), but the thin tight shirt had *shifted* during her sleep. As the dusky rays of predawn filters in through the poorly hung blankets and hurriedly assembled boards covering the windows, he can plainly see that her breasts have pushed up and *almost* out of the shirt's swooping, curving neckline. If she were to shift *ever so slightly*, Pete is almost positive one of her bare tits will slip out of there, and he'd have himself a little top-of-the-morning, free as punch-and-pie Ho-Show.

Unfortunately, and annoyingly, he also has to piss like a Russian race-horse. Which bears the complication of making a decision: Stay for the show? Or get up and hope it's an intermission, and the act will still be on stage upon his expedient return?

His brain begs to stay, but his bladder screams at him to *go*.

"Damn it," he murmurs. He slides out of his sleeping bag quietly as he can (leaving his boots alone) and all but tiptoes across the living room floor.

"Where you going?" a loud, deep voice says from the kitchen.

Pete rolls his eyes and looks to his right at Liam and Jim, hunched over the card table, obviously in deep discussion.

Making plans! Plans that may, or may not, include good old Pete.

"I'm taking a piss, you wanna come?"

Jim laughs and shakes his head. Liam studies whatever it is they have laid out on the table, oblivious and uncaring of Pete or his nature call.

★ ★ ★

Freezing!

Pete wraps his arms around his chest, feeling incredibly stupid for not putting on his boots before stepping outside. The sky is a sun-bleached pale blue. Pete eyes the line of trees twenty yards away, the glistening dew-specked wild grass that covers the ground between the house and the forest line, then looks at his bare feet.

"Yeah, no thanks," he says, and shivers. Instead he steps off the porch and walks briskly to the corner of the house, wanting privacy because now that he's up and walking, there's a great internal debate raging in his lower intestines as to whether this morning squirt is going to turn into a morning squat. He debates going back inside to grab toilet paper, but instead decides he'll go ahead and just piss for now. He'll figure out what he's gonna do next once that deed is done, his bladder empty, his feet no longer wet and cold, so he can damn well think clearly again.

He turns the corner and grabs at his fly. There are small bushes here, tall grass that pushes up against the side of the house. He heads for a small cluster of foliage and stops.

Pete stares stupidly at the ground, fingers frozen on a zipper at half-mast.

Now, how in the hell did we not see that*?*

Half-covered by weedy grass and wild bunches of tall, yellow-flowered buckwheat is a *door.* Two doors, in fact. Right in the damned ground.

Pete moves to the side, studies the doors more closely. He kicks aside a clump of the buckwheat and freezes all over again at what he sees. "Oh, shit." The chill moves from his feet and up his legs, shrivels his balls and sends icy daggers into the back of his neck.

Next to the double doors is a small, moss-covered window looking down into an earthy crawlspace. Pete bends down (momentarily ignoring the screaming pressure in his bladder), and peers through the window, pushing aside some of the tall grass to have a clearer view. A slanting beam of new-day sun streaks down from over Pete's shoulder, through the dingy glass, and comes to rest on the floor of the room below.

Blue-panted legs, awkwardly bent, rest flat in the dirt. Unmoving and broken as a discarded scarecrow.

That's a man, Pete thinks. He stands, pulls down his fly, and urinates against the side of the house, his brow wrinkled in thought. A distant part of him revels in the release of the pain and pressure, but the rest of his brain is trying hard to come to terms with what exactly he's seen.

And what it means.

"Jim's gonna be pissed," he says quietly and puts himself away, forgetting to zip back up and not much caring. "This is very bad, Pedro."

Pete takes two shuffling steps backward, looks from the doors to the window one last time, then begins to walk back around the corner of the house toward the front door.

Well, at least it explains the awful smell.

Pete starts to laugh, and then a pained expression crosses his face, as if he might scream, or cry. "Oh, shit, man," he says, and then decides he better stop walking.

And begins to run.

6

"Boss? We have a problem."

Jim looks over Liam's shoulder to see skinny-ass Pete standing in the doorway, shivering like a kid caught in the rain.

"What'd I say about keeping that door closed and locked?" he says, and his eyes dart to Liam with meaning in them, and Liam—always the smart one—catches it and turns around to study Pete.

"What's up, Pete?" Liam says calmly, and Jim is thankful yet again for having this man on his crew. Yeah, he fucked up yesterday, but the kid is easy to underestimate. He'd done it himself in a way, and it's not like he was gonna go anywhere. Little brother can't barely run fifty yards without blowing a gasket—Jim knows because he'd watch the little fucker, one leg all fucked up, running like a damn gimp during his PE class. Huffin' and puffin' and always behind everyone else.

Pete, on the other hand, wasn't the most stellar guy, and if it weren't for Greg's referral, Jim would have never brought on a gangbanger like Scalera. Jim liked having folks on his crew that could blend into normal society. Stand behind you at the coffee shop, watch you from a seat in the bus, follow you home at night. No worries. But hell, man, you see a tweaky Mexican dude like Pete, his neck slathered in a slobbering tat of a pit bull, his arms all inked up with skulls and knives and shit? Hell no. But they needed one more guy. A contingency guy in case things went wonky, one more set of legs, one more beating heart. Truth be told, with the addition of Jenny and Pete, this was more Greg's crew than his, which is why he's ever more thankful Liam answered the call and came running. And besides, with Jenny and Greg splitting their share, why not bring on a pretty girl who knows how to use a knife?

You never knew when a pair of great tits hiding a killer's black heart would come in handy.

Behind Pete, Greg and Jenny are waking up, brought to alertness by the room's sudden tension. Jim smirks at seeing Greg's hand—so deftly—tucked into his sister's sleeping bag. *Yeah, I know about you two,* he thinks without malice, without judgment. Isn't his damn business and besides, he knows everything there is to know about the people he works with, because that shit is useful in ways you don't even realize, until you do. Greg's affinity for Sister is simply something Jim needs to be aware of. Like Liam's soft spot for the kid. Yeah, he's aware of that, too. But that's fine, it's all good. Henry having an ally of sorts will keep him under control, and Jim knows—when the time comes—not to rely on Liam to do any dirty work.

Jim would take care of that himself.

"I need you guys to come look at something," Pete says, giving the siblings behind him a cursory glance before focusing nervous eyes back on Liam and Jim. "It's beneath the house."

★ ★ ★

Henry wakes up afraid. He stays very still, not wanting to move from the bed, unsure of the danger he senses, of what unseen traps he might set off by sudden movement, or by lowering a grimy-socked foot to the wood floor. He tries to clear his mind, but he feels ... funny. His thoughts are fuzzy. Distorted. Like a TV with bad reception, the picture and sound snowy and choppy from a storm or a bent antenna. He makes an effort to relax, to open himself up and see if he can figure out what's happening.

As the tension releases from his body, his mind calms, and the inner eye opens wide, absorbing the Other like a black sponge.

Swirling black fear like a broiling storm cloud distorts his reception. Henry's antenna is going haywire now ... a cloud jumps with flashes of electricity, pushing against his open eye—BLINK BLINK—the eye tries to see past it, see through it. There's so much fear, *so much* need.

Henry slowly integrates himself with the one he now thinks of as Baby.

The unborn.

Baby is upset, hostile, terrified. Henry closes his physical eyes and allows himself to connect, to plug in, to let Baby's thoughts and feelings become *his* thoughts and feelings.

This is dangerous, son . . .

Henry ignores his father's voice. He's mad at his daddy. Mad because he left Henry alone, didn't answer when he needed him, when he was being kicked and beaten and maybe could have been killed. So he ignores the familiar phantom that lives inside him, that shows him things he never asked to see, and instead focuses all his energy on the *other* specter, the one shifting inside a womb—no, a *cocoon*—down below, in the earth, where no one can see him.

But someone *has* seen.

Someone has seen, and they're coming.

★ ★ ★

Before following Pete out the front door, Jim leaves orders for Greg and Jenny to stay put, watch the front, make sure Henry is secure. Now he, Pete, and Liam stand beside the house, staring down at a pair of cellar doors the idiots hadn't seen when they set up the place, and a window that looks into a small cellar that appears, no doubt about it, to have a dead body stowed deep inside its brick-and-dirt belly.

"God *damn*, Pete," Jim says, not as upset as he probably should be, but still plenty annoyed. Isn't like a dead body is going to interfere with anything, and Jim guesses it's likely some homeless crackhead who probably tucked away down there before they came on the scene, a doper looking for a nice private place to shoot up and die quietly. "I told you to secure the house, brother. Now you're showing me dead bodies and shit."

"I know, man, I know," Pete says, shuffling his feet in the grass. "But me and Jenny, we checked every inch of the house, the big old shed over there, we even went down into the cellar. Hey, tell him, Liam!"

Liam shakes his head in disbelief and shifts his focus from the window to the cellar doors.

"Anyway," Pete continues, licking his lips, "we were talking about it yesterday, you know? The kid said it stunk. And now we know why, right? But I'm telling you, there wasn't any dead guy down there. This must be, I dunno, separated or something."

Jim straightens up, stretches his back until a couple vertebrae pop agreeably. "Only one way to find out," he says, then goes over to the doors to stand with Liam. "Can you open that?"

Liam kneels and grips one of the weathered metal door handles. "Doesn't appear locked." He pulls and the door swings upward with a graceless ease until one of the rusted hinges snaps, sending out a tiny cloud of red dust. Liam lets the door go and it flops over onto the grass with a *whump*.

Jim immediately smells the decay and takes a step back. Something in his guts is screaming up at the red flag receptors in his brain, and he's beginning to worry about this dead body a little bit. Now that he can smell it, get a sense of the reality of the corpse, Jim feels the slightest twinge of nervousness. Of concern.

"Want me to go get one of the flashlights?" Pete asks, and Jim thinks the offer is less to be helpful and more to get the hell away. But the question also pisses him off, because the flashlights, and their batteries, are meant to be saved. To be used as needed for emergencies. Jim doesn't want to find himself running through some damn forest in the middle of the night, trying to escape the police while swinging around a damn camping lantern because all the batteries are dead. "Go get a lantern, man, I told you to save the flashlights. Make it quick."

Pete scuttles off. Liam and Jim exchange a wary glance, then Jim bends and grips the handle of the other door, pulls it up and out. The door belly-flops into the buckwheat, leaving the gaping maw of the stinking cellar's entrance wide and welcoming.

Enticing, almost.

Like a damn mouth, Jim thinks sourly, ignoring the pinging electricity in his nerves that normal people would associate with fear, an emotional response Jim has spent decades building a stalwart tolerance against.

"After you," Liam says, and Jim watches with mild interest as he pulls the gun out of the back of his jeans and holds it loosely at his side.

"You shoot me in the back," Jim says as he steps over the concrete lip and onto the first of the broken steps, the ones leading down into the stinking, musty dark, "and I'll kill your ass."

"Noted," Liam says, and follows him down.

★ ★ ★

Henry sweats into the blankets. He shakes his head jerkily from side to side, eyes closed tight, mouth bent into a snarl of fear. "Stay away . . . stay away . . ." he mumbles breathlessly, and feels a surge of revulsion so intense that—were he in complete control of his consciousness and bodily functions—he might have leaned over the edge of the cot and barfed onto the splinter-riddled floor right then and there.

Because, although his eyes are closed, he can *see* the men. Their writhing colors are dark green snakes: caution and violence. Their features are vague, their bodies nothing but black blurs of shadow against a harsh, hazy white light coming in from the far side of the room. The vision is further distorted by the obstruction of the cocoon itself. To Henry's mind, it's like looking at the world through a black veil, the kind an old widow might wear at her dead husband's funeral.

As Henry sinks deeper into the consciousness of Baby, he begins to pick up on other senses as well. Not directly, but strong enough that his own mind attempts crude translation into human equivalents of smell, taste, touch.

It's as if *Henry* is the one balled up inside the cocoon, surrounded by thick, sticky fluid.

The outside world is so close, but he's still too weak; too frail, his skin too thin, his eyes, lungs, and organs not yet fully developed. Baby's heart beats fast, faster—much faster than a human heart could and survive—and Henry's own heart begins to speed up dangerously, his body beginning to respond to the brainwaves of the thing in the cellar, his breath coming quick and jagged.

As Baby watches the men, it feels ripe, acute *fear*. Ancient instincts broadcast the danger they bring, the deadly nature of their proximity. But Baby feels something else while he watches them come closer, ever closer, to his shelter.

Hunger.

He salivates for their flesh, for the pulsing blood in their veins, the stringy meat of their muscles, the soft, succulent tissue of their guts and organs.

Henry whimpers as these sensations pass into him. He wants to scream, to babble denials, to cry out in terror and revulsion. Were he conscious, he would be repulsed to feel his tongue dart out and slide across his dry lips, to hear his stomach grumble. Like Baby, Henry is hungry.

And the men stepping ever closer will be his next meal.

7

Jim bends at the knees to see the corpse more clearly. He hears Pete clatter down the steps, the flicker of lamplight dancing along the far dark wall as he descends the fractured stairs. The body is set in such a strange way, and so warped by trauma, that Jim has a hard time understanding exactly what has happened to the man in the cellar.

The man's head, Jim reflects, looks like someone had stuck a grenade in his mouth and pulled the pin. Except the walls aren't splattered floor to ceiling, the way they would be, if his head had, for sake of argument, exploded.

An axe, maybe. Swung down by someone strong—strong as me, I'd wager, to bust it open deep down like that, to the chin. Clean stroke, baby. That's a clean stroke.

The corpse's arms are spread wide to either side, hands stuck against the wall with glue or cement. The hands that look distorted, like they'd been blowtorched, melted to whatever the epoxy adhesive is. Hard to say without touching him, and Jim isn't there yet.

Both legs have been badly broken. His knees likely shattered with a sledgehammer or something equally powerful, the way they are bent. *All askew like that? Fuckin' ragman.*

"Ah, gross, it smells like shit and sex down here. Jim, I got the lant— sweet Jesus! Look at that fucking guy!" Pete says as he descends to the dirt floor. "That's a torture deal, I bet. Someone secured his hands there, then cracked up his legs real good. Once they had their info or whatever. Hey, Jim, what could do that? Shotgun in the mouth?"

Jim stands, nods thoughtfully. *Maybe. Sawed-off stuck up in there good could do that . . . interesting. Very interesting.*

He turns to find Liam running a hand along a brick wall separating the small cellar space they stand in and the rest of the open area beneath the house, and now that the room is fully lit by the incoming sunlight and Pete's lantern, it's easy to spot why the body hadn't been discovered on Pete and Jenny's first pass through the house.

They'd come down from the kitchen, from the inside. From the other *side of that wall. There are probably a few more that run the length of the house to support the crossbeams.*

Jim takes the lantern from Pete and holds it up high, studies the ceiling.

"I'm surprised this whole damn place hasn't collapsed," he says, eyeing the decayed wood of the thick beams that run beneath the floor above. "These brick walls are for shit, the posts are rusted, the support beams rotten. I guess that's why it's condemned, huh? Still as good a place as any to murder some dumb bast—"

Jim stops abruptly. He squints into the dark shadows stuck to the low ceiling.

"The hell?"

Wedged high into the furthest, darkest corner of the room is a long, thick, cylindrical mass, seemingly made from black dirt, leaves, and other debris. Jim approaches it slowly, letting the orange flickering light of the lantern illuminate its entire length. "What the fuck is that?"

The strange object, nearly four feet long, sags slightly, but seems nonetheless solid. Purposeful.

The lantern light glistens against its shell, and Jim clearly sees the moist conglomeration of leaves, paper, mud, and thick, gray paste the object is made of. *That's the shit on the dead dude's hands,* he thinks, and feels the unfamiliar tingle of worry tickle the back of his neck.

There's a *drip-drip-drip* of black liquid slipping from its surface, dropping down to form a growing, inky puddle in the dirt below.

That's a goddamn cocoon, he thinks. *Or a nest, maybe.*

And I'll be damned if there isn't something moving *inside there.*

Liam comes closer to stand beside Jim, as does Pete. They all stop a few feet away from the thing, studying it as if it's an old, dusty bomb that has miraculously never gone off. Interesting, sure, but in all likelihood extremely dangerous.

Possibly even deadly.

"I just realized what's been bothering me about this whole scene," Liam says absently, his eyes traveling the length of the fat, mud-packed shape.

"There's whole buckets of shit wrong with this scene," Jim says.

"Yeah," Liam agrees, looking around. "But that body's been here, what? At least three days, right? Whatever happened here, it was *before* Pete and Jenny arrived on Wednesday."

"So?"

Pete waves a hand at the meaty, pungent corpse. "So where are the flies? The air should be thick with them. That head should be crawling with maggots, maybe worms and other bugs."

"Christ, Liam," Pete says disgustedly.

"Well, it's weird, innit? Fucking strange."

"Yeah, well. Add it to the list," Jim says. "What do you think about this thing?"

"Looks like a bug nest," Liam says. "Jim, we should get out of here, seal those doors and forget about all this mess. We'll be gone in a couple days."

Pete studies the floor, then picks up a long, gnarled stick trampled into the dirt. He waves it at the corpse like a wooden sword. "If it's a bug nest, it wouldn't be dripping like that," he says. "Let's give it a poke and see what comes out."

"Pete, you're ten kinds of stupid," Jim says, but stands his ground, watching curiously despite himself.

Liam backs toward the stairs, ready to bolt at the first sign of a hornet, wasp, or whatever the hell has built that massive nest. "You guys are both crazy," he says, and Jim chuckles. "Pete," Liam says cautiously, but Pete only scowls and steps closer to the strange object.

"Chill, amigo," Pete says and, having reached poking distance, lifts the branch slowly, extending the tip toward the mass stuck above his head, nestled between a wooden crossbeam and the heavy rock and concrete of the cellar's outermost wall.

"Touché, motherfucker."

Pete jabs the thin stick into the cocoon with a quick thrust. It sinks in smoothly and black treacle pools at the incision, spills over the stick. When Pete pulls it free, the tar-like liquid leaks from the newly formed hole like blood.

Pete turns back to the others, grinning that gold-toothed grin. He's about to speak when they all hear the scream—a bloodcurdling screech of pain, and terror.

The cry—the long, anguished shriek of a child—filters down through the floor above them, filling the small underground cell.

All three men look at each other in surprise.

"That was Henry," Liam says, and sprints up the chipped concrete stairs, into the light.

8

As Liam slams through the front door of the abandoned farmhouse, sprinting toward the stairs while Henry bellows bloody murder from his locked room, Jay Munoz, the longtime mailman of Dave and Mary Thorne, has just delivered Mrs. Krubel's usual mid-December packet of year-end bills along with a holiday card from her daughter in Florida, the receipt of which delights her (as she has told him repeatedly over the last decade), because it always includes an updated photograph of her grandchildren who she never sees (due to the high cost of travel these days) but it is so nice to see them growing up, don't you think?

And now Jay the mailman leaves Mrs. Krubel's front porch and heads, whistling as he goes, for the Thorne home.

The last couple days he's made a point not to dawdle, what with all the police cars and press beginning to creep in. The last thing he wants is to interfere with what those poor folks are dealing with. Still, as he digs into his satchel and pulls out a rubber band-bound packet of letters, he is a little surprised to be stopped on the sidewalk by a tired-looking guy in a dark gray suit, his hand flashing an open wallet that shows a reflective white badge: FBI.

"I'll take the mail," the FBI agent says, and Jay—after only the briefest of hesitations—hands the packet over. "Thanks," the agent says, and turns up the walk toward the front door, where two police officers have been stationed, seemingly day and night. At least, they've been there every time he's come around.

Jay watches the agent walk away (head bowed as he peruses the letters Jay has delivered) and wonders if there is any news on the kid's abduction. He hates to think it, but part of him is beginning to wonder if he'll be delivering sympathy cards to this house sooner than later, stuffing outgoing funeral announcements into his satchel on their way to friends and family. God, he hopes not.

Jay has decided that bothering the agent with questions is a bad idea—and is already fishing into his satchel for the next packet to drop at the Snellman residence next door—when the FBI agent stops in his tracks so abruptly the officers on the porch look momentarily alarmed.

Jay watches, stupefied, as the agent rushes into the Thorne home, saying something Jay can't hear to the two officers as he goes by. He pushes open the door and yells out in an urgent voice, then slams the door shut behind him.

Curious, but also a little freaked out by the bizarre intensity of the agent's reaction, Jay decides it's best if he continues on his way toward the Snellmans.

He's gone two steps when one of the officers on the porch yells for him to stop. Insanely, Jay has the instinctual thought to *run*, for no good reason other than someone who looks anxious and a little pissed off (and wearing a gun on his hip) is coming straight for him.

Quickly.

Of course, he doesn't run (that would be crazy) but instead waits, with what he hopes is a look of patience beneath his jittery nerves, for the officer to catch up with him on the sidewalk.

"I'm gonna need the name and phone number of your supervisor," the big cop says, already pulling a small notebook from his chest pocket. "And I'm gonna need to confiscate your mailbag."

Obligingly, Jay sets his bag on the ground and gives the officer the information. When a second officer comes over to scoop the bag up and carry it away, Jay realizes that the Snellmans, and everyone else on Graham Avenue, are going to have a long wait for today's mail.

9

Liam takes the stairs two at a time. Henry's screams have not relented. If anything, they're increasing in volume and hysteria. When he notices the bedroom door standing open at the end of the hallway, he fears the worst.

Greg and Jenny are killing him. They've gone crazy and are in there right now, Greg holding him down while Jenny plunges that ice pick of hers into his belly, again and again.

Liam hears pounding feet behind him and knows Jim is following close behind—albeit for reasons different than Liam. Whereas Liam is genuinely concerned for the boy's well-being, he knows Jim's biggest fear is less concerning Henry's health and more that Henry is still intact. Would be pretty tricky to negotiate a ransom if the kid is butchered.

When he reaches the open door and looks inside—*my God there's blood everywhere! On the walls, on the floor; and there's Henry, dead and mutilated, Greg and Jenny covered in the boy's guts*—Jenny stands in the corner, eyes full of fear, her ice pick nowhere in sight. Greg kneels next to the cot, holding Henry's arms as he screams and screams. Greg is also screaming things like "Shut up, kid!" and "Henry, what the hell is wrong?!" and "Henry *god damn it!*"

As Liam hurries across the room, Greg turns his head toward him. His face is pale, his eyes wide. "I don't know what the hell's wrong with him!" he yells over Henry's throat-tearing shrieks. "We were downstairs when he just started screaming, I swear to God!"

"Move," Liam says, and Greg shifts aside.

Liam grabs Henry's face in his hands, peels open his eyelids to reveal blank whites.

For the second time in as many days, Liam cocks his hand and slaps Henry hard across the face. The screams stop as if they'd been controlled by electricity and Liam just jerked the plug from the socket.

Henry is panting, sweating. Embarrassed for the kid, Liam notices he's wet his pants. *And isn't that just great—I suppose a run to Kmart for new clothes is out of the question, hey Jim?*

"Henry? Talk to me, say something, come on."

No one in the room speaks, although Liam can sense the hair-trigger nerves of the entire crew standing around him in the room, watching him, watching Henry.

"Coming . . ." Henry mumbles, drool running down the corner of his mouth. "Coming coming coming . . . she's coming . . . she's coming to . . ."

"Who's coming?" Jim says abruptly from behind Liam's shoulder. "What the hell is he talking about?"

"I think he's just, I don't know, hysterical or something." Liam says, his eyes not leaving Henry's face. "Yesterday, before you came, he had a fit, of sorts."

"Fit? What are you talking about, man?"

"Like a seizure."

Pete said from the doorway, "That's true, Jim. I even tried to get him one of my pills. One second he was just sitting there, the next second he's jerking around like he'd been hit with high voltage."

"I been watching this kid close up for months," Jim says evenly. "Ain't never seen something like that."

Jim thinks it's an act, Liam realizes. But to what end? So he can piss his pants and scare the shit out of everyone? Henry is no fool—he knows there wouldn't be any emergency room runs on his behalf. They'd let him die first, and the kid knows that. So why play games?

No, this is something else. Something's up, and it isn't good.

"Henry? Can you wake up?" Liam says. His hands rest gently on Henry's chest and shoulder, trying to will the kid to snap out of it.

"She's coming," Henry mumbles, but more quietly now, his voice a steady whisper. "You need to leave, you need to leave . . . she wants you out, wants all of us . . . *OUT.*"

Liam starts to ask what he's talking about when Henry's eyes open. They're clear and focused. His breathing has slowed and Liam, with one hand resting on Henry's thin chest, can feel the beating of his heart shifting back to a regular, normal rhythm. Liam lets out a breath he didn't realize he'd been holding, feels relief rush through him. He's surprised at the severity of it.

Take it easy, mate. Don't get attached—he's just cash, nothing more, nothing less.

"Henry," he says. "You okay? What the hell happened?"

Henry's eyes flick from Liam to Jim, standing behind him. He looks over at Jenny and Greg across the room, sees Pete standing by the door.

"You have to leave this house," Henry says.

Jim laughs and Liam stands, takes a step away from the cot. Henry sits up, studies his wet crotch, and Liam hears him sigh heavily. That old man sigh of his that's just a little bit heartbreaking.

"What's he talking about?" Pete asks, but Greg and Jenny are already heading for the door. The boy isn't dead and he hasn't escaped. Case closed.

"Nothing," Liam says, but without conviction. "He had a crazy dream or something."

But Henry is shaking his head. He looks up and meets Liam's eyes. "If you don't leave, something real bad is going to happen. That's all I know."

Jim takes a threatening step closer to Henry's cot, but Henry is either too exhausted or too stupid to care. "Tell you what, little man. You pull another stunt like this, or have another seizure or whatever the hell it is you're playing at, and we'll leave the house, alright. We'll leave, and leave you behind in a plastic bag, buried in the fucking cellar." Jim lowers himself so his face is even with Henry's own. "When they bring me that money, they won't know whether you're alive or dead. And by the time they find your bones, we'll all be long gone. We clear?"

Henry lowers his head. "I was trying to explain," he mumbles, like a pouty child, but then shrugs. "You'll find out, I guess."

Jim straightens and heads for the door. "Whatever, dude. Just keep your shit straight for another couple days and we're good."

Pete follows Jim down the hall, and Liam waits until he hears them on the steps. "I'll bring you something to clean your pants with," he says. "Some soap and water, okay?"

Henry says nothing. His legs swing slowly over the edge of the cot, his focus on the top of his filthy socks.

"You want to tell me what all that was about?"

Henry thinks about this a moment. "I don't think so."

"You said something was coming, that we had to leave. Tell me what you meant by that. I'll—" Liam pauses, debating the wisdom of the words, then continues. "I'll keep it between us."

Henry looks at him then, a look that makes Liam's skin crawl, the one that feels like Henry's inside his head, flipping through his brain like a Rolodex.

Seemingly satisfied, Henry nods. His eyes flick to the door, then back to Liam. He speaks quietly. "That thing you found? In the cellar?"

How could he know about that?

Then he remembers Henry's strange abilities. *Is it real? And if it is, how fucked up is that?*

"What about it?" he says, leaving the rest unspoken.

"It has a mama," Henry says. "I call the little one Baby and the other one Mother. But they're not really that . . . it's just easier to think of them that way. For humans, I mean."

"For humans?" Liam says, wanting to smirk, to laugh this all off. He finds a chill running up his spine instead.

"She doesn't want us here," Henry continues. "She wants us to leave . . . so that the thing you found is safe. Safe from us, from you, the others."

Liam thinks about this a moment. Recalls the cocoon-like shape of the thing. Suddenly he's curious to know what, exactly, is inside that shell.

Or is he being played? The kid is smart, and he has some freakish abilities.

I mean . . . doesn't he?

Liam is no longer certain about what he knows or doesn't know. About what he believes. How can any of this be possible? And why the hell is he standing here listening to this kid talk about . . . what? Monsters in the cellar? Some angry mother in the woods? What is this shit?

Pull it together, man. You're cracking up and it's gonna get you killed. You realize that, don't you?

"Okay Henry," Liam says. "Okay. Just relax, all right? This will all be over soon."

As Liam heads for the door, Henry mumbles from behind him.

"Just not the way you think," he says quietly, and lies down on the dirty, urine-stained mattress.

Liam closes the door, resolved to find the boy some soap and water, pushing the nagging questions plaguing his mind aside for the moment. As he heads down the stairs he can't help wondering which of the people in this madhouse is the batshit craziest.

Right now, his money's on the kid.

With himself a tight second.

10

Jim waits until Liam returns before pulling everyone together outside. He wants to be out of earshot of Henry, and truth be told the house stinks and he fucking hates it. Claustrophobic as hell in there.

You don't gotta retire here, Jim, you just gotta hide out for a bit. Get a grip, brother.

When everyone is outside, Jenny smoking and Pete looking at the trees like they're hiding goblins and ghouls, Jim lays it all out.

"We're in the last phase, okay? They got the letter by now. Greg and Jenny, you do your thing this afternoon, be back here by dark. Pete, I want you and Liam to drag that corpse out of the cellar—"

"What? Oh come on, Jim!" Pete protests.

At least I got his eyes off the damn trees. Motherfucker is beginning to freak me out.

"—and bury it in the woods somewhere. Bury it deep. I don't want some wild dog dragging a thighbone outta the dirt and dropping it at Ranger Rick's feet."

"I saw a couple rusted shovels in the shed," Liam says. "We should be good."

"Cool," Jim says. "I'll stay in the house and keep an eye on Henry while you all are busy. I think I've done enough bullshit to last me a lifetime. Tomorrow, me, Liam, and Greg will go to the drop. We know how to get in and out without being spotted, so we stick to the plan and it's all good. Pete, once we're all out, you dummy-check the house, the grounds, the garage. Then you burn the fucker like we talked about."

"Yeah yeah, no problem," Pete says, his face brightening at the prospect. "This place will burn like a preacher in hell. I'm sorta surprised it hasn't burned to the ground already."

Jim nods. "Then you and Jenny split. Meet us down south at Grandma's ranch in Rosario."

"Shit man, back to Mexico." Pete says, grinning, the ghouls and goblins temporarily forgotten. "Who'd have thought it? Sure, it's paradise for you creeps. For me it's a goddamn family reunion. And get this, I'm the successful one!"

Greg sniggers and Jim notices even his crazy bitch sister is smiling a little. *Good, I want you all nice and relaxed. That way no one panics, no one messes up. In two days, it's huevos rancheros in the morning and tequila at night, then it's adios muchachos and you assholes will never see me again.*

Jim is feeling pretty good himself. He's thinking about the small house he's already rented in Barra de Potosi where he'll lie low for a few years, enjoy life, get away.

"And the kid gets dumped where?"

Jim's good feelings evaporate, blown away into the air like wispy smoke off a dying fire. Liam looks from one face to the other, Greg looks at his feet, and Jenny looks at Liam with a quizzical look Jim doesn't much care for; it's the kind of look he usually gives someone when he's trying to figure out how to kill him.

Pete laughs.

"Don't worry, Liam," Pete says, still grinning. "The kid gets let go, like we talked about. I ain't gonna burn the little dude. What, you think I'm gonna lock him in his room when I blaze the place? Come on, man. I'm sick but I ain't that sick."

Liam says nothing, turns to Jim. "We talked about dropping him at a main road. So he could walk out. Find a way out."

"Shit, dude," Jim says and points to the small fire road at the edge of the trees, the one so thick with overgrowth only low-riding cars can get through. "That's the road right there. Pete will give him an apple or whatever and tell him to scoot, like we said before. Then he torches the place and hightails it out. No problem. Cool?"

Liam tilts his head, as if trapping a stray thought, squeezing it tight between his ear and shoulder. "No, I don't think that's right."

Jim's face hardens, and suddenly there are no smiles, no wisecracks. Even the forest seems to go silent with tension. "What's the problem, son?" Jim says, the affability drained from his voice, nothing left but threat.

"If Pete lets the boy go, he'll start running. I'm supposed to believe Pete's gonna give Henry a head start like that? What, *then* he burns the place? That could be fifteen, twenty minutes. No, Pete would never do that. He'd rather let the kid fry."

"Hey, man!" Pete protests, but Jim holds up a hand, silencing him.

"Look. We discussed this. We all"—Jim looks each of them in the eyes—"discussed this. It's the same plan we drew up from Day One. No changes. No ad-libs."

"No?" Liam says, and takes a step closer to Jim. "Greg tells me the bartender was missing when he got there. Says maybe you tucked the chap away to rot in your apartment. That man, he was a friend of yours, I think. He was an old buddy, am I right? My question, then, is this: Was killing that bastard part of the plan? Or were you just—how did you say it? Ad-libbing?"

Jim takes a deep breath and forces himself not to look at Greg—that would scream guilt when right now all he wants to show is cool. Still . . .

Fucking. Greg.

Jim breathes in and out through his nose, squints at the sky, works hard to keep himself calm. To keep himself under control. He does not like the way Liam is talking to him. He especially does not like the way he is talking to him in front of the others.

No no no, my Aussie friend. This won't do. This won't do at all.

"Tell you what, Liam. You and me got history, we've done some good jobs and you always had my back, so I'm gonna let this sand run out, understood? I'm gonna let this go. I'm gonna let this *drop*. I told you what's gonna happen, and that's what's gonna happen. If it makes you feel better, the last thing I need on my ass is a bunch of cops and FBI bastards tracking down a child-killer. Bad press, if a child-killer gets away. I don't want that heat, okay? *We* don't want that heat. Makes things hard. Disrupts the plan."

Jim sneaks a peek at Greg, praying the idiot never went up to the apartment, never saw the *second* body he'd dumped there. *That's what happens when I'm rushed, I get stupid and sloppy. And now my own man is pressing me. Bunch of bullshit, what this is. All of it.*

Greg looks dazed and guilty, but not complicit. Not like he's holding back another man's lie. *Naw, he never went up there. He'd be gawping and staring at me with wide old doe eyes right now if he had. Dude's about as subtle as fireworks on the Fourth of July.*

"For all our sakes," Jim continues, "the boy gets cut free, like we discussed. He gets back safe, now we're nothing but thieves, dig? No dead kids in the newspaper. No manhunt. That's the way we want it, the way *I* want it. In two days I want to be yesterday's news, you copy?"

Liam studies Jim a moment, and Jim badly wants to punch that dumb Aussie motherfucker right in the mouth. To knock his teeth in and bloody up that pretty nose, hell yeah. Bust his head in like a piñata, leave his white man's flesh to the birds.

"Okay," Liam says and lets loose a brilliant, disarming smile. "You're right. I'm sorry. I'm . . . I'm a little tense, with the body and the kid having fits. I'm on edge. Apologies, boss."

Jim smiles as well, his thoughts of violence slipping away like distant memories easily forgotten. "All right then, so we're cool."

Liam nods. "As ice."

★ ★ ★

Henry sits on the cot in the locked bedroom.

He's removed his T-shirt, suddenly hating the feel of fabric on his skin. His shoes are on the floor, tossed carelessly along with the shirt.

The air is frigid and still; there is no breeze, no ventilation. The room smells like urine. Henry's pants and part of a blanket are damp with it, and the stink mixes with the ripe smell of preadolescent sweat and filth from two days of not showering. He sits with his bared lower back against the cold, coarse wall, feet dangling over the edge of the cot. He rocks slightly, clutching his bare elbows in the opposite palms, pressing his arms against the small bulge of his stomach.

"You don't think I see you but I see you," he whispers. "You don't think I see you but I do yes I do." His eyes are closed. His breath comes fast and ragged, his chest expanding and sinking like a frightened animal.

In his mind's eye he sees what *she* sees.

His view is from high above them, a short distance from where they all stand in a circle, talking, branches and leaves obstructing his clear view, but he can see them regardless. He hears them talking, their words not decipherable, just broken murmurs on the wind mixing with the paper chimes of leaves in the surrounding tree. The tree where she hides, and watches.

Henry can read her mind because she allows it. Because she has welcomed him and—in a way only a mother can—taken him into her care. But her child is also in danger. Grave danger.

He senses the power within her, the blinding power of her mind, the forces of the earth she's tapped into, that are hers to control.

Her and others like her.

The ones who wait in the dark beneath the cities and the people and the stink of humanity, the poison of man.

In his room, shirtless and cold, stinking and hungry and exhausted and terrified, Henry sees all this.

He knows what's coming.

His hitching breath slows, his heart rate steadies.

And he smiles.

II

Dave and Mary are forced to read the letter while it is held up by one of the latex-gloved forensic techs. Mary takes one look at the scrawled handwriting slanting across a torn sheet of grade-school notebook paper and runs to the bathroom, vomiting up the tiny amount of breakfast she'd been able to get down earlier that morning.

> THORNE FAMILY,
>
> We have your son.
>
> He is alive and unharmed.
>
> You will pay us two million DOLLARS in cash—small denominations, no bills over $50—to a spot which will be revealed in a future correspondence.
>
> If the cash is not dropped at the exact time and exact place we tell you, Henry will be killed, his body destroyed, and you will never hear from us again. You will never see the boy again. All of us ghosts. All of us gone forever.
>
> GOOD NEWS! We will release Henry once we are certain the FBI has not tampered with the money in ANY way. We can test this very easily and know their procedures.
>
> TELL THEM NOT TO DO THIS OR YOUR SON DIES.
>
> DO NOT FUCK WITH US OR YOUR SON DIES.
>
> DO NOT BE LATE, DO NOT MISS THE DROP, DO NOTHING TO INTERFERE WITH OUR RECIEPT OF THE MONEY OR YOUR SON DIES.
>
> You will hear from us soon.
>
> God Bless.

"Why are they making us wait?" Dave asks, sitting down and trying to control the tremble in his hands.

"Because they don't want us having too much advance notice of the drop area," Sali says, nodding to the forensic tech, who begins packing up the letter for further testing. "They think they're being smart, but it's actually stupid. Now they'll need to contact you again, which gives us even more to work from in trying to find out who they are and where they are."

Dave is concerned because he can't feel his feet, his hands, his heartbeat. He is literally numb and he wonders if this is a condition of mild shock. He puts a hand to his forehead and is surprised at the amount of sweat on his skin.

"Dave?" Sali asks, concern etched in his face. "You okay?"

"I can't—" Dave starts, then takes a deep breath, lets it out. "Can I get some water? I . . . I don't think I can get up right now."

"Of course. The medic is checking on your wife. She's okay. Just upset. Hold on."

As Sali steps away, Dave watches the forensics team put baggies into a file box. One of the clear baggies holds the letter, the other secures the envelope it came with. He's pretty sure they confiscated the mailman's bag, which he feels badly about. He doesn't want anyone else to suffer, and being close to the holidays—

"Dave?"

Dave looks up, startled. *How much time has passed? Seems like seconds.* Sali holds a glass of water in one hand and a small white pill in the other. "Oh," Dave says, willing his mind into motion once again. Willing his hands to stop trembling, for the feeling in his extremities to return. He wants to feel his heartbeat.

"Drink this, and take this. Please," the agent says, eyes pleading.

"Will it knock me out or—"

"No sir," Sali says. "Sadly, I need you awake. I need your help. Mary's, too. It's just a mild sedative."

Dave plucks the pill from his palm, swallows it with the cold water, which tastes like heaven.

"I need to talk to you and Mary, okay? I need to catch you up on some things. Some potentially *good* things, okay?"

"Yes," Dave says, feeling a little better. "Where's Mary?"

"I think she's lying down for a bit, but I'm afraid this can't wait. Why don't we go talk in the bedroom?"

Dave allows Sali to help him stand. He feels a hundred years old—his muscles weak, his bones frail, his mind polluted with age, deadened by a life of taxation.

In the bedroom, Mary sits on the bed while a medic takes her blood pressure. She looks up and gives him a weak smile, and Dave's frail muscles flood with strength, his clouded mind blows clear, and he steps quickly to his wife to embrace her.

They cry for a few minutes and at some point the medic must have removed the arm band from Mary and left the room, because when Dave is able to let go of his wife and control his tears there is no one there but Agent Espinoza, calmly holding out a tissue box.

Dave and Mary both pull a few tissues, and Mary excuses herself to the bathroom.

Making sure she doesn't look a mess, he knows, and it makes him glad she's still thinking of herself. He thinks it's a positive sign and he forces himself to wipe away any stray tears or snot, to take a deep breath and organize his thoughts. Blubbering in the back bedroom isn't going to help Henry. They need to be on their toes, to think clearly. To help as best they are able.

When Mary comes back, she does look better, and Dave smiles at her reassuringly. He is relieved beyond measure when she offers a small smile in return.

Gonna get through this. Gonna get through this, Lord. See if we don't!

"Sali says he has some news," Dave starts, then quickly adds: "Good news, maybe. Isn't that right, Sali?"

The FBI agent nods. "I want to keep you guys updated, both for your own personal solace and in case anything I tell you spurs a thought, or an idea, okay?"

Mary sits next to Dave and they look at him like expectant children, hoping whatever this man is about to tell them doesn't hurt too badly.

"First things first. We think we found the van that was used to abduct Henry from the school."

"Oh my God," Mary says, and clutches Dave's hand.

Sali continues, "The moment we received the ransom letter we got a location on the post office it touched first, okay? That was in Riverside, real close to here, a couple hours north. So, we know when Henry was taken and the time, we know approximately when and where the ransom letter was dropped, give or take a few hours. We figured they'd ditch the van, swap cars. This time it was a hunch. Long-term parking lots are our first thought. But storage centers are in the mix. It's usually not a private residence, because if we make a hit on associations of the perp, we can narrow down stuff like that. We also know, thanks to street cameras, that there was a 1979 brown Chevy Duster in the parking lot of the bar where the perp was living. Probably belonged to an accomplice. Okay, I'm rambling. Point is this: We put out a notice to all the parking garages and storage facilities in the *area where the van was heading.* And since we knew the timing, we narrowed down possibilities pretty good. So, who had a white van come *in* and a brown Duster go *out* between this time and that time? See? Boom, less than an hour ago we get a hit."

"Then you know where they are?" Mary asks, and Sali shakes his head.

"No, ma'am. But we know a hell of a lot. We know where they *were*. We now have a limited radius of where they could be holding Henry, you understand? But that's not the good news."

"What's the good news, Sali? Please," Dave says, trying to keep the tremor from his voice. Mary squeezes his hand urgently.

Sali begins to pace. He can't hide his thrill at things coming into focus, and Dave is *loving* it, taking it into his heart like a sweet song that lets him think that maybe—just maybe—things will turn out okay.

"These storage places have cameras," Sali says as if ticking off boxes in his mind. "They see everyone that goes in and out. They also photograph license plates. We already know the janitor, Jim Cady—aka Fred Hinnom—is the main perp. But now we also know who was driving the van, a known accomplice of Cady's. We have APBs on the Duster, Jim, and this other guy, whose name is Greg Lanigan. Even better? Lanigan has a sister who is no good, believe me. When we go to question her, guess what?"

Mary speaks first. "She's gone."

"Into the wind. Landlord says she took off about a week ago and he hasn't seen her since. He lets us into her place: empty. No furniture, no personal things. All gone. She's vanished. Regardless of whether she's involved, we absolutely want to bring her in for questioning. Now we have multiple leads to work toward, which is good news, because the more we know about this crew, the easier they'll be to find. We also know they're most likely still local, no more than a few hours from Henry's school, either inside the city or just outside it. So close, close enough that I've already got HRT standing by—"

"HRT?" Dave asks, feeling that contagious adrenaline, letting himself go with it, letting himself *believe*.

"Shit, sorry. A new unit the FBI has developed. HRT stands for Hostage Rescue Team. These guys are total badasses. Think Navy Seal-types. I mean, they're pretty much the FBI's Delta Force. Once I call them in, once we have a location, they'll be wheels up within minutes from any military base where they have men currently stationed at and be on the ground here in SoCal within a couple hours."

"That fast?" Mary says, curious despite herself.

"Yes ma'am, they can be anywhere in the country within a few hours. These guys do not mess around, and even though they're new to the FBI, the teams we use have a good track record, believe me. It is quite literally a military operation. Once they have a target, they move quick and sure. They'll deal with these people who took your boy, and they'll get Henry back.

"Oh, and the best part? In about three hours, the three perpetrators we know about are going to have their faces all over the five o'clock news."

Sali allows himself a small smile, his first in days. "It's time to turn on the lights and watch the cockroaches scatter."

Greg opens the large, shed doors. The Duster is on the right, shined up and ready to bolt like a caged animal. Unfortunately, it is also most likely hot as hell by now, and Jim is not about to let it out of the shed until it's time to make for the border. Greg shifts his gaze to the left and sighs. Jenny's puke-green Pinto wagon lurches there like a dead cricket stuck to a log. Greg gave it a tune-up before she'd driven it out here, and new tires with not one but two spares in the rear hold. He knows it will run, but that's pretty much all it'll do. The damn thing will hack and spit its way through these dirt roads, never hit fifty on the freeways, and, if they were lucky, not snap their backs like twigs with every bump its sad, shot suspension bounces over. He is an idiot, he knows, for letting her bring it up here in the first place. But the damned thing only has to make one short ten-mile trip, and then they can bring it back here, shoot it in the radiator, and leave it for dead.

Or better yet burn the damn thing along with the rest of this godforsaken place.

"You gonna look at her all day?" Jenny purrs from behind him, palming one butt cheek through his soiled khaki pants. "Or are you gonna get inside?"

Despite himself, Greg smiles. Jenny can always put a bug in his blood (not to mention a jolt in his cock). He turns around, shoots a quick look toward the house, and pulls her deep into the shade of the large shed. He brings her in tight and kisses her, hands sliding up her back, under the thin sweater and the somewhat sweat-moistened tank top she wears beneath. She pushes him away with a smile when one of his hand lowers to her hip, his fingertips resting lightly on the nub of the ice pick she always has sheathed there. "Easy, tiger," she says. "We got work to do."

"Yeah, yeah. I was just thinking I should have never let you drive out here in that little piece of shit."

"It'll be fine baby, I'll go real slow over all those nasty bumps," she says, grabbing his ass one more time and squeezing.

"Good lord but you're saucy," he says, pulling the second shed door open wide so the Pinto can roll out.

Pete stands behind the door, grinning wide.

"Shit!" Jenny yells. "Jesus, man."

Pete holds an armful of assorted, mostly rusted tools: two shovels, a scythe, and a long-handled axe.

"What the hell, Pete?" Greg asks. "Scared the shit out of us."

Pete's smile never wavers as he steps into the light. "Thought if I stayed hidden a bit longer I might get me a show." He sighs dramatically. "Ah well, I still have my imagination."

"You're disgusting," Jenny says apathetically, not really giving a damn who knows about her and her brother. *None of their damn business, anyway.* "What's with the tools? Making a garden?"

Pete's smile fades, partly at the memory of what lies in front of him, partly at her lack of annoyance at his spying on their conversation. "I gotta go bury a fucking body, don't I? And with what? A couple rusty shovels and whatever this thing is." Pete pulls the scythe free and drops it into the grass.

"What's with the axe?" Greg asks as Pete steps past them with his bundle of tools, making his way toward the house, and the cellar.

"Here, take it," Pete says, turning around. "Throw it back in there. You never know when we might need to chop some wood."

Greg grabs the axe off the pile of tools in Pete's arms, hefts it as Pete wanders off, whistling an unrecognizable tune.

Greg looks at Jenny and smiles. "You wanna chop some wood, sis?"

Jenny laughs as Greg tosses the axe into the weeds next to the shed. "Just wait for me out here and I'll bring it out. No room for you in this shitbox," she says.

Greg winces at the wrenching sound the door makes as Jenny climbs into the small car. The whine of its engine grates on him and his jaw clenches, but it rolls out smoothly enough and the new tires look good and fat, so he figures maybe it will be okay after all.

She stops and he climbs in the passenger side, pulls a pair of cheap sunglasses from his shirt pocket and puts them on, shoves the Padres hat lower over his forehead, and slouches a bit, hoping folks might take him for a teenager. Of course, the moustache will ruin the illusion to a degree, but he wouldn't shave it off for the world, and certainly not for Jim Cady.

Jenny likes the tickle of it too much, for one.

"You got the package, girl?"

Jenny unclips the faux-leather white purse she'd set on the seat between them. Greg looks in and sees the clear freezer baggie and the yellow office envelope folded within. "Did the kid give you shit about the photo?"

Jenny closes her purse and puts the Pinto in drive. "Hell no, he was asleep. Little bastard. I hope Jim kills that kid. I don't like the idea of him having seen all of us."

Greg feels a chill at the careless way his sister discusses such things, as he always does when she nonchalantly mentions killing this person or robbing that store or stealing a thing, as if she were mentioning a shade of blue in the sky or an interesting news item from a magazine. "Well, honey, I got news for you. If the FBI don't know who we are by now, they're gonna know soon enough. Jim blew the interview with a fed and he's been leaving more bodies lying around than a mortician. At this point, it's a smash-n-grab kinda deal. We get that cash and we haul ass to the border."

"Then it's mojitos and sunshine, right?" Jenny says giddily, and Greg wonders how long the novelty of Mexico will last for his sister. Soon enough she'll want back into the States, and he, of course, will let her talk him into it.

Well, we get caught, we get caught. C'est la vie and all that shit.

But that was the thing with Jenny. No matter how bad, or how *dumb*, the shit was they did together, they had never, ever been caught. The only time Greg had gone to prison was for a job with Jim that Jenny had been cut out of, and look where that had gotten him.

He grins, puts a hand at the plump intersection of her thigh and crotch and gives a squeeze. She squeals and slaps him playfully on the hand.

"You know what you are, Jenny? You're my good luck charm."

"Don't forget it, baby," she says, and the interior of the car falls into shadow as it passes beneath the canopy of the woods and begins bouncing its way down the fire road.

Greg turns and looks behind him, sees the farmhouse drifting further and further away, and feels a sudden elation at being gone from it.

Maybe we should just keep going, her and me. Head for the border now. *Get out of all this mess. Come on, man, you can feel it, right? This whole thing feels* bad. *Feels like a puddle you step in thinking you're gonna wet your shoe and next thing you know half your leg is underwater. Not to mention that kid gives me the grade-A heebie-jeebies.*

Turning back around, he looks out his window toward the deep woods, at the passing trees, the broken, slanted sunlight. He squints and thinks, for a moment, that he sees his dead father lying in the distant mud, a hole in his neck spurting blood with the final pumps of his dying black heart. And there's him and Jenny, standing side by side, watching him die. Jenny holding the ice pick in her hand, still covered in blood.

"He was gonna kill you," she'd said, and he hadn't disagreed.

At the ripe, hormone-pumping age of sixteen (only a few minutes separating them in age—she the elder and Greg being what she liked referring to as the "leftover squirt" of her own mighty birth), their father had found them doing it in the woods—similar to the forest surrounding them now—behind their house in Topanga. Their father was what the kids today might call a Real Piece of Shit, and ever since their mother had died giving birth (Greg blames Jenny for this as well, but in a teasing sort of way), Dad had been one serious asshole to the both of them.

He was a religious man, but more the Old Testament variety. Liked to yell and scream about blacks and Hispanics and, worst of all, the homosexuals. Those were the guys and gals that got his knickers in a twist, and there was a lot of fire-and-brimstone sermonizing in their small cabin home during Greg and Jenny's formative years.

Of course, the man had no one to blame but himself for what went on between his twin children. For one thing, he made them share a bedroom, right up through their teenage years, and if a man didn't know what twelve- and thirteen-year-olds were thinking about when they lay in bed at night, then a man didn't know much at all, did he? Hell, Jenny gave Greg his first blowjob while the old geezer was watching *The 700 Club*, blaring from the living room. Part of Greg was waiting for a meteorite or lightning bolt to fry them both where they rutted in his single bed, nothing separating their evil deed from their father but a paper-thin bedroom door with no lock and a Mighty Mouse comforter so old and worn it was more like a thick sheet than a bedcover.

So when he found them a couple years later, out in the woods downslope from their crappy old house, he'd gone ten kinds of ballistic. He leapt on Greg and started hitting him in the face, in the chest, in the balls and the stomach. Jenny, buck naked as a wild deer, screamed at him to stop but the man had lost all reason and Greg, now half-conscious with a sagging broken jaw and a right eye full of blood, could barely make out her flesh-pink form rummaging through their cast-off clothes.

As the old man was winding up for what might have been the deciding blow, Jenny scuttered up slick as a blue-tongued skink and punched a rusty, eight-inch ice pick into their father's jugular. She slid it out and was about to have at him again when he rolled off Greg and onto his back, blood shooting out of him like a geyser. Even Jenny was surprised at the velocity of the fluid's exit.

"Must have poked a vein," she said softly, and watched stoically as he gurgled and panicked in the leaves of the forest floor, his eyes white eggs, his mouth flapping open and shut like a fish tossed onto a dock.

After a moment, maybe after the initial shock had worn off, big dumb Bible-beatin' Jim Lanigan started to get up, to maybe try to make a case of things, organize his thoughts on punishment, et cetera. Well, Jenny took care of that by sticking him fast as a viper.

One-two.

The first one slid in and out of his heart, the second went into the right eye and stayed there.

Hell, maybe we should keep driving.

Greg looks at Jenny a moment, then his eyes go to her hip. She'd shined up the pick real nice after they buried their father. And to the best of his knowledge, she hadn't been without it since.

"If they don't want to kill that boy, you and I can do it," Greg says, pleased to see Jenny throw him her sexiest smile.

"Yeah?"

"Hell, if it's what you want," he says and pulls the cap lower on his forehead, staring forward to watch the dense forest split before them as if by sheer force of their combined will. "I don't mind at all."

PART SEVEN: PLAGUES

1

Balancing a paper plate topped with a bologna on white and a handful of Frito-Lays in one hand, Liam knocks on the door with the other, out of habit more than niceties. Well, maybe it is a *small* amount of niceties. After all, the kid has been through the ringer and Liam still feels a mild burn of shame at losing his shit on the boy. Unfair, that, grown man kicking around a little tosser. The can of Coke squeezed into his armpit is getting colder by the second, however, and niceties or not he throws the large bolt and opens the door to Henry's room. His nose wrinkles from the first sniff of air.

Christ, the smell.

It's also cold and, despite it being late afternoon, dense with heavy shadow. Liam looks first to the cot, expecting to see Henry lying there as usual, covered in blankets and exuding the musty essence of *go fuck yourself.*

He feels a chill—one that has nothing to do with the icebox quality of the air in the room—when he sees the cot is empty.

Instinctively, his eyes dart to the corner to his left first, being the closest blind spot from which Henry could come at him. When he's comfortable it's clear, he takes another small step into the room and searches the far wall.

And sees him.

Henry stands ramrod straight in the far darkened corner, just outside the reach of a few desperate sunbeams slanting inward through the boarded window. As Liam's eyes adjust, he realizes Henry is naked, his clothes lying in a pile next to the bed, ten feet away. The boy's hands are at his sides, and he's staring back at Liam with hooded eyes, like he's in a trance, or sleepwalking.

"Henry?" Liam says, and slowly, carefully, sets the food and the can of soda on the floor. *I give it about a minute before it's crawling with bugs, but first things first.* "Henry," he repeats, "what's going on, mate? Why are you undressed?"

While talking, Liam closes the door behind him. He can't lock it from the inside, but he'll be damned if he'll let the kid slip by him a second time. He realizes Henry—whose flesh looks more gray than brown in the dim light—is shivering. Badly. Liam hears his teeth chatter from across the room.

"It's *freezing* in here, Henry. Why don't we get you under the blankets and I'll turn your heater on, eh? You have enough fuel? Is it empty? Maybe put your clothes on as well?"

"They smell," Henry says, his voice small and shaking. "I peed in them, and I've been sweating in them, and they're dirty. I stink, but the c-c-clothes are worse."

"All right, all right. Tell you what. You put on your pants, yeah? And I'll go get you one of my own shirts. It'll drop to your knees, but it'll be dry and it won't stink. Then you and me, we'll go downstairs, where I have a bar of soap, and we'll pour a bit of the drinking water in a bucket or a cooler or whatever we can find, and we'll wash your undies and your shirt at least, okay? They can dry outside overnight and tomorrow you'll have them back. They won't be perfect, but they'll be better. And I'll take your bucket out for ya, okay?"

Henry sniffles. "I hate it here."

Liam sighs and drops his head, feeling suddenly exhausted and, truth be told, beginning to wonder why he'd ever agreed to this fucked-up plan in the first place. He is no soulless killer, and he is no abuser of children. *Thought it would go differently, did you? Fantasies of putting some rich brat kid in a closet a few days, picking up a suitcase of cash and dancing all the way to Mexico. Easy as pie, right? Hell if it is.*

"This will be over in a few days, Henry. Before you know it, you'll be back home and you can forget all about this little adventure and go back to school and girls and Dungeons and Dragons and all that shit," Liam says carefully, as if Henry is a fragile vase balancing on the edge of a tall table, a vase he definitely doesn't want to knock over, because that would lead to problems. That would be messy. He just wants to scoot the boy back a bit, get him stabilized, then let the good times roll until they're done with this whole thing.

"She won't wait a few days," Henry says quietly, looking ashen and ghostly in the corner.

The way Henry speaks about this strange creature he believes in, combined with the eerie ghostlike way he's half-hidden in the shadows, gives Liam pause and raises the hairs on the back of his neck. It's as if Henry is talking about the gods he believes in, the spirits of the earth that men like Liam couldn't see if their lives depend on it. And what Liam feels... it isn't fear. Not exactly. But it lives in a neighborhood that could certainly be considered fear-adjacent.

"Oh no?" he says, keeping his voice level, his presence calm and patient.

Henry shakes his head slowly. "No, you won't make it that long." He sniffs, wipes his nose. His eyes go to the cot, as if considering. "None of you will."

Not knowing what else to say, and beginning to feel the first tickles of annoyance in the back of his brain, Liam ignores this and gestures toward the bed. "Why don't you get under the blankets and I'll crank up that heater. It's like the fucking North Pole in here."

"I tried to start it," Henry says sulkily, as if disappointed by his own ineptitude. "But it smelled gassy and it wouldn't light."

"I'll fix it, I promise. Please," Liam says, more forcefully this time, and motions again to the cot, willing the little bastard to *move*.

Surprisingly, Henry does just that. Seemingly unconcerned about being seen naked, as many small children are, especially in front of strangers, Henry crosses his arms over his chest and walks briskly to the cot, begins piling blankets up over his small body. "The blankets smell, too," he mumbles, but Liam chooses not to address that one. There were limits to his hospitality. His ... niceties.

Liam checks the fuel of the heater, then pulls a yellow box of wood matches from his pocket. He opens the small door, like an oven in a fairy tale, and lights a match. While depressing the pilot button he holds the lit match above a small pipe just inside the door. It lights with a small *woof* and, after a few seconds, Liam turns the temperature knob all the way up and closes the door. The red eye glows hot behind the smoke-scarred safety glass.

Liam lifts the heater, carries it by the thin handle toward Henry's cot (careful to keep himself between Henry and the door), and sets it down.

After a moment's hesitation, he hands Henry the yellow box of matches. "You see how I did that?"

Henry nods.

"If it goes out again—"

Henry looks at the matches, then sets them down next to him on the bed.

"Don't get cute and light your room on fire. Promise?"

Henry nods again.

"And don't let the blankets touch the heater, they'll singe," he says and goes back for the food, setting the plate and the Coke gently on the mattress next to Henry, who lifts himself on one elbow and picks up the sandwich. Eyes tracking Liam's movement with renewed interest, and a touch of suspicion, Henry takes a bite.

Liam watches Henry eat, rubs the growing beard coating his chin, and begins to figure out how to execute his shitty plan of attack for getting the kid's clothes cleaned up, or at least wearable. "Let me go get that shirt. Can you put your jeans back on? You don't need underwear. I won't tell."

"Okay," Henry agrees, then takes two or three swallows of Coke, belches like a two-hundred-pound rugby player, and seems to regain some of his color. "Why did Jenny take my picture? I pretended to be asleep, but she did it anyway."

Liam debates lying, but doesn't see the point. "To prove you're okay. To prove we ... that you're with us."

Henry watches Liam closely for a second, and Liam has that creepy feeling again, the one he gets when Henry appears to be studying his insides. Then the boy just starts eating his chips, satisfied. Like he's been given an answer to a question nobody asked. Liam sits at the edge of the cot while Henry devours his lunch.

"Any more thoughts about that thing in the cellar, or its . . . what did you call it? Mama, right? The one so impatient to regain the solitary use of this wonderful, shitty old farmhouse?"

Henry says nothing, but shoves more chips in his mouth, chews them thoughtfully. "Not really," he says, and sips some Coke.

"You sure?" Liam says, and lowers his eyes to catch Henry's own.

"All I know," Henry says, and Liam would swear on a stack of bibles that the kid is smirking, "is that I'm glad you brought me this sandwich."

Liam laughs and stands. "Right, you're hungry, I get it."

"Well, yeah," Henry says, and now Liam can hear the smirk in his voice. "But that's not what I mean."

Crossing the room, Liam grabs the bucket gingerly, sees the dull white of soiled toilet paper in the urine, feels something solid sloshing around at the bottom. Below his disgust is the now-familiar pierce of hot shame. *Well, if the kid hadn't run, he'd be doing his business outside like I told him. Don't get soft, Liam. Not now, mate. That ship has sailed and made port in a distant land far across the sea. It's gone, baby, and it ain't coming back.*

"What *do* you mean, Henry?" he says, heading for the door, only half paying attention to the boy now, his focus on emptying this bucket and finding the kid a clean shirt. "Or do I not want to know?"

"I think I'll keep it a secret for now," Henry answers, and finishes off the last of his bologna sandwich. Liam chooses to let this go until Henry whispers: "Okay, Dad. I know."

Liam spins around so fast the stuff in the bucket sloshes and bumps the sides, perilously close to the lip and freedom. Despite knowing the impossibility of there being a third person in the room, he checks the dark corners automatically, spending an extra moment studying the black rectangle of an empty closet, before being satisfied the kid is messing with him. Or, as he'd previously surmised: batshit-crazy.

"Who are you talking to, Henry?"

"My dad," he says, light-hearted annoyance in his tone. "He's always telling me to *zip it.*"

"I see," Liam says, feeling his own cruel smirk creep onto his face. He doesn't like being frightened, and a primal part of him doesn't like being made a fool. It's that dark, nasty part of who he is, who he'll always be, the part wanting a little payback for Henry making him dance, making him scared. Not to mention making him play nursemaid. "Is this the same dad who threw himself in front of a bus with you wrapped in his arms?"

Henry sips the Coke, eyes on a distant wall.

"Yeah, Jim told me that story," Liam continues, his tone taunting. "He must have been one crazy fucker, your dad. You tell him I say hello, okay?"

But Henry doesn't respond. Doesn't cry or scream or whimper. He sits in the blankets, the light from the heater glazing his cheeks, igniting his brown eyes with a dull red glow. Liam waits a moment, hoping for a reaction, then shrugs.

As he turns to close the door, something icy cold rubs across the back of his neck, and although his mind rejects it, he swears he hears someone—some*thing*—whisper tight to his ear, no louder than a puff of stale air. The voice of a lover, or a ghost.

Gonna get you for that.

Liam stops, considers turning back to make sure Henry is still on the other side of the room, settled on his cot—*that wasn't Henry's voice and you know it, chum*—but decides enough is enough. Without a backward glance, he closes the door and slides the heavy bolt.

By the time he reaches the stairs, he's dismissed the voice as his mind playing tricks, and ignores the goosebumps scaling his flesh.

2

As the sun swells fat and languid on the horizon like a leech loading up on the ocean's red blood, the six o'clock news of all three major networks are flashing a triptych of mugshots onto TV screens across Southern California.

At the Texaco gas station off Exit 5 of the Escondido Freeway—the one that spills cars off the 15 onto Mission Road, then into the benign San Diego suburb of Grantville, home of the Patrick Henry Patriots and a lion's share of cherubic white nuclear families—Channel 7 broadcasts the three faces on the station's customer-facing television. It's always Channel 7 because the gas station's owner and full-time operator, Chuck Wilson, is particularly fond of that newscast's meteorologist, Sarah Raines, and especially fond of the tight red dresses Sarah wears while she gestures toward giant childlike suns splashed against a map of Southern California, pointing to them as if they held all the answers to life's great questions. Before Sarah's segment comes on, however, the anchors always give a grim-faced rundown of the local news—the *real* news—and today all the hubbub is about a young boy who's been kidnapped. It seems to Chuck, as he leans against the counter staring at the muted set in the upper corner of his Refreshments area, that the whole damned world is out looking for the boy.

The bell over the customer door jingles and Tim Shepard strolls in, stinking like he always does and gently rubbing his clean, freshly shaven jaw, a grooming procedure he tends to in the Texaco restroom with Chuck's blessing. Chuck has nothing against a man wanting to better himself, whether that man be homeless as a skunk or rich as a Trump, and Tim always leaves things neat and never makes a fuss. Not that it does a whole hell of a lot for Tim's general appearance: his sun-leathered skin, patchy white splays of hair, and baggy, stain-splashed clothes do not transform a street-lifer beach-bum into a businessman on holiday, sadly.

Hell, if a clean shave gives the poor guy a little dose of self-respect, and if that's
what it takes to keep to his own personal "drive to stay alive" marathon humming
along, who am I to judge?

"Hey there, Chuck," Tim says, and eyeballs the Pepsi cooler.

Chuck turns his gaze back to the television, where the smiling visage
of one Henry Thorne is peeking over the shoulder of the anchor, whose
solemn face contrasts sharply with the chubby-cheeked, toothy grin of
the young boy behind him. "Soda is fifty cents," Chuck says absently,
knowing Tim has this information branded with a hot iron into whatever
brain cells remain to him, but he likes to say it anyway. It's sort of the way
he says "hello" to the guy, without actually having to say it.

"Yeah," Tim says. "That the crooks?"

Chuck had spaced out for a moment, and his attention snaps back to
the television screen, now filled with the three pictures the FBI released
only hours ago. From left to right are the unsmiling mug of a slightly
younger, slightly skinnier Jim Cady, a sweaty-faced and moustache-free
Greg Lanigan, and—last but not least—the petulant, borderline pissed-
off glare of Greg's only sister, Jenny Lanigan. The three of them are set
neatly into stark white frames atop a blue graphic backdrop that bears the
repeated, slanted phrase "ACTION NEWS" drifting forever downward,
like slanted rain.

"I guess," Chuck says, and turns away from the screen to see what
needs doing before the sun goes all the way down. "You eat today?"
Chuck asks Tim (and if *"soda is fifty cents"* is their version of "hello," then
"you eat today?" is commonly accepted as Chuck's rendition of *"see ya later,*
man. I got shit to do").

"I'll eat later," Tim says, which is what he always says.

Chuck is about to respond with the next line of dialogue in this daily
two-man play of theirs: "Well, grab a bagel from over there. I think they're
old anyway," he'll say (they aren't—Goldstein's brought them fresh that
very morning, as they always do), but then there's a disruptive *ding-ding* of

the signal bell that chimes when a car rolls over the black pneumatic tubes in front of the station pumps. Both men turn to watch the puke-green Pinto wagon glide to a stop in front of pump 3.

"Customer," Tim says.

★ ★ ★

Greg knows they're making a huge mistake.

How do you not check the gas gauge, dummy?

He's been beating himself up about it ever since they left the doctor's office a half hour ago. While Jenny had been making the delivery, Greg had been thrumming his fingers on the scuffed black steering wheel to Supertramp's "The Logical Song," the Pinto's small engine clattering softly like a dying mechanical kitten, when he caught sight of the gas gauge, the red needle sagging far too much to the left—like, all the way—to the big E.

"Oh, brother." Instinctively, nonsensically, he'd turned around to look for the two cans of unleaded fuel he'd put into the trunk of the Duster.

I'm not in the Duster and I forgot to check the fuel and holy shit we're gonna need to actually pull into a mother-humpin' gas station and pay for actual gas. Good lord if Jim ever finds out about this he'll kill me dead, and that's no lie.

When Jenny stepped off the doctor's shadowed porch, looking ridiculous in a sunhat and oversized black sunglasses, he'd felt sick to his stomach with worry, guilt, and self-loathing. True to his sister's nature, she didn't freak out when he told her about his mistake, but he knew deep down she was seething, or whatever counted as seething in Jenny's head. He'd never seen her lose her temper. Even when she'd stabbed their father to death with an ice pick, she was never completely out of control. No, there weren't any red flags with Jenny. Greg knew she was the more clinical type—as in, clinically psychotic. His sister didn't get upset, she simply made decisions. Cold, calculating decisions. One second, she'd think you were the cat's meow, the next she was sticking an eight-inch ice pick through your eye for spilling a drink on her favorite blouse.

Greg had tried to keep Jenny's tendencies from the guys when pitch-ing her as part of the job, but he has a feeling Jim knows more than he's let on about his sister's past. He also knows that knowledge might have been what persuaded Jim to bring her aboard (with her split coming out of Greg's share, of course). He thinks maybe Jim—being the quick-to-kill type himself —wanted someone else he could rely on to play rough if the situation called for it. Lord knew Pete acted tough, with that stupid-ass dog tattoo of his and the gold teeth and all the gang slang, but Greg had seen Pete cower a few times during their stretch together. Pete is rough, and he is a bastard, but he isn't a coldhearted killer. Not like Jim.

And not like my sister.

As for Liam? Shit. That guy is cool as ice cream cake and smarter than all of them, well, except for maybe Jim himself, but Greg doubts he would ever kill a kid. If push came to shove, maybe, but not because Jim told him to. No, Liam isn't much of an order-taker. He thinks too much. Feels too much.

Greg wonders if *he* could pop the kid if Jim told him to (or if it was what Jenny thought best) and he figures he could probably do it. Especially for Jenny. He'd do anything for her, and he'd meant what he'd said to her about knocking the kid off even if it wasn't the "plan." He owes her that. That much and more. They love each other, and that is that. Forget the taboos and the polite society bullshit, they are in love and always will be. Case closed.

Still, he keeps half an eye on her lap as they drive—feverish to find a gas station before things go from bad to worse and they run out of fuel in the middle of the damn 15 Freeway—just to make sure her fingers don't creep toward the handle of the ice pick. That would be no bueno, folks. No bueno and then some.

Now, as they pull into the shittiest-looking Texaco station Greg has ever seen, he allows himself a sigh of relief that they made it safely and— thanking all the angels in heaven—that he hadn't been sucked into playing cards with Pete and Jenny. Meaning he still has the eighty-four dollars he'd stolen from the bar's register while Jim had been playing janitor at the elementary school. Of course, this is probably another action he should leave off any final reports handed over to the big man, something he'll keep to himself, thanks very much. And, hey, it's all working out for the best! Right?

"Stay here, keep that ridiculous hat on, and don't look at anybody," Greg says as he turns off the car. "I gotta go pay. Be right back."

"Shouldn't I do that? I mean, if one of us is hot it's you. You're Jim's buddy, after all."

Greg thinks about this a moment but doesn't like the idea of cops seeing that stupid pink sunhat his sister has on at the drop-off *and* the Texaco station. Not that he sees any security cameras, but still, better safe than sorry and all that.

"Nah. I got this. Stay put."

Jenny shrugs and says nothing as Greg gets out and closes the door.

Inside the station, he digs the thick fold of cash out of his front pocket, peels off a greasy-looking ten-dollar bill, and hands it over to the guy behind the counter. "Ten bucks on—" Greg looks out the window, sees Jenny sitting quietly, her face tilted downward. *Good girl.* "Pump three, I guess. And a paper."

The guy takes the money, taps a couple buttons. "You want a receipt?"

"No, thanks."

Greg grabs the daily paper from a stack on the counter next to the register and hustles toward the exit. On the way out his eyes flicker to a fish-eyed security mirror in one corner that more than likely has a camera behind it, recording all of this. He glances to another corner, sees a large television bolted to a black stand over the soda coolers. It's showing a commercial for Mr. Clean, and Greg thinks nothing of it as he tilts his face down as much as he can without looking like a damned criminal and pushes through the door. The bell above jingles as he does so, and the sound fries his nerves.

A few stressful minutes later, Greg is pumping unleaded into the dry tank of the Pinto, trying with all the cosmic energy he can muster to will the rolling numbers to go *faster, dammit, faster!* But this is an old station and the gas comes out at only one speed, each tenth of a penny casually flowing from 1 to 9 with all the energy of a drunk sloth.

"Come on, already," Greg mumbles, squeezing the gas pump handle so hard his knuckles are bone-white. He bounces up and down on his toes and tries to ignore Jenny turning around—repeatedly—to glare at him from the front seat, her judgmental gaze only partially obstructed by the wagon's algae-tinted rear window.

As 7.52 slowly rolls its way up to 7.53 and so on, Greg smells something sour—something besides the stench of gasoline fumes—and turns to see the homeless dude from inside the station staring at him from the opposite side of the fuel dispenser. Greg has a sudden, panicked flash of a cop car pulling into the station to grab coffees or donuts or whatever the fuzz eat these days when they aren't being pains in the ass, and even goes so far as to glance toward the station's entrance, just to confirm the nightmare is all indeed in his head.

"Hey buddy, can I have fifty cents? I want to buy a Pepsi," the homeless guy says, and Greg can't believe his bad luck.

"No man, fuck off," he says, keeping his cap visor tilted downward. *Like the homeless guy is a threat to match me to some police APB,* Greg thinks, and actually scoffs. *Guy's probably hopped-up on alley-crack and Thunderbird. Pepsi, my asshole.*

"Come on, buddy. Hey!" he says, as if the idea of the century has just popped to life inside his sun-addled brain, "I'll wash your windows for ya! How's that sound? I do it all the time here for folks, and sometimes they'll buy me a Pepsi for it. Chuck don't mind, he's the owner. He and I are friends."

"Uh-huh," Greg says, and thankfully sees the pump roll up to that blessed $10.00 mark and stop as softly as a tired old man settling into a

La-Z-Boy. "How about you fuck off like I said? You touch my car I'll break your goddamn arm, you comprende?"

The homeless guy has the balls to look offended as Greg smiles broadly and shoves the pump handle back into the dispenser with a loud, metal-on-metal *clack*. "No need to be rude, man!" the guy says, and stumbles back a few steps.

"Whatever." Greg screws the gas cap back onto the Pinto's tank and claps the access door shut.

"What was all that about?" Jenny asks sullenly as he gets into the wagon and starts it up, letting the engine whine, then settle a bit before putting it into drive.

"Nothing, some beggar," Greg says, and takes his foot off the brake as he slips a hand onto Jenny's thigh, thinking maybe he'd endeavor to see if sis was game for a pit stop before they headed back to the house from hell. The wagon did have its advantages.

"Watch it!" Jenny screams, and Greg instinctively slams on the brake.

Greg's eyes shoot forward to see the homeless guy standing in front of their car, his mouth turned into a saggy frown, his bloodshot ice-blue eyes blazing. He's pointing at the two of them through the windshield, his knees only inches from the Pinto's front bumper. "You're bad people!" he yells, loudly enough for them to hear him but not so much as to bring the owner of the station running to see what the hell is going on at the pumps.

Greg sees Jenny already has a hand on the door handle. *Sweet Jesus, that's all we need.* "Jenny, relax. Just stop."

She glares at him, but her fingers leave the chrome flip that opens the car door. "Fine," she says sulkily, and settles back into the seat.

Greg, about as done with this little comedy as a man can be, pushes down on the accelerator. The car rolls forward obediently.

The homeless guy squawks, still frowning, mumbles what Greg is certain is a horrible thing about him and things he can do with himself in private or in public, then skips out of the way in the direction of the station. He slaps at Jenny's window—hard enough to make her yelp—and Greg pushes down on the gas and slides out of the station, aka Crazyville (Population: 1).

His stomach does the slightest do-si-do when the guy screams something at them as he pulls the Pinto back onto Mission Road in the direction of Cleveland National Forest, their temporary home.

To Greg, it sounded an awful lot like the old fuck screamed: "I know you!"

Which is ridiculous.

Have another drink, pops, he thinks, and is thankful not to see Jenny offer any reaction to the man's final cry of defiance. If she had, he might think differently. Might think that maybe the guy had indeed said what it sounded like, which in turn might mean they have a large problem on their hands.

But Jenny says nothing, and Greg figures he's imagining the worst, just like he'd imagined the cop car pulling in while pumping gas. He smiles and puts his palm on Jenny's warm thigh once again, but forgets all about inquiring about a quick stop. They've turned the evening into more of an adventure than it needed to be already, and there's no reason to tempt fate.

★ ★ ★

Of course, Fate has already made an appearance, already intervened in the lives of the kidnappers, the station owner, and the down-on-his-luck homeless man named Tim Shepard.

It was Shepard who had, at the last moment, recognized the couple in the car as the ones he'd seen splashed across the television screen in Chuck's Texaco station mini-mart. Later he would tell the cops, whom Chuck immediately called after Tim told him what he'd seen, that "It was the two of them together that made it click for me. Both of them frowning and bitter, staring at me like I was a piece of filthy trash stuck to their windshield. They had disguises—hats and sunglasses, but it was them all the same. Then they just slunk away, back to bad business, I imagine. Yup, bad business is what those two are all about," he pontificated as the officers took notes.

It was Chuck himself who provided video footage of the man in question, as well as footage (along with the license plate number) of the car as it fueled up. Chuck felt damn good about it, too. Felt like maybe he and Tim had done something good, had maybe even done something that might help save that poor little boy. He made a mental note to give Tim Pepsi-Cola on the house from now on if this thing ended well.

As for Tim, before he wrapped up his detailed (and exceedingly sober, since you asked) report, it was one last thought that made his sunbaked but well-shaven face split into a large grin: "Except now that sucker's got himself a moustache," he said as the cop made scribbles in his pad. "Oh, and P-fucking-S, man . . . they headed *east*."

3

In the dark damp beneath the house, the creature pushes through the opening she's made in the brick wall, low to the ground and no bigger than an oven door. She reaches back for the object she's brought with her. It hums beneath her fingers. She chitters and clicks softly, speaking to it, then places the object—a large misshapen ball of dried leaves and mud—beneath the rotted wood of the stairway that leads up to a closed door. Voices float down from above, but she is quiet. And careful.

Leaving the object hidden beneath the stairs, she pushes back through the hole in the wall, leaving the broken remnants of brick and chipped mortar in the dirt where they fall. It has taken time, and patience, to scrape through the old mortar, to chip almost silently away at the brick. And now, the first job done, the creature sinks to the floor, golden eyes closed tight. She rocks back and forth, speaking in rapid successions of moans, clicks, and a sound not unlike chattering teeth.

She climbs up one of the cellar walls and onto the ceiling.

Just above her, only a few inches of floorboard away, is the kitchen. The creature places two palms flat against the wood and whispers a series of her clicks and coos, over and over and over.

Two floors above, Henry lies in his bed, his mind connected to the creature, but only enough to feel its presence. He is afraid to get closer, to open his inner eye any further. He fears being swallowed by the dark of its mind, fears having his own mind invaded, possibly controlled.

It could do that, he knows. Maybe not to humans, but to other things. Animals. Insects. Creatures he has never seen or heard of, that live below the earth's crust—below the cities and parks and schools, lying beneath the awareness of mankind in the deep bowels of the earth.

Henry's brow furrows. He tries to understand—to *see*—the language, to make sense of the sounds Mother makes beneath the house. He thinks, at first, it is singing. Or maybe a prayer. There is something complex about the rhythm of the sounds, the way they string together, the colors binding and knotting to create something like music. In the end, he thinks he is close to being right, but not quite all the way.

It's a damned curse, his father says into his ear.

Henry doesn't disagree.

4

Jim paces behind the large shed. The star-filled night sky rolls on high above. The air, crisp and brutally cold, prickles the bare skin of his forearms, pinches his ears with icy fingers. But he needs to be out of that house for a while. Needs to clear his head and think. He doesn't like the way things are going.

It doesn't feel smooth.

First, the FBI agent smoking him out—a not unplanned-for event, but in the back of his mind Jim had hoped to slip through the cracks until the school went on break. Then the weirdness with the kid acting bizarre as fuck, the dead body in the cellar, and now Greg and Jenny late coming back from the drop. Making things worse, Jim is exceedingly concerned about Liam, who is usually solid as they come, but is reacting poorly to the kid; too generous one second, out of control the next. Jim had counted on Liam and the boy being friendly, not acting like an old married couple lost at sea. Greg is also on his radar. Bringing in Jenny was a mistake. Jim didn't think through her influence on little brother, and Greg is distracted, unpredictable. Again, Greg's best virtue is literally his predictability.

Damn. Can't get good help these days.

Jim laughs and takes another pull on the joint. It occurs to him that the only one of these assholes he truly trusts anymore is that sack-of-shit Mexican. Pete isn't smart as Liam, or predictable as Greg, or savage as Jenny (although he tries his damned best to appear so), but Jim has discovered a steadiness in Pete. He's like a junkyard dog—apropos given his dumbass tattoo—that tucks his tail when his master is nearby and bares his teeth at anyone else.

Yeah, Pete's a good dog. And besides, best-case scenarios are for pussies, man. Gotta roll with the shit. Downhill, baby. Always downhill.

Jim allows himself another pull on the joint, then pinches the tip and tucks the remaining half into his pants pocket. He learned early on not to smoke indoors. He'd been beaten enough times during his years in juvenile detention—for smoking a cigarette in the john or trying to sneak one during lights out—to have it well ingrained into his DNA. *I guess we're all dogs in the end*, he thinks ruefully.

Besides, he doesn't want to share his shit.

Jim rubs his hands together and is about to go inside when he hears the familiar low whine of the Pinto's engine, the soft thumping of tires coming up the bumpy fire road. Instinctively, Jim takes a step backward, into the deep shadows behind the shed.

And waits.

Using the low beams, the Pinto pulls from the shelter of trees and into the overgrown clearing at the front of the house. It steers toward the large shed, pauses at the entrance.

"Go ahead and park it, I'm gonna have a smoke." Greg's voice carries easily through the thin wall of the shed. Jim feels the heat of the running engine, smells the exhaust as it slips through the cracks of the boards and into the night. The lights go out and the engine gives a soft rattle, then goes dead. The driver's door opens and shuts.

"Let me have one of those," Jenny says, and Jim slides quietly along the rear wall, closer to where brother and sister are having their palaver.

The *snick* of a lighter, the exhale of a woman's breath. "They'll be waiting for us to come in. We're late, you know."

"We could be later," Greg suggests, and Jim can almost hear their bodies move closer together. A soft gasp from sister, then kissing noises mixed with enough moaning that Jim's stomach sours and he grimaces. A deadened slap—palm on fabric—and Jenny's tinkling laughter.

"Enough." Exhale. "We need to get in there."

"Yeah, okay." A pause. Jim tenses. He rests a palm against the wall of the shed, listening close. "So, what do you think? Do we ride this out?"

"We're here, aren't we?"

"I guess. Still, tomorrow's a new day."

Another pause as the siblings smoke the last of their cigarettes. Then Jenny again: "Let's regroup tomorrow. If it feels wrong, we sneak out tomorrow night and split. You'll need to put down the kid. Or, screw it, I'll do it if you want."

Put down. Jim lets the words play inside his mind, thinking again of dogs.

"Fine," Greg says, "let's see how things go. I'm freezing my ass off here, and I'm sure Jim's in there wondering why the hell we're late and why we're not getting inside. No need to make the man suspicious. He's uptight as it is."

Jim smiles at this.

"Fine, God, we'll tell them the truth. We had a quick smoke. Jesus, Greg, you're a worrywart."

Jenny squeals and Jim pictures Greg pinching her ass. He wonders if one of these days Greg's gonna pinch that girl when she's in a mood and he'll find himself with an ice pick through the brain for his efforts.

Jim waits, motionless, as the two close the shed doors and shuffle toward the dark house. The front door squeaks open. Distant voices. The door shuts. Jim brushes wood shavings off his meaty shoulder, decides to walk the perimeter just to give himself an excuse for being out here. If he went in now, they'd be nervous as hell. *Did he hear us? Where the hell was he?* Jim laughs, thinking of their discomfort, and begins tromping through the tall grass toward the hulking specter of the farmhouse.

As he strolls behind the house, he debates whether he needs to kill them. It can't just be the girl, it would have to be both or neither. They'd done what he needed them to do. At this point they're essentially liabilities. Pete won't give a shit. More money for him. Liam might be a concern, and Jim realizes he'd have to clear it with the man first. Liam isn't expendable; too smart, too loyal. Someday, perhaps. But not yet. Good help being hard to find and all—

THUNK.

Jim's inner monologue comes to a sudden halt and he freezes, hidden from the moon in the building's heavy shade. The sound came from the side of the house, where they'd discovered the cellar doors earlier that morning.

The sound is easy to imagine: One of the doors has dropped into place. Not loudly, probably not loud enough to hear from inside. But he's near the corner, no more than twenty or thirty feet away.

There's no mistaking it now: footsteps in the grass.

Coming straight toward him.

Jim presses himself against the side of the house. No more than ten feet away, separated by worn siding, peeling paint, and termite-bitten two-by-fours, he hears the voices of his crew inside the house. Laughter. Jenny giving Pete shit about something, Greg and Liam in murmured conversation, most likely passing the bottle of Jack around the kitchen table. But out here it's as though he's on an island. It is pitch black and frigid. His shoes are sodden from the damp grass, but his skin is hot and prickly, his bald pate itches, and he can almost feel his body warming up with tension and anticipation. Whoever it is outside the house isn't one of his. It is someone else. A trespasser.

Part of Jim prays it isn't an FBI agent, like that prick who'd enjoyed playing with him at the elementary school. A bigger part of him hopes it is. If so, then the woods are already filled with feds and the game is over. But in a few seconds he's gonna get his big hands on one of them, and jail or no jail he's gonna snap the fucker's neck.

His fingers twitch involuntarily and he feels his dick stiffen at the thought of killing a man. *Yeah baby, come on. Bring that shit to papa.*

Jim's heart pounds but he remains motionless, his breathing steady and quiet. The corner of the house is only a few feet away, and whoever is coming toward him is nearly within reach. *Just a few more seconds.*

The footsteps stop.

Jim's eyes widen. Somehow, they know.

Somehow, they sense him.

There is a clicking sound, as if someone is cracking their knuckles. *Or loading a gun,* Jim thinks. *Fuck it, let's dance, baby.*

No longer worrying about noise, Jim lunges around the corner of the house, mouth carved into a snarl, fingers bunched into fists, muscles tense, blood pounding behind his eyes.

"The fuck are you?" he demands, pulling the gun from his waistband and stepping forward. The thing scuttles back, moving quickly, its eyes wide and focused on the metal in his fist.

The thing facing him is not something he can get his mind around. It is thin and short. It wears a ratty cloak . . . *no, not a cloak. Not clothes at all. A shell.* Its black carapace flows like ink over its limbs, canopies over its skull, shadowing sunken yellow eyes that come no higher than Jim's chin. Its body is black as pitch, a negative space in the dark night, covered in oddly shaped plates, like soft armor. Long, clawed fingers extend from the ends of what Jim can only think of as sleeves, or bracers of some kind.

He's shaken, and badly wants to kill this thing. Kill it and drag its body inside the house. Study it. He's curious, and his curiosity is getting the better of his buried fear.

Quick as a whip, he snatches for the thing's arm and hears that chittering, clicking sound again as it dashes further back, just avoiding his reaching fingers. *Yeah, I'm quick too, baby. Wait and see.*

But then the thing looks up, its golden eyes glowing beneath that strange hood. Jim doesn't care for how this weird-ass thing is looking at him. It feels . . . hostile. Like it wants to come at old Jim. Come at him and see what kind of damage it can do.

"Well," Jim says, fist tightening around the butt of the gun, the muscles of his forearms tight cords beneath his skin, "why don't you come on? Why don't you come on and we'll see what happens?"

As if in response, the creature hisses. Jim takes a step back, hesitating, before raising the gun.

That's all it needs.

The creature spins and runs for the trees, sprinting on four legs like a puma. Jim raises the gun further. Before he can properly aim in the dark, it's a dozen feet away. By the time he's able to locate it and target, it leaps for a tree and disappears.

"Damn!" he yells, and runs toward the forest's edge. Huffing, he stares up at the tree where the creature vanished, only a few stirring leaves giving any sign the thing had even been there in the first place. *Crazy bitch jumped ten feet straight up*, he thinks, not realizing he's already thinking of it as female.

For a moment, he considers following. Perhaps going back inside the house, getting a flashlight and Liam, but he knows it's pointless. Whatever the thing is—animal, alien, or something else altogether—it's long gone.

For a few moments, Jim stares at the trees where the strange creature fled, his mind temporarily numb with shock at what he'd seen, the unreality of it.

Then his mind recalibrates, refocuses. As he's done his whole life, he dismisses the impossible and focuses on the necessary. On the *job*. And whatever the hell that thing was, animal or alien, to him it was one thing and one thing only:

Unexpected.

And Jim didn't like unexpected things turning up in his plans. For now, that was enough to allow his mind to dismiss the bizarre and laser-focus on the practical.

He turns and looks to the cellar doors.

For one, what the fuck were you doing down there?

Grimacing, he decides to wait until morning to find out. Then he'll head down there with one of the boys. Wait until there's some decent light so he can be sure there's nothing else down there to worry about.

As he stalks back to the farmhouse, he decides he'll keep the incident quiet for now. No reason to get everybody freaked out, especially when it's obvious Greg and Jenny are just looking for an excuse to pull the plug.

He walks past the cellar doors with only a brief glance. He wipes his mouth, his forehead, feels the sweat chilling there. His stomach feels full of acid and his muscles are twitchy.

The smart thing, he knows, would be to go under the house now. Grab some lights and go down there and see if everything is clear. But he doesn't want to do that, and the fact he doesn't want to do that worries him. Angers him. Makes him feel like a fool. A coward. Regardless, he keeps right on walking toward the front door, only turning back once to make sure he doesn't see any yellow eyes watching from the dark forest, from the high branches of a tree.

Nothing.

Maybe Greg and Jenny are right. Maybe this whole thing is going tits-up. It *is* weird, and getting weirder by the second.

As he climbs the porch, Jim makes a note to keep his gun with him at all times from here on out. No one can be trusted, and if he runs into that creature again he wants to be prepared to blow the damned thing's head off. Kill it so he won't have to think about it anymore. Won't have to think about the truth—that the thing scared him. Scared him bad enough he doesn't want to go into a dark cellar at night. Like a little kid afraid of the dark.

Jim reaches for the door handle, notices his hand is shaking.

This pisses him off even more.

You come on back, baby, he thinks, rage and shame flooding through him. *You come on back and I'll show you who's scared. Right before I put a fucking bullet through your head.*

Jim steps inside and closes the door behind him. He turns and locks it with the heavy deadbolt and hates himself for the relief he feels at doing so.

5

Dr. Ryo Hamada is late and annoyed. His cat Kilroy, a six-year-old Burmese with fur the color of cocoa and eyes as gold as pirate coins whom he loves dearly, was being a real pain in the keister this morning. During his breakfast, she'd jumped onto the table and knocked his juice glass into his lap—which meant a change of clothes and a quick mop job on his ceramic-tiled kitchen floor before leaving to meet his friend Martin at the museum downtown for the new Barbara Kruger photo exhibit, which they'd bought tickets for months in advance. Otherwise, he frankly would have canceled. Given what was going on with Henry Thorne, he was much too worried to enjoy art or, for that matter, be good company. And now, on top of everything else, he's late, and Kilroy is a bad cat but she is also a very lucky cat, because it is impossible for Ryo to stay mad at her. Partly because the feline is his only true friend, and partly because she happens to be the world's greatest snuggler.

As he rushes out the front door in his *second* favorite pair of khaki slacks and a button-down white oxford that makes him feel like the squarest gay man in Southern California, Ryo nearly trips over a small package left on his front stoop.

"Damn it already!" he yells, flustered. He catches his balance and turns to close the front door—too late—as Kilroy shoots out the gap during the delay, down the three steps leading to the sidewalk, and immediately beelines for Mrs. Darley's house next door, where Kilroy's friend Maxie lives, much to Hamada's constant disdain.

"Kilroy! God *damn* it."

Now he will most definitely be late, and Martin will be pissed (and rightly so). But he can't leave Kilroy out all morning. He doesn't know when he'll be back, and there is no way he'll let his kitty eat the fast-food Friskies Mrs. Darley gives her overweight Siamese.

"Huh," Hamada says, momentarily forgetting about Kilroy, the museum, and whatever the hell it is Mrs. Darley feeds her cat. He bends down and picks up the manila envelope that has neither an address, a name, or anything else printed on its surface.

Something slides around inside when he turns it over, and Ryo feels his mouth go dry and the small hairs on the back of his neck stand up. The envelope is dirty, used, and bent. This is not a delivery from a service, or a hospital, or anything else of a professional nature.

This is something else.

He pulls up the metal tabs holding down the flap, lifts it, and reaches a hand into the envelope. His fingers brush against a tri-folded sheaf of paper and what feels like a Polaroid photograph. Feeling queasier and more terrified by the moment, he pulls both objects free from the envelope.

When he sees Henry's tired, overexposed face looking back at him, his small body sitting limp atop a pile of filthy-looking blankets against a bare gray wall, Ryo doesn't scream or cry out, but when he opens up the papers and reads what is written there, he leans over the small railing of his stoop and vomits his early breakfast into his bare-branched bed of roses, dormant at this time of year.

When done, he stumbles back inside, puts the envelope and its contents on the kitchen table, and starts to call the Thorne home. His finger stops, suspended over the keypad, his brain chiming in to remind him that he doesn't *know* the number to the Thorne home, and his client address book is in his briefcase, which may or may not be in his office upstairs or, barring that miracle, his bedroom.

"Ah, frack it," he says loudly and to absolutely no one (not even Kilroy, who is indeed gobbling down a plate of fast-food Friskies at Mrs. Darley's house next door).

Without further hesitation, Hamada punches in 9-1-1.

6

Henry wakes to a flickering memory, as if from a dream. He thinks perhaps it wasn't a dream, but something else. Someone *speaking* to him.

"Dad?" he says, tentative in the strange dark.

The room is its usual icebox-level temperature, and he looks to the one-eyed heater and sees a black window that should be pulsing with fire-red warmth.

Only silence responds to his feeble query.

"Darn it all to pieces," he mumbles, and is glad to at least have relatively clean clothes on again, even if they feel like sheets of ice rubbing against his skin.

Liam had been good as his word on that, even if the heater sucks it big-time. His jailer brought up a red, cracked plastic bucket he found in the large shed, half-filled with drinking water, along with a squeeze bottle of Joy dish soap the kidnappers had brought along for washing their hands as needed. The bucket had a hard crust of dirt along the bottom, but the inside was clean enough, and the crack was near the top so the water stayed in for the most part. Henry did the work himself, scrubbing his clothes as best he could, happy to have something to take his mind from his horrible situation, his constant fear.

Of course, Liam took their time together to needle him more about his abilities. Henry thinks Liam actually—well, at least partially—does believe Henry. About his gift, about the thing in the cellar, its protector in the woods. Being an adult and a kidnapper and a massive jerk means Liam also has to ridicule, to taunt and bully. But Henry knows from reading his thoughts, from the colors his feelings project, that the taunts are meaningless, the response of a grown man facing something he cannot fathom. Something he fears. Men don't like to be afraid, Henry knows, and it makes them lash out at anyone and anything they can—preferably weaker things—which is the modus operandi of almost every bully and a-hole Henry has ever encountered in his brief, traumatized existence.

For the most part, Henry was able to ignore Liam's teasing.

"If you can read minds, how come you didn't know Jim was going to take you? How come you didn't know his true intentions?"

Henry had only shrugged. "I don't pry. I don't invade people's privacy. I almost did, once. But he was a good faker. You can fake what's in your head, you know. You do it, too. Sometimes."

"Bullshit," Liam said, hanging Henry's sodden shirt over the worthless, broken doorknob. Henry didn't bother to answer or defend himself. Not only did he not care whether the man believed him, he had slowly begun to realize it had been a mistake to tell him anything at all. He'd thought, maybe (and stupidly), they would be friends. That if he opened up to Liam, he might help Henry. Protect him. Keep him alive.

But now Henry knows he was being a dumb kid. Naïve and silly. No one protects you but yourself. No one in this house cares about him. Even the creatures who he'd communed with (he could think of no other word that fit quite right) were nothing but monsters.

Dangerous monsters.

"And all this business about talking to your dead father? You know that's insane? Like, you should be in a hospital, Henry. You need . . . whatever, shock therapy. Drugs. It's like you're hallucinating all this stuff, and it's terrifying. I mean, don't get me wrong, I think you have an uncanny knack for intuition, guessing numbers and the like, I believe there's certainly something special about you. I'm not thick, you know? Chatting with dead parents is one thing, seeing them is something else altogether. That makes you crazy. Once this is over? Do me a favor and get some professional help."

Henry had kept his mouth shut and squeezed the ice-cold water from his underwear. Covered only in the long black T-shirt Liam had loaned him, he made a point of keeping his bare behind as close to the kerosene heater as possible without burning himself. It felt good to be dry and warm, and he was eager to be back in his own clothes. Plus, the soapy water, disgusting as it was, did a fine job of cleaning his hands, which had been so grimy that Henry didn't even like touching his own skin. These small comforts allowed him to ignore Liam's barbs, even if the stuff about his dad was wearing thin.

Very thin.

"It's not so strange," Henry had said. "I loved him and I miss him."

Liam said nothing to this as Henry handed him the relatively clean underwear. He dunked his pants into the water, wondering if it was even cleaning anything at this point as the water had turned brown and smelled—albeit faintly—of urine and lemon. A combination that made Henry's stomach gurgle uncomfortably.

"Besides," Henry continued calmly, "you're a father. If you died, wouldn't you want your son to remember you? Maybe even to talk to you late at night, when he needed comforting?"

Henry braced for Liam's feet to come stomping toward him, maybe a kick in the shoulder or another slap in the head.

But Liam didn't come toward him, and when Henry reached out, he didn't see rage or hate coming from the man—only soft colors: the green of new grass, the pastel orange of a sunset.

Henry said nothing further as he scrubbed the crotch of his jeans in the water. When he handed them to Liam a few minutes later, Liam just nodded and gathered the other clothes, picked up the bucket they'd used for cleaning.

"I'll lay these in the sun and get them back to you when they're dry," he said, and left the room without looking back, without another word.

He had returned, and Henry had felt almost luxurious putting on the sun-warmed clothes.

Now, after a night in the cold room, those same clothes are frigid once more.

Henry goes to the heater and tries to mimic what Liam had done the day before. He opens the glass door, lights one of the matches from the yellow matchbox Liam gave him and holds it steadily over the thin metal pipe with the cut in it. The pilot. He turns the handle and presses—and *holds* this time—the primer button. A hiss of gas comes from the small pipe and he moves the match closer. There's a soft *whoomp* as the fire catches and he pulls his hand free, puts out the match, closes the small door.

Soon, the dark glass of the heater's window awakens, opening its wonderful red eye.

Henry sits on the floor, palms up to the warmth seeping from the heater, and lets his mind focus once more on the lost thread that had eluded him upon waking. He recalls a memory, a forgotten occurrence that happened when he was much younger, when his mother and father were still alive.

They'd gone to the San Diego Zoo, and even though he'd been only four or maybe five, he remembers the trip vividly.

It was one of the best, and worst, days of his early childhood.

He's sitting in a booster, strapped into the backseat of their old station wagon. His parents are talking in the front seat while he looks at a picture book called *Animals of Antarctica*. He'd hoped to see some of them at the zoo (penguins and polar bears quickly became his favorite creatures on earth shortly after his mother gave the book as a birthday present). Something about seeing them on all that *ice* and *snow* . . . miles and miles of bright white ground below the bluest sky he'd ever seen. So different from their world in San Diego, where it was always hot and bright, and snow was something you saw in picture books.

When they arrived at the zoo, he'd been put into a pink plastic stroller shaped like an elephant. The pink elephant held his drink, his small coat, and a bowl of snacks. Cheerios.

And while the memories of being pushed around to see the animals— of being lifted from the shade of the elephant by his father and held high to see the giraffes and rhinos, the monkeys and the great tigers—were vivid, it was the memory of what occurred at the penguin house that stayed with him. He'd been so thrilled to finally see the penguins, so *taken* with them—swimming through clear blue water and waddling around behind the glass on their fake shelf of Arctic ice—that he hadn't noticed the black-and-yellow fuzzball crawling out from beneath his blue corduroy shorts.

When he finally felt the tickle of the whatever-it-was crawling slowly, lethargically, over his narrow thigh, he wasn't alarmed, just fascinated. He thought the big bug was one of the coolest things he'd ever seen. He knew what a bee was, of course, but he'd only ever seen the small, skinny ones that crawled on flowers in the park. This bug was so fat and fuzzy that he wondered if maybe it wasn't a bee at all, but rather a squat little caterpillar.

Sold on the idea of it being a creeping caterpillar, he reached down with two tiny fingers and tried to pluck it from his leg. For a closer look, obviously.

A red-hot prick of pain lanced his thigh and Henry pulled his hand away and *screamed* at the top of his lungs.

The rest was a blur.

His mother and father shouting, wrestling him out of the plastic elephant as he screeched and wailed. He recalls all the people in the penguin exhibit turning to look at him, wide-eyed, their mouths black O's of surprise and concern, tears blurring their faces. He remembers feeling bad for the penguins. He hated to scream and thought he was probably scaring the little creatures, so he began to reach out his hands toward them while wailing (further confusing his parents as to the cause of his distress), as if even through thick glass and a guardrail he could somehow comfort them, let them know not to worry, not to be scared.

When his mother, searching frantically for the cause of his anguish, brushed his thigh—and the small black, broken stinger still stuck there, protruding like Arthur's sword from a swollen red mound—his screams doubled in intensity.

"Jack!" his mother screamed, and he was passed from his mother's hands to his father's.

And then things got bad.

Henry realized, through his tears and screams, that something was happening with his throat.

It was closing.

Squeezing shut as if gripped by a large, invisible hand. He began to choke, the screams shrinking into wheezes. His boisterous wails became raspy breaths as his tongue and his throat swelled, sealing off precious air-flow to his lungs, cutting him off from life.

He vividly recalled his mother's face growing more and more dim. *She* was the one screaming now, her fading face a mask of terror Henry would never, ever forget.

There were loud shouts and something stuck his leg. Rough hands moved over the place where he'd been stung and it hurt *really* bad but he was becoming sort of separated from the pain, from the hands, from the voices. From his mother's terror.

Later, he woke in an infirmary with his parents sitting beside him. There were about a dozen people in the room, different kinds of doctors and nurses. Henry thought some of them were animal doctors, and some people doctors. A couple of them—a man and a woman in blue shirts and cool baseball hats—stood the closest.

They smiled when he opened his eyes.

"Welcome back, Henry," the man said, and Henry smiled and reached out to touch the man's face.

When they put him in an ambulance to take him to the real hospital ("just to be safe" the man in the baseball hat told him), he learned he'd been stung by a honeybee. And that he—like many people—was allergic to the venom. He learned a lot about EpiPens and allergy shots over the coming weeks (much to his dismay), but recovered okay and had never had a problem since that day at the zoo, in the penguin house. Frankly, he'd almost forgotten all about his allergy to bee venom, that a single sting could potentially kill him if he didn't have his annual shots. With everything else that had happened to him in his short life, this particular detail had all but completely slipped his mind.

Until now, that is.

His eyes drift to the door and the thin crack running beneath it, knowing what he'd see there.

A single yellowjacket wasp—long and ugly—crawls curiously through that crack, wanders nonchalantly into Henry's room.

Henry walks slowly to his bed and curls his fingers around one of the scratchy green blankets, his eyes never leaving his insect visitor.

GO AWAY!

The wasp's antennae rise with its black-eyed head, twitching like a dog sniffing the air. Then it turns and crawls back under the door, and out of sight.

Henry runs to the door, breathing heavily, not aware he's whimpering as he stuffs the blanket into the crack beneath the door, sealing it as best he can.

In this moment, he recalls the dream.

The warning.

He remembers, and knows what is coming.

7

Liam chokes down the burnt coffee, tries to focus his attention on the front page of the newspaper. Sitting here, the morning light slanting in, a tin cup of relatively hot coffee in one hand and the daily paper in the other, he feels almost human. Almost normal. As if he is just some guy named Joe sitting in his kitchen on a pleasant Saturday, waiting for the kids to wake up and demand waffles or pancakes, and he grudgingly obliges them, what with the missus having run off to an early morning yoga class and all.

He wonders absently if his fictitious wife is having an affair. Was that cologne he smelled on her when she got home late last night from "drinks with a client"? Perhaps the publican was wearing a prodigious amount of aftershave and had kissed her on each cheek, or simply laid a hand on her shoulder when dropping off the pints or cocktails or whatever the fuck his nonexistent cheating fantasy wife drank at midnight during a bloody work meeting—

"What the hell is that?"

Liam snaps out of his thoughts, sips his coffee—now cold—and looks up to see Jim holding his own cup of coffee and staring hard at the card table Liam had been fantasizing was part of his normal-guy kitchen.

He doesn't care for the look on Jim's face, and hopes he can attribute it to the shite pot of coffee he's brewed. "What's what?"

Jim steps toward the table slowly, lifts one giant paw, extends a long, meaty finger, and sticks its tip onto the *San Diego Union-Tribune*'s front page. "What . . . the *fuck* . . . is that?"

Liam glances down at the paper, at Jim's big finger poking into Reagan's smiling, wrinkled face, and considers the question.

Then realization comes. *Shit.*

"They must have stopped," he says lamely.

Jim's lips press tightly together, his eyes showing too much bloodshot white around his charcoal-colored irises.

"Jim . . . wait . . ."

"Greg! Jenny! Kitchen! Now!" Jim slams his hand onto the table. "*Now, god damn it!*"

Liam stands from the chair, steps away from the newspaper as if it's made of poison ivy. As he steps deeper into the kitchen, slightly behind Jim, there's a sound he can barely make out. At first, he thinks it's his nerves, the pulsing of his own blood making his brain hum. But it isn't that. It's something else.

Despite not being summoned, it's actually Pete who enters first, his black hair matted to the side of his head, his thin T-shirt stretched over his wiry frame. Baggy gym shorts and bare feet give him the appearance of a child, and for the first time since meeting him Liam takes a moment to wonder how old Pete really is.

Before he can spend too much time considering, Greg and Jenny stumble in together. Jenny in nothing but panties and a tight, nearly transparent wife beater, Greg shirtless but—thank God—at least wearing sweats and white athletic socks.

"Jesus, man, where's the fire?" Greg says, and then notices Jim's hand resting on the paper. The sleep goes out of Greg's eyes as if wiped away. As he starts to explain, Jenny rolls her eyes, turns, and leaves the room.

"Where are you going?" Jim asks, not kindly.

"To put some fucking pants on. If I'm gonna get yelled at in front of a bunch of dudes it's not gonna be in my underwear."

And possibly to grab that weapon of yours, Liam thinks, and glances at Jim, who, meeting Liam's eyes for a heartbeat, obviously has the same thought. Almost unaware of his motion, Liam reaches around his waist to the small of his back and wraps his fingers around the butt of his Glock. He leans back, almost casually, against the far wall, and sets his tin cup of cold coffee onto the rotting countertop.

"Jim, look, man, it's no big deal. The paper was sitting on the sidewalk, that's all. We grabbed it."

"On the sidewalk," Jim says.

Jenny returns, now in jeans, a flannel shirt thrown over the wife beater. "Jesus, what's the big deal?" she says.

"Did you stop anywhere?" Jim asks, more calmly now, perhaps sensing a possible escalation. Liam watches as Jenny crosses her arms, the fingers of her right hand dangling precariously close to where he knows the handle of an eight-inch needle rests, ready to fly free from its hidden sheath.

Jenny starts to answer, but Greg holds up a hand to stall her, looks Jim in the eyes. "No, Jim. We didn't. We dropped the package at the doctor's house. There was a newspaper sitting on the sidewalk. I almost tripped over the thing. I picked it up and brought it with us. I wanted to see if maybe the kid was getting some press. I thought you'd be down with that. I'm sorry if I screwed up, but man, I don't think it matters one bit. It's not like they don't know we were there."

Liam's focus wanes. The buzzing in his head seems louder now, and he sees Pete turn around, his attention also drawn away from the human drama and toward . . . what? An electric current? That's what it sounds like to Liam.

Maybe it's not in my head after all, he thinks, and takes a step away from the wall, letting go his grip on the gun. He cocks his head as he steps toward the table. He and Pete look at each other a moment, then both their heads turn toward the kitchen door.

The one leading to the cellar.

"No, we did not stop," Greg is saying, enunciating as if speaking to a slow child. *Mistake, that*, Liam thinks absently as he shuffles closer to the door. The same door they had barricaded. The one they'd pushed a blanket against to keep the stink of the body from permeating the kitchen—before they knew it was a body.

Pete steps in close as Liam reaches out a hand—slowly—and places his fingertips gently against the door's old wood. He withdraws it with a gasp and meets Pete's eyes once again.

What? Pete mouths, but Liam only shakes his head and places his hand—full palm now—back onto the door.

"It's . . . vibrating," Liam whispers, and his eyes move from Pete to the others who, he notices somewhat uncomfortably, are all staring at him. *We must look like fools*, he thinks, wincing inwardly at the image of him and Pete hovering by the kitchen door, heads cocked, Liam's hand resting shakily on its surface.

"What's up with you two?" Jim asks. Liam notices a strain of tension in his voice. Not a carryover of the anger he was venting to Greg and Jenny, but something deeper, something more rooted in fear. An emotion he didn't think Jim capable of.

"There's something behind the door," Liam says, and removes his hand, takes two steps back. "Can't you hear it?"

They all stop. Stop arguing, stop shuffling their feet, stop breathing. The room is completely, totally silent.

A sonorous buzzing sound, a deep *hummmm* vibrates through the door from the cellar. Jim pulls a gun from his waistband and walks over to the door. He doesn't press his ear against it, doesn't feel it with his fingertips as Liam had. Instead, he points the barrel of the gun toward the door with one hand and presses the toe of his black military-style boot against the door's base. He drags the barrel of kerosene oil away—the one that has been keeping the door firmly shut—and grips the doorknob with his free hand.

Liam takes another step away, surprised to feel a wall against his back, and wishing he could retreat further. Greg and Jenny actually move closer to Jim, eager to see the mystery that waits in the dark.

As Liam watches, something skinny and black crawls out from the blanket stuffed beneath the door. It twitches, as if testing for damage, then rises into the air and begins to circle the heads of the unwitting group of criminals and killers. For Liam, time seems to slow, his vision narrowing to almost preternatural focus, his senses stripped to raw nerves—the air hurts his skin, the light blinds his eyes, the *sound* erupts in his ears.

The wasp hovers, spins, and lands on the countertop a few feet from where Liam rests his hand. He turns to study it more closely and feels a chill at the flicker of its antennae, the glossy shine of its long body, the black needle sagging in its rear. It appears to tilt its head toward him, alien eyes meeting his own.

Liam gets the impression the thing is pissed off.

At the door, Jim is hesitating.

"Open it, man," Jenny says, smirking. "If you're afraid, I'll do it."

Jim's dark eyes flick to Jenny, promising a slow death.

"Wait," Liam says weakly, watching helplessly as Jim's fingers tighten on the old chrome doorknob. "Jim, wait!" he yells, finding his voice.

"Bullshit," Jim mumbles, and yanks the doorknob.

Liam's first thought is that someone has laid a black blanket over the other side of the door. The next volley his brain throws at him is that perhaps it's mold, black and fuzzy and completely covering every inch of the peeling white paint he should be seeing.

Except it's *moving*.

Jim steps back quickly, too quickly. He knocks into Pete, who falls heavily to the floor, inadvertently kicking the back of Jim's knee as he does so. Jim's leg bends and his gun fires.

The roar of the gun is deafening in the enclosed room, and when the bullet strikes the mass of black-and-yellow insects blanketing the door, they erupt into the air as a writhing cloud. The electric-wire buzzing triples in volume and before Liam can even think of what to do next—

They attack.

Jim spins, swatting at the air, and falls into the card table, splitting it in half as if it were made of cardboard. He thunders and bellows as the swarm spreads out and descends onto any and all exposed arms and necks, faces and legs; they land in hair and crawl toward scalps before puncturing deep with their venomous stingers.

Liam starts to run but trips, crashing into the moldy cabinets beneath the countertop. He feels the give of rotting wood as a gust of musty air blows into his mouth and nose. There's a piercing pain in the back of his neck and he doesn't know if he's been stung or if a splinter from the broken cabinet has driven into his skin. Something long and black lands on his cheekbone and crawls up onto his eye, partially obscuring his vision. He holds his breath and tries not to move as the insect keeps crawling, over his eyebrow and forehead, before tickling the edge of his hairline. Without moving his head he lowers his eyes to inspect his arms and legs, and horror slams into his brain like a crashing black wave. A dozen wasps are crawling over him.

Screams fill the room and he slowly looks upward. Pete is spinning madly, hands flailing. Greg has run from the room and Jenny is on her knees, screeching and wailing. Her bare arms and shoulders are covered with the things; they crawl in her hair and over her face.

Jim lifts a full bottle of bourbon and throws it at a window draped in a dull pink sheet. The glass shatters as bottle, sheet, and a handful of wasps all flow out of the room.

"*Fuuuuuuck!*" Pete bellows and turns, running out of the kitchen. He plows hard into Jenny, his knee meeting her chin with enough force that Liam hears a *crack* as her head snaps back into the doorframe. Her screams cut off and she slumps to the floor, lifeless. The wasps continue their savage feast on her as Pete runs to the front door of the farmhouse and throws it open, his screams growing distant as morning light filters through the kitchen entryway.

Liam feels more stings, one on his ankle. Another on his lower back. An especially painful one flares hot on his wrist. He knows they won't stop and he looks around for anything that might help him. The blanket from under the door is near his feet, crawling with bugs. The lantern that had been on the card table—now destroyed—lies sideways on the floor just a few feet away. Next to it is a mess of newspaper.

Not wanting to run, to desert Jim and Jenny, Liam instead digs into his pocket, squashing at least two insects in the process, and pulls out a cheap Bic lighter. He takes a deep breath and leaps for the blanket, grabs it, and yanks it back. He cries out as his thumb feels the pierce of a wasp sting while the insect's brethren hover off the blanket like a mist. Liam gains his feet, takes three steps and—swinging it like a cape—brings the blanket over his head and shoulders, then spins and scoops the lantern and the newspaper off the floor.

Jim is screaming at him but he can't stop—not yet. He ignores the barbs stabbing his skin as he throws the newspaper into the sink, then lifts and smashes the lantern down on top of it. Glass shatters and kerosene spills—as he hoped it would—darkening the strewn pages of the *Tribune*'s front section. He flicks his lighter and lowers it to the kerosene-soaked paper.

Flames erupt from the basin and dark smoke rises from the sink. Liam raises his arms, fists clenching the fabric of the blanket, creating an umbrella over himself that catches the smoke and holds it.

He shuts his eyes tight, and holds his breath.

There's a loud *buzz* in his ear and a red-hot poker stabs his neck just beneath the earlobe—not wanting to open his mouth under the blanket, not even to scream in pain, he grits his teeth and waits for the smoke to do its work. After ten seconds the smoke is thick and he no longer feels, or hears, any wasps. The rest of the newspaper catches quickly. The heat is strong but he forces himself to stay close as long as he's able. He knows the smoke will likely piss them off, but it will also choke and confuse them. He had to remove a couple of nests back in Australia while doing construction work, and although smoke worked when they were docile, it tended to piss them off proper when agitated. But he needs to get Jim and Jenny out of here, and he prays this will help.

Finally, unable to hold his breath any longer, and praying the smoke is thick enough to keep the insects away from him, he slowly lowers his hands, lets the smoke escape into the room, and takes in a breath.

He opens his eyes. The air is dense with smoke and frantic, buzzing wasps, but there are far fewer than there had been.

"Jim!"

Jim is crawling toward the door, but his trajectory is off and Liam wonders if they've gotten his eyes. He steps through the rubble of the table and grabs Jim's arm, hauls him to his feet. Many of the wasps are on the ground, crawling and confused. Liam can feel their bodies crunch beneath his sneakers.

Liam gets Jim to his feet and pushes him toward the door. "Run, mate! And *keep* running!"

Jim runs for the door, arms crossed over his face.

Liam drops to a knee beside Jenny's limp body, which lies facedown on the floor. He doesn't know how many times he's been stung—more than a dozen, he'd guess—and is beginning to feel sick, not to mention the pain coming from the stings on nearly every exposed part of his body.

But Jenny has it much worse.

Tiny stingers protrude from her neck and arms, the swelling bumps deep red and big as knuckles. A few bugs still crawl over her skin. He brushes them away as best he can, then drapes the blanket over her body, flips her over, and slides his arms beneath her legs and neck. A wasp climbs into his ear and he shakes his head; another lands on his cheek, sinks its stinger in deep.

Liam screams as he lurches from the smoky room, toward the promise of light and fresh air through the front door, and into the goddamned daylight.

★ ★ ★

Henry sits on his bottom, knees locked, legs straight as steel rods as his heels press the blanket to the bottom of the door. He knows one sting could kill him, although whether he's as allergic to wasp venom as honeybee venom he doesn't know. The doctors he saw after his childhood incident had liked to say things like "Always assume the worst when it comes to allergies."

Using that logic, he isn't going to take any chances. He smells the distant stink of smoke, and wonders if the house is burning down. It's hard to tell exactly what's happening from the chaos erupting downstairs: the screams, the bright flashing colors as he bounces from mind to mind. He thinks the girl might be dead but doesn't have the focus or concern to try to dig deeper. Her thoughts have gone out like a candle flame on a birthday cake, and part of him hopes she *is* dead. Hopes they all die, or run and keep running. Keep running and never come back.

That's what *she* wants, after all.

He giggles a little, feeling bad about it but enjoying their pain, their panic. He hates them. His father's voice hums in his head. *Yeah, you hate them, and so does she. So does her little one. She's feeding off you, off your hate. You know that, right, son? Can you feel her pulling off your powers?*

Henry doesn't want to listen to his father anymore, so he instead listens to the screams coming from outside. Through the boarded window of his room, from his own tired mind as he reaches out to the kidnappers and relishes their misery. It makes him giddy. It makes him feel strong. Like he isn't just a scared little kid. A victim.

He can be the aggressor as well. He and Mother can do such amazing things.

The wasps?

The wasps, Henry knows, are nothing at all. A warning they can heed or ignore.

This is only the beginning.

8

"Things are moving fast now," Sali says to the tired, emotionally drained, and increasingly frustrated couple sitting at the kitchen table. "Dave, Mary, this is good news, okay?" He chuckles, lowers his head a bit, forcing them to meet his eyes. "I mean, *really* good news."

The report had come in the previous evening: Greg and Jenny Lanigan had been positively identified at a gas station outside Grantville around 4 p.m. yesterday afternoon.

Sali couldn't believe what a huge break he'd been handed. Assuming the siblings had been returning from dropping off the envelope at the shrink's residence just south of Mission Valley—or on their way *to* the shrink, perhaps—which was approximately five miles from the gas station, logic dictated the rest of the gang wasn't holed up any more than a couple hours' drive from that point. Which made a lot of sense considering the location of Henry's school, the janitor's apartment, and the location of the first drop.

There's no way they're doing all this shit outside the city. The gas station was likely a last-minute screwup, one I desperately needed.

"Based on what we know, I believe they have Henry somewhere very close. Within an hour or two by car, is my guess. Probably secluded—I don't think they'd risk having him seen going in or out of an apartment or even a neighborhood-type house, okay? I highly doubt it's downtown or anywhere west. My hunch? They're in the hills somewhere, either using a ranch house or an empty barn . . . somewhere with no foot traffic, no street cameras, that sort of thing. You with me?"

Dave nods and Mary does her best to feign attention, but Sali knows these guys are near the end of their emotional ropes. It doesn't look like either one has slept much the last four days, and he hasn't personally seen them eat anything. He makes a mental note to ask around about that, make sure they have food in their systems. He needs them alert and active.

The hardest part of this whole thing is yet to come, and he'll need one or both of them to bring this thing home.

"Now, we have a photo of Henry and the final ransom demand. All things considered, the boy looks good. Does not appear to be abused or malnourished. Our team is practiced at identifying things like that from something as simple as a look in the eyes, and all signs point to Henry being treated fairly well."

"I want to see the photo!" Dave blurts, and Sali grimaces.

"Not just yet. When our team is done we'll provide a copy, okay? Seeing your boy exhausted and stuck in a room somewhere is going to do absolutely zero for your peace of mind, believe me on this."

Dave doesn't nod, but he lowers his eyes in acquiescence.

"Now, based on where the drop is, my hunch is they're gonna pick up the money and run for the border. This is also good news because it gives us another line of defense to try to catch these guys before they hit Mexico. I'm fairly sure by the time this happens Henry will no longer be with them—"

Mary gasps, her eyes water, and Sali curses at himself internally. *Mind your words, asshole.* He holds up a hand and moves on quickly.

"What I mean is they'll have left him in this hideout. Likely secure him somehow so he can't escape, then make a run for it."

Sali doesn't like to lie, but sometimes it's necessary. He knows the chances the kidnappers would leave the boy alive are infinitesimal. But like the Thornes, even he needs to hold onto a little hope, no matter how sparse, no matter the statistics, or the odds, even when the statistics are flashing in bright neon. Sometimes you need to avoid the bright colors and focus on the dark instead.

"They're supposed to leave instructions on his whereabouts at the drop, in exchange for the money," he continues. "Once we have the location we'll move in and get your boy. Meanwhile, another team will track the movements of the kidnappers. We'll likely nab them before they reach the border, if not at the drop. Also, we work closely with Mexican authorities. It's not like they cross the border and that's that. We'll get them, trust me."

"If you don't find them first," Mary says, hope welling in her eyes. "You said they're close, you have leads. The ransom demand is for tomorrow . . . maybe you can still find them, right?"

"That's correct. We have APBs focusing on the areas I've talked about with you. This narrows the search tremendously and allows us to focus our resources. It's a huge win, guys. They screwed up, and we were there to catch them. The news did their job, just like we hoped."

"I'll do the drop," Dave says. "They wanted one of us, right? I'll do it."

Attaboy.

"Okay," Sali says. "You have a deal. The FBI has the money. But I'm hoping it doesn't come to that. I'm hoping—like Mary says—that we see one of these bastards in the wild and get a tail to their hideout. If we can narrow it down even a little, I can bring in planes and choppers, start searching that way. I have one chopper in the air already looking for that ugly car of theirs, as well as the brown Duster we know they were driving a couple days ago."

"You said they had a green Pinto," Dave says, almost to himself. As if confirming hard facts will settle his mind, give his swirling emotions somewhere to latch on.

"Yeah. Another reason I don't think they're far away. I mean, come on, are you really gonna travel more than a few miles in a piece of shit like that?"

Dave chuckles and even Mary offers a half-hearted smile.

Good enough, Sali thinks, and pats Dave on the knee. "You two get some food into you, please, for me. I'm gonna go check in with all departments and get some updates for you."

Hang with me, guys. One way or another, this thing is going to be all over in twenty-four hours. Win or lose, the game is coming to a close.

I sure hope we win this one, and I think we will.

I think we've got these bastards on the ropes, and I'm winding up.

9

Jim looks at his miserable crew and tries to figure out just what the hell is going on around here. Jenny has finally come around from what he guesses is a serious concussion. The back of her head split when Pete knocked her against the wall, and there's a baseball-shaped blot of clumped, bloody hair amid all that white-girl blonde. But all she's doing, now that she's awake, is moaning and drooling. Of all of them she got stung the worst. By *far*. It was like when she went down the whole army of wasps had camped out and just stung and stung and stung. Greg lost count but he said it was right around fifty stings, which Jim figures could kill a person. Liam made sure all the left-behind stingers were removed from her skin, but there weren't that many. A dozen, maybe. Jim pulled one of those fucking things out of his own arm and it wasn't pleasant.

Now Greg won't leave her side, pouring water into her mouth, over the wounds, holding her wrist as if to make sure her heart doesn't stop altogether. Jim thinks maybe it could, but honestly doesn't give two shits. She's been poisoning the well, that one. Turning Greg against him, preaching mutiny. Even if she does live, Jim figures the chances are good he'd end up killing the traitorous bitch anyway.

As for the others—they'll live. Pete is whining and pissing about how much pain he's in, but whatever. That dude had been the first to escape, running for the trees like he was being chased by death itself. Hasn't gotten more than ten stings, but you'd think he was covered in them the way he goes on and on. Greg, miraculously, got away with only a few, and Liam and himself have their share. He would've had more if Liam hadn't picked his ass up and all but thrown him out the door. Dude probably saved Jenny's life as well. She would have lain there getting pricked by those black-and-yellow bastards forever if Liam hadn't carried her out. Liam's neck and face are bad, though, and he'd thrown up right after he dumped the girl's body into a clump of grass a hundred feet from the house.

The wasps had hung around, chasing them a bit, but out in the open they were pussies compared to being inside. The smoke had filled up the kitchen good, and they'd either choked to death or scattered for open air.

By the time it seemed safe to venture back inside, Greg was crying about taking Jenny to a hospital—*not happening*—and the fire in the sink had gone out. The smoke was bad, which made Jim nervous. *Very* nervous. Smoke signals to nearby Ranger Rick assholes was not what he considered a good thing. But from outside the smoke was hardly visible, and he relaxed about it.

"Think she's gonna pull through?" Liam asks, gently dabbing one of the swollen red nubs on his cheek with an ice cube.

"Yeah, man. She'll be alright. How's the kid?"

First thing Liam had done was run upstairs to check on Henry. Jim was okay with that—all they needed was to find the little dude covered in stings, his skin nothing but boils and pus, his tiny weak heart dead as cooked meat.

"He's fine. I mean, he said he was okay. I just knocked and hollered. You know what he did? He stuffed blankets beneath the door."

"So? I told you he was smart."

"Yeah," Liam says, leaving the rest of his thought unspoken.

Jim nods but frankly he doesn't give three shits for the kid, for Liam, for the whole damned crew. Tomorrow they'll get out of this hellhole, get the money, dump the kid (alive or dead—but Jim was leaning toward dead), and skip out of the States forever.

"Oh man! Oh man oh man! Mother *fucker*!"

Jim stands, alarmed, and spins toward Pete, who's staring down into one of the boxes of food with such disgust Jim thinks he must have found a dead rat.

Or worse.

"What?" Liam says, going to look. He bends over, nearly sticking his head into the box, then turns and looks at Jim with haunted eyes. "You've got to be kidding me."

"What the hell you two on about?" Jim asks, feeling butterflies in his own stomach at the looks on their faces. "What the hell's in there? Dead babies?"

They both back away as he comes to look. He grabs the box by the corner and tilts it toward him, part of him wondering if these two assholes are playing a joke on him, having some fun with old Jim.

Then he sees the maggots.

The Wonder Bread bag is filled with them. The plastic sags like a full diaper when Jim lifts it by the tied-off end. Unlike a diaper, however, the bag is *moving*.

He looks at the other food. Oatmeal, peanut butter, a box of Frosted Flakes, Oreo cookies, a giant bag of Frito-Lay chips . . . all of it covered in white, gummy slugs.

Must be hundreds of them, he thinks, and drops the bag of bread, dusting off a few grubs that had wormed onto his fingertips. "Musta left the bread open," he mumbles, knowing it still made no sense. *How could there be so many so fast?* He has a sinking feeling in his gut. "Check the other boxes," he says sharply.

To their credit, neither Liam nor Pete hesitate or stop to ask dumbass questions. Pete pulls a box out from behind the spare kerosene tank, looks inside, and curses. Liam stumbles across the room, kicks through the rubble of the table, and glares into the box they'd had on the counter—mostly liquor, but there are some crackers and shit—

"Oh my God," Liam says. "It's impossible."

"Jesus, man. They're *inside* the jelly!" Pete says, holding up a glass jar of Welch's Grape, the lid screwed on tight. Jim can see the white wiggling bodies floating inside, pressing against the glass, and feels bile stir in his normally ironclad stomach.

"All the food," Pete says. "They got all the food. I don't know, Jim." Pete brings his fingers to his temples, rubbing them hard against his skin. His eyes are wide and glazed, and Jim can see him shaking. "I'm beginning to think this place is haunted," Pete says, a quiver in his voice. "I mean, this shit ain't natural, brother. The wasps? Now this? Uh-uh. Ain't right."

"Relax," Jim says, but his tone is uneasy. Using two fingers, he picks up the jar of peanut butter from the box he'd been looking at. He brushes off a few of the grubs sticking to the side, then unscrews the lid. The jar was about half full, they'd been pretty much surviving on PB&J, but what's left is smothered in peanut butter-smeared maggots. He drops the open jar into the box with disgust. He feels uneasy, unsettled. This isn't possible. Food doesn't get infested in hours, and inside the sealed jars?

It's *sabotage.*

But how?

He feels like a man lost in a great dark sea who can't get his bearings, can't find a toehold on reality, on something that makes *sense.*

"All right, let's get all this shit out of here. Dump it out back in the grass."

"But this is our food, Jim!" Pete yells, slamming a box of Cheerios to the ground in a fit. Jim sees grubs spew out of the box along with the little O's and spray across the floor. His stomach starts to churn like hot stew again. He turns away from the mess and meets Liam's eyes.

Liam looks scared, or at least worried as hell. Jim figures his own face looks similar. Pete, though . . . Pete looks panicked. Pete looks like a guy who is about to *lose it.* Like a guy who might be cracking up a little bit.

Jim holds his patience the way a cowboy holds the reins of a bucking horse, keeping it in control. For now. "I don't know what happened, but we've got water, and we've got booze. We got one, two more days here, tops. We'll be fine."

"Two days?" Pete's mouth twists into a pouty frown and Jim sees the ten-year-old version of the boy formerly known as Pedro Scalera: his face red, the ugly welts of wasp bites dotting his skin, his hair greasy and his breath bad. Jim hates Pete in that moment. *The horse is bucking, boys. It's bucking hard and the cowboy's grip is getting a little loose on the reins.*

"Like we discussed, man. Tomorrow we get the dough. Once it's secured, we're gone. But if there's a problem, we come back here, right? If there's no problem, if you don't see me for a day, then you torch the place and bust out. Like. We. Discussed."

Pete looks like he wants to say something—something not particularly pleasant—but then just nods wearily.

Good dog.

"Come on, let's get this shit out of here. Makes me sick," Liam says. Carrying one of the boxes by the edge, held away from his body, he makes for the front door.

"What the hell?" Greg asks from the other room, and Jim rolls his eyes. "Where are you taking our food?"

"Go," Jim says to Pete, who picks up the other box in one hand, the one Jim had been inspecting. "Dump that shit far away, dig?"

"Yeah yeah," Pete mumbles, and walks out of the kitchen.

Jim feels a chill. A breeze pushes through the broken window, the one he threw a bottle at in an effort to clear out the wasps. He forces himself to unclench his hands. *Gotta get shit under control.*

He begins to organize the debris of the kitchen when his eye catches the cooler, the one holding their soda, beer, and water. He lifts the red lid with one finger, expecting the worst.

But he sees only ice. He bends down, picks up a can of Budweiser, cracks it open, and downs half the can. He belches, feeling a pleasant lightness, a calm returning to his worried mind. He barks out the broken window as the top of Pete's head bobs by.

"And pick up that bottle of Jack I threw!" he yells, and chuckles. He finishes the beer and sees a weary-looking Greg slumped against the door of the kitchen, watching him with haunted eyes.

"The fuck is going on?" he asks.

Ain't gonna rattle my cage, baby. No way, no how.

I'm solid.

Jim smiles, grabs two more beers out of the cooler, and tosses one to Greg. "Nothing, baby. We all good. Drink that, you'll feel better."

Greg does as he's told, looks over the devastation of the kitchen.

"Gonna be rich real soon, buddy. You hold on to that thought," Jim says and begins to feel that fire again, the strength that hate and rage and revenge gives him; the nasty old dragon he keeps inside, the one who needs to remind him every now and then who the fucking boss is around here. Not that freaky thing in the woods, not the wasps or the maggots, not Jenny or the know-it-all brat locked away upstairs. No, baby, Jim is in charge. Jim and the dragon and nobody else.

A few minutes later, Pete returns holding the bottle of Jack Daniels. "Thing didn't even break," he says, smiling his gold-toothed smile, a red blister teeming with wasp venom distorting his upper lip. "Must be our lucky fucking day!"

10

While the rest of the crew sifts through what's left of their food store—consisting primarily of water, a half-gallon of milk, beer, and liquor—Liam decides he'd better bring Henry whatever breakfast is still available.

In this case, that means a red plastic cup filled halfway with milk.

And the milk smells like it might be turning. But it isn't chunky, so small miracles, etc.

"Henry?" Liam calls as he slides the bolt. He pushes the door inward, feels the resistance of the blanket sliding along the floor at the door's bottom. "Henry? I'm back," he says, then gasps as the boy sits up in the bed.

Although it has been less than twelve hours since Liam last sat with Henry, he's shocked at the noticeable physical change. *He looks like he's been stuck in this room for weeks, not days.*

Henry's eyes are bloodshot, sunken and ravaged with dark circles. His hair looks brittle. His cheeks hollow, his skin gray. Liam wishes he was holding a platter of pancakes instead of the measly two swallows of milk (now rationed), but luck or fate or something much darker has pushed against them, and they are all paying the price now.

"Jesus, kid. You look terrible."

Henry *feels* terrible. Like something inside him has been eaten away. Gnawed to the bone. After the screaming stopped, he'd gone back to his bed (leaving the blanket along the door in case a stray wasp had been left to wander). The room had the usual stink of piss and shit and burning kerosene, but there was another scent beneath these more obvious well-known odors. At first, Henry couldn't place it. Thought maybe it was just his own BO, or perhaps the mold in the walls, or mildew from the heaped cardboard boxes sulking in the corner.

Then he thought maybe it was the smell of death. His own death.

Am I dying? he asks himself—himself and whoever else might be listening.

No one answers, and he decides not to dwell on the question—or the answer—in order to keep his sanity relatively intact.

"I'm fine," he says weakly, and notices, without surprise but with an overwhelming disappointment, that Liam carries no food.

As Liam closes the door behind him and steps into the room, Henry notices the dude doesn't look ready for a Saturday night out himself. He has welts on his arms, neck, and face from the wasp stings; his skin is waxen and pale as the bare walls surrounding them. He looks oily and his hair is clumped at the side of his head, and when he gets close enough Henry smells *his* body odor without any effort at all.

Liam hands him the cup of milk and sits at the edge of the cot, looking down at his own hands, as if pondering a problem. Henry drinks the milk in three gulps. It's a little sour, but it's cold. He wonders if it's the last meal he'll ever receive. The last thing he'll ever put into his body.

He prays he can keep it down.

"Henry," Liam says, and Henry looks with interest at the clashing colors of Liam's feelings: the dark gray of doubt, the crimson streaks of fear, the writhing peach and orange snakes of confusion. Henry thinks, in that moment, that the world would be much different if everyone could see the things he saw. It would be a lot more honest, for one. And perhaps a lot better, assuming it didn't drive folks insane. "I need to ask you . . ." Liam says, hesitant, then continues in a rush: "I want to know everything you know about the thing you've communicated with. The thing in the cellar . . . and the one you call Mother."

"Why do you want to know now? You didn't care before," Henry says, giving Liam his most defiant tone. He didn't like when people made fun of him, and now that the man is scared, now that maybe he *believes* what Henry has told him, all that kicking and screaming is supposed to be erased? Now Henry is supposed to *help* Liam? After all the crapola he'd done?

No way, hombre.

"Henry, I know you don't like me very much," Liam says, as if he's the one who can read minds, "but I need to know if this thing is dangerous. Some weird shit is going on, and I'm beginning to worry how all this added stress will affect, to be frank, your safety. You don't want these people pissed off at you, Henry."

Henry hands the empty milk cup to Liam, who takes it solemnly, then lies back down. He is so *tired.* "Don't know what you're talking about," he says, and almost smiles when Liam scoffs.

"Don't be stubborn, Henry. I'm sorry I lost my temper, okay? I really am. It's not cool to be hitting you and . . . and I promise it won't happen again. Look, you can read my mind or whatever, right? Look at me and tell me if I'm lying."

Henry turns his head, meets Liam's eyes. The guy looks even worse close up, and Henry turns away quickly. "Fine," Henry says, having dipped quickly into Liam's head and seen the truth of it, or at least that he thinks he's telling the truth. Henry knows those are different things, but he's too exhausted to explain it to a grown-up.

"You asked me who Timothy was," Liam says, his tone different than Henry has ever heard it. He sounds human. Like a normal person. Despite himself, Henry flips over, puts his hands behind his head, elbows cocked outward, as if Liam is about to read him a bedtime story. He raises his eyebrows, his expression matching his posture: *Well, I'm waiting.*

Liam takes a deep breath, then sinks back so he's resting against the wall. In a different world, in a different place and under different circumstances, a bystander who peeked in on the scene might think them father and son, or perhaps age-gapped siblings. Possibly friends.

"Timothy is my son," he starts, the words coming slowly, as if dragged to his lips from a faraway place. "He'd be about the same age as you now, perhaps a year older."

Henry, always curious, feels excitement grow in his belly. His mind conjures up a thousand questions, but he holds them inside for now, not

wanting to interrupt the story, realizing the new ground of this relationship is tenuous, as fragile—and dangerous—as thin ice on a cold lake.

"He and his mum—" Liam pauses, then quickly continues, a strange
smile on his lips. A *dreamy* smile. "They live in Australia. I had to leave
when . . . well, it's complicated. Anyway, I haven't seen him in a while. But
when you saw . . . whatever it was you saw when you were playing around
in my head, that's what it was. He's my boy. Timothy's my son. So, you see?
I'm not a complete monster. I raised a child, which makes me a tiny bit
human, doesn't it?"

"You miss him, huh?"

Liam sighs, stares into the empty red cup as if it contains the right
answer, an answer he can live with.

"Every day," he says quietly.

They stay that way a few moments, both of them quiet, both lost in
thoughts. Then Henry says, "I told you what she wants. She wants you,
me, *all* of us, to leave here. She'll keep doing what she's doing until we go
away. That, or—"

Liam shifts his body weight, hunches over his knees. Head bowed.

"Or what?"

Henry shrugs. "Leave and live," he says calmly. "Or stay and die."

"Wasps and maggots aren't killing anyone, Henry," Liam says, and
Henry hears the old steel in his voice return. The threat that lies buried
deep inside the man, waiting to be beckoned, waiting to come out.

Henry just shrugs again, not seeing the need to reveal what he knows.
Not sure it would do any good, anyway.

"Besides," Liam says, sitting up, "you can talk to her, right? You guys
have a little psychic connection going on, as batshit loony as that sounds. I
think maybe you tell the old girl to lay off, eh? I'm sure she'd hate to see
anything happen to that thing in the cellar. You tell her that. And remember, Henry . . ."

Liam stands, looks down at Henry's small body, his tired eyes. "What happens to us, happens to you, mate. You understand?"

Henry says nothing for a moment. A tear spills from the corner of his eye and he quickly wipes it away. He turns his back to Liam, faces the wall. "I'm dead anyway," he says finally.

Liam looks around the room, still searching for answers. Guidance. He sees the piss-bucket, the tired old heater, the mold clinging to the walls. "That's not true, son," he says quietly, no longer sure of anything.

"I'm not your son," Henry says into the thin pillow. Then he turns over, doing it so quickly that Liam takes a half step back. Henry's eyes suddenly don't look tired, or bloodshot, or sad. Or scared. Liam thinks they look hard as steel.

"And I hope she kills every single one of you."

11

Pete enters the dark cellar. He holds the flashlight before him like a divining rod, steps carefully down each concrete step. He knows Jim would be peeved at him wasting battery power, but Pete is pretty far past giving a damn what Jim thinks. This whole thing has gone south, and Pete's confident something's going on that's being kept from him—from him and Greg and Jenny, that is.

He figures it has something to do with the thing in the cellar.

He reaches the dirt floor and there's a soft *crunch*, as if he's stepped on dried-up popcorn or broken potato chips. *You got food on the brain, Scalera. Best get off that train 'cause it's going nowhere.* He turns his light to the ground and his brain shrieks, his body jerking backward as he retreats to the lowest step.

They're dead, dummy. They're all dead.

The ground is littered with hundreds of dead wasps, most of them nothing more than desiccated husks, as if they'd been dead for days or weeks. "Weird," Pete murmurs and, deciding it's safe, moves off the step.

Crunch.

"Gross." He's glad to have his thick-soled boots and nothing flimsy that a stinger—even a dead stinger—could slip through. He's had enough stings to last him a lifetime. "Well, at least the dead guy's gone."

Pete and Liam had used one of the blankets to cover the bastard and haul him out to the woods. Liam had brought the shovel, but when they got fifty yards out or so they both agreed just to toss the fucker on the ground. Let the animals have him. They smoked and shot the shit for fifteen minutes to make it look good, then headed back for a snort of whatever liquor was left and a few hands of five-card stud.

Gonna need another drink after this. A double. Hell, a triple!

Pete forces himself a few more feet, each step raising the hackles on the back of his neck and making his teeth grind. He turns the beam of the flashlight toward the brick wall. "What the hell, man?" he says, spotting the gaping hole in the once solid wall, the scattered bricks cast into the dirt, the small chunks of mortar. The hole is low to the ground, sectioned out in a way that is unnatural, done purposely by someone. *Or something.* The idea tastes like fear, and he swallows it down hard.

After glancing quickly around—lighting up the corners and shadows where the sunlight doesn't reach—he assures himself he's alone and relaxes. He carefully approaches the broken wall, thinks about kneeling down and lighting up the other side, but the thought of kneeling on dead wasps is not his idea of a good time, so he demurs. Plus, he isn't crazy about what he might see through that hole. Perhaps something—maybe the same something that had torn out all this brick—is still there, waiting for him, a dark face grinning back from the shadowed flipside of the cellar. *Yeah, fuck that.*

He takes a deep breath, lets it out, and turns. He points the beam toward the upper corner of the room, at the object he's come to investigate.

The freaky cocoon.

He moves toward it, the hot white beam of the flashlight giving it an eerie sheen he hadn't noticed before, as if it's wet, the leaves and mud moist to the point of—

"Oh my God." His eyes trail with the light from the cocoon to the dirt below, where a small, milky-white puddle has formed. "The damned thing is leaking," he says, noticing a thin string of mucus secreting from the damp shell, drawing a shiny line to the dirt.

Pete stuffs his free hand into his pocket, feels the heft of the switchblade he keeps there. He pulls it free, and the blade *snicks* to life, glinting in the raw filtered sunlight like a warning. He starts toward the cocoon.

"Pete!"

He jumps and spins around, a held breath releasing with a sickly gasp. He's sweating, his gut tight as a drum.

Jim's elongated shadow falls across the concrete stairs. "What are you doing, man? Get your ass up here. We all need to talk."

"Yeah, one second," Pete says, turning back, wide-eyed, to the cocoon. His breath catches in his throat because for a brief second—the space from one heartbeat to the next—he thinks he saw something *move* inside that shell. Like a baby's foot kicking against the stomach of a woman coming up on the nine-month mark.

"Now, Pedro. I ain't asking you."

Jim's shadow disappears and Pete scowls at the cocoon one last time. Grudgingly, he pushes the back of the blade against his thigh and snaps it closed with a *click*. "I'll be back, amigo," he says in a whisper. "I'll be back because you and I are gonna have a little talk. Okay? You feel me, *cabrón*? I'll be back real soon."

Pete turns and hustles up the stairs, ignoring the crunch of dead insects beneath his feet, and slams the door of the cellar, sending the underground chamber once more into muddy darkness.

★ ★ ★

Henry stands at the boarded-up window, staring into cracks of daylight broken by a distinctive shadow.

Looking at the face of Mother, who stares back.

Henry shakes his head slightly. "I don't know, they don't tell me," he says in a barely audible whisper. The creature looks more alien than Henry could have imagined, but he likes her eyes. They remind him of Blink, his old tabby. The one he'd left behind when he and Dad moved to the apartment. From what he can see of her face through the one-inch gaps, her features are squished and brown, like how he imagines an ant's face might look close up, but without the antennae and the choppers where a mouth would be. *Mandibles.* Henry remembers the word and smiles.

He's glad Mother doesn't have those, it would probably freak him out. There are two nubs protruding at either end of her forehead, but anything beyond that is obscured by a thick black shell, like a hood. Her mouth is similar to a human's, but wider and straight across. No lips. Just more of that dark, heavy skin.

He can't understand the sounds the creature makes, but the thoughts are clear, the fears, the demands, easy to translate.

GO!

It is almost time.

Which means that for Henry, and the group that brought him to this place, time is running out.

★ ★ ★

Jim eyeballs the tattered remnants of his crack squad of criminal masterminds. Jenny lies semi-conscious and moaning atop her sleeping bag. Her brother sits cross-legged, her head in his lap, stroking her hair like she's a five-year-old. Liam sits on the stairs, elbows on knees, head hung low. Jim figures he's thinking, probably thinking too much. Probably thinking about the little piggybank they have stowed upstairs.

Gonna have to keep an eye on that.

His eyes move to Pete, who's twitching like a junkie and, for reasons unknown, prowling the damned root cellars like he's looking for buried treasure.

They all look like hell, they're all hungry and tired. But Jim needs them for one more day. He needs them to hold it together just a little longer.

★ ★ ★

Henry takes two steps away from the window and concentrates.

Can you help me? WILL YOU HELP ME?

The response Henry gets is garbled, he can't make sense of it, but something hard taps against one of the boards outside the window.

TAP.

Then again:

TAP! TAP!

Henry watches with a sense of awe as the fingers of one gnarled claw slide between the highest board and the windowpane. He thinks those claws are more like talons than fingers, and he wonders if he's right about the creature being more insect than animal.

There's a soft *ween*, like metal bending, then a *SNAP* as the board across the top of the window pulled cleanly away.

Henry laughs.

The creature grabs the next board, and Henry sees—too late—that this one has been nailed directly into the frame. As she pulls, he can see the thin old glass waver.

"Wait!" he yells.

The nail pulls free, and the window shatters.

★ ★ ★

Liam springs to his feet, turns and looks toward the second floor. He looks back at Jim—mouth open, eyes wide. Jim is already moving toward the stairs.

"Go!" he bellows, and Liam goes.

★ ★ ★

Henry runs to the window, waving his arms. "Stop!"

The creature lifts its head so it can look down at him from where the top board—one of five or six nailed against the outside to prevent Henry's exit—had once firmly resided. Henry starts to say something more but, finally seeing her face in its entirety, is mutely transfixed. Her eyes—a brimming gold with black slits for pupils—lock onto his own. Despite his fear that someone might have heard the breaking glass, he smiles.

"I—" he starts, and then hears the loud *clunk* of the bolt on his door being slammed to the side, and Liam bursts into the room. His eyes go wildly from Henry's empty bed, to Henry, and finally to the window, and the creature that still hunkers beyond it.

"Fuck me," Liam murmurs, then his eyes narrow and he reaches a hand toward the small of his back.

"No, please!" Henry screams, running at Liam, waving his arms. But Liam is already swinging the Glock around, aiming its barrel at the creature's head.

He fires.

Glass and wood explode outward.

The creature is gone.

They both look to the ceiling as heavy footsteps pound along the roof. Liam points the gun at Henry, who looks ready to make another dash for the half-open door. "Don't," Liam warns.

Henry stops, instinctively putting his arms—already half raised in the air—straight as goal posts, his terror-filled eyes locked on the point of the gun.

Liam takes two steps back into the hallway, slams and bolts the door.

Liam ignores the sound of Henry's pounding fists and desperate cries to "leave her alone" and "not shoot her." He sprints down the hallway. Jim stands at the top of the stairs, both of them following the sounds of heavy footsteps crossing above their heads.

"Go, Jim! Go, goddamn it!" Liam yells, and notices Jim has his own gun drawn and fisted in one big hand.

Jim needs no further encouragement; he turns and bolts down the stairs. Liam spares a glance over the railing that looks down into the living room, sees the stunned faces of Pete and Greg looking up at him.

"What the hell's going on!" Pete yells, but Jim blows past him and out the door.

Liam takes the steps two at a time, leaps near the bottom, his boots hitting the floorboards hard. He runs for the open door. "Keep an eye on the kid!" he yells at both men—not caring which one accepts the command—and runs into the bright amber sunlight of the dying afternoon, ready to kill.

A couple feet ahead, Jim jumps the porch steps and hits the ground at a sprint. While still in the shadow of the house he spins and points his gun toward the roof, looking from one end to the other for any sign of movement. The side of the house is dressed in shade. The windows look down on him with dull, blind eyes. He backs up slowly, slips out of the skewed rectangle of shadow and into the sunlight. He barely registers Liam running up beside him, his gun also pointed up toward whatever it was running across their roof—and Jim thinks he has a pretty good idea what they'll see.

"What the hell's up there?" Pete yells from the porch, then jogs out to meet the other two men. Jim lets his eyes flick down to Pete for a second, a flash of metal catching his eye, and sees Pete gripping a long switchblade in one hand. *Don't think that thing's gonna do jack shit, but if it makes you feel better.*

"Where's Greg?" Jim asks.

"He's got a lap full of cooch, man. He ain't moving."

"Jim," Liam says, almost nonchalant.

Jim looks back to the roof, and sees her.

The creature is hunched over, as if on all fours, staring down at them from the apex of the pitched rooftop. It has made it all the way to the near edge, where it has stopped to survey the scene. *Looks like a goddamned gargoyle*, Jim thinks, and shudders.

"Just say the word," Liam says in that same calm tone, borderline conversational. Jim figures he doesn't want to spook the thing, and once again he's glad to have Liam there with him. He doesn't know what that thing is, or what exactly he's going to do about it, but at least he isn't alone.

There's another adult in the room and that's damned reassuring, despite the bizarre circumstances.

"Good Christ," Pete gasps. "Is that a human?"

"I don't think so," Jim says, lining the dark figure up with the front sight of his Smith & Wesson. *You ain't slipping away this time.*

The creature stares down at the three men, crouching low but not moving. Jim can't make out its face any better than he could the previous night, backlit by the dying sun, but he sees two glints of gold under that hood—the thing's eyes watching them.

Slowly, the creature moves forward, as if testing to see their reaction. The limbs are quick and agile, and when it moves it's like ink spilling—fluid and dark. If they didn't know it was there, Jim wonders if he'd have even noticed it moving flat and black against the gray shingles of the old roof. It's nothing more than a phantom; a shadowy stain, nearly invisible when not hit with direct daylight.

"Don't lose it," he says, and knows Liam has the thing sighted as well.

The creature reaches the eaves of the house overhanging the front entrance where it momentarily pauses, then continues to crawl over the eaves and down the chipped white siding.

"Oh, hell no," Pete says, and Jim feels his genitals shrivel so tight it feels like his nuts want to crawl inside his asshole and hide.

"That's not possible," Liam murmurs.

Jim agrees.

The men watch in stunned horror as the creature creeps effortlessly, like a man-sized spider, across the side of the house. It stays high but moves quickly, skittering above the roof of the porch, along the east side, moving higher, then back onto the roof, where it turns, gold eyes addressing them solemnly.

"Fucking thing is showing off," Jim says, and believes it. *It's trying to frighten us, intimidate us*, he thinks, swallowing hard. *And I'll be damned if it ain't working.*

"Jim?" Liam, asking permission.

Jim's eye narrows along the sight. He's got a clean shot of its head. *Just gotta aim for those creepy yellow eyes.*

"Kill it."

Jim and Liam open fire.

The creature moves like a blur across the roof. Jim and Liam continue to shoot. One of them misses badly and blows out a second story window—luckily a room they aren't inhabiting.

Like the flash of a black, wind-blown cape, it scampers across the eaves and disappears over the side.

Jim and Liam hold their fire and run for the edge of the house, arriving in time to see the creature crawling down the side so fast it could be falling if not for the rhythmic *taptaptaptaptaptap* of its limbs beating against the siding. It reaches the bottom, turns its head, and *hisses* at them. The sound is so horrible, so defiant, that Jim actually lowers his weapon for a moment, his face twisted in fear and disgust.

"Jim!" Liam screams, and Jim snaps out of it. The thing is now sprinting through the high grass toward the woods, going for cover the way it did when surprised by Jim the previous night.

Jim aims his weapon. He has only three more shots and knows reloading is not an option. He targets the flowing black shape as it flies over the green like a giant dog sprinting for home. He fires once, twice. Liam with his semiautomatic Glock is getting off more shots, but he's wild. Jim lets out a breath and lines up his last bullet.

The creature is almost to the tree line when it leaps.

This time, Jim is ready.

Like a pheasant breaking out of the brush, he thinks, and fires.

There's a scream that's almost human and the creature spins in midair, its smooth leap interrupted, as if a string pulling it aloft was suddenly cut. It slams awkwardly into the low branches of a tree and vanishes.

Liam starts to run toward it.

"Liam, no!"

Liam stops, turns around, face red, eyes wide with terror and shock. "We gotta kill that thing," he says.

Jim shakes his head. "Not in the woods, brother. That's its home, its playground. It'll fuck you up you go in there."

Liam looks toward the woods again, then back at Jim. A scared, frustrated child. "How the fuck do you know that?"

Jim starts walking back toward the house. "Leave it. We scared it more than it scared us, am I right? And I ain't running through the damned forest chasing it just so the thing can drop down on me from above. No thanks. Let's go. We got to talk."

Liam gives a last look toward the rustle of branches where the creature landed, then reluctantly follows.

"Did you kill it? I heard a scream," Pete says, jogging around from the front of the house to meet them.

"Jim hit it, I think," Liam says, deep in thought.

"Jim?" Pete says.

"We just gotta get through one more night," he says, tucking his .357 into the rear waistline of his cargo pants. "I think we better figure out a plan."

"Plan for what?" Pete asks, folding his knife.

"Defense," Jim answers. "For when that motherfucker comes back."

As they head back inside, Liam considers telling Jim he agrees with him. He also believes the creature will return, and the reasons why. He remembers seeing that board ripped free from Henry's window, the way Henry ran at him, arms waving, telling him not to shoot, to leave her alone.

Seeing that . . . animal, monster, whatever it was, it turned the stories Henry had been telling him into truths. And if Henry was telling the truth about her, he was likely telling the truth about everything.

The creature wants them gone.

When they enter the house, Liam closes and bolts the front door. *Not that it will do much good, not with the way that thing can crawl all over the house like a wolf spider.*

But he does it anyway.

Once inside, he decides not to tell Jim, or the others, what Henry has confided. What he *thinks* he knows. Not yet. Part of him doesn't want Jim, or Pete for that matter, to know the monster was trying to break Henry out of his room. Or how it wants to protect the thing wrapped up in that muddy chrysalis below their feet.

Liam wonders if keeping this information to himself is a decision made in the spirit of self-preservation—he certainly doesn't need Jim and the others thinking he's lost his bloody mind—or one of protection.

If Jim knew, he'd beat the information out of Henry. Then he'd kill that thing in the cellar. Then he'd kill its mother.

Liam scratches his forehead, rubs the bump behind his ear where the wasp sting is slowly receding, the venom cleaned by the natural flow of his blood. He's conflicted, confused. He can't figure out for the life of him how he's arrived at this place, but here he is nonetheless. Trying to decide what is right, what is wrong, and what is smart.

Trying like hell to decide whose side he is on.

And isn't that a son of a bitch.

PART EIGHT:
THE VERY
WORST THINGS

1

In Southern California, winter is the bringer not of snow and ice, but of the early dark. The days are pushed around by the brutish season like impish schoolchildren, bullied into taking away the surfer's late-day spotlight and filling the rush hour freeways with the thousand-eyed snake of white head-lights instead of the metallic reflection of a San Diego gloaming smeared against a seemingly endless row of sunshine-blazoned automobiles.

Folks in Southern California are raised on sunshine, they breathe it like they breathe polluted air, every day, all day. Therefore, the winter months are annoying, if not necessarily cruel. The dark is oppressive in California. For its inhabitants it creates uncertainty, an almost awkward, embarrassing unease. And when it comes early, before that drive home from work or the end of happy hour, it can even be eerily disquieting for those used to seeing a bright yellow sun overhead as a sort of constant, an evident God.

In the winter months, the early night seems to bury the city alive, along with the long beaches, the suburbs, and the hills of deep forests that create a natural eastern barrier to San Diego's metropolis heart. As the night tide rolls over the city and its fringe environs, those living within are more susceptible to brooding, or worry, or fits of weeping; they will be eager for sleep, praying to the vanquished sun god for solace, for the bliss of unconsciousness, until the light returns again.

At the Thorne home, Dave and Mary must endure another cold, damp night without their boy. Another night knowing that somewhere Henry is alone, and scared, chilled by the early dark, unloved as the coldest, farthest star.

By midnight, a now mildly sedated Dave and Mary find slumber in the warmth and safety of their bedroom, leaving the police and FBI tech-nicians to monitor their house, their phone, the surrounding neighbor-hood. They leave the night behind.

In a two-bedroom third-floor apartment near the Gaslight District, Sali Espinoza sits on the couch drinking his third glass of Dewar's and would have had a fourth were it an option, but the bottle has been finished off with that last, robust pour. He stares at a television that shows, for the umpteenth time, the faces of those wanted by the FBI for questioning in the abduction of ten-year-old Henry Thorne. A few minutes later, the empty glass falls to the carpet, the hand holding it devoid of strength or command as its host sleeps.

Less than twelve miles away, at the southern end of the woodland ridge designated as the Cleveland National Forest, hunkers a rundown farmhouse, the structure standing for the sole reason that it had once been given historical landmark protection by a one-term congressman whose great-grandfather had harbored there, for a handful of days, over a hundred years prior. The congressman's ancestor had been chased to the house by members of the First Regiment Cavalry of the Union Army while attempting to secede from the Union, cross the desert, and go fight for the Confederates based out of Texas. He and three other men hid out along with the hostage host, a middle-aged widow named Helen Butterfield, before shooting her dead during a late-night attempt to escape and, to hear the sympathizers tell it, alert the Union Army to their position.

Although the home was given historical designation, it never did receive its plaque of notoriety, the congressman from the Fifty-first district having been voted out of office after only a single term.

But plaque or no, the house stands.

Uncared for. Unloved, unwanted, unnoticed.

Until now.

To the old house it is simply another night. Another early winter evening falling down like a trap door on a mild, golden, San Diego afternoon.

To those inside the house, however, the dark feels ominous. A threat that needs tending, as if the night might suddenly spring to life and pour inside, smash through windows and break down doors to invade without mercy, devouring all those within.

As the cold bites the fingers and numbs the feet, chills noses and cheeks, the people who harbor there feel trapped rather than secure; the besieged rather than the besiegers.

The window Jim busted out is covered once again with a sheet, but the cold air pushes through without effort. The house does little to insulate its interior, the walls thin and shielding as cardboard; the cellar beneath them an icebox, forging damp cold that pushes up through the sieve of gapped floorboards. Wind sneaks beneath doors and poorly sealed window frames like a vengeful spirit.

Jenny is awake and alert, which calms Greg's nerves and allows them all to focus on the cold and their gnawing hunger instead of Jenny's welfare.

The kitchen stinks of smoke and the only viable table in the house is now smashed to worthless pieces. The occasional maggot rolls aimlessly around the floor or countertop. The air seeping through the broken window and from the cellar below completes the job of making the room uninhabitable. Liam has gone so far as to use Pete's hammer and remaining nails to secure a spare blanket over the empty doorframe in order to keep the frigid, stinking kitchen air from permeating the rest of the house.

"It's probably forty degrees and we're acting like we're camping in the Arctic without a tent," Greg says amiably, and Jim grunts acknowledgment.

All the heaters and fuel have been moved to the living room. The cooler was also carried out.

The food is completely gone.

Jim has already laid out the plan for the night: Liam will take the first shift, then Jim, then Greg, then Pete. Jenny, although feeling better, needs her rest, and tomorrow is a big day—the biggest—so she will forgo a shift.

Jim has ordered that under no circumstances will they all be asleep at the same time. Someone will keep watch. Will listen. Check the kid every hour, be aware of any strange sounds coming from upstairs, from outside. From the cellar.

No one is to investigate without waking up Jim or Liam.

No one is to go outside alone.

Liam sits in the corner playing solitaire. He listens to the snores and heavy breathing of the others, surprised any of them can sleep at all. Three different times he's stood up with the intention of going to check on Henry, to *talk* to Henry, to find out more about the creature, find out everything he could.

Three times he has sat back down, picked up the deck of cards.

Not yet, he thinks. *Maybe later.*

He doesn't understand the reluctance, the fear of seeing the kid again, of simply talking to him. A deeply buried part of him wants to save Henry, to make sure he gets through this, that he lives. Another part of him craves the indifferent, callous man who has lost everything and cares for no one. The man he had become so adept at portraying.

As he wins his third game of solitaire in a row (only cheating once that last time), he thinks wistfully of his son, wonders what he'd look like now that a few years have passed. His brain orders him to cease and desist with these thoughts, but he shuffles the deck and ignores the order, allows his imagination to show images of him and his boy together, in a life far away, in a reality he knows will never come to exist.

★ ★ ★

Upstairs, things fare no better.

Henry's teeth chatter beneath the blankets as the heater, dragged to within inches of his cot, belches stale warmth into his body that has as much effect as a box fan pushing against a strong wind. The small heater is no match for the flow of frigid night air pushing through the broken pane of glass, sliding across the floor and up the legs of the cot to crawl over Henry's flesh, press down against him like a frigid ghost, eat him alive with ice-crystal teeth.

Even worse, this frozen specter is the only company Henry has, the loneliness and boredom having become as draining as the cold. Other than a cursory visit from Liam to ensure the missing board didn't allow space for Henry to make a heroic escape, he has been left alone, and hasn't seen anyone.

In a burst of desperation, Henry runs to the window, stuffs his thin pillow into the broken pane, then leaps back onto the cot, pulling the three blankets over himself so he's covered from head to toe. After blocking most of the incoming wind, the heater finally seems to be doing some good, allowing Henry's body, and mind, to slowly relax.

As he falls into unconsciousness, hungry and tired, his mouth dry as a bone, his stomach clenched and his bowels cramped, he prays to his dead father.

"Help me, please. Help me, please," he says, again and again.

Soon, he falls asleep, and the prayers cease, and he does not dream.

2

Henry does not dream, but he does feel.

He feels Baby, and he feels Mother.

Baby: Alert, anxious, scared.

Mother: Hurt, angry. Violent.

Close.

Henry, wake up. Let me talk to you.

Henry stirs, reaching. For Mother, for Baby. Seeking comfort, seeking sanctuary.

Wake up, son.

His mind drifts to the people downstairs. They're asleep, some dreaming, some not. Only Liam is awake. *I won't let them hurt you, Henry.*

Henry's brow creases. He moans, and his eyes open. He slowly pulls away the blankets covering his face. Silver-penny eyes stare down at him. The dark shadow, the memory of his father, stands above his bed.

"Daddy," he says, and the dark figure smiles. Those silver eyes gleam. Henry sits up and the shadow steps back. *I'm here. Let me help you.*

"You can't help. You're not even real." Henry sighs in the dark. "I'm crazy. I should be in a loony bin."

His father chuckles, and Henry can see his breath frost in the cold air, which means it is near freezing in the room. He stays under the blankets.

I'm real, son. I live inside you, but I can come out on occasion. You know, you've seen. Maybe I can help you yet. Perhaps, yes, there's a way.

"Where's Mom?" Henry asks, pulling the blanket up over his face again, the cold nipping at the inside of his nostrils, his lips, his ears.

Well, you know. She's waiting. Waiting for you. Waiting for me. Listen, son, you're tired. Get some sleep. Tomorrow's a big day. There's something I got to do.

But I need a little push, like when I'd push you on a swing, you remember? Can you give your old man a little push, Henry? A little help?

Henry lowers the blanket one last time, studies the shadowy figure, the one he'd seen so many times since the accident. The one responsible for the things he can do, his gift. The things he can see. The colors. For everything that's happened to him.

"Will you come back?" he asks, and a small hand slips out from beneath the blankets, reaching.

A firm, cool hand grips his own and Henry gasps, shuts his eyes tight.

He imagines the *before*. Holding his dad's hand, being lifted into the air. Laughter. Love. Walking to the park, through a crowded mall, down a busy sidewalk to the first day of school. Kisses. Hugs. Warmth. Love.

"I miss you," he says.

Like I said, I've got something I need to do. I'll see you soon. I just need a little push, baby.

The hand is gone, the cool touch erased like a mistake on a chalkboard. Henry pulls his own hand back under the blankets, curls it up, and cradles it to his chest. His stomach growls, but he ignores it. He wants to go back to sleep, to forget where he is, what's happening, and what will probably happen tomorrow.

He is almost sure he will die, and he badly wants to say goodbye to Dave, and to Mary. To tell them he loves them. To tell them he's scared, that he misses them very much.

He starts to slip back into sleep, into ten-year-old dreams, knowing it will probably be the last time he will ever fall sleep, the last time he will dream in this life.

But before he does, he musters up what's left of his strength, and he *pushes.*

3

Liam has played enough solitaire to last him a lifetime.

He watches the others sleep and debates whether he should even bother waking Jim. It's past 2 a.m., the time he was meant to be relieved, but the truth is he isn't remotely tired. If anything, he's antsy. He's also starving, and wary of drinking anything stronger than a beer with no food in his stomach.

Now would not be a good time to get sloppy.

Still, he doesn't want Jim angry with him, and the big guy will definitely be pissed if Liam lets him sleep past his shift. Jim is a man of details, of plans and orders being followed to the letter, and his wrath is historic.

Grunting, he pushes up from his sitting position against the wall, his only company the last couple hours being the deck of cards, a dinged-up kerosene heater, a low-lit camping lantern, and his poisoned thoughts. He isn't sure how this game is going to play out, but having time to think it all through has allowed him to construct some boundaries, some rules about what he will allow.

And what he will not allow.

He *will* allow the drop to go off as planned. God knows he can use the money, and they all know it's FBI money, anyway, so who gives a shit. That's protocol, regardless of what the movies said. Sure, it would be twelve kinds of marked, and probably traced, but both he and Jim had experience with that. They already have an appointment with a cleaner in Mexico who, for a double-digit percentage, will wash it all clean.

No problem.

He *will* allow the house to be burned, because fuck this place. It should have been torn down years ago, and if Pete happens to start a forest fire doing it? All the better to distract the world, and the local PD, while they all slip across the border. Of course, officials will be monitoring the main traffic arteries bleeding into America's southern neighbor, but Jim has this covered as well. He's already paid off an old coyote to usher them into Mexico, easy as pie, and right here in the great city of San Diego. The borders are a joke, and a little cash—especially for those trying to get *out* of the United States—goes a hell of a long way with the American patrols.

Liam hits the pause button on these thoughts while he crosses the room to where Jim lies atop a couple army blankets, a denim jacket bunched up for a pillow. He watches him for a few moments, wondering if the guy is as deeply asleep as he appears. Liam has a feeling Jim sleeps lightly—anyone who did serious time in prison does—and is likely well aware of his surroundings even when he is, or appears to be, unconscious. Watching the man's chest rise and fall, debating what to do next, Liam closes his eyes a moment, reviews the promises he's made to himself.

The things he has decided he will *not* allow.

He will *not* allow Henry to stay in the house with Pete and Jenny once they've left. He will take the boy with them to the drop, stick him in the trunk if necessary, and they'll all leave together for the rendezvous, assuming there are no problems. Liam is fairly sure he can convince Jim of this, using the argument of having insurance (or, put another way, a hostage) if things go sideways and they have to shoot, or deal, themselves out of someplace or another.

He will *not* allow Jim to kill the boy.

Henry will live. He'll finish school, go to college, and become a scientist or some smart shit like that. Cure cancer, who knows.

But he will not die for money. He will not be killed by some criminals looking to score a retirement plan.

Like a prayer, Liam thinks: *I won't let them hurt you, Henry.*

He kneels and touches Jim lightly on the shoulder. Jim rolls over and his eyes open easily, clear and focused, as if he may indeed have been pretending all along. "You're late," Jim says.

Liam looks at his watch. It's 2:14 in the morning. "Sorry. Not that tired. Debated letting you sleep another hour."

Jim sits up, rubs his bald bowling ball of a head. "Fuck that, man." He looks Liam in the eyes. "Glad you aren't tired, though."

"Yeah?"

Jim gets to his feet and stretches, hands reaching skyward, muscles and tendons straining his tight T-shirt, rippling beneath the skin of his bared arms and neck. Liam marvels at how massive the guy is, at the strength of him, and looks away awkwardly. That old tingle of fear prickles his gut.

"Yeah, bro," Jim says, reaching down for a bottle of water. "You and me? We gonna have a little chat."

"All right."

"Let's walk the perimeter, then you can get some sleep."

"You sure that's—"

"Just a few minutes, man. Ain't no shit gonna happen, and we ain't going far."

Liam doesn't press. He knows Jim wouldn't tell him anyway, so he waits patiently while Jim laces on his boots, then follows him out the front door.

The night is cold but Liam is immediately relieved that Jim wants to talk outdoors instead of inside the house. It's fresh out here, and the scent of forest is a nice change of pace from having to smell his own stink, the stink of the others. He didn't realize how used to the fetid house he'd gotten—unwashed skin, mildew, and smoke seemed to permeate from the floors and the walls as much as from the people. The open grave stench coming from the cellar was another unwelcome layer he was glad to be temporarily free of.

Thinking of the cellar offers an image of the decomposing body they'd had to dump, and of the strange chrysalis that may be the key to the bizarre happenings of the last twenty-four hours.

That thing you found? In the cellar? It has a mama. I call the little one Baby, and the other one Mother.

Liam shudders, tries to blame it on the cold.

Jim walks a half step ahead. "Let's walk around once, make sure our friend isn't hanging out on the roof or nearby. Also, I want to check the cars."

"The cars?"

Jim shrugs and says nothing further as they stomp through the high grass, the house offering no light, the moon nothing but a dim fingernail clinging to the edge of vaporous cloud, the surrounding trees a silent dark army.

"You and Henry been talking a bunch," Jim says finally, and Liam lets out a sigh. He hates to feel so exposed. It's one thing to have Henry pry through his thoughts, pulling his personal memories out like cards from a deck, but to think he is so obvious to Jim is worrisome. And dangerous.

"Yeah," he says, deciding not to take the bait. If Jim had something to say, he could damn well say it. Liam wasn't about to start defending himself without a direct assault.

They arrive at the shed. Jim pulls open one of the large bay doors. The hinges creak gently. An owl hoots from the far trees, jolting Liam's frazzled nerves. "What are we doing here, Jim?"

But Jim ignores the question, instead silently studying the two cars—the brown Duster and the Pinto wagon. He reaches into the pocket of his cargo pants and clicks on a small, metal-cased flashlight. It's pitch black in the shed except for the beam emanating from Jim's closed hand. He walks to the driver's door of the Pinto, opens it, and reaches inside. Liam hears the sound of the hood popping even if he can't see it, or anything else.

"Everybody's got secrets, man," Jim says, in a sullen tone Liam finds troubling. "I'm trying to get us all paid. Spent half a goddamn year setting everything up, getting everything planned, and it's like you all a bunch of little kids. Scared little boys and scared little girls."

Jim lifts the hood of the Pinto, flashes the light inside. With his free hand he begins digging into the heart of the small engine.

"So what I want to know from you, my brother—"

Liam hears a squelching *pop* and the smack of metal on metal. Jim steps back, lowers his head so as not to bang it on the upraised hood. He holds what looks like two or three skinny black snakes in his free hand, barely visible in the glow of the flashlight beam. He closes the hood softly, turns around and aims the light at Liam's face, blinding him.

Liam puts a hand up to shield his eyes. "Jesus, man."

"I want to know if you're scheming anything with the kid. If maybe you and him have come to some sort of *understanding*, you know what I'm saying? Some sort of secret pact, maybe you got a handshake and shit." Jim chuckles, mirthless.

"You wanna get that fucking light out of my face?"

There's a soft click and the light dies. The contrast from the bright spot of white to the total darkness throws him off balance, and his eyes are slow to adjust. *If he was coming at me right now, there isn't a damn thing I could do about it.*

"Great," Liam says, deciding for levity, "now I'm blind."

"Well, come on outside. Let's finish our rounds. What do the Aussies call it? A walkabout?"

"Eh, sort of," Liam says and staggers outside, where the soft moonlight brings things back into focus—the jagged tops of the trees, the gray block of the dead farmhouse. "Can I ask why you just pulled the plugs out of the Pinto?"

Jim starts to walk away, back toward the house, and Liam follows. "Jenny and Greg are talking about bailing. You know, running away in the night. Like young lovers, or double-crossing thieves."

Liam feels his heart quicken. "With the kid?"

Jim shakes his head, a sliver of reflected moonlight dancing on the back of his shiny skull. "Nah, just bail out, you know? I don't think they like all the—" Jim waves his large hand toward the forest. "Weirdness. And that was before that thing showed up today climbing all over the house, freaking everybody out. Thank God those two stayed inside. If they'd seen that? Oh shit, they'd be long gone by now."

Jim holds up the plugs, gives them a shake. His way of saying: *Of course, that's all behind us now.*

"What about the Duster?"

"I got the keys to that, no worries." Jim pats his front pocket, then sighs heavily. In a way, it reminds Liam of Henry and his heavy, old-man sighs. "Anyway, they ain't going nowhere now. I'll give these to Pete when we leave for the drop, but not before. Man, it's like no one wants to *win* this thing."

"In their defense, Jim, it's been a bizarre couple days. Some of this stuff can't be explained."

Jim turns suddenly and Liam stops short of bumping nose to chin. "That's what I'm saying, Liam," Jim says softly, as if pleading. "Folks gotta focus on the *job*. All this other stuff is bullshit, man. All that matters is that *kid* and that suitcase of *money*, you dig?"

Liam nods. "Yes, I do. That's why I'm here. And it's also why I'm a bit confused about the questions you're asking me."

Jim lowers his head, as if thinking. When he raises it again, he's smiling a wide, toothy grin. He puts a large hand on Liam's shoulder and squeezes hard enough to show off his strength, but not quite hard enough to hurt. "Because I don't trust anyone no more, Liam. Not Greg or his slippery little sister, not that dumbass Mexican, not the kid, and not you, my brother. And I *always* trusted you."

"Jim," Liam says, "you can trust me. I'm in a hundred percent here. That's why I came halfway across the country to do this job, and why I will make sure the job is done as planned. If it's just me and you, then that's what it is. But I promise you, I'm not going anywhere. Okay?"

Jim removes his hand from Liam's shoulder, lifts his eyes to study the roof, as if making sure there aren't any slinking shadows above them, watching. "And what about the kid?" Jim says. "What if I decide the best thing to do is to smoke his little brown ass? You gonna have a problem with that?"

Liam knows better than to hesitate. "No. No problem. Whatever you decide, I'm in."

Jim lowers his eyes, looks at Liam questioningly, then smiles again. This time it warms his features; the mouth less sinister, the eyes brighter. "My man," he says, and pulls Liam into a tight, quick hug.

"Okay," Liam says, and Jim releases him with a chuckle.

"Shit, man, I don't know," he says, and commences their walk around the house. "Maybe I'm getting a little rattled, myself, you know? All this trouble makes a man worry too much. Think too much."

"Nah, it's fine. We're cool," Liam says, relieved.

They walk side by side around the remainder of the house, both of them noting that the cellar doors are closed, and the surrounding area clear of any phantom creatures dashing through the smattering of long shadows.

Despite the fresh air and the disgust he feels for the house, Liam is relieved to be going back inside. He's cold, and he's tired.

Lying through your teeth takes a lot out of a man.

At the edge of the forest, a hunched shape watches the two men walk to the shed, go inside, then continue on, eventually disappearing around the back of the house.

She waits, unmoving.

After a few minutes, they appear again.

Finally, they go inside, seal the doorway.

Still, she waits.

After a few moments, the creature scoops dirt from the earth, cupping the soil in the palms of her hands.

She holds her closed hands to her mouth and speaks quickly, quietly, for several minutes. Her warm breath fills the sealed sphere until she feels *life* emerge from the soil.

The insects she has brought to existence are frantic, impatient. She continues speaking into her hands, a temporary prison for the newborn bugs, until their agitated movement slows, then stops. The incantation goes on for several more minutes, until the creatures are diseased with her spirit, her command.

Only then does she uncurl her long fingers and lower her open palms to the earth.

Five full-grown cockroaches crawl away from her, through the dirt and between the clumps of tall, dry grass toward the house. Toward those that lie sleeping, unaware, inside.

4

Dave sleeps, but his mind is restless, anxious. Mary had finally convinced him to take one of the Valium her doctor prescribed, and after ten minutes of lying in bed, absolutely certain the pill would have no effect whatsoever, he falls heavily into sleep.

Into the subconscious world of dreams.

He sinks deeper and deeper into a much-needed REM state, the chemicals of the drug dragging him down like a heavy anchor through layers of sleep spindles, his body temperature steadily dropping, his brain waves slowing, expanding, until . . .

Dave is flying.

He doesn't feel his body. When he looks down at himself, he does not see his hands or his feet, legs or chest, as if he's invisible. A spirit. He has no sensations of comfort or discomfort, hot or cold. Though he's moving at great speed he doesn't feel the push of air against his skin, has no internal sense of movement. If he didn't see the world slipping by all around him, he might think he was floating, stationary within an enclosed room, numb to his surroundings, the gliding earth nothing but an all-encompassing projection.

But part of him knows that it's not a projection, that it's real. He looks off into the distance, toward the bright hot light of the sun to the west, a sweltering red disc hovering above the razor-edged blue horizon of an ocean frozen in time—the great body of water motionless as a photograph; a film reel stuck on a single frame. There are no boats, no people on the beaches, no far-off oil rigs, no black-comma birds in the sky. No waves, no sound.

Below him—a thousand feet between himself and land—the geography flows past glacially, like a slow-moving river of city grids, broken green hills, and deserted highways that stretch toward the northern horizon like gray ribbons rolled out carelessly along the earth.

Dave squeezes his eyes shut, then opens them as the world below tilts, then *rolls,* as if he's perched upon the tip of a child's top near the end of its spin, the wobble growing more and more erratic until Dave loses any sense of up and down, east or west. Space contracts to a point and he shoots through a blurred funnel toward a singular speck of light pulling at him like gravity, as if propelled downward from a great height. He's frightened, and he crosses invisible arms in front of his eyes and screams.

Suddenly the feeling of motion stops, the suck of gravity abates, and he senses his body once more. A brush of air rustles against his skin, a damp cool caresses the back of his neck, his scalp. His eyes open slowly, fearfully, and lowers his arms from his face.

Dave.

He turns his head one way, then the other, and is relieved to find himself on the ground, surrounded by trees, the earth gratefully firm beneath his feet. Dense black oaks crowd the perimeter, their spindly arms reaching skyward and outward, pressing toward him as if alive; angry and vengeful. Dense shrubbery lay thick along the ground in all the colors of military camouflage—dark browns, bright greens, muddy yellows.

Dave.

Streaks of sunlight break through the tall dense trees in elongated hazy rays, like white spears tossed into the dirt by angels. Twisted branches provoke the sun, then grasp at its leavings. Dave takes a few uncertain steps to where he thinks the voice is coming from.

A hundred feet away, a silhouette slips from behind a tree.

This way.

The voice is as indistinct as the shadowed specter it emanates from, yet both are somehow familiar. Not recognizable—not in any way Dave can pinpoint—but familiar by *feel.* The feeling you get when someone you know, someone you know intimately, comes through the front door—even if you're in a different room and can't see them enter, there's a part of you that knows there's no need for alarm, no underlying tension or worry about them having entered your home.

Versus, say, when a stranger walks through your door.

You could be in the basement, or the attic, and if a stranger entered your home some instinctual part of your brain would just *know* it was wrong, red flags waved by the sentries of your nervous system, the hairs on your arms might rise from your skin and that sixth-sense warning siren mankind has been developing for thousands of years would start to whine in the back of your brain, softly wailing: *Danger. Danger. Danger.*

But Dave feels no such danger from this presence, this voice repeating his name; calling him, guiding him, somehow far away but also very close. Mysteriously, it's as if the voice is right next to his ear, whispering directly into it.

Dave swears he can feel its breath.

"I'm coming," he says, but first takes a moment to study himself. There is a grounding in seeing his physical form: his hands, his button-down white dress shirt, his dark slacks, his leather wingtip shoes. Office attire—but casual. No tie, no jacket. A Saturday afternoon at work, a weekend lost while preparing a case—

Dave!

His eyes snap up, his thoughts refocused. The shadow is further away now, and Dave jogs to catch up. He slides past thick, coarse tree trunks, ducks low-hanging branches thick with dark green leaves that look, to his dreaming eyes, like green hands; slapping at him, reaching for him. His wingtip shoes kick through the rough brush, pound into brown puddles hidden by layers of dead mulch. He's panting. His socks and shoes are soaked through with the cold sweat of Mother Earth. His face, scratched and bleeding, stings with the salty moisture of his own adrenaline-laced sweat. His dress shirt sticks to his skin and his lungs burn as he runs, but he knows he can't lose whomever it is he's following, so he forces himself to keep up with the flickering shadow slipping between the trees, always just ahead . . .

Because it's taking me somewhere . . . somewhere I must go. Keep up, you old bastard. Don't lose him! Don't lose him now!

Dave picks up speed, sprints through the trees faster and faster, a hard wind now pushing at his back as if willing him to push beyond his limits, to go beyond, perhaps, what he thinks possible. The dark trunks on either side of him begin to blur, the dense undergrowth turning to mist that his pumping legs pass through effortlessly. Still the shadow dances ahead, but close now. If he wanted, Dave could reach out a hand and touch it, grab its dark cloak and tug it back, reveal what lies beneath.

Ahead is a clearing and the figure races toward it, an escape perhaps, an ending; the proverbial light at the end of the tunnel that is Dave's quest, Dave's desire to . . . what? To find out what lies at the end. To find out where this phantom is leading him. To find, to find—

The world gasps and releases its breath.

There's a *pop* in Dave's ears, as if he's broken through a membrane of sight and sound into a bubble of existence outside the dream. Or, possibly, inside.

He stands in a broad clearing. Tall grass, brittle and patched with scrub, deerweed and coffeeberry brush cover the ground around him. There are splashes of yellow honeysuckle; clumps of purple sage wave in a breeze he does not feel.

Panting, Dave studies the place he has been taken, the dream inside the dream.

The figure stands ten feet ahead. Smoky tendrils wisp off its arms and head and shoulders, but Dave can easily make out the shape of a man.

Past the man is a house.

An old, rundown, forgotten farmhouse in the middle of a forest. The doors and windows are boarded, the bone-white paint on the wood shingles peeled and cracked; the house itself showing dark weathered skin beneath dried, flaky curls of off-white. Nearby is a large shed, unpainted and walled with broad, dark oak panels. It has two large bay doors and Dave thinks it must be an old coach house, or perhaps a stable. It's big as a two-car garage, but brittle as the house. Dave thinks a stray match thrown within ten feet of either structure would ignite them as quickly as if they were soaked with gasoline.

The trees surrounding the structures are like guardians of some old, shitty kingdom, forgotten and decayed. An artifact from a world left behind.

He focuses again on the dark figure, the shadow, the rabbit he has been chasing through this strange dream. As if sensing his gaze, the shadow turns to face him, and Dave recoils in horror at the thing's glittering silver eyes, the broad, gleaming white teeth buried deep in the smoky black face.

Dave, do you see?

"Who are you?" Dave says, his voice stale and leaden, as if the air in this dream world does not vibrate, does not carry sound.

Still, the shadow seems to hear him. It steps closer until they are only a few feet apart.

Not much time now, I think. Not much time left.

"What is this?"

Those silver eyes continue to study Dave, as if curious, or hungry. But the smile goes away, buried beneath wisps of darkness.

One last time, then.

"I don't understand," Dave says, then stops as a stinging wind strikes his cheek. He shivers, but quickly loses all sense of discomfort and his eyes widen in shock as the wind buffets the shadowy form as well. Like shifting gray clouds revealing a bulbous white moon, the shadow stands still even as its disguise is pulled away like a silken shroud to reveal a body and a face he knows well; it is a face he has known since he was a child, looked at and looked up to. Looked at and loved.

The last tendrils of smoke drift away and leave his brother. It is Jack who stands before him; Jack and his intelligent, cautious eyes. Jack and his high cheekbones and small ears, his cunning smile; the smile of a big brother who said he would always be there to protect you, who said he'd never ever leave you, then left you in the very worst way there was.

"Hey Dave," Jack says, and Dave looks at him with wonder, and hate, and love—so much love that his throat clenches and his eyes water and flow. He steps closer to this spirit until they are almost touching.

"Jack," he says, or thinks he says. Sound and thought are intermingled here and it's hard for Dave to know what's real and what's illusion, what senses are being triggered. What are thoughts, and what are sounds.

What is dream. What is real.

Jack smiles, happy and contrite—the smile of a kid who aced the test but knows he cheated to do it. "Yeah," Jack says.

Jack is wearing a blue oxford shirt and Levi's 501s. White sneakers.

It's what you were wearing on the day you died, Dave thinks, and isn't surprised to see Jack nodding.

"That's right, that's right," he says, and puts a finger to his chin, reflective. "There are so many things to remember," he says. "So many things to forget."

Dave throws his arms around his brother, filled with joy to *feel* him in his grasp, feel his warmth, his physical body—muscle and bone—the smell of him, the fabric of his shirt beneath his fingers. "I'm sorry I wasn't there for you," Dave says into his ear, finally saying the words he'd always wanted to say from the moment he saw Jack's broken body in the morgue. "But I hate you! I hate you for what you did, Jack. For what you did to Henry."

Jack gently pushes Dave back, his face solemn and downcast. "I know," he says, and offers no more.

"But more than that, I'm sorry," Dave says, unsure now, not knowing what to say, what to feel. "I'm so sorry, Jack."

When Jack's eyes meet Dave's they flash silver again, and he's smiling. "I don't have any more time, and neither do you, and neither does Henry." He turns, looks behind him at the house. "Find him, Dave. Find our boy."

Dave looks to the house with new understanding. His features brighten. "Here? This place?"

Jack nods, but he's already drifting away, like the shadow mask blown away by the mysterious wind, so does his flesh tear apart, drift into the air before Dave's eyes. "Find our son."

"Jack." Dave feels the strength drain from his body. His eyelids are suddenly heavy—*too* heavy to keep up—and he doesn't even realize he's falling away. Down to reality. Out of the dream that is not a dream.

"I love you, Jack," he thinks, or says. It's irrelevant now, but he hears Jack say it back, if only a whisper, soft as the sound of leaves rustling in the wind.

I love you too, little brother.

Now find him.

5

The gap beneath the farmhouse's front door is surprisingly narrow for a century-old home that's been warped and weathered by over a hundred years of sun, rain, and, in a few rare instances, ice and snow. Even so, the half-inch gap is still tall enough for a gust of northern wind to spread across the floorboards, or the yellow heat of direct sunlight to illuminate the separation into a glowing bar for the duration of a lemon-yellow morning, turning hazy as it dims a few inches in, tilting lazily during the progression of a summer day.

The gap is also just tall enough to allow entrance by scuttling insects, slim snakes, or other such creatures inhabiting the rich forest soil. In the dark of this night, it allows the entrance of five full-grown cockroaches, each focused on their destination, antennae twitching and carapaces shining in the dark, black eyes intent on the soft, fleshy giants who slumber nearby.

None carry disease, but each holds a curse. A crude spell old as mankind, passed through the centuries, first by those above—soon lost—and then by those below.

The bugs fan out as they approach the humped, snoring figures wrapped in sleeping bags, or twisted among blankets.

The first cockroach to reach his target pauses, then crawls over the edge of the shining blue fabric encasing a woman's feet. In a few moments it crests a wave of cloth near a hand, an arm bent at the elbow, exposed. The dirty fingertips of the hand are pressed against the bottom lip of a mouth partly open, the head turned toward the floor, greasy blond hair falling over the forehead and eyes. She inhales and exhales steadily.

The cockroach climbs onto the back of the hand, crosses to the lower lip. Its antennae brush the moisture there. Oil-slick eyes stare into the warm dark crevice that calls to it. A moist tongue slips out once, flicking the dry lower lip as well as the head of the lingering insect.

The tongue slides back inside, and the cockroach follows.

Jenny does not sense the invasion—not consciously.

The large bug all but fills her mouth but pushes deeper, back across the slippery warmth of tongue to the throat and burrows down, as if slipping down a slick tunnel, wiggling into the woman's esophagus.

Jenny gags, then instinctively swallows; the salivary glands push the bug down like a kid on a waterslide. Her breathing resumes, steady and unbroken.

The dying cockroach quickly dissolves in the acids of Jenny's empty stomach, her small intestine eagerly accepting the tainted (but relatively nutrient-rich) juices, releasing the proteins into her system—first through the bloodstream, then touching base with the liver before hitting her sleeping brain like black ink squirted onto a sponge, altering her dreams into the very worst thing her subconscious can possibly imagine.

"Jenny? Greg? What the hell is this? What—oh my God—what the *almighty hell* are you doing!?"

Jenny, panting and naked and covered in sweat, looks up to see her father standing only a few yards away from where she hunkers on her knees in the dirt, grinding her crotch against her twin brother like a cat in heat.

"Oh shit!" Greg yells. He bucks and twists, pushing Jenny off his hard, narrow cock and dumping her on her back in the leaf-and-branch-strewn forest floor.

"Ow! Asshole!" she yells, a sharp stick jabbing one bare ass cheek.

Were it not for the fact they are both naked (and screwing), one might have supposed, upon coming upon them in this way, that it is was nothing more than an innocent, old-fashioned sibling tussle—two teenagers wrestling in the woods outside their rustic cabin home, possibly over a tease gone too far, a friendly punch in the arm thrown with too much heat.

Their father is under no such illusion.

With a roar the lanky older man falls upon his son, driving his knee into Greg's guts before raining blows with his hammer-strong, bony-knuckled fists into the boy's face and head. Greg screams in terror and pain; legs kicking wildly, arms arched over his face to block the punches from connecting with his bloodied nose and mouth.

Jenny watches in horror, screaming at the bastard to *stop! Please stop!*

Like he has any right! she thinks, knowing damn well why the old guy is angry. Yeah, it's partially self-righteous rage, incest and all that. But it's also *jealousy*. The big dumb bastard, the one who sang hymns from the third pew of First Baptist every Sunday morning and Wednesday night, who prayed before every meal and literally thumped his big leather bible whenever he admonished the kids for some indiscretion—a curse or a minor theft, being caught in a harmless lie—also liked to visit Jenny some nights. Had been doing so ever since their mother passed, going on a decade. Greg knew, of course. What details he couldn't ascertain from listening through paper-thin walls Jenny filled in for him. Of course, there were many nights she would sneak into *Greg's* bed and worry their father might go to her room and find it empty. A part of her, deep down, perhaps hoping he would do just that. Get it all out into the open.

It was a joke, really. They were nothing but a house full of perverts and sneaks. A house so filled with pain and darkness it was a wonder they didn't drown in it.

But the cat is out of the bag and all hell is breaking loose, just as she'd known it would. And now that the time finally has come, Jenny doesn't hesitate.

The shit needs to stop.

She scampers through dirty leaves and stony earth to her clothes, throwing a Judas Priest concert tour shirt aside to locate her frayed jeans and the rusty ice pick she's carried every day for the last year or so, ever since Ben Burnham and two of his buddies had cornered her in the girl's bathroom at their high school after hours, all of them having served detention for a variety of dumbass reasons. Ben and his friends had forced Jenny to do some things in a stinking bathroom stall, under physical pressure and the threat of extreme violence, that she'd never told anyone, not even her dear brother. Later that same night, ashamed and pissed off, she'd been digging through the toolshed for a claw hammer her daddy wanted and had come across the rusted ice pick, lying in a wooden crate along with ten handfuls of old nails and an ancient Dazey butter churn (the sealing jar long lost) that her mother had used once or twice, thinking it quaint.

Trying to tune out the sounds of flesh smacking flesh behind her, she clutches the narrow wood handle of the pick and swivels like a snake toward her father, who is still swinging—albeit tiredly—at her brother. Greg's arms, she notices, are no longer up and shielding the assault, but lie limp at his side. Looking at his blood-spattered face, Jenny thinks, in that moment, that her brother is dead. Murdered.

With a howl she lunges, thrusting the tip of the pick straight for her father's open throat, her senses already leaping in ecstasy at the thought of seeing the old man's blood spew from his neck.

She doesn't even realize she's smiling.

In the memory, things go as they went on the timeline she and her brother are currently tripping along. She sticks her father once in the neck and once through the eye. He dies. They bury his body and flee, never to return.

Life goes on.

Dreams, however (especially cursed nightmares), are not held by such rules as time and reality the way memories are. Dreams have their own rules—some good, many bad. In dreams, you can be married to a completely different person than the one sleeping next to you in bed; you can be a professional athlete wondering how you ever made the team when you're just a little kid; you can live out your wildest fantasies or be consumed by your worst fears.

Or you can die horribly, even if, in reality, you escaped unscathed.

When Jenny feels the iron-tight grip of her father's hand on her wrist, the point of the rusty pick still a bewildering three inches from the pulsing vein of his jugular, her first response is astonishment.

But that's not what happened, a confused part of her mind reflects. And when he turns his large head toward her, with his gray crewcut stacked neatly above impossible red eyes, the space inside his open mouth *writhing* with a thousand tiny bugs, Jenny doesn't laugh in triumph, but screams in horror, her mind snapping somewhere in the distance, like the popped vein of an aneurysm; a blown tire on the speeding sports car that is her sanity.

And when those little black bugs begin to pour from that horrendous mouth, crawling like tiny spiders out and over her father's cheeks and chin, down his neck and up into his hair, it seems all Jenny can do is scream and scream and scream.

"How about a kiss for daddy?" growls the thing atop her beaten, and most certainly dead, twin brother. *(And yes—so sorry sweet memory—but in this draft, you see, Greg's eye socket is bashed in like a dented fender, one eye burst like a broken egg spilled gracelessly over a cracked cheekbone, and he is most certainly not breathing in this new and improved version of Jenny's well-worn footage, her life-changing scene of patricide and freedom.)*

Jenny tugs and tugs but the hand of the thing holding her, the thing with fiery red eyes and a mouthful of squirming wet bugs, is too strong—*impossibly* strong.

With a sudden jerk, it twists its hand and Jenny feels the bone in her wrist *snap*. She's already shrieking for her life and her sanity, but when that pain strikes her nervous system, she manages to reach down and find one last gear, one last level of terror resting quietly in the back of her mind that comes wide awake and springs forward, blowing her thoughts to shreds and ripping her throat as she drops to her knees, helpless and fighting off the shock the damned must feel when they first meet the devil and those flames start burning the soles of their feet, climbing hastily up their legs.

Her eyes bulge as the face comes closer. The red eyes intensify with hunger, and the bugs pour out of the mouth in such volume that the thing's face is covered in them. Jenny watches them skittering over her father's arm, the hand that clenches her own, then feels the tickle of them moving up her bare skin, racing toward her body, her face, her mouth.

"*Come on, sweet thing. You know I love you,*" her dead father says in a gravelly, almost indistinct voice, and when his mouth moves the bugs are pushed out in bunches, some split open by whatever passes for teeth inside the monster's maw.

Jenny tries to cry out for mercy as her father's face presses into hers. Those horrible red eyes fill her vision; he reeks of rot and sour earth, like a corpse exhumed.

As his mouth clamps over her own the scream is cut off by his invading tongue, his foul breath, and the thriving mass of insects scrambling pell-mell into her own mouth, biting mercilessly at her cheeks, her tongue, a multitude pushing down her choked, silenced throat.

His body presses down on her exposed flesh, shoving her down; her panicked, broken mind screaming at her that she is . . .

★ ★ ★

. . . *choking to death*.

Pedro gags on something lodged in his throat, then swallows hard; a bitter squirt of gritty fluid slicks the back of his tongue, prompting a gag reflex. He wakes up rubbing his face, disgusted by the taste in his mouth. He spits into the dirt, the metal Coca-Cola sign popping in protest as his body weight shifts on the old paint-flaked aluminum. His long hair is slicked over his head with warm sweat. His brain feels pressurized, like it's swelled up and pressing against the inside of his skull, pushing at the backs of his eyeballs, clogging his nasal passages.

It's sweltering inside the makeshift lean-to he'd erected in the back-yard that afternoon, tired of sharing a room with an army of siblings and strangers. He isn't a kid anymore, a child who changes clothes in front of a bunch of snotty baby boys and prepubescent girls, the latter constantly gabbing like pigeons about makeup and how their tits were gonna come in soon and the mystery of periods—

"OW!" he yells.

Something frickin' bit me.

Pedro sits up on the worn cot, throws off the quilted blanket. *Too dang hot anyway.*

"OW! Shit! Ow ow ow!" Now there's something *crawling* on him—a *lot* of somethings. He feels them on his bare arms, his legs, beneath his shirt, his shoulders, chest, and belly. Tickling up his thighs.

Breathing heavily, the first glimpse of panic unraveling in his brain, he begins swiping at his flesh. He brushes flecks of something off his legs ... bugs?

Then they're biting again, and it feels like his whole body is on fire. "Damn it!" he yells, sobbing now; frightened and confused, the pain searing, the darkness total, the heat oppressive.

I gotta get out of here!

Pedro stands, still swiping at his arms and clothes, tiny hot pinches erupting on his feet, his calves, his back and arms. His chest and neck.

He steps off the sign and into the dry grass, pushes against the blue tarp, ready to bolt for the house, for help.

But there is no tarp.

Instead, there is a wall. Firm and solid as the wall of any house.

"What the hell?" he says, confused, thinking maybe he's gotten turned around in the dark, and maybe he's hitting one of the plywood walls by mistake? *Built this thing too well,* he thinks, his brain offering one last moment of levity in order to keep things loose, keep the knifepoint of full-blown panic from stabbing too hard, from penetrating his rational mind, from screwing up his decision-making.

"Okay, okay," he says, and turns around, takes three steps, arms extended.

Another wall.

"That's *impossible!*" he screams, banging a fist on a wall that is neither tarp nor plywood. *Feels like concrete!* he thinks, brain swinging smoothly into freak-out mode.

The biting isn't getting worse, but it's sure as hell not getting better. He can feel the bugs crawling into his long hair, tickling his scalp, but ignores that for now. *Shuts that shit out* for now. Because if he thinks about it—*really* thinks about it—imagines an army of small angry bugs crawling over his slick skin, beneath his clothes, along his scalp, tangling with strands of hair . . . well, he might completely lose his shit.

"The flashlight," he says, using all his willpower to keep his voice steady, despite the sensation going on way down below, beneath his bare feet—the sensation that maybe he's stepping on something that isn't grass, or dirt, or his mattress, or even that crappy aluminum Coca-Cola sign. Something that feels a heck of a lot like it's *moving.* "Just need to find the flashlight, and I can get out," he says, but now his voice has a little hiccup quality. A little skip on the record. A hitch in its giddyup.

At this point, panic has taken off its coat, kicked off its shoes, pulled up a seat, smiled that maniacal smile, the one showing too many bright white teeth, to let you know it really *likes* it here, and it's decided to stay a while.

Pedro takes a step back, up onto the cot, and is momentarily relieved to feel the fluffy fabric beneath his toes. Even when sleeping inside with the others, he had a habit of keeping a flashlight above his head so he could reach it to read comics when the others were asleep. In his new setup he'd continued that routine, just in case he needed to make his way to the house for a drink of water or a whiz in the middle of the night. He bends over (*totally* ignoring the feeling of insects crawling beneath his shorts—exploring the crack of his ass, the little soft spot behind his balls, the crook of his crotch) and feels the pillow. He takes a half step forward and reaches again, finding the hard metal of the flashlight.

That's the good news. The bad news is that whatever's crawling all over him—*biting* him—is also crawling all over the flashlight. Regardless, he needs to see, so what choice does he have? He picks it up, feels for the metal switch, and slides it forward with his thumb.

The light bursts to life, igniting the small interior of his private abode with a comforting white glow. Pedro is crying now, but things are moving quickly, and he needs to keep his shit straight and get the hell out of here.

Wincing at the continuous needle bites in his legs, feet, and hands, he spends the first few seconds aiming the light at the structure surrounding him. His fifteen-year-old brain can't fully comprehend what he's looking at, because it seems he was right about the walls. There is no tarp, no wobbly four-by-eight sheets of plywood. The walls here—the ones erected for the sole purpose of this dream—are cracked, and peeling, and old.

But solid, baby.

They look just like the walls of an old house, ones you might need a sledgehammer to break through, or at the very least you'd need a lot of time to punch, kick and claw—

Pedro hisses loudly and slaps at his neck. In response, two more quick bites sink in: one on his throat, one at the meat of his shoulder. His feet feel like they're buried in hot needles. Tears and snot and sweat pour down his face, and he swipes at something crawling over his chin.

He aims the light at the ground and—when he realizes what's been feasting on him—his chest constricts, his throat closes. The feeling of being someone *else* takes over, the out-of-body sensation that accompanies the first stages of shock takes his hand and holds it tight.

The ground is covered with giant, bright red fire ants.

Pedro hears a long, sinuous moaning sound. Like a fire engine in the distance, or a ghost slipping out of a dark closet, waving its transparent hands in the air as it approaches your bedside.

That's coming from me, he realizes, but he cannot make it stop. The primal moans continue as he studies his feet with the light and sees the ants are no longer just blanketing the ground, but are now almost completely covering the thin mattress he stands upon—like a life raft slowly losing air, or a stray piece of wood in a quagmire of quicksand being sucked down, inch by inch. Except Pedro and his mattress aren't sinking. At least, he doesn't think so.

Which means the thrashing floor of red ants must be *rising*.

"How many are there!" he screams, sobbing loudly but afraid to move, unsure if stepping off the mattress is something he *can* do, something he *should* do. His shallow breaths come too fast and spots appear in front of his eyes. He swipes at his forehead, feels the first of the insects crawling free from his hairline and down onto his face. Another climbs up his right ear, over the lobe, and into the waxy tunnel leading to the brain. He sticks a finger in the ear and feels the satisfying squish of the ant but not before it bites him hard, deep inside the canal. He howls in pain and realizes things are getting out of control. He has no choice—he needs to find a way out—and *fast!*

He spins in circles, but no matter how many times he looks at them the walls are all the same—white and solid. He aims the light straight up, expecting to see the blue tarp ceiling, but there is no ceiling; there's nothing there at all. The walls simply continue up and up into cloudy darkness, as if he's at the bottom of a deep well, one with no ladder, no dangling rope to cling onto.

No escape.

"Help!" he screams. "Help me!"

His voice sounds dampened, as if he's screaming from far below the earth. He looks down again and sees with horror that the level of ants has reached his shins. He can no longer see the ground, the mattress, his pillow, or his own feet.

"STOP IT!" he screeches, high and scratchy. He begins smacking the rising floor of insects with his flashlight. He lifts one foot from the bed of bugs—the foot is slick with blood and writhing. A persistent few have pushed into open wounds and are crawling *beneath* the flesh, giving his foot the appearance of something monstrous and foreign, something that could not possibly be his own. With a howl of rage and despair he smashes the foot down, crushing as many of the red bastards as he can.

But it feels to Pedro as if he is standing in a deep tub with the water spout turned all the way on, jetting down so fast that it's filling too quickly for him to stem the tide.

Despair settles in as the floor of ants rises to his thighs. He can no longer feel his feet. He's tired and dizzy. His body is covered from head to toe with the insects and they are all biting, biting, *biting*. They're in his ears and in his nose. He does what he can to keep his lips closed tight but he knows it's only a matter of time and he must do *something*. Call for help again. Scream for someone to save him.

He looks around desperately for inspiration and sees the walls are no longer white, but red. Red and dancing with shadow. The ants have swarmed the glass head of the flashlight, and the hand holding it has become so very heavy. Pedro slowly lowers his arm to his side and the ants swallow it because now they have risen past his waist. They are on him and they are inside him and still they are coming.

He looks upward one last time, toward the eternal darkness, but tiny bodies crawl over his eyeballs and soon he cannot see anything.

In death he opens his mouth to say a prayer for his soul. They infiltrate this last orifice greedily.

He is sinking, and the numbness and the dark have almost taken over, but a few moments of life remain.

He swears he hears the ants clogging his ears and mouth *laughing*—chatting giddily as they consume him. He thinks they're saying: *Hold on. Hold on. Not yet . . .*

There is still so much for you to experience.

6

Greg has lived with Jenny his entire life. They were born minutes apart
(Jenny hitting the dirt three minutes and forty-five seconds before Greg
emerged), both of them swollen and pissed off and bawling like their
skin was on fire. As little kids they'd lived in a trailer near Bakersfield,
California. When their mother died, their father sold the trailer home,
threw them in his old red pickup (whatever belongings they had tossed
into the bed like the garbage it was), and headed north.

Their new home wasn't so much a house as it was a cabin, and
although it was surrounded by woods and a gentle spine of green hills,
to Greg and Jenny it was just about the ugliest shithole they'd ever been
dragged to. School was a forty-five-minute bus ride—each way—and the
only things to do for fun once you got home were watch television, read
comics, or go mess around in the woods.

When the kids got older, and things became physical between them, it
seemed, to the siblings anyway, the most natural thing in the world.

How many nights had they slept side by side? Thousands, Greg figured, over the years. As kids, teenagers, and adults. He knew, for instance,
just by listening to his sister breathe, whether she was fast asleep or just
skimming the surface. He knew she sometimes talked while dreaming, at
times grabbing him tight and mumbling fast, nonsensical words into his
ear, her breath hot and him thinking she must be talking in tongues, like
a person possessed.

So when Jenny starts to moan and thrash around in her sleep, Greg is
awake and alert within seconds, because in his experience this is abnormal
behavior.

Something is wrong with his sister.

His first thought is that it must be a reaction to the wasp stings, the venom hitting her heart or her lungs, some sort of allergic response that wasn't immediately apparent. But the more she thrashes and gasps and moans, the more he begins to think it might be something else, something not physical.

Sitting up, Greg starts to say his sister's name. His mind tries to say, "Jenny!" but his mouth isn't cooperating—his tongue is caught on something *inside* his mouth, something moving slick and prickly toward his throat. His eyes go wide and one hand claws at his neck before he gags and, reflexively, snaps his teeth down on the impediment, biting through the intruder and spilling its insides like a chocolate-covered cherry between his cheek and molars.

"*Gaaah!*" He retches, coughing up what he can before it slides down his throat, spitting the entire bitter, gooey mess onto the floor. "*Jesus Christ!*" he yells, eyes watering as he works up more saliva and spits again.

Jim, who had been sitting at the top of the stairs in order to keep an eye on both Henry's door and the front door of the house, runs down, heavy boots pounding. "What's wrong, man?"

Greg, on hands and knees, holds up a "gimme a second" finger, belches, then twists his body away from his writhing sister and pukes into the corner.

Jim approaches, his face a mask of disgust and confusion as he looks at Jenny in the dim light. She's twisting and turning, as if fighting someone in her sleep, moaning horribly. It brings a chill to the back of his neck. "Greg! What's going on? What's with Jenny?"

Greg stands shakily, wiping his mouth. "Lemme see a lantern."

Jim turns, spots one sitting on the other side of the room. He runs over and grabs it, lights it up to full power.

"Bring it," Greg says, waving Jim over and pointing to a spot on the floor.

Jim brings the light closer and stares down, not sure what's he seeing. "Is that vomit, man? I don't need to see—"

"It's a fucking cockroach," Greg says. "Or what's left of it. Fucker was *in my mouth*. I almost swallowed the damn thing."

"Looks like you tried to eat it instead," Jim says, studying the floor. At the edge of the frayed circle of light, another cockroach skitters straight for his boot. He casually lifts his foot and brings it down on the insect; the crunch of breaking shell is audible.

"By accident, yeah," Greg says. "Listen, I'm gonna wake up Jenny, she's having a bad nightmare or—"

"AAAAHHH!"

Pete's scream tears through the silence of the room like a buzzsaw. Jim sets the lantern down and runs over to him. "Pete! Dude, *wake up*!" Jim drops to his knees, shaking Pete, yelling at him.

Greg, meanwhile, turns his attention back to his sister, who is now weeping in her sleep, her face smeared with tears. As he watches helplessly, she clutches her throat, as if choking.

"Jenny!" Greg says, kneeling next to her. "Wake up, baby! Wake the fuck *up*!"

"Greg, help me, man!" Jim yells, and Greg looks over to see Jim with his hands spread in the air—a gesture saying: *What do I do?* In front of him Pete is convulsing, his body arched and shaking in spasms. A dribble of white, foamy saliva leaks from the corner of his mouth. "I think he's choking on his tongue," Jim says, and Greg watches him shove two meaty fingers into Pete's mouth. With his free hand, Jim digs through Pete's worn gym bag, yanks out a prescription bottle. The Klonopin. He shoves one into Pete's gurgling mouth, cussing him out the entire time.

"I—" Greg starts to say.

Liam cries out frantically, incoherently, from the other side of the room. "NO! I didn't . . . oh no . . . oh my god no no no NO NO NO . . ." His arms shoot straight up into the air and he gives a terrible, chest-wrenching cry, the likes of which Greg has never heard. It's a scream of unfiltered, unforgettable pain.

Greg rests trembling hands on his sister's hip as his eyes dart from Liam, to Pete and Jim, then back to his sister.

Jim is half turned toward Liam, one hand slick with foamy saliva, but Pete appears to be breathing. Jim starts to stand, takes an uncertain step, then stops, as if he's being pulled multiple directions—like he's lost, or stuck, unsure where to go, what to do. His wide eyes find Greg's, and Greg knows what he sees there but can't believe it.

It's *fear*. And if Greg didn't know any better, he would have bet anyone in the room a hundred dollars that Jim Cady—the original Big Nasty—was straight-up terrified.

"Greg," Jim says, almost a whisper. "What do we do, man? What do we do? I mean, holy shit, tell me what the hell is going on here."

Greg shakes his head, more exhausted than afraid, but also more certain of his next move. Over the last ninety insane seconds Greg has decided exactly what he's gonna do before dawn breaks. First, he's gonna wake up his sister and make sure she's okay. Next, he's gonna figure out a way to somehow get hold of Liam's gun. And then he and his sister are gonna get the hell *away* from this house.

And if Jim or anyone else gets in the way, he'll kill them.

"I don't know, Jim," he says. "I really don't know."

7

The man's name was Shaw. He was an older geezer, and up until a few months ago, he and Liam had been close mates. Business partners. Or, perhaps more accurately, partners in crime.

The two of them had done a slew of odd jobs together—mainly robberies. Their specialty was pawnbrokers, and they, along with whatever crew they assembled for a particular job, were adept at turning a nice penny off smash-and-grab operations all over Queensland.

What had soured the relationship was a particular load of stolen jewelry, a job they'd spent months planning. It was Liam who'd actually gone into the shop to grab the jewelry, with Shaw and one other—a digger named Marcus with a bad case of PTSD and an itchy trigger finger—having disabled the security, removed two night guards from the equation, and readied the getaway.

Liam was still inside when he heard the sirens and realized one of the guards—not as dispatched as he was led to believe—must have tripped a silent alarm. Now he needed to get the jewelry and get out—and what should have been five minutes quickly became sixty seconds. He went as fast as he could, focusing on speed versus precision.

He had just emptied the last tray of diamond rings, necklaces, and other such finery into a black sack when he heard the gunshots.

In all the years doing jobs they'd always carried weapons only for intimidation purposes, and had certainly never fired one. Now it sounded like a damned shootout was taking place outside, and he was stuck in the building like a trapped rat. He took the time to peek out the front window through iron bars that had done nothing to prevent the robbery, but were now prophesying the view he looked forward to if he was nabbed.

He watched in horror as Marcus was shot in the neck and chest, falling hard to the street's pavement. Shaw packed himself into the Monaro he was so proud of (now strewn with a barrage of pockmark bullet holes along its shiny black siding) and tore off in a screech of smoking tires.

It was to Liam's credit that he was a careful person, and a smart planner. He always had an alternate escape route for any job; a backup route for him, and him alone, were things to go south. This job was no different, and Liam wasted no time executing Plan B in an effort to escape the incoming—and hostile—police.

The ceiling at the rear of the shop hid an old trapdoor, what was once a ladder leading to roof access. Some years ago, likely for safety reasons, the shop owner had the access door on the roof bolted shut and wired for alarm, the ladder removed, and ceiling panels placed below the previous access point. Three nights ago, Liam had come on his own, scaled a drainage pipe to the roof from the exterior of a neighboring shop, bolt cutters in tow, and carefully snipped the protruding heads off the bolt ends, thereby (he hoped) allowing the access door to be utilized with a good push upward from inside, the alarm being triggered a superfluous problem if it came to that. Because if Plan B was enacted, it meant the shit was well beyond hitting the fan; it would be spraying the goddamn walls.

To his delight—and no small amount of surprise—the backup plan worked as he'd hoped.

By the time the checkered caps were yelling from the front door two stories below for him to "*Come out with hands raised!*" Liam was making his way to the next rooftop, then the next, and the next, until dropping down in a darkened alley almost two blocks from the scene.

Still clutching the sack of jewels.

He didn't know what happened to Shaw, and he didn't care. The guy had brought a loose cannon in on the job, and now they were likely labeled cop-killers in addition to thieves, and that was a huge problem.

Besides, in his hands he held a run-fund for him, his wife, and their son. Enough to get far away from Queensland, enough to live off for at least a few years while he found real work, *legal* work, that could sustain the long haul and finally get Kaaron off his back about leaving Shaw—and crime—forever.

A day later, he and his family left the apartment in Brisbane with everything they owned and headed south. Kaaron's parents owned some land in Bega, near Eden on a rough patch of coast, and an old mill with an empty caretaker shed. It was just the place to hide out while things cooled down. Liam had seen photos, and understood it was far from a permanent solution, but one that would do for now.

At least, that's what he'd thought.

Instead, it became the horror-show setting for The Dream. The recurring nightmare he'd had over and over the last handful of years, the dream that followed him from Australia, then to England, and persistently over the great Atlantic Ocean to America, like a dark spot in his mind—an obstinate, nagging tumor that would never leave him no matter how far he ran or how much time passed by.

It was The Dream he was having again now.

Unlike the others, however, the poison from the bug he'd swallowed did not alter the previous memory that changed his life forever, like it had Pete and Jenny. They dreamed of truths that became twisted into horrible, maddening lies.

Liam's dream was a lie that, once altered, became a maddening truth. A real memory—not the fabrication his mind had conjured up—of the day his life changed forever.

He's with Timothy and they're running.

Always running. Laughing. A game.

Three shots—*bap bap bap*—echo from the direction of the mill, and the caretaker's shed attached to it. The shed they've been using as a temporary home.

They've found us.

"Timothy, *run!*" he screams, and the boy runs, obedient. He knows enough of his father, of his father's past, to understand there is always the possibility of danger. His mother has cried about it on countless nights, and countless fights have stomped through their old apartment over the years, like monsters in the night. So he runs, but then—without warning—he's falling.

Liam reaches Timothy at a dead sprint, drops to his knees on the sandy rock face to see his son's body trapped between two large rocks in a shallow crevasse, a gap in the shoreline rocks. The sea crashes twenty yards away, the splash of each wave warning him. *They're coming! They're* coming*!*

"I'm hurt!" Timothy yells from below. A small hand reaches up from the darkness. Liam lies on his stomach, not daring to turn back toward the mill, not wanting to know how much time he has because time is irrelevant. All that matters is getting his boy free, getting him out of harm's way. He doesn't think about the three gunshots, does not imagine what has happened to his wife.

He focuses on the hand.

A large, heavy boot stomps down onto his back, the heel grinding into his spine between his shoulder blades, pinning him. Three long shadows stretch over the tan rocks, their gray heads breaking apart in the bog grass that separates the beach from the low ridge. His son cowers in the dim light of the crevasse, and now Liam's only hope is that they don't see him, that he remains quiet while his father is killed.

In the recurring nightmare, a creature emerges from beneath Timothy, wraps slick black arms around his face and chest, and drags him down into the dark.

In *this* dream, the poisoned dream, lies the truth, the *real* memory he'd run from, across continents and over oceans. Through time and space he has fled from it, turned his heart to stone and thereby become the worst kind of criminal: a killer, a stealer of children. A buried, hidden part of him hoping that by turning himself into a monster, he could forget the human he once was.

In this dream, however, there is no creature in the dark.

There is no lie.

He struggles to free himself until the butt of a gun smacks the back of his skull. The world goes gray, hazy, and his body goes limp. His eyes roll but he is still conscious, still aware enough to look down and see his boy's terrified face, to hear his son scream for the men to "Stop it! Stop!"

Don't speak, he thinks. *Please stop yelling. They hear you, Tim, they see you now.*

"You awake, Liam?" Shaw's voice, like tire on gravel. "Can you see, brother?"

Then comes the crash of a shotgun.

Liam screams but it is muffled because his ears are ringing, half-deafened by the blast. To his ears it's as if he's yelling from a distance, as if the entire world has been somehow deadened. He stares at his son's twisted, bloody body, and he cries his name: *Timothy! Timothy! NO NO NO NO NO . . .*

He doesn't feel the boot leave his spine, doesn't acknowledge the men as they walk away, leaving him to his misery, leaving him to live with the consequences of the man he'd been, the death of the man he'd hoped to become.

Later, in a shocked haze, he climbs down to retrieve the body, sobbing and cursing at the dying sun. He cradles it in the dark, his arms wrapped around his boy as his mind splinters like breaking glass.

In this dream, there are no lies, there is only the truth, and guilt, and shame. There is no creature in the dark. There is only the man he'd lost, but has now found once again.

8

Dave opens his eyes, surprised to find the room still bathed in darkness. He rolls onto his side and sees the shadowed shape of his wife sleeping next to him, her breathing soft and consistent. He looks at the clock. Nearly 4 a.m.

The dream is so fresh in his mind he can almost feel the cold dew from the forest floor on his feet as he slides them out of bed, his dead brother's smiling face alive in his mind—a three-second film reel on loop—and his final words imprinted like a scar in his memory:

Find him.

Dave gathers his Adidas track pants from the floor and slips them on. He slides bare feet into kicked-off slippers and pulls a sweatshirt over his head, the front blazoned SDSU, his alma mater.

He opens the bedroom door carefully, not wanting to wake Mary, then closes it even more carefully behind him. Quiet voices murmur from the living room. He figures the morning shift isn't likely to arrive until six, if they keep the routine of the last few days, and the officers and techs out there now are probably haggard and tired, sick of his house and his brand of coffee; strained from being constantly ready for an incoming call, for a threat from the outside . . . for anything and everything.

Dave detours to the guest bathroom to pee and—the idea of going back to sleep wholly dismissed—brush his teeth with one of the disposable travel toothbrushes Mary keeps in the cabinet below the sink. His nose wrinkles at the mild after-stink of someone's early-morning shit, and he sighs at the scraps of toilet paper strewn on the floor, the overflowing garbage pail, the well-thumbed magazines puffed with dots of moisture sitting on the sink next to the toilet.

Time to call in a house cleaner, he thinks absently as he urinates, the primary part of his brain already formulating the conversation he would soon be having with Agent Espinoza, trying to figure out exactly how he was going to explain his hunch, his—*call it what it is, Dave*—his vision.

What it means. What it *could* mean.

Moments later, he's greeting the officers, some of whom he's never met, and is relieved to see the coffee maker still percolating the final drips of a recently brewed pot. He pulls a mug from the cabinet and pours himself a cup, then leans on the counter, head down, finalizing his thoughts on the matter. He walks into the dining room where an FBI tech sits at the table next to a recorder hard-lined into the house phone.

"Hey there, I'm Dave Thorne," he says, not knowing how else to start.

The man rises quickly, holds out a hand. "Agent Mitchell. Good morning, sir."

"Good morning, or night, I guess. I hate to ask this, I know it's early, but I need to call Agent Espinoza about something. I wanted to let you know I need a line."

"Yes, yes, of course. He won't mind," Mitchell says, already fiddling with switches. "Knowing Sali he's probably up pacing the bedroom floor himself. Uh, here," the agent says, handing Dave an industrial-looking phone that feels heavy in his hand, and is most certainly not his own sky-blue, plastic-shelled house phone. "I'm opening a second line for you now, so that your primary line won't be affected should . . . well, should someone call."

"Of course, thank you. And, I'm sorry, I'm very tired, and I think his card is in my pants, which are in my bedroom, and I hate to wake my wife—"

"Oh! No problem, here, I'll dial his number for you, sir. This is his home phone. If he's awake, he'll answer."

Agent Mitchell dials the number, then hands Dave the phone. Dave realizes he only has a few feet of cord, and that he hasn't thought this all the way through. He clears his throat as the first electronic ring chirps in his ear. "Agent, I need to apologize again. I should have asked before. Do you think I could speak in private?"

The agent smiles and stands, pats Dave warmly on the shoulder. "It's your home, sir, no need to apologize for anything. I was gonna go have a smoke anyway. The boys in blue over there"—Mitchell indicates the open door leading to the living room, where Dave can see two officers lounging on his furniture—one looks asleep and the other is reading what appears to be yesterday's sports section—"will let me know if a call comes in, so you take your time."

"Thank you," Dave says, then there's a click, and the weary, but not sleepy, voice of the agent in charge.

"Espinoza."

"Sali? It's Dave Thorne."

There's a slight pause, then Sali responds in his most upbeat, everything's-gonna-be-fine voice. "Good morning, Dave. Tell me what's on your mind."

★ ★ ★

Sali had not been awake, but not far from pacing the floors, as Agent Mitchell theorized. His brain was skimming the surface of that deep green lake of dreams, but even more, it was sifting through information, revisiting facts, looking for a clue or a lead he might have been missing. To his frustration, he was having little success with either endeavor. Sleep evaded him, and chasing clues around in a tired mind was the equivalent of running through a topiary maze and finding nothing but dead end after dead end. It didn't help either cause that he was slightly hungover, which made him feel flu-ish and muddle-headed. He was normally pretty good about keeping it to two drinks a night when working a case, but this case had been particularly trying. For one thing, it was going on too long, and that weighed heavily on him, on the parents, on everybody. For another, the points of contact were too few and far between. Just two messages—one stupidly mailed, the other smartly dropped at an associate not being monitored by the police or FBI.

The drop was supposed to be later today, but Sali's intuition was telling him something was goofy, something was not right. He had the strong feeling he was being jerked around by the janitor and his crew. Either that or they'd caught wind of their newfound fame on the nightly news and it spooked the shit out of them.

Maybe they were running. Maybe not.

Regardless, Sali put the odds of the drop going off as scheduled at about one in ten.

And now Dave Thorne was calling him at four in the morning. Normally he would put this down to nerves. Maybe Dave had been up all night fretting about some detail or other and had been sitting around waiting until a somewhat decent hour to approach him with some random question or concern.

Or maybe it was something else.

From the moment Sali picked up the phone he had the strong feeling Dave was going to tell him something of importance, something that could possibly affect the course of things.

Checking himself in the reflection of a darkened window, he's slightly surprised to see himself still dressed in yesterday's shirt and slacks, having never made it off the couch. He clocks the scotch glass laying like a dead soldier on the carpet and winces. He desperately has to piss, and even more desperately needs about ten cups of coffee.

But none of that is gonna happen until he hears what Dave Thorne has to say. All that stuff can wait, because Sali's Spidey-sense isn't just tingling, it's banging like a goddamn gong.

"Good morning, Dave," he says, walking to the kitchen on his cordless to at least get a sip of cold water, wash the filthy taste of bacteria and scotch out of his mouth. "Tell me what's on your mind."

"Well," Dave says hesitantly, "you're gonna think I'm nuts." Dave chuckles a little and some static interferes with the connection. Frustrated and eager, but patient, Sali pours a glass of water at the sink, then moves back into the main room where the reception sounds less like Dave's calling from Siberia.

"Dave," Sali says reassuringly, "think of me as a psychiatrist and a priest mixed together, my friend. You can tell me anything and I swear I will not think you're crazy or anything else. And I promise, unless you tell me differently, that it will stay between us. Between you, me, and my shitty leather shoes, right?" Dave laughs a little, as Sali hoped he would, and some of the tension leaves the electricity flowing down the phone line. "Seriously, you're thinking hard on something. Let me guess: you thought of something absolutely ridiculous and there's no way it'll mean anything, but you think you should tell me anyway. Am I close?"

"You're close," Dave says, still sounding tentative.

"Okay, so let me be clear. There is no such thing as insignificant information. There are no bad hunches, bad guesses, or bizarre coincidences too insane to not be of value. And I'll tell you something else," Sali says, pacing now, his body and brain warming up, his hangover fleeing to the rear to give out its sulky pulses of protest as adrenaline takes over the driver's seat of the agent's mind. "I've solved more cases based on gut feelings, crazy hunches, or weird, absolutely stupid hypotheses than you'd care to know, believe me. There's a reason I talk to my shoes, Dave, okay? There's no such thing as crazy when it comes to an investigation. Now, have I comforted you? Do you feel better about what you're going to tell me?" Sali swallows the rest of the water and sets the glass on the coffee table.

"I guess," Dave says.

"Good. So, Dave. What's on your mind?"

There's a pause, static dances on the line, and Sali all but bends over the phone's main housing unit, the two antennae nearly touching.

"Well," Dave says, and Sali hears a loud exhale of breath, one the poor guy must have been holding tight in his chest all this time. "The thing is, I had a dream last night. A very vivid dream."

"Go on," Sali says, trying hard to mask his disappointment.

"My brother . . . the one who passed? Henry's father? Well, it's a lot to try and explain; you'll just have to believe me about something, and then I'll tell you what I think."

Sali is pacing again, that little gong banging away once more. There's something here. This is *something*. "I'm listening. I'm all ears."

"Okay. The thing is, Sali, our Henry has some unique . . . oh boy, this is gonna be harder than I thought."

Sali waited, said nothing. Paced.

"Forget all that, it's too much. Here's the deal: I had a dream, like I said. But it was more like a vision, you know what I mean? Very real. I suppose I said that."

"It's okay, take your time. You mentioned your brother."

"Right! Yeah, so Jack is there, and we're in a forest. The middle of a forest. And we're in front of this old house, sitting right in the middle of these trees. Like a witch's cabin in a fairy tale, you know? But a real house. White, two stories. There's a large shed to the side where they probably kept a carriage or some horses. Pigs or whatever."

Sali couldn't help himself. His mind ticked off boxes. *House in a forest. Abandoned? What forest? East. What kind of house would be in the middle of a forest?*

"And Jack, that's my brother, he starts going on about how I need to save Henry, to find him, and he's showing me this *house*, Sali. I think—"

"What?" Sali's pulse quickens. *You've gone insane, Salvador. You've truly lost it if you're getting jacked about a grieving father's dreamscape vision.*

And yet.

"Dave?"

There's a pause, and when Dave's voice comes back it's lost some of the uncertainty. Some of the embarrassment. It's a lawyer's voice. A sane man's voice. A father's voice.

"I think Henry is in that house, Sali. The one in the dream, in the forest. I can describe it to you in great detail if you want, but there's something else."

"Okay."

"I'd say you're gonna think it's crazy, but I think that train has left the station, don't you?"

"Not at all, Dave. What else?"

"I'm not a hundred percent sure, and I'd have to give it some more thought, but the thing is—"

Sali's already looking around his apartment for his coat and car keys. "Uh-huh," he says, sitting on the couch to slip on his shoes, which are all but screaming at him.

"I think I might even know where it is."

9

Liam jerks awake, breathing heavily. His mouth is pasty and dry, his throat aches, his head pounds. He's reeling from the horrible nightmare, the *memory*. As he glances around the room, which glows softly with a sapphire light that seeps through the frayed blankets covering the windows, illuminates the crack beneath the door with a bar of ghostly blue, he counts four shapes, all humped and silent.

He's not sure what time it is, but by the coloring of the light from outside he'd guess it's predawn.

They're all asleep. No one's keeping watch. I need—

His brain slips out of gear and he winces, remembering the awful moment he'd tried so hard to destroy, to hide away in a dark cabinet of his mind and forget, unseen, forever. "Oh God," he whimpers and pinches his burning eyes, the tears that escape down his cheeks warm against his chilled flesh. *Timothy, I'm so sorry.*

And hot on the heels of that: *Henry!*

Liam throws aside the blanket, filled with a sharp desire to run upstairs and check on the boy, to make sure he's safe.

To save him.

It's only then he realizes that something is terribly wrong.

It's subtle at first. Like a soft breeze rubbing your skin, ruffling your hair. But as his senses slowly come alert, one by one, he knows it's something else. His scalp itches and it feels like something is crawling along the ridge of his hairline. He scratches at his head, feels the tiny insects catch in his fingernails. He removes his hand, studies it.

Lice?

The small crushed bugs are on his fingertips, dug under the crescent white moons of his nails. One crawls sleepily over the pad of his index finger. There's a similar itching in his legs and he pulls up a pant leg. Tiny red welts cover his shin and calf.

"The hell?" he says and stands, stepping away from his folded blanket. He scratches his head again, then gasps when he feels pain up both legs, on his arms, his back, his chest. He takes a step forward and kicks at the blanket.

Liam has only seen bedbugs once.

When he was a kid, he went away to camp one summer, and after all the boys in his cabin had complained loudly enough about getting bitten to death in the night, the counselor inspected each mattress. As a point of scientific interest, he had shown the boys the brown spotted markings in the seams of their mattresses, pillows, and sheets. Bedbugs. There was nothing to do but burn the mattresses, the counselor said, and fumigate the whole cabin.

Looking closely at his blankets, he makes out similar markings. Even in the dim light he sees infinitesimal specks of brown dust and black spots that, if magnified, would reveal blood-sucking bugs that fed off you, crawled beneath your skin, and laid eggs.

Great.

And now he's infested with them. And—because why the hell not—he's somehow contracted lice as well. Liam knows he needs to get out of his clothes, get a hot shower, and likely shave his head to the scalp. But none of those things are going to happen, not today, so he scratches at his head, his arms, his belly, his ass, and goes to wake up Jim.

This time Jim isn't faking, or sleeping lightly. He's *out*. Liam notices the glint of metal protruding from one of Jim's front pockets. He kneels, waits a beat to make sure Jim isn't going to roll over and stare at him with large open eyes, then reaches for the small hoop of metal and pulls it gently away. He stands, waiting for the roar of anger, the unanswerable questions, but it doesn't come. Liam stuffs the car keys into the pocket of his jeans.

Finally, it takes Liam all but kicking the bastard before Jim eventually blinks sleepily, turns, and winces at Liam with annoyance. His eyes are heavily crusted, and it doesn't take more than a momentary inspection to see that the same bugs roosting in Liam's hair are crawling around in Jim's black stubble. Usually shaved clean, Jim's head has built up a quarter-inch of hair over the last week or so, and Liam can't believe how infested his scalp is. He's seen a few on one head before, but this is like an army. He actually sees them squirming over Jim's scalp. There is even one in his eyebrow, and Liam almost gags at the sight of it.

"The fuck you looking at, man? It's the middle of the damn night," Jim says, then his eyes widen and he yelps, rolling himself out of his blankets and standing quickly, slapping at his legs and arms. He lifts a hand to his head and stares at Liam with what can only be described as childlike horror, the look a small boy might wear if the boogeyman stepped out of his closet one dark night, holding a bloody axe in one hand and the head of his sweet mother in the other. "What the *fuck*!" Jim cries, swiping madly at his head.

"What happened to keeping watch?" Liam says angrily.

Jim's look of horror turns to rage. "To hell with you, Liam! Maybe if you weren't crying like a little bitch in your sleep all night you might have helped us out! It was fucking crazy in here, man! Damn! What the hell's been biting me?"

"Bedbugs," Liam says, and isn't surprised to turn and see Greg also awake and having similar issues as Jim, if not worse.

We've all been infested.

"Hey man, there's fucking bugs all over me!" Greg yells, and Jim and Liam share a look that's almost comical. Almost.

"That bitch," Jim says, and they both know who he means.

Liam walks over to inspect Pete, who looks horrible. He's pale and there's a pool of something brown and slick by his face, like vomit but without substance.

"Pete had a seizure last night, damn near swallowed his tongue," Jim says, and Liam, without thinking about it, kneels down and puts two fingers on the guy's carotid artery, right around the mad eyes of the pit bull tattoo, to feel for a pulse.

It's there, but it isn't strong.

"Jesus, he's not looking so good."

"It ain't just him, man," Greg says, pushing himself out of his sleeping bag like it's on fire. "Damn, thing's crawling with bugs and shit." He touches a finger to his hairline and his eyes widen. "Oh, God . . ."

Liam does his best to ignore the sickening feeling of his own scalp crawling. "What happened? Why didn't you guys wake me? Is the kid okay?"

"Fuck that kid, man!" Greg yells, suddenly fully awake and amped up. "Jenny almost *died* last night, Liam! Fucking Pete was jackhammering on the floor, foam coming out of his mouth. It was a real shitshow, brother. And lucky you, you slept through the whole thing. Jim tried like hell to wake you, but you were all curled up, crying and yelling . . . Jesus, it was like a madhouse."

Liam looks at Jenny and Pete comatose on the floor. "I better go check on Henry." He turns and starts for the stairs, but Jim steps in front of him, his eyes blazing.

"Hold up."

Liam freezes, not liking the expression on Jim's face, nor the cold chill in his guts.

"You know something, Liam? You're taking all this shit in stride, and I know you're cool, but you ain't *that* cool."

Liam shrugs. "I don't know what to say. I didn't infest the place with bugs."

"No, I know who did that shit. But I want to know *everything* that *you* know. What has the kid told you?"

Liam's gaze drops to the floor. Jim steps closer, points a finger at his chest.

"I'm getting good and pissed off, brother. Good and pissed off, you understand. And right now, I'm caring less and less about the goddamned money, or that kid, and more about cleaning some house around here. Is that thing out there—is it somehow—" Jim bites his lip, not wanting to go there, not wanting to admit, for even a second, that something out of his realm of knowledge, something unnatural, possibly *supernatural*, is occurring. "It's that *thing* doing this."

"Jim, that's nuts," Liam says, his tone not selling the lie.

"You're right, it is. This whole thing is nuts," he says, and he stares at Liam with blazing eyes. "Now you tell me what you know. Hell, man, tell me what you *think* you know. But do it right goddamn now."

Liam takes a breath, turns, and sees Greg standing close behind him. Liam realizes, with a twitch of despair, that he's left his gun by his tossed bedding.

A heavy hand clamps down on his shoulder. Not gently. Liam isn't surprised to see Jim has pulled his own gun free, and is now pointing it at Liam's left eye.

"Tell me everything, my brother. Or I will shoot you in the fucking head."

Liam looks toward the stairs, then back at Jim.

"All right," he says, and as the first sliver of dawn breaks outside the farmhouse, igniting the fuse on one final, bloody day, he tells them everything.

10

Sali studies the map spread out on the kitchen table, Dave right next to him, Mary sitting down, looking not at the map, but at her husband.

She's wondering if he's cracked, and maybe he has. Maybe I have as well. But desperate times call for desperate measures, and I've made cases on crazier assertions. Sali hadn't been lying to Dave about that. He once found the body of a murder victim named Joanna Spriggs, missing for more than six months, when the woman's sister called him, frantic that she had seen her sister's face in the folds of a dress hanging in her closet. The face in the dress said that her missing sister had been murdered—strangled, to be specific—and buried near an old well.

One afternoon, with nothing urgent to do, Sali spent some time looking for existing wells within a two-mile radius of where the sister had disappeared. When he spotted one—at first glance looking like nothing more than a pile of gray rocks nestled adjacent to a weathered red barn, just a half mile or so from the paved road where Joanna had been jogging the day she vanished—he investigated.

It wasn't hard to spot the large patch of newly dug earth amid the half acre of wild grass surrounding the well, one the farmer swore up and down he hadn't used in over a decade, and that went for the decrepit barn as well.

Which was true.

But his son had.

Along with Joanna Spriggs they'd found the bodies of two other missing persons, a few lost dogs that had been reported to the local shelter, and a small room hidden beneath the barn floor where the young psychopath had kept souvenirs, along with certain body parts he'd formed into a sort of half-animal, half-human configuration. When asked about the bizarre manipulation, he stated it was an offering to an interdimensional being in the hopes it would come to earth and enslave humankind. Sali would never forget the old farmer shaking his head, lamenting that his son had always "read too many damn books."

Ever since breaking that case, Sali had begun talking to his shoes whenever things got a little rough, much as the sister had listened to the dress to provide key information to solve a dead-end mystery. At first, he did it as a gag, something to ease the tension in a particularly stressful case, and then it became a habit, a quirk. Over the years, he'd learned that being a little quirky often gave stressed-out family members something else to focus on, seemed to jumpstart their brains when lost in their own misery and fear. Sure, once or twice they'd asked for (and been denied) a new agent, but those things were easily soothed away. After all, if they were talking to him, they had bigger problems than an FBI agent who asked his wingtips for advice.

In some ways, being a little quirky had opened up Sali's mind a bit as well. Allowed him to think outside the box on things, not discount anything he heard—no matter how strange, how deep from left field it might come. Sure, it could be a waste of time on most cases, but on some cases (more than a few, in fact) odd lines of inquiry often led to a new train of thought, a blind spot they hadn't noticed the first time around, a new perspective that allowed for an influx of clues, ideas. In other words, *hope*.

Sali liked to stock whole barrels of the stuff.

So upon hearing Dave's dream, although eyerolling on the face of it, it didn't bother Sali as much as it might have other agents. For one thing, Sali was smart enough to know that dreams, or "visions," were direct by-products of the subconscious, and the subconscious was an *excellent* hoarder of random information. Patterns. Things the conscious mind wasn't paying any attention to, wasn't looking at. If it took a dream, or a wrinkled dress, or his damn shoes, to bring forward a bit of information hiding deep in a person's subconscious mind—then that was information Sali would accept any day of the week. That was *hope*.

"I want us to focus on these mountainous areas over here."

The map of San Diego and Los Angeles Counties is one Sali likes to keep handy in the trunk of his sedan. It was a little outdated when it came to certain street names, and it may not have all the newest developments as suburban sprawl crawled ever forward over the coast to the west and foothills to the east, but he likes that it's a topographic map—showing gradients of mountains in different colors, differentiating elevations, detailing rivers and lakes and depths thereof. That information has come in handy more than once. Finding bodies, alive or dead, is a lot easier if you know the kind of ground you're gonna be traversing.

Right now he shows Dave the forest regions east of the city—the Cuyamaca Rancho State Park, Pine Valley.

It was a forest, and not a small forest. I'm not talking about a little park, I'm talking miles and miles of trees. I saw it when I was hovering above, you see. Before I landed.

Sali had rolled his eyes big-time at that "landing" bit, grateful he was talking to Dave over the phone and not in person.

"No, no, see the city here?" Dave shows how downtown lies directly west of the area Sali is pointing to. "It wasn't that close, it was . . ."

Dave thinks for a moment.

I don't know if the guy has cracked or not, but whatever he saw, he sure as hell believes he saw something, Sali thinks, and waits silently.

Mary's worried eyes never leave her husband.

"South," he says finally. "Yes, downtown was southwest. I remember . . . well, it doesn't matter. Here." Dave shifts the map to reveal another massive patch of green forests and higher elevations. "What's this?"

"Cleveland National Forest," Sali says, a growing sense of rightness bubbling in his gut. *That would make a lot of sense, based on where we've seen these guys. Holy shit.* "Uh, okay. Look, here's Escondido, where the first package was mailed. And here!" Sali points excitedly. "This is where we spotted Greg and Jenny Lanigan fueling up the car outside Grantville, near the university. And if they were dropping the second package at Hamada's . . . *here* . . . then that would mean they were heading northwest."

"Okay, okay," Dave says.

"And if they were getting gas, which I'm sure was not something they were *supposed* to do—I'm positive that was a risk they had not planned for—then they needed to get at least another ten miles or so, right? I mean, enough to qualify the risk. What else?"

"Well, the house. I described it to you. It looked boarded up, old. Worn down. But it was also *remote*. Nothing else I could see anywhere near it. No roads, no other homes. Why would a house like that be in the middle of a damn forest?"

Sali shakes his head. "Can't really say, but here's the thing. If we think these guys might be holding out somewhere in this area, that's about ten miles of unpopulated forest. And we're talking about a concentrated group of people."

"I don't see what you're getting at," Mary says, leaning forward, now studying the map as anxiously as the two men.

"I can have a plane fly over this area equipped with military-grade thermal tech. It'll do a visual search but it will also be able to identify any warm bodies down there. It'll pick up animals and maybe the occasional hippie who wanders away from Lake Escondido and gets lost, maybe a ranger or two . . . but three, four people together? That would stand out."

"But if they're in a house, like Dave says? What then?"

Sali is already doing the calculations, thinking about the area he wants the pilots to focus on. "They'll have heat," Sali says, as if to himself. "Heaters, something. That house will be glowing like the north star, Mary. Compared to the forest surrounding it, you're talking about a small structure with the compounded warmth of a group of people, plus whatever heat sources they're using. If they're in those woods, they've been freezing their butts off for the last few days. They'll have something." Sali looks at Dave, smiles, then checks his watch. "It's 5 a.m., so I want to make the call now and get them in the air before the sun comes up. It'll be easier before daybreak, like looking for a bright light in a dark sky. Meanwhile, we continue to prepare for the drop this afternoon."

"And what do I do?" Mary says, and Sali does his best to meet her tired, scared eyes.

"For now?" he says, offering a weak smile. "Just sit back, wait, and hope. If they're hiding out there"—his eyes fall to the map one last time, to that green stain of forest—"we'll find them."

11

Tucked deep in his blankets, which he knows are crawling with vermin but not giving a rat's ass, Pete listens. Eyes closed, breathing steady, he eavesdrops as best he can as Liam spills about Henry's unusual abilities, and his ears perk up when Liam hesitantly mentions that the kid is good at reading people, maybe connecting on levels that are beyond normal understanding.

Pete thinks of the card game, and is surprised to find that it's not so hard to believe.

Nothing is, anymore.

Then Liam talks about how the kid claims to have a connection with that thing in the woods, the insane demands for them to get out of the house.

"He calls her Mother," Liam says, and Pete can almost imagine his face reddening from embarrassment. "He calls the other one, the unborn thing in the cellar, Baby. For obvious reasons."

Pete's mind, now broken, warped and bent like a vinyl record held over a hot fire, screams at him to *do something*. But he knows he must wait, play possum for a little bit. Be cool. Wait until the coast is clear, until there's no one around to stop him.

Then he'll go into the cellar and kill that thing. After that, he'll find the thing in the woods and kill it, too.

He smiles, thinking about his revenge, and imagines slicing the little kid open.

Shit, maybe he'll just kill *all* of them.

His gold teeth sparkle in a ray of sunshine slipping between two loose boards covering a window, and he doesn't even notice—or care—when one of the lice crawls over his eyelash and settles along the bottom of a sunken eye socket, cozy as a kitten.

The bites on his body are nothing compared to what he's already been through, and he can take it. *No problemo, amigo.* All's good with Pedro. All is squared up and tight.

He hears the footsteps of the three men heading up the stairs, going to talk to the kid. He reaches a hand into the pocket of his jeans to feel the folded knife secured there.

Just gonna wait for my moment, gonna lie here a while and wait for my time. Then shit's gonna get real, boys and girls. The dance floor is gonna get real full, you hear that? And Pete? Pete's ready to dance, brothers and sisters. He's ready to get down and boogie.

Ten feet away, Jenny moans and pushes her face into the dirty floorboards.

Pete's smile widens, thinking of all the things he's gonna do when the music finally starts, and it's time to dance.

★ ★ ★

Henry feels them coming.

He's hardly slept all night, and he's more tired than he's ever been in his life. There was a brief period where he thought he might have been unconscious, lost in his own dream—a dream of Uncle Dave, of his dad—but then he woke abruptly to waves of pain and confusion. Despite his best efforts, he wasn't able to ignore the bright lights of the nightmares occurring one floor below—it was like trying to sleep with a spotlight pointed at your eyes, the colors of the light flipping and swirling and flashing so fast that it's like a mad, kaleidoscopic disco ball spinning in your brain, a strobe effect of horror and fear and despair and shock.

Henry knows what Mother has done, but had no idea how charged the results would be. He'd hidden beneath his blankets as he felt Pete's mind torn apart, like a veil of hot colors ripped and shredded to ribbons by a savage monster, leaving only a bottomless black, a dull pulsing violet Henry translated as madness.

He felt Jenny's horror, her mind shattering, her heart twisting with pain and disgust and a sense of total loss.

But Liam . . . Liam was the worst of them all.

Like a clean sheet torn off a bed to reveal a pit of slick, slithering snakes, the reveal of Liam's most tragic memory, the death of his family, of his *child*, was too much for Henry to bear and he had shouted at the creature in his mind: *Turn it off! Please, make it stop!*

But she had not. She caused the infestation of bedbugs and lice, and Henry is dimly aware that even he has not been spared this curse. His head itches and he can feel the dull burn of bites on his legs, neck, and arms. Anything exposed is fair game, and he's about to throw off the blankets and climb out of the bed when he feels *them* coming, a hateful storm cloud of violent colors, flashing like lightning. Through all that hate and threat of violence, however, he can also feel that Liam is nervous, worried for Henry and for himself, which scares Henry even more.

The bolt is thrown, followed by the loud slam of Jim kicking in the door. Terrified, Henry screams and leaps from the bed, runs to a corner, cowering. He doesn't want to die, he doesn't want this man to kill him.

But Henry sees that's exactly what Jim wants to do. He's *considering* it.

Henry shakes with cold and fear and exhaustion and hunger. He puts his arms over his head, as if already warding off the blows he knows are coming. He can already feel those massive hands gripping his neck.

So can Jim. Henry sees Jim's plan clearly as a lunch menu:

Get the information.

Kill the kid.

Get the money.

ESCAPE.

"Get your ass on the bed!" Jim orders, and without hesitation Henry scurries back across the room and sits on the bed, doing everything he can to comply in order to calm him, perhaps change his mind. His eyes find

Liam's and he does his best to make him see *his* thoughts for a change, his brain screaming: *he's going to kill me!*

Liam grimaces but does nothing. Jim stomps forward and grabs Henry's thin T-shirt at the chest, hauls him up so hard his head snaps back and his ass rises a foot off the cot. Only his toes manage to reach the floorboards.

"You're gonna tell me what's going on, Henry. You're going to tell me right now or I'm gonna break your neck like a goddamned chicken. SNAP! You believe me, son?"

Henry nods feverishly as tears spill down his face.

Jim drops him, takes a step back, and folds his massive arms. Waiting.

"Henry," Liam says softly, and Henry turns to him like a beacon in a storm. "Tell them about Mother. About Baby. They already know what I know, but tell them everything you might have left out."

Henry looks up at Jim, then down at the floor. He wipes his running nose, ignores the feeling of bugs crawling through his scalp. "The thing in the basement, that's hers."

"And what is *she*?" Jim demands. "She a witch, a monster, some weird animal, what? Because I seen that bitch close up, and she ain't human, Henry. Nasty fucking thing."

"I don't know. I have no idea. She ... I think maybe she's very old, something that hides from us, from people. I think it was a mistake, us being here. It's her child, I think, in the cellar. She wants us to leave so it's safe."

"The bugs?" Greg asks, his face red with frustration and anger. "She can do this with the bugs? The wasps, the lice?"

Henry nods. "And the nightmares. And ... other things."

Greg's eyes widen with understanding. "That cockroach that crawled in my mouth?"

"I think most of you swallowed them," Henry says abashedly.

"Henry?" Liam asks.

"Uh-huh, you too. Sorry." Henry sees Liam's green wave of sickness and wonders if the man's gonna puke. When he doesn't, Henry goes on. "If you leave, it'll stop. But I think time is running out, because once Baby is born, she'll know. And then . . ."

Henry stops talking. His mind spins and widens, the black eye in his mind shoots open in alarm, in fear. Something is happening.

"So let's get out of here," Greg whines. "I mean, fuck this, right?"

"And go where?" Jim grumbles, beginning to pace. "Where the hell we gonna go? By now we're all probably on the damn news, man. The only way out of all this is to make the drop, get the money, and hit the border as fast as we can."

"The *drop*?" Greg says, laughing. "And who the hell is gonna do that? You and me and Liam? Jim, Jenny's probably *dying* downstairs. And Pete, for all I fucking know, is already dead. This thing is blown, man, it's totally blown!"

In two steps Jim is at Greg, punching the side of his head with a mallet-sized fist. Greg crumples to his knees and Jim kicks him backward.

"*You wanna leave? Leave, motherfucker!* Take that nasty skank of a sister you love so much and get the hell out of here. Go on. *Go on!*" he shouts, kicking at Greg as he scrambles backward toward the open door.

Henry barely registers any of this because his body has gone limp, just before it rolls to the floor with a soft *thud*.

Liam runs to him. "Henry!"

Jim hears the cry and it cuts through his rage. He spins away from Greg, who takes the reprieve to find his feet and throw himself down the hallway at a sprint. Jim walks to Liam, who's bent over the boy.

Henry's eyes are open but show only bloodshot whites. He's trembling and his mouth is moving a hundred miles an hour.

"Move," Jim says, and shoves Liam aside. He slaps Henry hard in the face.

"Jim!" Liam yells, but Jim ignores him and hits Henry again.

Henry is drowning. Fluid fills his lungs.

His eyes, heart, mind . . . are no longer his own.

Then, miraculously, total darkness becomes total light. There are new smells, new sights. In a rush, he vomits the fluid out, breathes in for the first time, sucking in the fresh, life-sustaining air.

A thousand feelings surge through his body, but one is paramount above all others:

He's *hungry*.

He reaches out and, like the intertwining of mystic threads, he finds her, instinctively wants her comfort. But she is not coming. He senses her fear but doesn't know what to make of it. He doesn't know what fear *is*. He basks in her from afar, calls to her.

Finally, gratefully, she answers.

"Henry?" Liam says, having gotten Jim to back off. He puts his hands on the boy's shoulders, shakes him. "Henry, come back, mate. Come back."

Jim gives Liam a knowing, hateful look, but says nothing.

Henry gasps, as if he's been underwater too long and has come up for air at the last possible second. He stops trembling and his eyes roll down to focus on Liam.

He looks scared, but not of the two men.

"What is it?" Liam asks, his gut churning. "What's wrong?"

Henry sits up and leans against the bedframe. His eyes linger on Jim, as if wondering what he might do when he answers Liam's question. Debating, most likely, whether Jim will reach out and end his life.

"Henry, it's okay," Liam says gently, and gives Jim a "back off" look. Jim doesn't move, but his face softens a bit, and his fists uncurl. *Good.* "Come on, kid. What?"

Henry licks his lips, then gives his head a little shake. "I think it's too late."

"What do you mean?" Jim asks.

"I don't think she wants us to leave anymore."

"The fuck you talking about?" Jim says hotly, fingers curling into fists once more.

But Henry no longer seems to regard Jim as a threat. If anything, he seems resigned, and it frightens Liam terribly.

"I think now she has a different plan."

Jim puts a fist to his mouth, thinking. He looks at Liam, the slightest tint of worry in his eyes. Confusion. Maybe, perhaps, even fear. "You can talk to this thing, right?" he asks. "You and she have been using that ESP shit or whatever."

Henry pauses briefly, then nods.

"Okay, good," he says, pacing. "Tell her to stop. Tell her we're pulling out. Today's the day, brother. We're all getting out of here, dig? You tell her that. Tell her to back off and we're gonna get out of here like she wants. Okay? Tell her, Henry. Tell her to *stop*."

Henry stares at Jim, then the most unexpected thing happens:

He smiles.

Henry, no, Liam thinks.

If Henry hears the warning, he ignores it. His eyes don't leave Jim's, and his mischievous, hateful smile broadens. His voice, when it comes, is chilling.

"Why would I want to do that?"

12

In the damp darkness of the cellar, the end of the mud-caked chrysalis splits open. A sticky, milky fluid gushes out and slaps to the floor.

Two long, bent black limbs emerge, spread the split of the womb wide.

Outside, the red sun breaks the eastern horizon like a wrathful god. The shadows of the trees stretch across mossy earth, and the black abyss of night is pushed away by a violet cloak trimmed in gold. The new day is rising, flexing its muscle of light and promise.

The drone of a small plane moves off in the distance, its work complete.

As the voices of the forest pepper the air, and a tepid, earthbound breeze shakes the multitudinous leaves of the forest, Baby is born.

PART NINE: BABY

1

Sali takes the call in the kitchen. Mary, unable to sit still knowing this whole ordeal will be over—one way or another—in a matter of hours, has gone to take a shower and change into fresh clothes. She's determined to come to the drop with them, and although Sali is giving the Thornes the okay to tag along, he leaves out the fact they'll be in a van a mile away from the alley where the pickup is supposed to take place.

He and his support team of agents have thoroughly dissected the drop point and have their ideas about how Jim Cady—or whoever shows up—is planning to get in and out. They'll be seen, but as long as they have the boy, they'll also be untouchable.

Temporarily, anyway.

Right now, however, all of Sali's attention is focused on the incoming call via his secure line. He looks at his watch—just past six in the morning, meaning the surveillance plane has only been in the air, at the most, an hour. Getting back to him this quickly is a good sign.

They're excited. They found something.

But what?

Agent Miller hits a button and gives Sali the handset.

"This is Espinoza," he says into the industrial phone, his eyes shifting to the left as Dave walks into the kitchen. There's a look of pained anticipation on his face, the look of a man watching his child perform a high-wire act on a windy day.

Sali's eyes meet Dave's as he listens.

"Where?" he says, and can't help himself. He turns his head to Dave. They lock eyes, and Dave *knows.*

They found him.

"Okay, is it federal land?" Sali says calmly despite the excitement leaping in his chest. "Yeah, okay. Send a Suburban to the Thorne home with an experienced driver, someone who can handle those back roads. I'm calling in HRT, who should be on the ground here by eight at the latest. I'm going to meet them at the airfield and we'll go in together. Yeah, send them everything we've got on persons of interest, and the boy. Yeah."

Dave puts a hand over his mouth, his eyes wide. He steps forward and rests a hand on Sali's arm, as if he needs to touch the man to make sure he's real, to make sure what's happening is real.

Sali places his own hand over Dave's. The adrenaline is pumping now and he needs a little stability himself, a little grounding.

The next few hours will decide it all.

When he hangs up, he turns his full attention to Dave. He was going to ask him to get Mary, but she walks in just as he ends the call. Mary notices Dave's hand on Sali's arm, sees the look on her husband's face.

"What?" she screams suddenly, unable to control herself. The policemen in the living room turn toward the kitchen, concerned. "Oh God, what's happened!"

Sali tries to give her a smile somewhere between ecstatic and encouraging. *We still don't know about the boy. We won't know until—*

"We think we've found them," he says, and Mary bursts into tears and clutches at Dave, who embraces her. They're all so tired, the tension of the last few days so great, Sali feels ready to burst into tears himself. He takes a deep breath, continues. "The thermal did its job, and the surveillance team found the kind of heat signatures we were hoping for." He turns to the kitchen table, grabs the map they'd looked at earlier, and unfolds another panel, exposing more terrain. "Here."

Dave and Mary stare at the point of the map where Sali's finger lies, two inches south of a heavy line of text: CLEVELAND NATIONAL FOREST. On the map there are no roads, no clearings, just the dark green color denoting hundreds of acres of trees and undeveloped land.

"North of the 74, southwest of Lake Elsinore, there's this valley, and this stretch here is called the San Juan Trail. It's federal land, although not technically part of the National Forest. We think they used old fire roads that haven't been touched in years, but somehow, someway, they knew about a house stuck in the middle of all this forest. We'll have an experienced ranger with us, it won't be hard to find them."

"Did they see Henry?" Mary asks, desperate.

Sali shakes his head. "No. They saw a house that was extremely warm compared to the surrounding area. And they registered heat spots outside the house consistent with human movement—meaning someone had walked the grounds recently. There are people there, and there shouldn't be."

"But," Dave says, the struggle of playing devil's advocate, when all he wants to do is scream with joy, apparent on his strained features, "how do you know it's them? I mean, it could be kids, or bums. Anybody."

Sali knows this is possible, but his instincts overpower these doubts. Still, better to temper expectations. "True, but it lines up with everything we know so far—where they've been sighted, the timing of their appearances. Plus, they can't have been there too long. You can get away with holing up there a few weeks, but longer than that? Nah, they would have been spotted. But look, you're right, it could be a houseful of squatters, or drug addicts. But to be honest, I don't think so. My surveillance tech says the place was lit up like a Christmas tree, which means they probably had multiple heating sources, and without power that takes planning—heaters that use gas, or kerosene. One other thing, they think there might be cars in a nearby shed, close to the house. They had faint readings that indicate a vehicle driven in the last twenty-four hours, give or take. Still warm enough to show up on the thermal. So, if these people have driven out there, and are hiding their cars—anyway, there's only one way to know for sure."

"You're going," Dave says, hope replacing his brief moment of doubt.

"Yeah, but first I've got to make a few calls. Detectives Knopp and Davis are being notified as we speak. I'm gonna get a Hostage Rescue

Team wheels up, most likely from Texas or Arizona, whoever is closest and ready. They should be here in a couple hours. We'll head out to a base here, then, once HRT is briefed, rendezvous with local police and the rangers *here*." Sali points to a different section of the map near the thin yellow ribbon that marks the only road going through the massive forest. "From there we'll go in on foot. We don't want to give them a chance to run, or ... well, we'll want to surprise them. Move in fast, take them out, get Henry. These guys in the HRT are the best, they've trained half their lives for this exact thing. They'll get the job done."

"I want to be there," Dave blurts suddenly. "I want to be there if— *when* they find Henry, I want to be there."

"That's fine. It'll be HRT's show, but you can ride with me and we'll take up the rear," Sali says.

"What about the money?" Mary asks.

Sali picks up the phone, begins dialing. "Mary, if these guys are who we think they are, there won't be a drop. This will all be over by lunchtime."

Mary buries her face in Dave's chest as Sali waits to be connected with the main office in Langley. It's time to push the cart.

"Sali," Dave says, and whether he means it as a question, a thank you, or a plea for grace Sali doesn't know, but he smiles all the same and looks the man in the eye when he replies.

"I know. Let's go get your boy."

2

While Jim and Liam screw around talking with the kid, Greg takes the opportunity to grab his sister and get the hell out.

His face aches from where Jim socked him, but compared to the wasp stings, the lice crawling all over his head, his insane hunger, and the fact there are thousands of microscopic bedbugs crawling beneath his skin, getting his bell rung is small potatoes.

He reaches the bottom of the stairs and is surprised to see Jenny sitting up, covered from the waist down by her sleeping bag. Her ice pick is gripped in one hand; she looks feverish and bewildered.

"Jenny!" he yells. He runs to her, drops to his knees, and grips her shoulders. He wills her eyes to stop roaming the room and focus on him. "Jenny, hey, come on."

"Where is he?" she mumbles.

Greg follows her eyes to Pete's bedding, which lies flat. He's gone.

"Pete? Did he do something?"

"I ..." She scrunches her face, gives her head a hard shake. Greg notices she hasn't escaped the lice, but holds back on commenting for now. They have much bigger problems. "He was crawling on top of me. When I woke up, he was on *top* of me, and his eyes ... he looked crazy."

"Jesus," Greg says, rage percolating. "Where did he go?"

"I don't know. I got him with this," she says, lifting the ice pick, "and then he ran off, laughing like an idiot, like I'd fucking tickled him."

For the first time, Greg notices that the business end of the pick is wet with blood. "Okay, look, forget him. We don't have much time. Do you have the Pinto keys?"

Her eyes finally focus on his and she nods. Greg is heartened to see sanity in those eyes, because for a minute there he thought she'd totally lost her shit—with her clumped, filthy hair (and infested—don't forget that one!) and the welts on her face, neck, and arms, she looks like one of the crazy homeless people who live on the beaches or, more appropriately, the crack addicts who harbor in the alleys downtown. She certainly smells the part.

"Okay, good. We're leaving. Right now."

Jenny nods again, then drops the pick in her lap, stares at her slick hands, lightly misted with Pete's blood. "I'm not feeling so good, brother," she moans. "I think, like, I'm gonna be sick. Something happened to me last night . . . Oh god . . . *that dream!*" she yells so suddenly that Greg removes his hands from her shoulders and shuffles away from her. Sobbing, Jenny buries her face in her palms. "What the fuck is happening to me?"

Greg stands, spots the Pinto keys lying on the floor next to Jenny's blanket and scoops them up. "Listen, you stay here and get your shit together. When you're ready, come out to the front. I'm gonna pull the car around. We don't have a lot of time, okay? Jen?"

"Yeah, okay. I'm cool. Get the car, I'll be right out. Oh shit, I think I pissed myself," she says, tossing the unzipped sleeping bag off her legs. Sure enough, Greg spots the soiled patch at her crotch spreading toward her thigh, the dark spot making him think insanely of the shape of Florida.

"Watch out for Pete, okay?" he says, looking around the room once more to make sure Pete isn't hunched in a dark corner, peeking out from behind a wall with his gold-tooth grin, the stupid dog tattoo riding up his neck. "I don't think he's all there."

"He ran out the front door, so maybe he's gone," she says, looking toward the gaping entryway, the early morning light breaking through the trees.

"I'll be back in a few minutes," Greg says and starts toward the door, momentarily debating whether to dig around for Liam's gun, but figuring that speed is currently more important than firepower, a choice he'd come to regret. "Get ready, okay? We're getting out of here."

Running toward the shed, hazy dawn giving way to a clear, blue-skied morning, Greg doesn't notice Pete crawling on all fours around the far corner of the house, the glint of sharp metal in one fist, the other pressed against a dripping hole in his stomach; a line of drool hanging like a yo-yo string from the corner of his mouth.

★ ★ ★

Pete *does* see Greg hauling ass for the shed, but ignores him. Pete isn't interested in Greg, and he's definitely had his fill of his cunt sister. He was only playing around! She didn't have to fucking *stab* him! And ho boy, does it hurt. It hurts bad. But that's okay. That is just peachy, because Pete has only one thing left to do, and then he's gonna clear out of here, let Jim and the Aussie Asshole clean up the mess.

The only thing Pete wants now—what he wants more than anything in the whole wide world—is to stick his knife into that goddamned cocoon, spill whatever is inside it onto the cellar's dirt floor, and then *gut* the thing.

Tear it apart.

Cut it into little itty-bitty pieces.

"Oh yeah, baby," he mumbles as he crawls toward the cellar doors. "Pete's got a little present for you. He's got a little package to deliver." He giggles as he reaches the doors, grabs one of the handles and tugs it open, lets it flop lazily into the grass. He stares down into the abyss, the stench of decay and filth wafting up and over him.

"You hear me?" he yells down the stairs. "Special delivery, Mama!"

Pete laughs again, cackling like a drunken witch as he crawls over the lip of the entrance and makes his way down the concrete stairs, into the cold, waiting dark.

★ ★ ★

Greg pulls open the shed door and makes his way to the Pinto. He climbs inside, sticks the key in the ignition, and turns it, foot already kicking the gas pedal.

Nothing.

"Oh no." He turns the key again, careful not to pump the gas this time, not wanting to flood the engine.

"No . . . no no no no . . ."

Greg pops the hood and slides between the two cars to reach the Pinto's front.

As he studies the car's engine in the damp dark, it takes only a moment to see what's been done.

Jim, you bastard.

Greg's shoulders slump in defeat. The game is lost; the big man has—unsurprisingly if he's being honest—outthought him. He'll have to go back in, make things right. Figure out a way to convince Jim that he and Jenny are good to go. Team players. No hard feelings.

What choice does he have?

Greg drops the hood with a loud *clang* and turns to leave.

At the entrance of the shed, silhouetted against the growing daylight, huddles Mother.

She's smaller than he thought. Based on how the others had talked about her, he expected something . . . taller. The creature is almost child-like, like a kid wearing a costume, her thin, bony limbs protruding like gnarled sticks. Her eyes are bright yellow—cat's eyes, or maybe like those of a lizard—he isn't exactly sure how to classify them. He's never seen anything like it, but right now he's got bigger problems, and whatever it is, it looks small. Weak.

I can take her, he thinks and steps forward, arms held out from his sides, palms exposed, showing he's empty handed. Defenseless. Not a threat.

"Hey there," he says, waiting to get within striking distance, close enough to grab her head and twist it like a top. "So you're the freaky thing causing all this trouble, huh? Well, guess what? We're leaving." He makes the motion of a plane taking off the runway with one hand, shooting into space. "We're *gone.*"

The creature cocks her head, but otherwise does not move.

He's only a few feet away now, and even with the hooded shell over her head he can make out the features of her face. The dark brown skin, the lipless mouth. *Looks like a bug fucked a monkey.*

He takes one more big step, and lunges.

The creature hunches and, with a loud hiss like a cat preparing to fight, shoots a stream of brown liquid from her mouth, directly at his eyes.

The fluid strikes his face and the effect is immediate.

While in prison, Greg had once heard about a guy who informed on some big mob boss or other, and one day they'd found him in the laundry room with half his face melted off, some sort of acid having been dumped over his head. The shock had killed him within minutes.

Greg isn't that lucky.

The sticky liquid burns like he imagined the acid had burned that mafia rat. He actually feels his flesh dissolving. He screams, wet and throat-tearing, and drops to his knees, clawing at his eyes, trying to pull off the hardening fluid. Too late, he realizes that his hands are also burning. *Melting.* The tips of his fingers have turned soft and gooey, are sticking to his skin.

He presses on, trying to do something—anything—to rid himself of the pain, but his fingers just slide against hard—*exposed?*—cheekbones, the flesh almost liquified. Panicked, he accidentally pushes too hard with his right index finger, a little too eager to get the poison out of his eyes, and feels a fingertip sink into one of the sockets where, only seconds ago, a perfectly good, bright brown eye had existed.

Blind, screaming in pain and terror, Greg begins to crawl toward the creature, or where he thinks the creature had been moments ago. He's almost sure he can hear melted pieces of skin dropping to the dirt beneath him, and his hands digging into the dirt are burning so badly—the pain so incredible—that he turns them over, using the backs of his hands instead, no longer able to take the pain of pushing damaged fingers into the soil.

He sobs and whimpers as the fluid hardens on his face. What flesh remains is being *stretched*, pulled tight, pulling his upper lip into a bizarre snarl, tugging his infested scalp downward as the skin of his face contracts to the area where his eyes—now nothing more than gobs of runny yellow snot curled onto his temple and chin—had recently been fully operational.

"*I'LL KILL YOU, YOU BITCH!*" he screams. Then, with a burst of energy born of desperation, he scutters forward like a crab through the dirt.

But the creature, which he would have known if he could have seen anything—anything at all—is gone.

She'd moved on. Other fish to fry.

So Greg just crawls blindly out into the morning light, moaning like a shot hound, searching for a way out of the nightmare that he knows, deep down, there will be no waking from.

3

The sun, still new and slanting down from the east, slowly warms the horizon with a peach-fused yellow, the mellow morning gently filtering over the land, the mountains, and the trees. Down in this dank cellar, however, it creates nothing more intense than a smoky gray ambience that Pete's eyes must adjust to as he reaches the bottom of the stairs.

Slowly, he rises to his feet. One hand clutches the long metal switchblade, the other holds his stomach, the wound bleeding freely, blood pulsing through his clamped fingers, spilling down his hip and leg, dripping onto his shoes and the dirt around them.

As he grows accustomed to the dark, he notices the strips of human skin still stuck to the concrete wall, drying now, curling and brown amid the remnants of whatever epoxy had been used to affix the poor bastard. Of course, Pete knows more now than he did then, and has some pretty good suspicions about the culprit behind the dead guy, the bizarre way he was glued to the wall, split open like the post-Halloween rotten pumpkins he used to kick off porches when he was a kid.

Screams come from outside, made distant by the earthen walls. Pete recognizes the cries as coming from Greg, but he ignores them, ignores everything from the outside, from the real world that once existed for him, for the boy he used to be, for the criminal he'd become. That boy had been eaten alive, the man stripped away like a dead branch shaved of its leaves and bark, whittled down to its primal core, a combination of violence and self-preservation.

Predator. Survivor.

Pete's mind is now driven solely, undisturbedly, by these base instincts—allowing him to focus on what lies before him in the dark, on the prey perched along the ceiling of the godforsaken cellar.

If the world has an asshole, I'm standing in it.

He shuffles forward a few steps toward the target of his hate—the strange cocoon that has taunted him since he'd first seen it. The mystery of it, the brazen, disingenuous *passiveness* of it buying itself time, keeping itself from violence by creating a false sense of helplessness, of neutrality. Of insentience.

But now Pete knows better. He knows a *lot* better.

Whatever's in there is *alive*. And it has protection. Worse yet, it's played a part in the nightmare of this job, this house. And that will not stand.

That *cannot* stand.

"La venganza es un placer de dioses," he whispers as he stalks forward, only a few feet away from the thing now. He squeezes the handle of the knife tighter. His smile widens. "Fuck you," he says.

He rams the knife into the heart of the cocoon, pulls the blade out, slick with brown slime, and thrusts it into the belly of the shape again, and again, and again.

On the last thrust the knife plunges so deeply—so *effortlessly*—that Pete's entire fist goes with it, right through the broken shell and into the gelatinous substance within.

"The fuck!" he says, taking a step backward.

Breathing heavily, a sheen of sweat on his face and neck, the dog's mouth tattoo covering his Adam's apple bobbing with each panting breath, Pete's face changes from one of vengeful fury to one of confusion. The anticlimax of his initiative is at first disappointing, and then worrisome.

It's only now—as the sun filters down into the small room, dissolving shadows, revealing details—that Pete notices the large split at the head of the cocoon. As if whatever had been inside the thing had (likely recently) emerged.

"No," he says, and with a guttural curse he grabs the broken remains of the chrysalis and tries to tear it down, rip it from the beam above and throw it to the ground. Instead, it falls apart between his fingers. He pulls away dirty clumps of filthy leaves, fistfuls of mud saturated with stinking, slimy fluid.

He stares into the opened chamber, the mystery exposed, and realizes there's nothing there.

Empty.

He drops the mess to the ground, notices the pool of fluid already settled there.

There's a rush of movement behind him.

He spins, knife held point-out at the end of a rigid arm, aiming it at dark shadows like a gun, a talisman.

Something slick, long and dark scuttles in the dark shadows bunched along the floor at the far side of the room. Then the black shape angles upward, climbing up the brick wall until it reaches a high corner. Small white eyes stare back out of the dark. There's a soft *hiss*, and an open mouth reveals tiny, sharpened teeth.

"What the hell, man?" Pete says under his breath, and takes a step toward the thing, knife extended, his gut wound temporarily forgotten, his other blood-smeared hand out to the side. He's ready to fight this . . . *thing.*

Ready to punch it full of holes.

Ready to watch it bleed.

Pete keeps a steady eye on the creature, still hidden in deep shadow, as more noises filter down from outside—yelling voices, cries of terror and pain.

Inconsequential. Irrelevant.

"Just you and me, fucknuts," Pete drawls. Sweat drips into his eyes despite the cold of the room. The knife handle is slick in his palm, but he grips it tighter, the bunched muscles of his skinny arm coiled and taut.

Baby moves a few feet to Pete's left so quickly that Pete curses and jumps back a step, knife raised higher, eyes showing whites, mouth curled into a sneer of anticipation.

"Fast little thing, aren't ya?" he says, eager.

Then the creature moves out of the shadows, into the light.

Pete gags as a spike of fear squirts acid into the back of his throat, his asshole reflexively tightening so that the contents of whatever is in his lower intestines doesn't shoot into his pants.

"What the hell are you, man?" he whispers, his broken mind not comprehending, not able to make sense of the strange beast snarling down at him.

Its eyes are small and white, tiny pupils twitching within. Its skin is dark, but more pinkish than black, as if semi-translucent, the pumping blood beneath dark and evident. Thick, ropy veins run through its entire body, already over three feet in length and thick as a four-year-old child. Its head is pointed at the top and spiked with bristles. Its torso is ovular, like a spider's abdomen, but this is no arachnid. If it were, there would be eight bent limbs sticking to the high corner of the cellar.

Baby has only six.

It hisses at him again and Pete sees the thin line of saliva slipping from its gaping mouth.

"You hungry, *pendejo*?" he says, showing teeth. "Yeah? Guess what, man? *Me fucking too!* So how about you stop screwing around, little froggy? Huh? How about you come down here and give Uncle Pedro a big sloppy kiss, you nasty cockroach!" Pete yells, thrusting his blade into the air between them. "HOW 'BOUT YOU JUMP, LITTLE FROGGY? HOW 'BOUT YOU JUMP, MOTHA—"

Pete's curses are cut off and turned into screams as the thing—with shocking speed—springs from the wall with such force and precision that Pete doesn't have time to position his blade, and instead catches the thing in his arms as it attaches to his chest and face, knocking him off his feet and onto his back. Pete's breath blows out of him. The knife leaps from his fingers as he slams into the earth.

"NOOOO! GET OFF ME, MAN!" Pete screeches.

Now face-to-face with Baby, he finally releases his bowels and bladder, his face stretched in horror with the knowledge that his death is imminent. Baby's jaw unhinges like a snake; its pointed teeth—as black lips curl back to reveal their full length—are much longer than Pete had originally thought. Its wild, savage white eyes are wide, and eager . . . *hungry.*

In death, Pete taps the steel that had served him so well over the course of his life one last time—the obstinate fury, the courage in the face of great odds, that allowed him to survive poverty, a decade of gang life, and years of confinement with men as bad or worse than himself.

"YOU WANNA DANCE, MOTHERFUCKER!" he screams, defiant, into the creature's face, his fingers scrambling for the fallen knife. "THEN LET'S DANCE!"

Baby hisses gratefully and clamps its mouth over half of Pete's stricken face. Long teeth sink into flesh, and when it closes its iron jaws, facial bones snap like pottery. Baby chews gratefully as the blood rushes into its mouth. The dying body convulses beneath its hard limbs, which grow stronger by the minute. By the swallow.

It gobbles Pete down and clamps anew for another taste, crunching through what's left of the man's head, swallowing bones, blood, flesh and brain greedily.

It is, after all, its first real meal.

And Baby is ravenous.

4

Henry sits on the floor of the bedroom, numb and scared.

When the screams started—first a man screaming from outside, then a woman (Jenny, he assumes) screaming from downstairs—Jim ran out of the room, followed by Liam, who turned back only to point at Henry and yell "Stay here!"

Unsure what to do, Henry sits on the floor, stares at the door of the bedroom.

It's wide open.

Cold snot taps his upper lip and he wipes at his runny nose with the back of a hand. Jim and Liam are yelling outside, near the shed. Liam sounds worried, Jim angry. Henry doesn't bother reaching out; he knows what they're thinking, what they're feeling. He knows what's happening, can almost feel the tickle of blazing reds and muddy browns of rage and despair, all of it streaked with inky black terror. Besides, he's too tired. His stomach is growling and cramped, his limbs feel weak, and his head is stuffy and hollow at the same time, like there's wet cotton where his brain should be.

He gets up and crosses to the open door. The dimly lit hallway looms beyond, an invitation to run, to *escape*. For a moment it's like he's not in the abandoned farmhouse at all, but in his bedroom at home, with Dave and Mary sleeping just down the hallway, and the nightlight overpowering the thick, creeping dark that all hallways seem to attract. He imagines that if he steps through the door he won't feel splintered old wood beneath his socks, but the plush of dark green carpet that softens his path from his bedroom to the bathroom when he walks there at night in his bare feet, clean and comfortable in his pajamas, excited to climb back into bed after he's done his business, crawl beneath the warm blankets and sleep the sleep of the protected and loved, the content.

He puts a small hand on the cold knob of the door and waits, listening. The screams and yells have stopped, but there's movement downstairs.

He hears the front door of the house burst open and Liam is screaming at someone, probably Jenny, to *MOVE! Move out of the way!*

Henry knows he's not yelling at Pete, because Pete is dead.

He sighs and leans on the door, thinking he'd give just about anything for a cup of hot chocolate and a plate of warm, buttery pancakes. With bacon and yummy syrup. It was what Dave and Mary made him every Sunday morning, and he *lived* for Sunday morning pancakes.

The noises from downstairs have lessened again, and Henry isn't sure if Liam and the others are even in the house anymore.

He thinks that he has never felt more alone in his life, and when he looks down the hallway now, it's not the dark green carpet and clean beige walls of home, but the cracked wood floors and peeling white paint of the farmhouse. And although it continues calling to him, beckoning him to flee, to run, to *get out*, he just stands there, very still.

Because something is coming.

A *lot* of somethings.

Henry cocks his head, eyes momentarily on the ceiling.

"Okay," he says.

And with one last glance at freedom, he takes a step backward, into his prison, and gently closes the door.

He only wishes he could lock it.

5

"Greg!"

Jim drops into the dirt next to Greg, who is crawling in drunken circles halfway between the farmhouse and the shed.

What the fuck's wrong with his face?

Liam watches from the porch, unsure of what's happened and unwilling—for the moment—to get closer to those horrible screams. Even from the front porch he can see that the top of Greg's face is bright red and somehow *blurred*. Like someone dumped a jar of glue on his face and rubbed it around, left it to dry. Liam takes a few steps toward them, then hears someone behind him and turns to see Jenny. Her face is a mess of swollen wasp stings, her greasy hair likely crawling with lice, her bare arms and the top of her breasts, bare above the curve of her tank top, pimpled with inflamed bug bites. Her eyes look vacant and dull, her mouth hangs open, and she has a weak shamble to her walk. She reminds Liam of a zombie movie he saw as a teenager, where the dead shuffled around and ate people's brains. Liam wonders how stable-minded she is at the moment.

If she'd had dreams similar to his own, he figures the answer is pretty close to *not very*.

"Jenny, wait," he says feebly as she brushes past him, her brother's screams now reduced to wretched sobs. He winces as Greg, on hands and knees, vomits into the dirt.

"Greg?" Jenny says, mildly curious, as if her brother has arrived back from a trip a day early and she's coming to terms with seeing him unexpectedly. But then her back straightens, that little shamble in her walk disappears, and she takes two long strides in the direction of Jim and her puking, weeping brother.

Liam can just make out Jim's words as he tries talking to the guy: "What the hell happened? Jesus, Greg, you're all fucked up, man. You're all fucked up! Tell me what happened!"

Over and over again, and now Jenny spins, gives Liam a deadly, questioning glare. Liam can only shrug. "Something's wrong with his face."

Jenny turns away and, with surprising energy given that Liam was only seconds ago considering her top-notch zombie material, sprints toward her brother, screaming *"Greg! Greg!"*

When she gets to him, he tilts his head up to her, and his face—or what's left of it—catches the sunlight. *Where are his eyes?* Liam thinks mildly—*too* mildly—as shock sets in, the internal question as unemotional as if Greg were missing his shoes instead of most of his face.

Jenny is still screaming, of course. Screaming and screaming. Jim is trying to lift Greg to his feet, half walking, half dragging the poor bastard back to the house.

Liam looks up, squints into the new day, taken aback at how bright and blue the sky is. He's reminded of a song that was a hit a few years back, "Mr. Blue Sky." He thinks maybe Mr. Blue Sky is up there right now, looking down at this pathetic group of assholes and laughing his big blue butt off.

Jim yells for Liam to get off his ass and come help; Jenny is crying and helping Jim carry her destroyed brother back to the farmhouse.

As if there's help here, he thinks, still in that mild tone. *As if dragging that freakshow who used to be Greg out of the dirt and into this godforsaken shithole is going to do him one tiny bit of good.*

Jim gets Greg to the porch and Liam can't even look at the mess of burnt skin popping on Greg's neck. He sees a glob of yellow snot the size of an acorn sticking to the guy's cheek and is pretty damn sure it's an eyeball, but he can't run with that idea because if he does then *he'll* be the one puking, and maybe it'll be *his* mind that snaps, the calm veneer of shock tearing apart like old paper to reveal the grinning specter of pure terror lying beneath. Next thing you know, he'll be wandering around like a goddamned brain-eating zombie from—

"HAAARRRROOOOOOOOO!" From the woods, but close.

They freeze. Jim stops in his tracks. Even Jenny shuts up for a second. All of them turn toward the tree line twenty yards off.

"Huh," Liam says, as cold fingers of fear crawl up his spine.

A dog stands at the edge of the clearing.

It's not an especially big dog, and it's not a wolf. Liam has seen wolves, and this isn't one of them. It isn't even much of a dog, more of a gangly old mutt. Scrawny. Feral. Liam can, even from a distance, see the shadowy indentations of a rib cage through matted gray fur. The animal is nothing but skin, bones, and stringy muscle. Its fur stands straight up on the back of its neck, and its black eyes are sparks, wet pebbles reflecting the daylight. Liam figures it's a wild dog; probably rabid, definitely hungry.

And oh baby, is it showing some *teeth*.

"Can we just get him inside?" Jenny says, her voice whiny with heat and emotion and not giving two shits about the mangy stray watching them. Greg moans his assent and Jim grunts as he wraps a big arm around Greg's midsection, all but lifts him up onto the porch.

Another howl ripples across the clearing, but Jim doesn't stop his forward motion, pushing past Liam and through the doorway. Liam hears the sound of a body being dumped to the floor, Greg's scream of pain and fear, Jenny's protests and flaring curses.

Liam, though, is focused on the dog.

Or, as it stands now: *dogs*.

Three new canines have joined the first, all of them standing a few feet apart, all of them baring teeth.

All of them looking at Liam.

One of the new arrivals, a black lab with a dirty white chest patch, raises its muzzle to the sky and howls. "HAAARRRROOOOOOOOO!"

From all around the clearing now: one . . . then two . . . then more and more respond from the trees with their own howls, their calls to action. Liam thinks he hears a dozen, maybe more. Suddenly he can't shake the idea that they are being *surrounded*. The shrill, voracious nature of the howls, the sheer number of echoing cries makes Liam's heart beat faster, his skin prickle with fear.

Good almighty God, what now?

Having picked up his gun before following Jim outside, he smoothly untucks it from the small of his back, lets it dangle casually at his side, fingers dancing on the trigger guard, debating which of the snarling, rabid mutts he's going to shoot first.

There's a lot to choose from.

6

Henry sits up straight on top of his bed, eyes closed. Rocking. His mind too filled to feel his head knocking against the hard wall—*bump, bump, bump.*

Baby is free.

Mother is angry.

Mother has decided they are a threat to her and her child, and she will do anything to counter that threat—sacrifice herself, if needed.

Sacrifice Henry?

Without question.

She is close, close enough to try to fetch her offspring, to get him away from the men and the guns, the promise of death.

It is her gift. It is her *right*. Hers, and those like her. Those that live beneath. The old ones, the sacred ones who have lived in the earth for millions of years, much longer than these humans have littered the planet.

Over time, many powers, many secrets, have been lost. Driven into the darkness the way she, and others like her, were driven into forests and caverns, underground worlds.

She can call on the insects, call on the animals. She could send a plague of snakes to chill their blood, strike at their heels. Throw a cloud of sparrows that would eclipse the sun.

Instead, she calls to those who are hungry, whose bellies worm with a lust for meat, who scavenge corpses and trash barrels, who are kicked and shot and burned and left in the cold to fend for themselves, to find a way.

She commands the wild ones who live in the forest and the ramshackle communities that surround it, the ones living in the alleys and gutters; the canine rats of vagrant camps and polluted sewers. The castoffs, the forgotten, the expendable.

She calls on the dogs to finish what she started.

7

"Where's Pete?" Jim asks.

Liam shuts the front door and throws the bolt. He leans against the cool wood, his head pounding, blood racing. The dogs continue to howl, but at the moment he has more important things to worry about. For one, with Greg out of commission and Jenny a blathering nutcase, it leaves only himself and Jim to handle the money grab.

And now Pete's missing.

"No idea," Liam says, staring at the empty blankets where Pete had lain that morning, before they interrogated Henry, before Greg had his eyes juiced and his face burned to a puckered asshole. "I'll check upstairs."

Liam crosses the room and takes the stairs two at a time, leaving Jenny to comfort her brother while Jim decides what to do next.

Henry's door is closed but not bolted, and Liam grimaces at the mistake. He doesn't recall if they even shut the damn thing when they'd hauled ass out of there, freaked out as they were by Greg's screams. With everything that's happened, none of them are thinking straight.

He opens the door, half expecting Henry to be gone. *Or dead, Pete standing over his shredded corpse with a bloody knife and a Jack the Ripper grin.*

But Henry is there, on his bunk, blankets pulled onto his lap, held tight against his chest. "Henry?"

"Close it, please," Henry says, and Liam does, wondering what has the kid so freaked out that he couldn't open the door and walk on out of here. *Maybe the howling scared him,* he thinks. *It sure as hell scared me.*

"You hear those dogs? Don't worry, they're just wild mutts."

Henry looks at Liam with something close to pity. "You better get downstairs," he says, like an apology. "I think they'll need you downstairs."

Chilled by Henry's tone, Liam anxiously squeezes the doorknob. "All right, mate. Don't worry. You stay here nice and tight. In a few hours this is a bad memory. Today's the day, Henry. Soon we'll be driving out of here, and by this time tomorrow you'll be at McDonald's getting twenty cheeseburgers."

Henry gives Liam that same sad look. That pitying look.

"I don't think so," Henry says quietly, studying his hands.

Liam doesn't know how else to comfort the boy, so he leaves.

Back downstairs Jim is pacing. He gives Liam a questioning look, and Liam shakes his head in response. "No Pete."

"Fuck," Jim says under his breath. "You think he ran?"

Liam takes out his gun, casually drops the clip and inspects it. He has a full load—seventeen bullets. Jim's .38, a powerful six-shooter, is most likely full.

"Dunno," Liam says. "You bring extra ammo?"

Jim shrugs. "Got a few extra in my pocket. Was in a bit of a hurry, you know? Why?"

"Bad feeling," he says. "Kid's got me spooked, I guess." Liam looks across the room, catches Jenny's eye. "How is he?"

Greg lies motionless on his back, but his breathing seems steady. Jenny sits next to him, cross-legged, holding his limp hand. "I don't think he'll die," she says. "But he's in a lot of pain. His eyes—" She takes a breath, pushes on. "Fuck, man, what do I know? He needs a hospital, obviously, but I'm guessing that's not an option with you dickwads."

Liam ignores this last dig and walks to a window, looks out between the cracks of two boards. He spots at least six dogs in front of the house. That he can see. "Well, I'd offer to go look for Pete outside," he says, "but I'm not crazy about the look of them woofers."

"Let's give it a bit." Jim sits down heavily against a far wall, absently scratching at his scalp. "Dude's probably taking a dump somewhere."

★ ★ ★

His meal finished, Baby crawls away from what's left of the meat. He looks toward the open door leading to the bright, painful light. Then he turns away and slips through a hole in the brick wall leading to more cool darkness.

Inside the larger room, there are stairs leading up to a door, beyond which he smells food. Curious, he makes his way up the stairs to the door that, when lightly touched, swings open easily, without even making a sound.

8

Sali sits in the backseat of one of two black Chevy Suburbans waiting on the sun-warmed tarmac. Behind them are two Humvees painted in dark green camouflage, their only current occupants two marine sergeants acting as drivers until the HRT take them over. Sali knows the team will bring their own vehicles in the belly of the C-130, but for the sake of speed he wanted them at least standing by. Beyond the vehicles are two Huey helicopters, also standing by, but Sali is going to try to convince the HRT that the roads will be the best access routes, given the terrain. Not that they're gonna listen—once these guys hit the ground they take control, and for good reason. Still, Sali will make his case and live with whatever decisions their team leader chooses to make.

As Sali ruminates, Dave sits quietly next to him, looking out the tinted bulletproof windows at the large swatch of gray concrete, the rocky crags of coastline in the distance, the horizon of blue ocean beyond.

"I'd only driven by this place," he says numbly, as if needing to talk, to get out of his own head. "Seen choppers, you know, coming and going. Never been inside."

"Well, don't take any pictures or I'll have to shoot you," Sali says, and Dave looks at him with a mixture of surprise, annoyance, and concern. "Sorry, bad joke."

"It's okay, keep 'em coming," Dave says, and looks eagerly to the sky.

Pendleton is one of many military institutions the FBI is authorized to utilize, but Sali has a particular fondness for this marine base, and he's relied on the goodwill and cooperation of the commanders who run it— with unparalleled efficiency—many times over the years. He is proud to see the armed services in action, and he counts himself lucky to be able to employ them when needed. In this case, they provide vehicles, personnel, and a landing strip big enough to welcome a C–130 transport aircraft bellied with twelve men, their only mission to save a child's life.

"Here they come," Sali says, and points out the windshield to the large plane coming in fast and low from the northeast. For the hundredth time that day, Sali looks at his watch. It's just under two hours since he'd made the call to bring in the Hostage Rescue Team. They'd geared up and been wheels up within twenty minutes of him hanging up the phone. This particular team came from a base in Texas, and Sali is eager to brief them and get rolling.

"My god, look at the thing," Dave marvels. "All that for us?"

Sali nods. "That's the C–130 Hercules, courtesy of your US Air Force. They'll roll two military vehicles out of the rear once they land. It's quite an operation, one many civilians don't often see."

"I'm honored," Dave says, his tone simultaneously sincere and awed.

"Your tax dollars hard at work," Sali quips as the large plane skids past them, brakes whining, wheels smoking, the engine so loud it vibrates the windows of the SUV.

Now fitted in rugged boots and a bulletproof vest strapped over his white button-down shirt, Sali pleads one last time with Dave, secretly hoping the man will opt out and stay out of harm's way. *When pigs fly*, he thinks, but tries anyway.

"You sure you want to come? I don't think it's dangerous, but we're going to be moving fast, and I won't be able to babysit you, no offense."

Dave—still looking out the window as the plane begins its turn before slowing to a stop, ready to release its elite force of soldiers to the ground—doesn't bother turning back to the agent in charge. "Just get them in the damn cars. I want to see my boy."

Sali smiles a moment, reassured, then casually flips a switch in his brain, entering an all-business mode that military personnel—even former military like himself—always have at the ready, to turn on or off as warranted. Had one never met the man, the look on his face in this moment would make one think he is of a perpetually pissed-off nature, a bull ready to be sprung from the cage.

From between his feet, he pulls a canvas bag filled with smoke bombs, extra ammo cartridges for his service weapon, and a black hat with the letters FBI stitched across the front. He pulls it on low and tight, then taps the driver twice on the shoulder.

"You heard the man, Charlie. Let's rendezvous with those bad motherfuckers and haul ass."

9

When it becomes clear that Pete is gone, things go from very bad to much, much worse. Greg has become strangely animated, refusing to sit still, to be quiet, to do anything but rave like a madman and crawl around the floor like a drunken cat. Liam wonders if whatever poison the creature had spat at his face—for Greg had told the story in spurts and starts of clarity amid his manic behavior—has corrupted his brain as well as his flesh.

He certainly *seems* mad.

But then, by this point, maybe they're all just a little bit off.

"He needs a doctor!" Jenny screams into Jim's face for the thousandth time. Liam finds it almost touching, as twenty-four hours previous it had been Greg screaming the same thing about his wasp-assaulted sister. She is right, of course. What Greg is going through now is almost one hundred percent adrenaline-fueled, and when his brain stops pumping that shit into his body he will collapse like a bled animal, and most likely never get up again.

Jim is resistant, though, telling whoever will listen that he needs some time "to think." As if there is a way clear of all this. A way for them to continue with the plan. Liam knows the best plan—at this point—is to cut and run. There is nothing tying any of them to the kidnapping, no witnesses, no hard evidence. No money has transferred hands.

Nothing but Henry.

Liam sighs, works the grip of the gun in his hand, and thinks about killing Jim. If it comes to that, could he do it? Or Jenny? If need be, he thinks he can, yeah. He won't let them kill the kid, and if Henry fingers Liam as one of the bad guys? So be it. He's done time before and, truth be told, he thinks he can likely wiggle out of it. A good lawyer would make mincemeat of the kid's testimony, and Liam could claim he had no knowledge of what was planned—the old "hired gun" defense, popular in bank heists gone wrong as the "I'm just the driver" gag.

Liam's homicidal thoughts are broken when Jim reaches beneath his blankets and pulls out the black plug cables he'd yanked from the Pinto.

"There! Take 'em!" he yells, tossing them onto the floor, petulant, staring at Jenny with fire and hate. "Take your brother and go! You'll be in a jail cell before the sun sets, but what do you care, right? So go. I ain't gonna stop you, fool. Me and Liam, we'll finish this thing. And when we're counting Benjamins in Mexico you'll be staring at a judge who will enjoy the hell out of making an example of you. The one who didn't get away. The one held accountable. Hell yeah, I like that. Your brother will be in some asylum somewhere and you'll be doing twenty to life. So hell yeah, go! I don't give a shit no more."

But Jenny hardly listens to Jim's rant. She scoops up the cables in one hand and reaches for her brother's arm with the other. "Come on, babe. We're getting out of here. Come on."

Greg stands, rocking on his heels. "I want to kill the kid," he says, almost apologetically. "I want to cut him open and take his eyes."

Jenny pushes him toward the door. "Right now you need a hospital. We're going, okay? Let's get out of this place."

"Yeah, okay, sis," Greg says, his voice slurred, and lets her lead him to the front door.

Jim gives Liam an exhausted scowl as he pulls the Smith & Wesson from the front of his waistband. Liam thinks the feeling Jim is conveying here is something akin to: *Do you believe the shit I gotta put up with? Now I got to kill these motherfuckers.*

As Jenny unbolts the door, Jim walks nonchalantly toward the middle of the room, stops a few short yards behind her.

He raises the gun and points it at the back of her head.

"Hey, Jim?" Liam says, taking a half step forward, tightening the grip on his own weapon.

Annoyed, Jim looks back at Liam as Jenny throws open the door. There's a blast of bright sunlight and Liam winces at the sight of it, but not before he sees the shapes hurtling toward them.

Snarling shadows leap from the light to push Greg and Jenny backward. Greg manages to keep his feet a few steps, then tumbles on his ass to the hard floor.

Jenny is on her back screaming bloody murder as one of the dogs buries its teeth in her shoulder and shakes its head frantically, desperate to pry meat from the bone.

"Jesus!" Liam screams. Instinctively he points the Glock at the dog attacking Jenny, but switches at the last second to the dog sprinting straight at *him*, eyes blazing, fur bristled, teeth bared.

He fires into the dog's chest and it's thrown backward, as if it reached the end of an invisible chain at a full sprint and was then snapped back.

Jim takes two long strides toward Jenny and shoots the dog in the head at close range. The concussion of the blast sucks the air from the room and makes Liam's ears ring as he watches the dog's head evaporate in a bright red cloud of brains and meat.

Jenny throws off the corpse and leaps to her feet, pulling the ice pick free of its holster in one swift movement.

"Close the door!" Liam screams and Jim kicks the door shut as two other dogs burst inward—the first gets all the way into the room while the second's body is trapped between the door and the frame, Jim's boot and the weight behind it leaning hard against the writhing beast as it tries desperately to go either forward or backward.

Mostly forward.

The lead dog—a large chocolate Labrador with short dirty fur and a scarred muzzle—stays on Greg. It sinks its teeth into his thigh as Greg screams and begins beating at it blindly. Before Liam can react, Jenny straddles the thing, ropes her forearm beneath its jaw, and jerks upward. The dog yelps—more in surprise than pain, Liam thinks—before she smoothly drives the ice pick through its brain.

Meanwhile, Jim is punching the dog trapped in the doorway as it snarls and tries to rip flesh from his pistoning hand. Finally, with a whiny yelp, the dog slips backward and the door slams shut. Jim slides the bolt and leans his back against the door, eyes narrowed to a scowl. Liam thinks Jim looks ready to kill the world.

"What the fuck!" he yells. As if in answer, the howls from outside the farmhouse fill the air. A multitude.

From all directions.

Jim tries for footing: "We've, uh, we've got to—"

The sound of smashing glass comes from the kitchen. The window to the left of the front door explodes inward, and Liam sees blood and fur battering like a mad devil against the loosening wooden boards.

The windows in the other rooms of the house, some of which are boarded up, some of which are simply covered in dirty blankets or stained sheets, start to shatter, one after another. There is pounding on the walls and the front door beats hectically as dogs hurl their bodies against it with insane abandon. The noise of the pounding and the mad barking is so intense that Liam wishes he could cover his ears to mute the tumult, to run and hide, screaming, from the impossible assault.

Barking comes from the kitchen and Liam spins to point his gun at the sheet separating the rooms as two blurs—one muddy orange and the other coal-black—burst through it. He fires into the ribs of the orange one and the black one leaps at Jim, who drops his gun to catch the thing in both hands. It snaps and snarls at his face while being held in midair. With a roar Jim raises the beast above his head and slams it to the floor with such force that Liam hears its bones snap.

Jim lifts a boot to stomp on its head and Liam turns away, disgusted, in time to see a far window burst inward, a dying dog lying half-in, half-out of its frame.

Amid the chaos, Greg crawls blindly around the floor, searching for and finding Jim's dropped gun.

"Jenny, behind you!" Liam yells and Jenny spins toward a short hallway that leads to the rear of the house. Two more dogs burst from the hall and she has a split second to raise her arms in defense as they leap in a simultaneous arc and drive into her head and chest, lifting her off her feet and propelling her backward, where she and the animals land in a whirlwind of teeth and skin and fur, shrieks of rage and snapping teeth. One of the dogs squeals as she stabs its chest with the ice pick, but the other is already snapping at her face with blinding accuracy. She punches at it with torn, bleeding hands as the corpse of the canine—the pick still buried in its torso—lies lifeless on her gut, leaking blood into her dirty tank top.

"Fuck YOU!" she screams as she punches madly, but a third dog (one Liam never saw entering) sinks its teeth into the abusive arm and jerks its head violently side to side as Jenny screams.

Liam shoots the dog at her neck just as it tears into her. It flies from her body as if kicked. The dog at her arm releases her and turns its face toward Liam, teeth bared and red. Liam fires into its belly and looks for more targets.

A rust-furred mutt, bony and vicious as a junkyard watchdog, is backing Jim toward the front door, and it's only now Liam realizes that Jim's lost his gun. From the corner of his eye he spots more dogs leaping through torn-apart windows just as three more attack from the kitchen. Claws scrape at the front door, which *bangs* in its frame, and it seems to Liam that within seconds the room has become congested with the smell of fur and blood, the clamor of continuous barking.

He watches sickly as Jenny, her neck and back slick with blood, her shirt torn from her body to expose gouged breasts and a torn stomach, limps toward him, arms extended, bloody face contorted by sobs. As she opens her mouth to speak—perhaps a last cry for help, for salvation—her eyes go wide and she is knocked down from behind by a German shepherd so malnourished Liam can make out the sores on its patchy fur. She manages to turn herself over before it sinks its teeth into her throat and rips flesh and tendons free, exposing a red cavern of muscles and tissue that pulses with her dying heartbeats. More dogs leap atop her and blood sprays the floor in a crescent as her limp body is twisted beneath the frantic, feeding animals. The last thing Liam sees is one thin, pale hand beating against the floor before the room is taken over by the invaders.

He fires at random, first at a few coming toward him at the base of the stairs, then at the ones leaping for Jim, who is punching and kicking at the animals, roaring and snarling right back at them with such vigor that a few seem hesitant—despite their bloodlust—to attack.

But Liam is quickly running out of bullets, and others are pouring into the house, some limping, some sprinting, many going to join the bountiful feast that was recently Jenny.

In the throes of the attack, Liam did not notice—just moments ago, while Jenny breathed her last—her brother Greg slouching up the stairs behind him, Jim's gun in one closed hand, the rail clutched in the other. When he reached the top, he disappeared down the second story hallway with murder on his mind and a tilted smile on his scarred lips.

Liam never had motive, or opportunity, to look at the ceiling, which Baby scurries across like a child-sized spider, untouched, and wary of the bedlam below, heading in a similar direction as the blinded man.

Whom he sensed as easy prey.

10

Henry hears the chaos from downstairs and is terrified.

STOP! his mind screams, but she has—for the moment—shut him out. Like she's thrown an invisible cloak over her mind.

Earlier, he'd sensed her power as she commanded the dogs. Now, he wonders what kind of destruction she could potentially sow on humankind. To call up insects from the air, or to *create* them as if she were a god was one thing; but to control animals for miles around, to force them to do her bidding, was something else altogether.

What if there are a hundred like her? he thinks, staggered by the idea. *What if there are a thousand . . . ten thousand?*

In his imagination, Henry visualizes a world never seen before: Nature versus Man. Mysticism versus Science. Psychic powers versus weapons, machines, technology. Or is he wrong? Is that how the world has always been? Since the beginning?

A secret war so hidden as to never be seen? Buried? Ignored?

Right now, however, all Henry cares about is getting out of this alive. If the dogs get into his room they'll tear him apart with the same ferocity and thoughtlessness as the rest of them. They won't see a little boy, helpless and hungry and alone. They'll see exactly what she's made them see: walking, talking meat.

Henry hears the soft *wisp* of the door latch, as if whoever's coming into his room is trying to be quiet, or careful.

Sneaky.

The door pushes inward and Henry gasps. He leaps off the cot, sneakers landing with a hard thump on the floor.

Greg's face twitches as he tracks the sound.

Henry can only stare in horror, mouth working but making no sound, as he tries to understand what has happened to this man. The top half of his face looks *melted*, nothing but red-hot inflammation, puffy and grotesque. Wrinkled, burnt skin where his eyes, brow, and forehead had once been.

"Henry?" Greg asks, a strained smile on what's left of his face, his voice slurred and thick. Henry notices his top lip is pulled up toward his nose, exposing his teeth like a monstrous rabbit from the hot meadows of hell.

Then he sees the gun in his fist.

Henry reaches out, then immediately pulls back, as if he's received an electric shock. The man's mind is broken, warped. Henry can't look at it, can't touch it. When he'd been allowed to commune with the creatures, he shared their fear, their hunger, their anger. And in doing so, *he* would feel those things, and it often overwhelmed him, gave him seizures, or caused him to simply black out.

But to touch madness? Henry shudders at the prospect of what that would do to his own tired mind.

With or without his gift, he knows Greg is thinking about only one thing: *murder*.

Henry takes two silent steps toward the window to his right, careful to set his feet down quietly, toes first, breath held. He prays that with the commotion of barking and screams and gunshots, any noise his shoes make will be well covered.

As he'd hoped, Greg's head doesn't follow him, but continues to stay positioned the same way—seemingly focused on the spot where Henry had been—momentarily fooled.

"Henry? We can fix this, kid. I think we can fix this, you know? Look, I have a favor to ask you." Greg steps deeper into the room, one hand fumbling along the edge of the door frame, the other lifting the gun and aiming it at the now-empty space Henry had recently occupied. "I was hoping you could ask your friend, the cunt who burned my face off?" he says mildly, pointing the tip of the gun at his slightly askew nose, indicating the face in question. "That you could ask her, pretty please with sugar on top, if she would be so kind as to give me back *my goddamn* eyes?!"

Like a man with perfect vision, Greg sneers and glides his arm to the left, pointing the gun directly at Henry, whose feet feel glued to the old rickety floorboards. "You know what, you little shit? Don't bother."

Greg fires two successive rounds, and Henry screams in terror and pain.

11

Liam is halfway up the stairs, walking backward toward the top, kicking furiously at the trio of dogs pacing him on the steps. By his count—and it is by no means a sure thing given how fast he's been firing off shots—he has one bullet remaining.

"Jim!" he yells, as the huge man catches and throws dogs ten feet across the room where they break into walls, or kicks savagely and without mercy at the ones who go for his legs and ankles. The door behind Jim is still pounding and Liam imagines a pile of dead dogs out there, killed by their own insane hunger to get inside, being overrun by live ones, a continuous onslaught. The bolt rattles, the wood screeching from the dragging claws. Liam is sure the dogs will break through—not if, but when. There will be a final wave, and that will be the end.

"Jim! Upstairs!" he screams, and Jim looks up, seeming to finally understand his peril—time is running short and the dogs are not slowing. One of his arms has a nasty tear; a flap of skin hangs off a bicep. His fingers drip blood, wet and red as raw sausage. His shirt is smeared with blood and gore.

The dogs have fared little better.

At a glance, Liam figures at least a dozen lie dead or dying on the floor of the main room, another four or five pulling and fighting for the scraps of whatever meat is left on Jenny's corpse, and more outside trying to find ways in.

If they can make it to Henry's room—the only one on the second floor that has a working door—they can barricade it and wait the damned things out. Then, possibly, get on to the roof through the window, figure a way to the ground and escape.

But down here it's a free-for-all. Down here is a slaughterhouse.

Two gunshots erupt from Henry's room.

Oh no, Liam thinks, and every nerve screams at him to turn and run, to find out what's happened. But the dogs snapping at his toes would be on him like lightning. He'd never make it.

Then, with a gladiator roar, the kind to fill a coliseum and send shivers down the spines of any waiting opponents, Jim runs for the stairs.

Two of the dogs on Liam turn their heads toward the sound, and Liam actually hears one of them whine, like a puppy who's been scolded for shitting on the carpet. Jim takes the steps in great bounds, knocking aside the gnashing teeth and blazing eyes of any of the dogs in his path. He leaps past Liam, who delivers one last solid kick to the jaw of a feral mutt that may have once been someone's pet, abandoned and left for dead in the wild, where these animals have almost zero chance of survival.

Despite his fear of being chased, he holds off firing his last bullet into the head of the savagely grinning animal closest to him, feeling sick and ashamed at having to kill so many of the creatures—despite their viciousness, their desire to tear his throat open and drink his blood. Instead he does his best impression of Jim and screams at the dog—who, surprisingly, instinctively, cowers.

A moment later the front door bursts inward and bodies spill into the house. Some dogs simply lie inert; others scramble to their feet, looking for targets.

Liam doesn't hesitate. He turns and sprints upward, hot on Jim's heels, as they run for their lives toward the room of the boy they've held captive, praying his prison will become their sanctuary.

12

Glass explodes behind Henry as the bullets miss him by inches and crash into the window, sending shards of shrapnel into his back, neck, and head. One of the remaining boards covering the window splits in half with the bullet's impact and swings downward on the hinges of the nails at each end. Like broken arms, they hang limply to either side of the frame.

Henry tucks into a ball as Greg aims again.

"Did I get you, Henry? Did I split your head open, you little freak?"

Not wanting to give Greg a third try to do just that, Henry flops onto his stomach and belly-crawls away from the window. Sharp slivers of glass pierce the skin of his exposed elbows and palms as he pushes across the floor toward the cot. Making as little noise as possible, holding back the whimpers of pain caused by sliding his body over the glass-strewn floor, he snakes under the rusted steel crossbar of the bedframe, holds his breath beneath the sunken springs.

Greg takes another step into the room. "Where you hiding, little dude?" he whispers. Henry—only able to see him from the knees down—watches, helpless, as Greg's feet move closer and closer toward the bed.

To Henry's horror, he kneels.

No . . . it's not possible!

The ghoulish face of what used to be Greg Lanigan turns its blistered red flesh toward Henry. A grin pries open, stretching skin and causing pus-filled blisters to burst and leak along the recessed areas that were once eye sockets. His teeth are stunningly white against the hot pink skin, and Henry wonders how he's not screaming bloody murder for all the pain he must be in. *Maybe it's so painful he's kind of numb, like his brain is in shock. Or he's just gone totally bonkers.*

"Hiya Henry," Greg says, and lies flat on the floor, the gun in his hand pointed casually at Henry's torso. "I can hear you breathing, you know," Greg says. "I can also hear you dragging your fat ass through glass. Hey, you sound pretty scared, man." He chuckles lightly, brings his fingers up to touch his temple. Henry winces as the fingertips seem to stick to the skin; he can actually hear the separation when he pulls them away, a wet *tut* sound, and he can't help but notice that some of the blistered red skin from his face is now stuck to those same fingertips. Greg laughs, abruptly and too loudly, which makes Henry shrink back even more. "I gotta admit, kid. I probably don't look too good! Right? I mean, hell, to be honest with you, Henry, I don't feel too hot either. I mean, *look at me.*"

Henry's inner eye twitches, and he instinctively opens himself up.

He senses Jim and Liam's panic far away, too far to be of any help. He brushes against Greg's murderous, broken mind and mentally shoves it away, moves past it to the *other* presence—the one getting close, the one that's a little scared, uncertain and confused in this strange new world.

Baby.

Henry shuffles forward slightly to see past Greg and toward the open door. He doesn't see anything, or anyone.

But he's close, I know it!

With a slight hesitation, and a sour feeling in his stomach that makes him grimace, Henry shuffles a few inches closer to the edge of the cot, away from the wall and toward Greg. He sees the door easily now, but this time he cranes his neck so he can see *up.*

Upside down, Baby crawls beneath the top of the doorframe and scurries up the wall toward the ceiling, all six limbs shuffling in rhythm, its head turned downward. *Like that girl*, Henry thinks. The one from the scary movie he's heard so much about. *The Exorcist.* In that movie, the little girl turns her head *all the way around.*

Or so he's heard.

Because that's what Baby's doing now. Its limbs stuck to the ceiling but its head turned, facing downward. Its gaping mouth shows off pin-prick teeth, and its bright white eyes are slowly widening at the sight of Greg just below.

"Hey mister," Henry whispers, his body shaking.

Greg moves the point of the gun up from Henry's tummy to his head, following the voice easily. "Yeah, little buddy?"

"You should probably . . . um, not sure I should say . . ."

Greg's grin widens, cracking skin and opening a fresh fissure of blood at the corner of his mouth. "Say what, Henry?"

"It's behind you," Henry whispers, and Greg's grin slips away.

He frowns and pushes to his knees, that horrible mask of a burnt, eye-less face thankfully leaving Henry's view. "Who's there?" he yells.

Henry hears a *thump* as Baby lands on Greg before they both tumble to the floor. Greg screams and there's another gunshot. The creatures hisses and Greg is lifted from the ground, so Henry only sees him from the waist down. There are loud grunts of a struggle, a wet-sounding curse, and then the loud *snap* of breaking bone. Greg's body stops struggling and goes limp. He collapses to the floor, back into Henry's view. His left cheekbone is bitten clean away, leaving a pit of red gore.

Baby chews as Greg moans.

He's still alive, Henry thinks. *Oh no please no.*

Baby finishes whatever part of Greg is in its mouth, then clamps down hard into the side of Greg's neck, ripping away a large piece of flesh and muscle.

Henry whimpers and Baby's head turns to find him beneath the bed. Its mouth is full of meat and blood as its bone-white eyes meet Henry's for the first time.

Henry can feel its surge of comfort—of *happiness*—at being near him, being close to something he understands.

A friend.

I'm so hungry, Henry hears, as the creature's jaw works the fresh meat.

Then you should eat, Henry thinks back.

He smiles reassuringly, but feels his stomach turn as Baby complies, and takes another bite.

13

Jim sprints down the hallway and easily hops the empty space in the floor through which a portion of a downstairs room is visible. As he draws near Henry's room, he notices the door wide open. Despite everything that's happened, he has a surge of anger that someone has been so negligent as to leave the kid's door unlocked.

Fucking amateur hour around here.

Liam's pounding footsteps are coming fast behind him, the sounds and scrapes of the snarling pack of dogs beyond that.

Jim rushes through the open door and stops so suddenly that his boots skid along the dusty floor.

The room is a horror show.

His brain registers three things simultaneously:

First is Greg, facedown on the ground, surrounded by a growing pool of dark blood. The back of his neck and head are nothing more than caved-in bone, gristle, and exposed brain.

Second is the thing on top of Greg, currently nose-deep into Greg's upper shoulder, chowing down on whatever bits of meat remain there. The creature is a dark red color spun through with pulsing black veins. It has six limbs, all of which are pinning Greg's lifeless body to the ground. Its spine is bony and arched, and Jim's twitching mind refuses to categorize it as animal, insect, or demon, and he momentarily sets that quandary aside.

Third is Henry.

The kid is huddled beneath his cot, his face ashen and dull-eyed. He's either dead or in some kind of shock, because Jim can think of no other reason the boy's not screaming his head off and clawing at the walls trying to get away from the monster turning Greg's body into a breakfast buffet.

Suddenly Jim's head snaps back as he's nearly knocked off his feet by a striking blow from behind. He hears a surprised *oomph* as Liam bounces off the bigger man and collapses in a sloppy heap on the floor. Jim spins, grabs the door, and slams it shut, putting his back against it just as the weight of the first dog slams into the other side. The industrial bolt lock being on the outside of the door is a problem, but at least Pete had installed a new doorknob, along with a spring-latch and plate which, for the moment, seems to be holding.

Still, Jim has no intention of removing his considerable weight from the door as more hard bodies slam against it, followed by a frenzy of frustrated barks and the clatter of snapping teeth.

"Holy Christ!" Liam screams, having finally seen what Jim discovered only seconds ago.

Liam leaps to his feet and backs against the far wall, staring in horror at the creature and what's left of Jim's mighty crew. The creature ignores the two men for now, so consumed by its hunger it either doesn't know or doesn't care that they've burst in on its feeding.

"Henry," Liam says. "Get out of there. Slide over here to me."

Jim notices the glass of the window has been shattered, and only two boards remain in place. He searches the floor, sees his gun in Greg's dead hand, and puts it together.

"He shoot your ass, Henry?" Jim asks, not really caring at this point if the kid is bleeding out or not.

"No," Henry says quietly, unmoving.

As if Jim's voice has finally broken through its feeding frenzy, the creature pauses and turns its head toward the big man. Jim feels a chill at seeing those ghostly pale eyes, the tiny black pupils trembling within. Instinctively he recoils, presses back against the door.

And then, feeling as slow as his alter ego Fred Hinnom, he finally realizes what the hell he's gawking at.

That's it. *The fucking thing from the cellar.* That's *the nasty-ass bastard all this mess and death and fuss is over? Damn, man, it looks like a piece of shit grew legs and teeth.*

Anger rising, tempering any wariness he might have felt when first seeing the bizarre creature, Jim takes a lunging step toward it. Testing.

Baby recoils with a hiss, eyes blazing, black pinhead pupils dancing madly.

Jim scoffs. "Shit, I killed snakes bigger than you, amigo," he says, his peripheral vision aware of the gun clutched in Greg's stiffening fingers, but still keeping a sharp eye on the creature, making sure it doesn't suddenly decide to attack.

I think you're looking a little full there, mongrel. Wherever the fuck your belly's at, its likely pretty heavy right now, am I right? With all that yummy Greg meat inside you—and likely some Pete meat, too. Yeah, I think you got some of Pete in there. Too bad. But maybe all that food gonna slow your ass down a bit, what you think?

"Jim, what are you doing?" Liam says, eyes wide, his gun pointed down at—what did the kid call it? *Baby.*

"You got any bullets left in that thing?" Jim asks, secretly knowing the answer but keeping it to himself for now. His eyes don't leave Baby who, having temporarily forgotten about his meal, eyeballs Jim warily.

"One," Liam answers. Then: "I think."

"All right, good. I'm gonna see if I can't wrangle this thing—"

"You're *what?*"

"I got a plan," Jim says, taking another half step toward Baby. "Jim's always got a plan, my brother."

Jim bends his knees and inches forward, ignoring the sounds of the dogs on the other side of the door, ignoring the flap of skin hanging from his bicep, the stinging bites and scratches from the mutts. He forces his mind to *focus.* He spreads his hands out wide to either side, eyes fixed on every muscle in the creature's long, skinny body. *Ugly damn thing. Like a*

*giant mongoose without the fur . . . plus a couple extra legs . . . I got you, mongoose.
I got you.*

Baby shuffles halfway off Greg's body, limbs moving in creepy unison.
But it doesn't move toward Jim, shuffling instead toward Henry.

As if afraid.

*Yeah, you afraid of old Jim, ain't you? You should be, Baby. That's right, you
should be.*

"Hey now," Jim says, and opens his right palm wide and holds it high,
shaking it to catch the creature's attention. Baby's white eyes flick up to
the hand, ready to attack, and that's when Jim flashes forward with the
left, grabbing the creature tight around the dark pink skin of its narrow,
muscular neck.

Its flesh is slick, rubbery as an eel, and it's stronger than Jim had bar-
gained for. But Jim is strong as well—he could break the bones in a man's
neck by squeezing one large hand, and had done so. The creature's eyes
bulge and its mouth drops open, showing long sharp teeth colored red
with blood and flecks of human flesh. It hisses so loudly it sounds more
like a scream as Jim, now smiling almost as wide as Baby's snarl, slowly
straightens his legs, easily lifting Baby off the ground.

Baby's six limbs writhe and kick, its jaws snapping at the air, longing
to sink its teeth into the arm holding it. Its long body squirms and wiggles.

*Yeah, Baby, you a little freaked out right now, huh? Ol' Jim's got you nice and
tight, and now we're gonna see what's what.*

We're gonna see who's playing with who.

Henry screams and Jim risks a glance down to see Henry beneath
the cot holding his hands over his ears, like he's being driven mad by a
high-frequency sound Jim can't hear.

"What's wrong with you!" Jim yells, tightening his grip on the back
of Baby's neck, willing it to calm the fuck down.

"He's screaming!" Henry wails. "He's scared! Let him go!"

Jim laughs. "Yeah, I don't think so. Tell me something, Henry," he says, his eyes hard, his grin a scythe with teeth. "Is Mama around, boy? Because I think if *you* can hear that shit, she can hear it too, am I right, little brother?"

Henry only sobs, but Jim sees him nod his head, almost imperceptibly.

"Liam," he says coldly, never taking his eyes off Baby. "Hand me my goddamn gun."

Liam steps away from the wall, giving Jim and the creature a wide berth, shoots a nervous look at the door and the mad braying behind it, then reaches down and pulls the gun from Greg's cooling fingers. He extends it toward Jim's reaching hand, the one that doesn't have Baby in a death grip, and Jim takes it. With his thumb, Jim rubs the release latch and the cylinder drops open. He glances down, does a quick count, then flicks his wrist to snap the cylinder back into place.

"Four shots," he says. "That'll be plenty."

Henry slides out from under the bed, careful to avoid broken glass and the bloody mess of Greg's body. He stands up and points at Jim defiantly. "Let him *go!*" he yells, eyes wet. A child throwing a hissy fit.

"Shut up, Henry," Jim says coldly, and it feels good to see fear in the kid's face again. He's been too slack. Too *nice*. Everyone thinks they can fuck with him when he's too nice. Greg and Jenny scheming behind his back, the kid yelling at him, Liam likely planning his own escape, that crazy bitch outside getting biblical with the bugs and dogs—oh yeah, he knows what's going on. No way a bunch of feral dogs gonna attack like that.

She's doing it.

She's ruined everything. Made him look like a clown. It's bullshit, and it's time things got *straight* around here. It was high-fucking-time Jim takes *control* of this situation.

"Liam? You keep an eye on Henry. Don't let him slip away now, and don't let those dogs get him and tear him apart. Because hell or high water, I'm getting my two million dollars, and if it ain't today it'll be tomorrow.

And if it's just me and you then it's just me and you. If the kid survives, peachy. If he don't? That's peachy, too. I'll still get my money, and so will you. We clear?"

Liam pries his gaze away from Greg, looks at Baby with disgust, and nods. "Yeah. We're good."

Jim turns to Henry, making sure his grip stays iron tight on the hissing, kicking monster. "Don't be dumb, Henry. I didn't empty trash cans and mop hallways and talk like Fuh . . . Fuh . . . Fred the dumbass so some alien bug can fuck up all my plans. You understand, son?"

Henry says nothing, but steps away from Jim, toward Liam.

"Good. Now get outta my way."

As he raises Baby high into the air, the creature, sensing danger, renews its thrashing, but Jim ignores it and approaches the broken window, now crossed lamely by two tired-looking boards. He lifts a big boot and smashes through the lower board, the cross-patterned old muntin hanging to the sill by a thread, and the last jagged teeth of glass still clinging to the frame.

Baby claws at Jim's face with the end of one limb, scratching through flesh, but Jim has no time for it. He raises his arm straighter, locks his elbow so the dangling creature is too far from his body to do any further damage. As a child, he'd held cats in a similar fashion, gripping the scruff of their little necks while they hissed and clawed and wiggled and kicked. Not one ever got away from him, and he got to lots of them. It was a sort of hobby of his as a young man. Killing cats. He hated those goddamn things.

And this? No different. Just an animal to be taken care of. To be handled. To be disposed of.

But first, Jim needs an audience. A very particular audience of one.

With the butt of his gun he knocks the higher board free of its moorings and clears the rest of the window innards away, leaving an open rectangle full of blue sky above and a pitched rooftop below, the muddy old shingles extending outward a dozen feet toward the shed and the forest beyond.

Jim steps carefully through the window, then quickly pulls his other arm through so the creature has no chance to grab the sides of the frame (another trick he'd learned when drowning cats: Never hesitate when putting them into the bucket). He pulls Baby clear of the window and holds him triumphantly skyward, smiling like a boy holding up a first-place trophy.

He turns and walks along the top of the pitched roof toward the far edge, eyes scanning the surrounding trees. He doesn't see her, but he knows she's out there. Watching. Waiting to make her move.

He spares a glance toward Liam and Henry, who are watching him closely—Liam with a furrowed, anxious brow, the boy with wide-eyed horror.

"She can see me, can't she, Henry?" he yells back.

Henry doesn't answer, but he doesn't need to. Jim realizes that the fear on Henry's face is only partially his own. Jim finally understands that, in a way, when he looks at the boy, he's looking at Mother as well.

Perfect.

"HEY MAMA!" he bellows, now standing only a few inches from the edge of the roof, holding his captive high, the newborn creature weakening with the effort of trying to free itself, its limbs moving slower, its hissing quieted down to heavy breaths, its wide white eyes fearful.

"I got something you want!" Jim yells, watching the trees for movement. "How about you come out and GET IT?"

A moment passes, then another. Jim's eyes watching. Waiting.

There.

No more than ten yards away, the creature slowly, cautiously, slinks from the deep shadows and into the sunlight, golden eyes locked on Jim, and on her child.

"Gotcha," Jim whispers.

Then he turns back to Henry one last time, and winks.

14

Henry tugs at Liam's shirt. "You've got to stop him," he whimpers. "They're both screaming, I can hear them. I can't take it." He rubs his temples, as if trying to push the intruding sounds away, force the creatures out of his head.

Liam scowls. "Honestly, kid? That *thing* out there? If it dies, or that crazy bitch in the woods gets a bullet, I couldn't care less. As far as I'm concerned, she asked for it." He looks back toward the torn-out window, watches as Jim roars from the rooftop, thrusting the squirming monstrosity high in the air. He's reminded of a painting he once saw when in primary —that of Perseus holding aloft the head of Medusa, with her snakes for hair that turned men to stone. He has a fleeting thought about how such myths came to be, how the stories originate, what mythical creatures may truly exist that could spawn such awful tales of mysticism, death, and revenge.

"Fucking gods," he mumbles. "Henry, listen to me."

But Henry's eyes are fixed on Jim and Baby. Tears run down his cheeks, snot leaks from his nose. He stinks of piss and there are lice in his hair and to Liam he's never looked more alone or more helpless.

"Henry!" he repeats sternly, and gives the boy's shoulders a gentle shake. "Listen, please."

Finally, Henry turns.

Liam takes a breath, gives himself three more seconds to debate. But he damn well knows he's already decided. "Henry, I'm going to get you out of here. I'm going to get you home."

Henry sniffles, wipes his nose with the back of a grimy hand. His brow furrows. "You?" he says, giving Liam a head-to-toe look almost comical in its contempt. "Why? I mean, why now? And how?"

"Never mind why. I just need you to listen, okay? There are two cars in the big shed, but only one of them is working. The brown one. Not the green one. You understand?"

Henry nods. "The brown one."

"Right." Liam digs into his pockets, pulls out a set of tinkling, shiny metal. "I took the keys from Jim this morning. He doesn't know. We're gonna take the car and get away, okay?"

"But what about the dogs? Jim? Your money? What about Baby and Mother?"

"Fuck those monsters," he snaps. "I'm trying to save your life, kid. We will only have one shot at this. So, do you want to get out of here, see your lovely aunt and uncle again? Or do you want to stay here and die?"

"I want to go home," Henry says quietly.

"Good. Then you *have* to listen to me. All right?"

"You're not tricking me?" Henry says, studying Liam's eyes.

"You're the psychic, dumbass. Look in my head. Tell me if I'm lying."

Henry's face grows solemn, and Liam gets the briefest glimpse of what the boy will look like when he's a man, assuming he doesn't die today. He studies Liam's eyes with a renewed focus, and Liam feels that uncomfortable sense of spiders in his head, the one he got last time Henry went rummaging around in his brain.

"Believe me?"

"Yes," Henry says.

"Good," Liam says, relieved. "For now, just be cool. When the moment comes, I'll tell you to haul ass. When I do, go to the shed and wait by the brown car. As a matter of fact, here." Liam hands the keys to Henry, who takes them silently, without question. "The doors are locked, but use these to get inside and wait for me. You might be safer inside."

"From what?"

But Liam only shakes his head. His eyes grow distant, as if trying to see the enemy through a thick haze, looking into the past for an unseeable future.

"I don't know," he says finally, then stands, a hand on Henry's shoulder, and waits for the outcome of the drama outside, waits for the moment he'll be able to do something right for once in his miserable, sorry life.

15

Mother approaches the house slowly, cautiously. Jim watches her come. If he chose to do so, he could put a bullet into her from where he stood.

She'd have no chance.

But what would be the fun in that?

Bitch has messed with him, messed with his plans. With his crew. Attacked them without mercy. Tried to drive them out.

Murdered them.

Greg, Jenny, for sure. Pete, almost certainly.

Time for a little payback.

"That's close enough!" he yells, tiny red sparks flaring in the back of his mind, telling him to be careful. He has no clue of what this thing can do. Best to err on the side of caution.

She stops and—in a perfect mimic of a human—holds her thin arms away from her body, her clawed hands open wide.

Look, no weapons.

Jim scoffs at the pose, but is also troubled by it. It's such a human response that for a moment his reasoning, his intellect, takes over the controls, grabs the steering wheel away from the raging bull and forces him to wonder what, exactly, she is.

How can such a creature possibly exist?

But then he thinks of Greg being snacked on by the monster held firmly in his left hand; of Jenny being overrun by rabid dogs, a swarm of teeth and fur washing over her in a wave as she screamed.

Not that she meant anything to him. None of them did, not really. It is a matter of *respect*. And this Mother, this *abomination*, stole his pride, made him look foolish; shrank him to the size of a gutter rat, a fucking insect.

"You surrender, huh?" he says loudly, even though he no longer needs to yell. The creature stands only twenty feet away, arms wide, hooded face unreadable but for the yellow eyes, which flicker from him to her offspring dangling from his arm, the very thing she's been trying so hard to protect.

She moves her head up and down slowly, as if imitating, once again, something she might have seen a human do—as if curtailing her responses in a way he will understand. Honestly, he's a bit impressed. Another time, another place, he would have trapped the thing and studied it. Out of curiosity.

Taken his time before killing it.

But he's out of time now. And out of patience. Out of every-goddamn-thing.

"The dogs!" he says, and the creature—Mother—nods slowly, then begins to emit a loud, piercing noise. To Jim's ears it sounds like bursts of static with an underlying pattern of clicks and shrill whistles. It makes his thoughts turn fuzzy. Were his hands not a little full at the moment, he would have covered his ears.

Then, from one moment to the next . . . silence.

No more strange sound coming from Mother, but more than that:

No dogs.

No barking. No snarling or banging from inside the house. Jim looks to his right and sees a few of the dogs wandering around the front of the clearing, smelling the grass. One lean black pit bull smells another dog's ass. A one-eyed German shepherd takes a piss on a tree and disappears into the shadows.

Just dogs. Nothing but dumb, hungry, feral dogs that no longer give a shit about the humans, or the beast who—somehow—had commanded them. Forced them to kill.

Jim looks back to Mother, who nods again. Hands still high.

She shuffles a step closer, gestures one black claw toward her child.

There, you see? We're all friends again. I do what you ask, and you let my baby go.

"Very impressive," Jim says, hardly loud enough for anyone to hear but himself and the whining creature in his grip. *By God, my arm's getting damn tired, son. Gonna have to end this, I'm afraid.*

Jim raises the gun in his right hand, points it at the back of Baby's head.

The creature starts to move forward.

"DON'T!" he yells, and she stops, arms raised even higher now. He can see her more clearly, her face—the eyes muddy and alien, her mouth opening and closing, as if talking to herself. As if praying.

Baby has gone limp; a soft whine curls from deep in its throat. Then, slowly, pathetically, it lifts its top two limbs, extends them toward the creature below. The whining grows louder.

Mother's arms bend forward, as if reaching.

"You made a big mistake fucking with me," Jim says.

"Jim!"

Jim turns his head quickly to glance back at Liam. There's no sign of Henry.

"Don't," Liam says.

Jim only grins, his eyes dancing with madness.

★ ★ ★

When the barking and snarling from the hallway and the sound of claws scratching against the door suddenly stops, Liam knows it's time.

He leaves the window and goes to the door, pulls his gun and aims it low, ready to see wild eyes and a foaming canine mouth, lips pulled back to show yellow teeth. He glances back at Henry, then grabs the doorknob and tugs.

The latch comes free and the door creaks inward. The paint on the other side is torn down to bare wood; streaks of paw-shaped blood paint the bottom half, the only remaining sign of the mad dogs who sought entry.

The dogs, however, are gone.

Gun still poised, Liam looks into the hallway, sees a gray tail disappear down the stairs toward the massacre below.

"She's called them off," Henry says, moving quietly to stand at Liam's side.

Liam looks down at the boy, tucks a finger under his chin, and raises his face to look at him. "This is it, Henry. This is our chance. It may be our only chance."

"Please don't let him kill Baby."

Liam ignores this. He drops to one knee, looks Henry in the eyes. "Go to the shed. Do what we talked about. I'll be right behind you. This is almost over, Henry. Listen to me now and you'll get out of this in one piece. Time to haul ass, okay? No more questions."

Henry glances down the empty hall, then back at Liam one last time. He reaches out a hand and puts it on Liam's stubbled cheek, studies his eyes.

"Please go," Liam says, his emotions stirring uncomfortably in his mind, his heart. "Go around the back, he might not see you."

Henry removes his hand. Without a word he runs down the hall toward the stairs.

Liam waits until he disappears, makes sure there are no sounds of him screaming or more dogs attacking—but he hears nothing from below, just the quick, soft footsteps of a boy running across a wooden floor, and away.

Returning to the window, Liam watches as Jim points the gun at the back of the skull of the wormlike, savage creature. In the distance, he can make out the top of the barn, toward which Henry will now be running.

He needs to distract Jim, buy Henry some time.

"Jim!" he yells.

★ ★ ★

Jim grins at Liam, then turns back to face Mother. There's a streak of blue cutting to his left. Henry making a run for the shed.

Fucking Liam, he thinks with cold regret. *Looks like I'll need those extra bullets after all. One for each of you dumbass traitorous motherfuckers.*

He looks down at Mother, and the smile turns into a scowl. "I'm sorry about this, I really am," he says, and moves the barrel an inch closer to the slick crimson head. "But the reality? The truth?"

Mother's arms drop and, in a blur of black, she sprints for the house, toward her child.

"No one, and I mean no one, fucks with me and lives."

The gunshot sounds like a cannon, and Baby's skull blows apart.

In Jim's hand, the creature's muscles go slack. The body feels like nothing more than limp rubber in his palm. With disgust, he tosses the thing outward, watches it fall, lifeless, to the ground.

★ ★ ★

Henry reaches the shed and yanks open the door. He hears Jim talking but then his head fills with a rush of such blind panic and despair he drops to his hands and knees, his vision of grass and dirt blurring.

There's the pounding crack of a gunshot and it feels as if half of Henry goes numb, like part of his mind has just disappeared, been totally blown away. But another part pops like a flashbulb, a blinding light of bright white—so bright that he squeezes his eyes shut reflexively, puts his hands over his eyelids and wills all his senses to *stop*.

He falls to his knees screaming in terrible, piercing pain; the worst agony he's ever felt, ever imagined.

★ ★ ★

Mother collapses to the ground in front of the lifeless body of her child. Her hands frantically paw over its limbs, its stomach, its blood-soaked head.

This is the first time she has seen her child. The first time she has touched it.

Feverishly, she tries to connect, tries to *think* it back to her, use her powers to push life into its motionless heart, hoping to see a spark in the one blank, staring eye that remains.

She pulls the lifeless body in her arms and cradles it, moaning and rocking the dead child she had wanted so badly to live, a child to exist with her in this world, a world in which she was terribly alone.

★ ★ ★

Jim watches the creature from above, listens to its whining cries, and feels nothing. He points the gun carelessly at its shelled back.

"NOOO!"

He looks up and sees Henry sprinting toward him with that awkward gait of his, waving his arms and yelling. "PLEASE! DON'T SHOOT!"

Jim gives Henry a little wave, then glances back down to finish the job.

Mother is gone.

Frantic, he looks around and sees a flash of black sprinting for the trees. He has a split second to see the limbs of the dead offspring dangling from her arms.

It's a tough shot, but he's made worse.

As he finds his aim, she leaps, one arm extended to catch a heavy branch. She swings wildly, a blur of motion, and disappears into the shadows.

Furious, Jim turns and stomps back toward the bedroom window.

He drops back inside, stares around the empty room with the angry eyes of a bull ready to charge.

"Liaaaam!" he roars.

But there is no reply.

PART TEN: HENRY FLOORS IT

1

Sali thinks the park ranger looks like a hybrid combat war veteran/ linebacker for the San Diego Chargers. When the ranger shook hands with each of the HRT members—all combat veterans themselves—they greeted him with a respect reserved for like-minded men. They'd shown similar respect to the SWAT team and the local police who had arrived in support, including Detectives Knopp and Davis.

It was the team's assault leader, Jim Parker (who could have been mistaken for a surf bum given his deep tan, unshaven face, and long hair, were it not for the nasty looking M4 carbine assault rifle held casually in his arms), who had taken time to speak quietly with Dave for a few moments. Sali didn't know what was said, but the way Dave patted the commander twice on the shoulder and nodded a reply, he assumed it was something to do with bringing Henry back alive or, barring that, killing everyone responsible if he was not.

Sali hoped it was the former.

Once the police had been given instructions by Parker (which was essentially the containment of possible escape routes along the roads and walkways leading out of the targeted forest area), the park ranger, Sali, Parker, and the SWAT team leader gathered around a map laid flat atop a weathered picnic table, part of the small public camping area—temporarily requisitioned by the FBI—where the team had rendezvoused.

The ranger, who had introduced himself to Sali simply as "Ranger Bob," shows Parker the location of the abandoned house, the overgrown fire road the perps had likely used to get there, and the best entry points by foot.

"It's almost ten hundred now, so if we move at a steady rate we can arrive at the house within an hour," Ranger Bob says, addressing Parker directly. "There is a clearing, if I recall correctly, at a radius of approximately thirty yards around the house, mostly low brush and over-grown ground cover, then you hit trees. Plenty of hiding spots for SWAT and your snipers."

Parker nods and, for the first time since the airfield, gives Sali his full attention. "Agent Espinoza, any theories about what's going on inside that farmhouse?"

"We know of at least three perps, but there might be as many as five. You looked at the files coming in, so you have IDs on the ones we think are inside. The boy is most likely locked away, but frankly he could be in the cellar or the attic, if there even is one. It's going to have to be a room-by-room search."

Parker nods again, undaunted, and points at the map. "Fine. I'll place my snipers Fowler, Davies, and Loeb here, here, here. SWAT?"

The SWAT leader lifts his eyes.

"Your guys cover the perimeter north of the house here, here, and let's have someone to the east, here. You'll be firing only on my command, understood?"

"Yes sir."

"I wanna get eyes on as many as we can before engaging, I think that gives us the best chance of recovering the hostage unharmed. We light the fuse too early, and this thing could blow up in our face, copy?"

The ranger gathers the map and moves off with Parker to address the rest of the team about the walk ahead. Sali joins Dave, Knopp, and Davis, who stand quietly aside, waiting to hear about next steps.

"We're gonna move out. Dave, you can stay with me, we'll be taking up the rear and essentially staying the hell out of the way while these guys do their job. Knopp, Davis, you're welcome to tag along in the caboose."

Davis lights a cigarette, shakes his head. "You have enough firepower to take out Iran, you don't need me. Good luck." Knopp nods in agreement. "We'll stand by, stay on top of the officers and any changes that may come down the line. Captain Harris is a good cap, he'll be sure SDPD are where you need them."

"Okay, good," Sali says. "Let's go ahead and have fire and medical standing by. Uh . . . hell, let's bring them in here now, and I'll ask Ranger Bob to have someone come meet up with them to answer any questions. They should be as close as possible—and for the love of God, make sure they know to keep it quiet. If I hear a firetruck siren I'll lose my shit."

"Copy that," Davis says. "I'll take care of it personally."

"Thank you," Sali says, and desperately searches his tangled, adrenalized thoughts for anything he might have missed. "Okay, we're moving out. Good luck. See you on the other side. Dave?"

Dave, who had forced down two granola bars and three cups of coffee before leaving the house that morning, looks as alert and energized as Sali has seen him since the whole nightmare began. "I'm ready, Sali," Dave says.

Sali looks at the sturdy, well-worn hiking boots, the tough denim jeans and Carhartt jacket. "Appears so. Great, let's do it."

The park ranger and the members of the HRT—all wearing green camouflage, goggles, and military helmets—are already vanishing into the dense forest beyond the campground.

"We better catch up. The last thing we want is to get lost and need rescue ourselves."

But Dave is already moving, and Sali falls into step beside him. As they enter the woods, he offers a silent prayer for a positive outcome. The last thing he wants to be doing at the end of this fateful day is offering condolences to the man beside him on the loss of his child.

2

"Liam!"

Jim's roar carries out the window and across the grass to find Henry, who still kneels at the edge of a dark gray quadrangle in the rough grass, the structure's shadow a symbol of defiance against the rising light from the east.

Jim calls out again for the man—the one person—who is willing to save Henry's life, to get him *home*.

Get to the shed. Get in the brown car.

Henry does his best to push away the horror of what he'd seen, what he'd *felt*, following Baby's murder, and the ensuing overwhelming grief that assaulted him from Mother upon seeing her child killed in front of her. He forces himself to his feet with a grunt, digs into the pocket of his jeans, and pulls out the keys.

He jogs to the shed's big double doors, grabs the splintered edge of one, and pulls it toward him. The large door swings open, surprisingly graceful on its old hinges, and Henry finds himself staring at the chrome bumper of the brown Duster. Next to it, sulking in the shadows like a shy kid at a birthday party, is a Pinto the color of ripe avocado.

Henry steps inside the cool, moist shed. The ground here is rough dirt, and he recalls Liam's threat on their first night—a night that seems a whole lifetime ago—to make Henry sleep out here if he was being bad. Seeing it for the first time, Henry agrees that in comparison to the shed, his stinking, freezing bedroom was a five-star hotel.

The slats that make up the shed's wall and A-frame roof are wrinkled like dead skin. Sun pours sickly through their cracks, and through holes low in the walls where a variety of varmints—probably rats, Henry thinks sourly—have chewed their way in, or out, through the boards. The wood is thick, however, and Henry figures if the thing stood this long without anyone doing fixes, it's likely a lot sturdier than it appears.

Releasing a deep breath, trying to focus on the escape plan, he looks back toward the house to see if anyone is approaching.

He sees no one, and wonders if Jim has killed Liam. Wonders if he could do such a thing to his friend. Or perhaps Liam is the one forced to kill in order to help Henry, to release him from the bindings of Jim's plan.

Henry pulls the door closed, and as the two doors meet the bright day is blocked from his sight, vanquished, leaving him alone with the dark.

He stands still a moment, allows his eyes to adjust. He checks his breathing, tries to calm himself, erase some of the pain still lingering fresh in his mind. The pain Mother left there is like a trail of slime.

As for Baby, while Henry didn't actually feel the bullet, he did feel the intense *fear*, the instinctive mad desire to *live*. In its last moments, Baby wanted nothing more than to be with the one who gave it life, the one thing in the world that loved it.

Its mother.

When the thoughts and fears and desires cut off, there was nothing. Just emptiness. The void of death that Henry recognized at once, having looked into the abyss himself before somehow, miraculously, finding his way free.

Thinking of Baby's pain and Mother's loss sends a flood of such immense sadness through him that he almost crumples to his knees again. But he fights against it, forces himself to be strong, to be brave, to steel himself so that he might survive when so many others have not.

Gotta be tough. The tough survive.

He lowers his eyes to the ground, closes his eyes, and squeezes his hands into fists so tight his arms tremble.

Then he releases his fingers, opens his eyes, and exhales.

Better.

Still focused on the ground, he notices a long piece of wood near his feet. With a kid's curiosity, he bends down to study the long, half-buried beam. It's almost as long as the two swinging doors and appears to be partially sunk in the mud. Henry imagines insects probably having made a home beneath the wood. Personally, he loves roly-poly bugs, and he would bet a dollar there are a bunch of them under the wood. Probably spiders, too, which he does not like.

Looking up to study the inner face of the doors, he notices the large, rusted metal brackets screwed into the wood.

"It's a . . . whatchamacallit. A crossbar," he says, his voice carrying in the quiet of the shed.

It's a lock. A lock to keep people OUT.

Henry thinks keeping people out, especially people who might qualify as murdering types, would be an excellent idea, and begins to work the beam free of the earth.

3

Liam walks through the nightmare. Canine bodies are sprawled around the house's front room like a postapocalyptic dance floor, lifeless and scattered as dead leaves blown in through an open door. They lie broken along the bottoms of walls, stuck in windows, bleeding on the stairs.

No living dogs remain.

Not much remains of Jenny. The torn shell of the woman she had been is splayed like an adult-sized flesh balloon dropped from a great height, bursting open upon contact, innards shooting outwards in a chaotic pattern. Liam debates covering her with a sheet—several are scattered about that were once covering windows—but is quickly deterred when Jim yells his name. He quickens his pace toward the open door and the blue sky of escape just beyond. From the upstairs hallway, however, he hears Jim's fast-moving footfalls grow louder, and at the last second rethinks his strategy. He doesn't much like the idea of Jim taking shots at him while he makes a run for the shed.

Turning at the door, he jogs toward the kitchen instead, careful not to step in blood (not an easy trick) as he goes, so as not to leave footprints, a trail for Jim to follow.

In the kitchen, he winces at the sight of another dead canine—what was once most likely a playful (and quite pretty, by the fur patterns) border collie, stuck half-in, half-out of the shattered window—but keeps moving to the cellar door. His stomach flips as he pulls it open, half expecting to see that blanket of wasps, but the back of the door is clear. His nose wrinkles, regardless, as it's hit by a sickening smell coming from the cellar, a stench he has zero desire to investigate.

He steps into the dark, pulling the door *almost* closed behind him, not wanting to be locked in, trapped on the cellar stairs with God-knows-what waiting down there in the damp darkness.

Perhaps that's Pete I smell, he thinks, the idea feeling right in his mind. Feeling accurate.

Sure, I'd guess Pete already met Baby, before more proper introductions were made upstairs with Greg, Jim, and myself. Unlike Greg, however, maybe Pete somehow avoided being a light breakfast. And maybe he's down there right now *watching me as I stand here like an idiot by this door, waiting for a pissed-off Jim to go by. Hell yeah, that's a solid idea, all right. Quite plausible. I can see it clearly: Pete's on the floor—badly injured, we'll assume—and he's lying there, just* watching me. *Maybe—and wouldn't this be a pisser—but* maybe *he's crawling toward me at this very moment. Soft hands on the stairs, face bloodied, stomach ripped open like a Thanksgiving turkey, sliding his way up toward my ankles with murder on his mind.*

Liam cracks the door open another inch, telling himself it's so he can hear Jim's footfalls as they head out the front door. He looks behind him just the same, expecting to see wide white eyes, the pit bull tattoo splayed across a torn throat, that gold-toothed grin . . . but instead sees nothing. Nothing at all.

Finally, Jim stomps through the main room, and Liam's attention snaps back to reality. The footfalls approach the front door, leak onto the porch, then fade away.

He's going for Henry.

Allowing his imagination one last snapshot of a gore-faced Pete Scalera reaching bloody fingertips toward the cuff of his jeans, Liam steps back into the kitchen, into the light, and—gun drawn—cautiously follows Jim's path out the front door.

He thinks of his son, reaching up to him from the dark. The blast of the shotgun. The spray of hot blood as it hit his face. His boy's blood.

My fault. My fault. My fault.

He promises himself, promises the sweet spirit of his dead child, that he won't let it happen again.

Not today. Not ever.

I'm coming, kid, he thinks, praying Henry's locked himself in the car and is hidden from sight. Because the game is over now, and if Jim sees Henry he won't talk, or bargain. He'll shoot to kill.

And Liam will be next.

4

Lifting the long piece of wood isn't too hard once he's unstuck it from the ground (there are indeed a few roly-polys, and a few spiders, as well), but balancing it just right so he can drop it into all four brackets—two on each door—is a bit more of a trick. He finally manages to do it just as a large shadow moves across the slanting bars of sunlight, stopping directly in front of Henry. A hazy figure made of darkness that blocks out the sun; a looming specter that appears, to Henry, to be staring straight down at him through the weathered boards.

Henry takes a step backward, then quietly moves to the driver's side of the car, there not being enough room between the Duster and the Pinto for him to climb in the passenger side. Once inside he could slide over; he did it all the time when Uncle Dave or Aunt Mary would drive him somewhere, when some "idiot" had parked too close next to them.

The massive shadow moves and the big door rattles. The brackets catch the crossbar, holding them shut.

"Motherfucker," Jim's voice says coolly, as if amused, from the other side of the wooden slats. "I thought you might have figured that out. Smart kid like you. Tell me something, Henry, do you muh . . . muh . . . miss your old pal, Fuh . . . Fuh . . . Fred?"

There's laughter, and Henry is grateful for it because it masks the sound of him twisting the key in the door lock and climbing inside, shutting the car door behind him as quiet as he can.

It isn't quiet enough.

The laughter—maniacal as a villain in a Saturday morning cartoon—cuts off sharply.

"He gave you the keys, huh? I'll be damned. Can't trust nobody anymore, Henry. You remember that. Uncle Jim? He's teaching you something right now: you can't trust *nobody*."

Jim's muffled voice filters to Henry though the car windows, sounding distant, but Henry has heard enough. Henry's pretty sure the guy has lost his marbles. *One can short of a six-pack*, as Uncle Dave liked to say.

You can say that again, his dad says. *He's gone around the bend for sure, if he wasn't already headed that way before.*

Henry turns to see his father sitting on the passenger side of the car's front bench. He's still shadowy, like normal, but Henry thinks that—when the dusty light sneaking in between rotten boards and the dirty windshield hits him in a certain way—he can also sorta see the *real* him. Skin and eyes. A nose. Lips. Hair.

He's wearing a blue oxford work shirt, and it's familiar to Henry although he can't say why. From the waist down he is all darkness, as the light doesn't reach into the footwell. But Henry imagines he's most likely wearing jeans, or khaki pants—his favorite ones with the broken belt loop and the patched knee he insisted gave them *character*.

When his dad turns to face him, his features are a blurry, writhing maze, a hybrid of shadow and reality. Henry sees brown eyes, and white teeth when he smiles, but there are cross-patches of heavy shade playing through the light, and if he moves his head a little to one side or the other, one of those brown eyes flickers to pure silver. If he lowers his chin, the teeth melt into black ink.

"Daddy, what do we do?"

Well, his father says, hands primly on knees, looking through the windshield toward the shed doors, where the silhouette of Jim Cady is moving off and away, perhaps to leave them alone, but more likely to find a way to gnaw his way in, like the rats who chewed through the old boards. *I suppose we have to sit here and wait a bit. Wait and see what happens.*

Henry brushes the steering wheel with his fingers, liking the feel of the grooved, hard plastic. "You went away," Henry says. The cool interior of the car, the feeling of confinement, of comfort and normality, makes him feel sleepy, relaxed. "I was asking for you."

Well, I'm sorry, his dad says, firmly but not sternly. *But I had to do something.*

"That's okay," he says. "I'm glad you're here now."

Yeah, I figured it was time, Jack says. *And listen, son, I need to tell you something. I need to tell you now, while we have a moment, here before the end.*

Curious, Henry looks at his father. The mouth is still there, but a play of the light has cut away the top of his face, transformed it into black smoke in the shape of a head. His silver eyes stare back earnestly, two north stars in a night sky. Henry sighs his old-man sigh, knowing it's not good news, whatever it is.

"Well," he says, feeling more tired than he's ever felt in his life. "Then I guess you better tell me."

★ ★ ★

Outside the shed, Jim finds the old axe where Greg had tossed it, lying in the tall grass. He picks it up and grips the handle. *Perfect,* he thinks, and walks back to the front of the shed, unaware of the broad smile on his face.

★ ★ ★

It's not easy for me to talk about, Jack says, looking at his hands as they work against each other, a writhing mass of flesh and opaque gloom. *But you need to know I won't be with you much longer, son. I'm sorry. My time is almost up.*

Henry caresses the steering wheel, not knowing what to say, what to feel. He stays silent and waits.

It's a matter of energy, Henry. You've only got so much inside you that can be expended holding me here. You're a badass battery, son, but when the energy gets low, the light goes out. Jack pauses, as if considering, eyes spinning from brown to silver, then back. *When I died,* he says quietly, *you used that energy to* hold on *to me, to hold on to me so* tight *that I was able to stay with you . . . at least for a while.*

"I'm sorry," Henry says softly.

No! No, Henry, I'm glad *you did. I'm glad I got to watch you grow, see Dave and Mary take you in, love you. Hey now, look at me, Henry.*

Henry looks. For a moment, his dad is almost completely whole. Almost himself. Henry feels joy and sadness run through him like a river made of hot and cold; the disparity, when intertwined, making one indescribable new feeling that has no word attached to it. A feeling you can only experience, never properly define.

You gave me an amazing gift, Henry. An amazing *gift,* Jack says. Then, almost slyly: *And, in a way . . . I gave a gift to* you.

Henry thinks a moment, then his eyes widen, and for a brief second he's forgotten about the danger outside the shed. About Jim and Liam, Mother and Baby, the slaughter of the dogs, the bugs, the wasps, the cold room in the farmhouse. For a brief moment, he's just with his dad, and the joyful release of that is all-consuming, mind and spirit.

It's *wonderful.*

"The eye."

Jack nods. *Yeah. The eye.* He points a finger to Henry's forehead, but does not touch him. *I know it's brought you heartache, but I think it's also helped, right? I mean, at least a little bit, I hope. And, to be honest, without that—* he points at Henry's forehead again—*you wouldn't be able to see me. Not a bad trade-off, huh?*

Henry smiles, knowing it's what his dad wants to see, and shakes his head. "No way, no how," he says quietly, sadness and loss hiding behind his love for the ghost, for all that remains of the man he once needed more than anything in the world. The man who took everything. The man he could forgive, that he would always forgive.

Jack laughs. *Anyway, the bad news is that soon, very soon, I won't be able to help you anymore, Henry. Won't be able to show you things—how people think, what they feel. You're gonna have to see those things with your own eyes, see the world plain, without cheating. Without getting the answers for free, you know? Because that's what life is, baby. Life is questions you don't know the answers to, and figuring things out is what makes us human. But I owed you, and I love you, so I guess you could say I gave you a little head start.*

Henry studies the steering wheel again, Jack focuses on his hands. Neither of them say anything for a moment, Henry fighting off an encroaching sadness, not wanting to give into it, but also not wanting to let go.

I wish I could hug you, Jack says quietly. *Hold you one last time.*

"Me too," Henry says, and wipes at an itchy, tired eye.

Jack sighs. *But I'm using up a lot of battery right now, buddy, and I used up a hell of a lot last night . . . but hey, listen to me.* Henry looks up at the specter, smiling wide beneath a shadowed forehead dotted with those silver eyes. *It worked, Henry. I got through. Your Uncle Dave? He's coming. He's close.*

"Really?"

Jack's smile fades. *But not close enough, I don't think. I don't know . . .*

Jack's attention is drawn back to the shed doors. He follows the shadow cutting off lines of sunlight as it moves across the face of wooden slats.

The shadow stops.

Recedes.

There's a blur of motion followed by a loud *crack* as the head of an axe punches through a panel of wood, knocking a giant splinter to the floor.

Jim's face fills the narrow opening, one bulging eye pressed close, staring into the dark.

"Hiya, Henry."

5

Jim pulls the axe back and swings it at the shed door—again, and again, and again. He waits to hear the sweet sound of Henry screaming in terror. He's put off—a little *disappointed* to tell the truth—to hear no such thing.

Don't matter. He'll be screaming soon enough. Oh yeah, baby, he'll be screaming plenty.

Jim swings the axe again. It lands with a *crunch* as another chunk of wood flies into the dark. He can easily put his hand through now. He clutches the crossbeam and lifts it out of the brackets. It drops to the ground with a thud.

Holding the axe loosely in one hand, he reaches for the edge of the shed door.

"That's enough, Jim."

Jim pauses, drops his hand from the door. He lowers his head. "Please, do not do this, my brother."

"I'm doing it," Liam says. "Now turn around."

Jim doesn't turn, but instead takes a small, slow step away from the shed's chewed-up doors. "We're almost there, Liam. The kid? He's right *here*. We're free and clear. We're *close*. All we got to do is get in the car, right now, and drive out of here. Go get our fucking *money*. Two million bucks, man. One for you, one for me. We meet up with my guy and the second we hit the border we let the kid go. He'll find a border patrol soon enough, and that will be that. We can *still do this*."

"I don't think so," Liam says. "Henry goes free now. We run. That's my offer."

Jim sighs heavily, shakes his head.

"Everyone in my life," he says.

Liam steps closer, head bent. "What's that?"

"Everyone in my life disappoints me," Jim says, muscled shoulders slumping. "Sooner or later, they all let you down, man. Everybody."

Jim turns his head halfway around. Liam has the gun pointed at his back. His eyes and hands are steady, and Jim knows he'll shoot without hesitation if he makes a move for the .38 tucked against his stomach.

"You sure about this?" Jim asks.

"Move away from the door, mate," Liam says. "Drop the tool, lose the gun."

Jim takes a half step, then stops. "Yeah . . . I don't think I'm gonna do that."

★ ★ ★

"It's Liam," Henry says, opening his inner eye, reaching out to the men talking in front of the shed. "He's going to help. He said so."

Jack points to the ignition. *Put the key in there, Henry, but don't turn it yet.*

Henry's confused. Nervous. "Why?" he asks, but Jack's eyes don't leave the splintered, sun-soaked wood of the shed's door.

Just do it, son.

Henry slips the key into the ignition—something he's never done before—and feels a certain empowerment as the jagged teeth of the metal key slide, albeit roughly, into the cavity. "Cool," he says.

Now, can you reach the pedals with your feet? The brake's on the left, the gas on the right.

"I know," Henry says (not being a hundred percent truthful, but also not wanting his father to think he's just a dumb kid), and stretches out his legs. "Yeah, I can reach, but it's hard to see."

Henry's backside is near the edge of the seat, his hands gripping the bottom of the steering wheel for leverage, his eyes just barely above the level of the dashboard. For the millionth time in his brief life, Henry wishes he was three inches taller.

That's fine, that'll do.

"Do for what?"

Put your foot on the brake, hold it down, Jack says in reply. *Now put a hand on that key and get ready to turn it. Okay? When I say. Now I'm gonna tell you what to do next, so you listen careful and do what I tell ya.*

"If you were still alive? You could teach me how to drive," Henry says, not trying to be hurtful, but speaking in that way young kids have of blurting out the truth. Wrapped up in finding a comfort zone with the pedals, he doesn't notice the look of total loss on his father's ghostly face.

Jack doesn't comment, but instead—calmly but quickly, for time is running out, oh yes, running out very fast now—he instructs his son on how to put the car in gear, when to use the gas pedal, when to brake. As he talks, his brow stays furrowed with concern, and his eyes never leave the shed doors.

As if he's waiting for something horrible to happen.

★ ★ ★

"I don't want to shoot you, Jim. I didn't want any of this, and I'm sorry I let you down, mate. I am. But I can't go through with it. I won't hurt that boy."

"I told you—"

"I don't believe you, Jim. I *know* you. You'll never let Henry live. That was never part of the plan and we both know it."

Jim tilts his head, as if thinking, then nods. A decision made. "Here's what I know, Liam."

With lightning speed, Jim spins his body full circle, smoothly swinging the axe around in a one-handed grip, like a man about to throw a baseball sidearm.

Without hesitation, Liam pulls the trigger of his gun.

Click.

The head of the rusted axe isn't anywhere near razor-sharp, or even sharp enough to split a fat log. But it's more than sharp enough—especially with the additional torque of Jim's swing—to split the flesh of Liam's stomach and punch hard into his guts, the front edge sinking so deep it taps the fragile bones of the lower spine, breaking a vertebra and spilling the contents of his lower intestines into his bloodstream.

Liam folds in half, eyes wide in shock, his mouth an O of surprise. A breathy *phwa!* escapes his lips as his legs turn to rubber and he drops to the dirt, first looking up at Jim with admonishment and despair, then down to the axe handle protruding from his body with a sense of detached horror.

He drops the worthless gun and—to Jim's astonishment and delight—begins to crawl away, sliding himself along the ground, his face a mask of torment.

Jim drinks in the fear, enjoying the show of his old friend dragging his body away from him, as though there was a possibility of continued threat from this man who had ended his life.

"Where you going, man?" Jim asks, and laughs. "Stop that shit. Just lay down, bro."

Jim steps forward, reaches down and picks up the Glock. He pops open the cartridge and turns it so Liam can see.

Empty.

"I figured you must have miscounted," Jim said. "But I didn't. You fired seventeen shots, Liam. At the dogs? You figured you had one more, huh?"

Liam tries to talk, but crimson blood spills out between his lips and spreads down his chin like a liquid glove.

"Shit man, that looks like it hurts. I'm sorry." Jim kneels, pulls the .38 out of his waistband. "You want me to end it now? Just—" He points the barrel of the gun at Liam's head. "*Pop.*"

Liam's terror shines bright in his eyes. He shakes his head, red spittle decorating his pale cheeks.

Jim stands, taps the gun against his thigh, as if considering. "Yeah, probably for the best. I need my bullets. Just in case, you know? Plus, I'll need at least one for Henry." Jim stretches his back, savoring the torment.

"Yeah, I'll probably do it at the border, dump his body in the dirt for the animals to eat. I actually sorta like the little dude, so I'll do it clean and fast, don't you worry." Jim thrusts the gun in Liam's direction as he says this, emphasizing his promise. "Nice and clean. To be straight, I kind of owe him one. Saved me from a rock in the head once, can you believe that shit? Anyway, I gotta get on with things. I gotta get *paid*, man. So look, you just stay down there and relax. I gotta get that little shithead out of the car before he hurts himself."

Jim turns his back on his old friend and walks back to the door of the shed. Without hesitation or warning, he yanks open the door.

Despite all he's been through—all the weird, impossible shit he's seen over the last few days—he still holds the capacity for surprise.

He's caught completely off guard, for instance, when he spots Henry sitting low in the driver's seat of the Duster, and some old black dude he's never seen in his life sitting right there next to him.

6

Now! Jack yells. *Turn it now, Henry!*

Daylight explodes into the shed as the door opens wide. Blinded, Henry sees Jim as an ethereal figure in the bright white light—

A memory returns to him, something so deep and hidden he didn't even know it was there, stuck in his subconscious like lettuce between teeth:

Shadows chase me as I'm pulled upward, upward . . . fast, flickering lights slow until they become just one—one impossibly bright, white light. The light burns against my closed eyelids . . .

So I open them.

And see a nurse—

Henry! Jack snaps. Coming back to the moment, Henry stomps his foot down on the brake pedal (*the one on the* left) and turns the key. The engine cranks and whines.

Give it a little gas, the other pedal. Just a little, now, Jack says, and Henry complies.

The engine rumbles, then roars to life. Henry is fascinated with the sheer power of the machine as he flexes his right ankle again and again, revving the engine so loud in the enclosure of the shed that it vibrates his vision, shakes the car's windows.

Okay, now press that brake hard and put it in drive like I showed you. Hurry!

Henry crams the toe of his sneaker into the brake again, grabs the thick knob at the end of the gear stick, pulls it toward him and brings it down—*click, click, click*—until it reaches the magic letter, the one that makes everything all right: **D**.

★ ★ ★

As the car rumbles to life, Jim raises the gun, undecided as to who to shoot first. He doesn't know who the asshole with Henry is, but assumes it's a cop who snuck in somehow, waiting for the right time to snatch the kid away.

Jim hates cops.

With a snarl, he slides the .38 Smith & Wesson to the left and fires two shots—*POP POP*—at the man through the windshield.

He doesn't miss.

★ ★ ★

There are two loud blasts, followed immediately by an ear-splitting *crack*. In his peripheral vision Henry sees something punch into the passenger-side cushion. A puff of white stuffing floats through his father, drifts down toward the seat.

"Dad!"

But Jack only shakes his head. *What an asshole. Floor it, son.*

Henry takes a split second to look through the windshield and his eyes meet Jim's—Henry's tight and mean, Jim's wide and filled with confused anger. Henry slips his sneaker off the brake and stomps down so hard on the gas pedal that it hits the floor.

The engine screams in savage joy and the car leaps forward—shooting out of the shed like a bullet from a gun.

★ ★ ★

Jim dives to his right, two seconds too late.

The snarling chrome bumper comes at him faster than he would have expected; the hard metal surrounding the left headlight catches his knee and shin, slamming into him with such force that he does a full horizontal spin in the air before landing in the grass, only inches from Liam's dying, blood-soaked body. Something in his knee snaps and his shinbone cracks as if struck by the full swing of a baseball bat.

"AAARRRGH!" Jim screams, clutching his leg as he rolls onto his back.

The Duster rips through dirt and dead grass, and Jim hears Henry whooping—whether in joy or fear, he doesn't know or care—as the front wheels of the car turn madly to the right and the rear end fishtails to the left, the churning tires throwing dirt ten feet in the air as the treads spin for purchase.

"FUCK!" Jim hollers, his leg badly twisted at the knee, his shin on fire where he fears a bone has broken.

No time to wallow, man! Get that little punk!

Jim raises the gun, does his best to steady his breath, and narrows his eye down the sight as the car swings one way and then the other, moving further and further away from him in the direction of the house, toward the fire road that leads to freedom.

"Uh-uh, little man," he mumbles, waiting for one of the tires to slide back into his crosshair, not chasing the flailing black rubber; patient despite his rage and the incredible pain in his leg.

The car swings hard again, and Jim has time to think: *Someone needs to teach that boy how to steer* as spinning black rubber lines up with the sight at the end of his .38.

He pulls the trigger.

★ ★ ★

Henry flings the wheel left, then hard to the right, the car swaying madly beneath him. He imagines he's trying to stay atop a pissed-off bronco, or a fast-moving shark.

Not so fast, Henry! Jack yells. *Get control, son!*

"I can't!" Henry says, his foot still pressed hard to the pedal, the world outside the windshield flying vistas of blue sky, green trees, and the top edge of the (fast-approaching) farmhouse.

Lift your foot!

This registers in Henry's mind—a command he can understand—and he suddenly realizes the problem. "Oh," he says, and lets up the gas.

A gunshot clap comes from behind them, followed by a nasty-sounding *BOOF*, like a giant belching into a drum. The car lurches and dips and Henry thinks he must have driven into a ditch because the whole world tilts at an angle. But that can't be right, because they're still moving. He loses his grip on the wheel as the car bottoms out, the rear right tire having been blown to shreds. The exposed rim grinds into the earth as the car takes over control of its direction, inertia yanking the wheel away from Henry's small hands.

The farmhouse races at them—too fast to avoid, too late for Henry to steer away, too late to save himself.

Stricken cold with fear, he looks, terrified, toward his father.

Jack looks back at him, a whole man, the shadows chased away by the light. Henry sees the father who left the first time, the father who will leave him again, this time completely, and forever.

I'm sorry, son. I tried, Jack says, the scenery of distant trees and perched clouds shooting past the window behind him. *It's on you, now. I love you, Hen . . .*

The Duster slams into the corner of the farmhouse and Henry is thrown forward, smacking his forehead into the steering wheel and twisting his right wrist awkwardly against the dashboard. His body crumples to the seat as flames bloom from beneath the hood. Oily black smoke fills the air as the engine begins to burn.

Henry's eyes flutter as he fights for consciousness.

"Dad?" he whispers, lifting his dazed eyes to the passenger seat, but there is no one to answer, because no one is there.

Henry is alone.

Jim limps toward the flaming car. The smoke flowing from the car's grill, along with the flickering flames beneath the crumpled hood, makes him slow his pace a bit. He doesn't want to be too close if the thing decides to explode, like they do in the movies.

But then the driver's door pops open and Henry stumbles out, falls to the ground. He looks up at Jim with a hard stare and half runs, half limps around the door, putting the flap of steel between his body and Jim's gun.

"Better get out of there, Henry!" Jim yells. "Unless you want to be blown to hell!" Part of Jim is sincerely hoping this happens, would love nothing more than to see the car explode with the cop inside and Henry crawling right next to it, his body blasted apart. Jim imagines parts of him landing as far as the tree line twenty yards away. He smiles at the image.

But the scheming part of Jim would prefer to keep Henry alive, at least for now. Just until he gets his money and gets to the border. Of course, now he'd have to drive the Pinto, which means finding the damn cables he'd torn out of there. Still, he has time now—yes sir, time is back on Jim's side. He has hours to get Henry locked up somewhere tight, think through things, and get this shitshow back on schedule.

He watches, almost carelessly, as Henry runs, blubbering, up the porch and back into the house, probably waiting to feel a bullet hit him in the back.

Jim doesn't shoot him, but instead keeps limping along, keeping an eye on the open car door for the stranger to appear, just in case Jim's two bullets didn't finish the job. He grunts as he walks, pissed off and in pain, knowing damn well his leg is broken, his knee twisted something awful and probably all torn up inside. Kneecap likely broken as well. But a hospital isn't gonna happen, so he'll just have to deal with it in Mexico.

What a goddamn mess, he thinks, and rage starts percolating inside him once more, and despite the cunning, planning, intelligent side of his brain telling him to *be cool* and *think things through*, the mad bull part of his brain is running a little bit hot at the moment, and it's giving him all kinds of bad advice.

Like maybe he should kill the kid now.

Yeah, that feels right, Jim thinks as he hobbles up to the side of the car, gun drawn.

"You dead in there?" he hollers, then quickly ducks his head to look through the window, expecting to see a man's bloody corpse lying across the seat.

But there's nothing. No one.

Confused, Jim looks in the back seat, then bends down next to the open door, wincing as his leg gives him shit for it.

The front seat is not only empty, there's no sign anyone was ever there. No blood on the upholstery, no corpse. Just two neat black holes where the bullets tore through the seat back, a small piece of flyaway white stuffing where a man should be lying dead. The passenger door is closed—sealed shut against the side of the house—the window rolled up. No way a man escaped without him seeing it. No way.

"I dunno about any of you folks," Jim says, out loud and to no one, "but I feel like I'm in the goddamn Twilight Zone."

He tries to laugh off his discomfort, his perplexity at the vanished man, but he's shaken. Unstable. As if reality has taken a little holiday, and he's just waiting for it to come on back, set things right again. But he's not inclined to dwell on it, and the stab of anxiety shooting up his spine tells him that maybe he doesn't *want* to know what's going on. That perhaps he should just stick to his plan and let all the weird spooky nonsense just float right on by, pass through him like cool mist while he walks straight on toward the light.

"Just keep on walking, that's right," he says, feeling better, making himself forget about the disappearing man, the monsters, the betrayals. "Get the boy," he murmurs. "Get the boy, get the money, get out."

Simple. You just keep it simple, Jim, and things will go right, my brother.

Jim clears away from the car, still pretty damn sure it could explode any moment, and hobbles gamely up the porch and through the open front door, murmuring like a homeless junkie: "Get the boy, get the money, get out . . . Get the boy, get the money, get out . . ."

Once inside, he immediately spots Henry standing at the top of the stairs, hands on the old banister, like he's waiting for daddy to come home from work.

Jim turns and shuts the door, then takes a moment to survey the room—blood, broken glass, broken bodies. Jenny's chewed-up corpse.

What a goddamn mess, he thinks again, disappointed in himself for letting it get so bad. This was not a clean operation. It was unprofessional, and definitely not up to his personal standards. He shakes his head, annoyed, but knows what's done is done, and there's nothing to do now but finish things.

He looks up at Henry, the clenched gun dangling at his side.

"Hey there, Son," he says in a devilish impression of fatherly love, a tight grin stretching across his face, one that shows too many teeth and doesn't touch his eyes. "Daddy's home."

Henry is trembling, and Jim *loves* it.

"How about you come give the old man a hug?"

★ ★ ★

Henry doesn't have much time. He runs through dogs and blood to the foot of the stairs and the two cans of kerosene sitting there. He removes the cap of the one that feels more full, then picks up the sloshy, nasty blue can and begins humping it up the stairs backward, tipping it the whole way, the clear liquid sloshing out onto the wood, which sucks it in greedily.

With the can's bottom edge bashing against his knees every step of the way, he duck-walks to the top, then sets it down gently by the banister. He hears Jim on the porch as he slides the can a little to the side with one foot, hiding it from view. He scans the hallway to his left. The railing runs about ten feet, the walkway overlooking the main room below. Past that is the hallway, then the open door of his room, where Greg's corpse is rotting. If he times it right, he thinks he can make it.

But it'll be close.

He yanks the yellow matchbox Liam gave him from his pocket and cups it in his sweaty palm.

As Jim shoves aside one of the poor dogs so he can close the door, Henry waits patiently, feeling horribly empty inside, as if part of his brain has gone numb.

Since the day he woke in the hospital, he'd constantly sensed the presence inside him—he's talked to it, listened to it, enjoyed its company, held onto it—like a baby's security blanket. But now the blanket has been snatched away, and things are different. The black eye is gone. The sixth sense of seeing people's thoughts, of seeing all the colors of their feelings, that's gone as well. To Henry's eyes, Jim looks *normal*, nothing but flesh and bone. And even though Henry tries—tries *hard*—to see what Jim might be thinking (if he means to kill Henry now or later, for example), he can see nothing at all. He is colorless. Just a physical body shuffling around looking crazy and angry.

Life is questions you don't know the answers to, and figuring things out is what makes us human.

Henry hates the emptiness, the castration of his gift, and hates his father for leaving him again, but he will have to worry about all that later. All of those emotions—the loss, the anger, the confusion—will have to wait. Right now, he has bigger problems.

He'll only have one chance, and he doesn't want to blow it. If it works, Jim will be dead. If it doesn't then, most likely, *he* will be dead.

Any way things go, it all came down to the same point:

One way or the other, it will be over.

The flood of relief at that notion is more than enough to give Henry the courage to do what he needs to do next.

As Jim approaches, looking up at him with a nasty grin, Henry notices the frayed sheet separating the kitchen and the front room turning dark.

Then pushing slowly, silently, aside.

Here comes the Wizard, Henry thinks. *And I think maybe that changes a few things.*

Forcing his eyes to stay focused on Jim—and not on the thing coming through the curtain (*The Great and Powerful Oz!*)—Henry's brain kicks into overdrive to finalize a brand-new plan, one he thinks might just have a higher rate of success.

Of survival.

When Jim asks him for a hug, Henry can't help but smile.

★ ★ ★

The fuck that boy smiling about?

Jim is at the foot of the stairs, and were it not for the reeking smell of dead dogs, he might have noticed—which would have been bad for Henry—the sharp stink of kerosene that covered the rotting wood steps.

Angry at the kid's defiant smirk, Jim points the gun up the stairs, knowing he could blow the boy's brains out at this distance without effort, maybe put one into that potbelly of his, let him bleed out slow.

That idea gets Jim feeling good again.

"I think I'm gonna kill you, Henry," he says, and waits for Henry to bolt down the hall, make a run for his bedroom and the window, crying and hectic, desperate for escape. Given the condition of Jim's broken leg, he might even make it.

"I don't think you should waste your bullets," Henry says calmly.

Jim takes a half step back, but keeps the gun aimed at Henry's guts. "You got huge balls, kid, I'll tell you that. Damn, it's like you woke up or something."

"I think," Henry says, "that Mother is really, *really* angry at you, Jim. You shouldn't have done what you did."

Jim laughs. "Yeah, well, that alien motherfucker shouldn't have eaten Greg, should he? Shit happens, though. You gotta pay the price."

Henry shows his palms. The yellow matchbox lies in his right. A single matchstick in his left.

For all his intelligence, all of his abilities of recognition and assessment, his skills at planning and the ruthlessness with which he carries out those plans, Jim can't for the life of him figure out what the *fuck* Henry's gonna do with a box of matches.

"You want me to come get you, boy? Is that it?" he says, but is suddenly unsure of himself. *I'm missing something—something—*

"No," Henry says, and Jim notices the boy's eyes moving up and over his shoulder, to focus on something *behind* him, before sliding back to Jim.

And there's that damn smile again.

"I think you should just stay down there," Henry continues. "You two have a lot to talk about."

There's a *click-click-click* from behind him and Jim spins, gun already coming around to fire at the hunched creature a few feet away. Mother springs forward in a dark flash and swings a clawed arm at Jim's gun hand.

The gun erupts before it's struck out of Jim's hand along with three of his fingers, torn away at the root by the creature's claw.

As the gun goes off, Henry strikes a match against the side of the yellow box, lets the flame bloom, then gently tosses it onto the steps. There's a WHOOSH as a runner of flame ignites the stairwell from top to bottom. Within seconds, the entire breadth of the stairs is covered in flames, and Henry has to scamper back from the intense heat, his eyebrows singed by the burst of fire.

Henry doesn't run to the room, to the open window that waits for him, that will finally take him away from this place and back to safety. To his life, his aunt and uncle. To his home.

Instead he lingers, moving cautiously away from the belching fire running up the stairs. He steps gingerly along the length of the banister, keeping his eyes cast down toward Mother as she prepares to take another leap at Jim.

After everything he's been through, he has no intention of missing what's coming next.

★ ★ ★

Jim screams and clutches at his destroyed hand. Blood jets out of the ports that recently lodged three thick fingers. He experiences a wave of dizziness and stumbles back a step, but in doing so inadvertently puts weight on his busted leg. The surge of newfound pain runs like an electric shock up his body, spikes his adrenaline.

"BITCH!" he screams, but the black-shelled creature only squats and throws her arms wide, hissing savagely, yellow eyes blazing. Jim looks around for the gun, sees it a few yards away, tucked against the cold flesh of Jenny's corpse.

He also notices two of his three missing fingers lying lazily beside it like dropped sausages. He has no idea where the third went.

Jim moves carefully in the direction of the gun, doing his best to keep most of his weight on the good leg. The heat from the fire the brat started is becoming overwhelming, smoke filling the air inside the large room, replacing the ceiling with a gray cloud. Jim figures the stairs have a few more minutes before they totally collapse and knows there's no way for him to get up there now. He offers a silent prayer the kid doesn't get out in time, that he burns with the fucking house.

The flames reach the ground level and start to spread, catching the fabric leading to the kitchen, crawling along the floor and sparking gleefully at every fur-covered corpse. The smell of burning fur and meat rolls through the air sickeningly, but Jim forces himself to focus, to forget about the stink and the smoke and the boy and the flames. To focus on Mother, who, if he's not careful, might just beat him.

And he can't allow that.

The creature stalks him, not coming too close, but close enough to jump when the moment is right. She has the appearance of a demon—her skin and strange shell coverings all black and yellows, reds and oranges as the fire reflects off her hands and arms, her shiny insect-like face.

I just need to get to the gun, he thinks, sneaking a peek at it.

In that moment Mother jerks her head back, like a guy hocking up a fat loogie, and spits a stream of gray liquid at his face. Remembering in a flash what the spew had done to Greg, Jim collapses backward, his ass hitting the ground so hard his teeth *clack* together painfully. His leg is screaming and his hand is painting the floor with thick red blood, but the acid shit misses him almost completely. A few drops must have spattered one ear, because he can feel it burning, and his hearing grows uncomfortably muffled, the sound of crackling flames and the groans of warping wood taking on an aquarium feel, like the whole ugly scene has just submerged beneath black waves.

Knowing it's now or never, Jim rolls over and lunges for the gun.

The creature sees what he's going for—her eyes flicker to the gun and back to him—and she leaps like a lion.

This time, though, he's ready.

He cocks his good leg back and jacks it into her chest.

To his surprise and delight, he connects perfectly. The creature—no bigger than a teenager, and a skinny one at that—is flung backward into the pool of flame at the bottom of the stairs.

Snarling with glee, Jim twists his body and reaches again for the gun. He grabs it in his good fist and starts to push himself off the floor.

"NOOO!" Henry screams, and Jim is so beyond reason that he turns and fires two shots up toward the boy, now nothing more than a hazy ghost behind a thick veil of blackening smoke. One shot blasts the railing; the other must have narrowly missed, because after a moment Jim sees his head peeking back up again.

Jim scoffs, then turns his attention back to the creature, who is stumbling out of the flames, the shells of her body ignited like tissue paper, boiling like hot molasses. Flames engulf her from head to foot.

He aims carefully this time, wanting to go for the head.

8

Henry watches Jim kick Mother into the flames and is just able to dive to the floor as Jim twists and fires two shots up at him. Splinters of wood spray from the shattered railing, and Henry hears the whine of a bullet pass by his head, but he doesn't think he's hit. Slowly, he raises himself back up, knowing he can't stay here much longer. The smoke and heat are getting to be too much, but he can't leave *her*, not without knowing she's won and Jim is dead.

He watches in horror as Mother staggers out of the flames, her body on fire, and Jim points the big gun right at her.

Not knowing what else to do, how else to help, Henry pulls his T-shirt over his head and wraps the cloth around his hand once, twice, three times. He hobbles to the stairs, to the blue can that has somehow, miraculously, not exploded from the heat being generated a few feet away.

Bathed in sweat and feeling as feral and savage as the dogs who attacked the house only hours before, Henry twists the cap to open the can and carefully grabs the handle with his cloth-covered hand. The heated metal is still painful to hold, even through the shirt—hot as an iron skillet over high flame, he figures—but he doesn't let that stop his momentum.

He is not the boy he was—mercilessly bullied in school, helpless and forlorn and damaged, ravaged as he laid full of tubes in a hospital bed, his uncle telling him that his father was dead, who wished every day to be *normal*, to be *accepted*—but the boy he's become, who can survive the very worst things imaginable, will do anything to defeat the aggressors, will *survive* despite all odds.

That's the child who throws the blue can, and its remaining contents of sloshing kerosene, over the railing and into the fire.

The can lands with a *clang* deep within a thick blanket of flames, ten feet from where Jim lies holding the gun.

Within seconds the heat becomes too much.

The can explodes with a *WHOOF* and a blinding burst of white heat.

Both monsters are blown off their feet as a cloud of roiling flame, thick with sizzling slivers of shredded metal flying fast as bullets, fills the air.

★ ★ ★

Jim is burning.

He can smell the burning hair and boiling skin of his own body as he's blown backward, the gun in his left hand disappearing as he slams into the base of a wall and drops to the floor. Razor-sharp shards of metal punch into his legs and stomach. He roars in agony and white-hot fury.

He forces himself to roll over and get an elbow beneath him, push himself off the ground. Slowly, painfully, he gets to the remaining good knee, then his feet. The room is spinning, his breathing harsh and labored. The air burns his throat, makes him want to retch. Through the miasma of pain, blood loss, and injury, he can just make out the blurred shape of the creature through the smoke and wavy heat.

Like him, she is also getting up for more.

He watches in mystified horror as she tears away what remains of the charred, warped shell casing that covers her arms, legs, and torso, then rips free the smoking hood protecting her head.

What she reveals terrifies and sickens Jim to the core; the strange, glistening black alien body beneath now fully exposed for what it is, what *she* is.

There are two additional limbs folded tightly to her torso, previously hidden beneath the ovular protective casing, tucked away between the ones that served as her legs and arms. These limbs are also clawed with the vicious, hooked nails. Some part of Jim's imagination had expected her body to be insect, jointed like a human-sized ant with a head, but what he sees is far more disturbing.

Her body is thin and angular. Black lumps of flesh sag from her upper torso and Jim realizes he's looking at breasts, the nipples black as charred metal, the skin tough like well-worn leather. Below her pelvis dangles a proboscis, stemming obscenely from a swollen abdomen. When she unfurls her middle arms Jim sees, lit harshly by the bright gold of surrounding flames, that her strange body had been *folded,* collapsed in the middle like a small ladder.

With her yellow eyes staring at him in pure hate, she *stretches* herself upward. There are loud, snapping *clicks,* like a spine being realigned, as her body unfolds and rises higher on her two legs while the other four limbs fan out in a euphoric release, and Jim is reminded of a tattoo of the Indian deity Kali, slick black arms holding a severed head, on the shoulder of his first cellmate, many years ago. He'd mocked it at the time, but deep down it had also made him nervous, and he was relieved when the cell mate was transferred, taking the goddess of death with him.

Like that horrible god, Mother rises before him. But she is no supernatural deity, to Jim's mind. She is something much more terrifying.

She's human, Jim thinks. *That fucking monster is a* human.

Fully upright, Mother stands a head taller than Jim's six foot two. She cocks her head to one side, as if debating what part of him to devour first.

Jim takes a hop-step backward, his leaking hand jammed against his stomach to stanch the flow of blood, his broken leg useless, his body burning with the heat, the slivers of metal, the nearly forgotten wasp stings. Energy drains as quickly as the blood from the jagged flesh of his torn-away fingers. Fatigue has turned him to putty.

I am so very goddamned tired.

Tired of the fucked-up heist, the impossible creatures, the inexplicable kid. Tired of having people turn on him, use him; people with no sense of honor or loyalty.

More than anything, he's tired of being disappointed. Let down by the world, by what it offers a man like him.

A different time, maybe, he thinks, calm at the end. *A different time, different place, I would have been a king. A warrior. But now? In this world, I ain't nothing.*

The creature steps toward him, a demon through the flames, and he laughs at her. "I'm like you!" he roars. Mother hisses at him, arms stretched, stepping closer. "I'm just a fucking bug!"

Mother puts one clawed hand on Jim's chin and squeezes, forcing his head straight. His eyes roll for a split second, then he focuses on her one last time. She lowers her face to his, looks into his eyes.

"Go on," he drawls. "Before I decide to fuck you up, you bug-eyed bit—"

Mother clutches another hand over Jim's mouth. Two more hands clasp the sides of his head. The claws of all four limbs grip his skull tightly. There is a muffled scream as she *squeezes*, snapping the jawbone on one side, the orbital bone on the other. In a last surge of survival instinct, Jim's good hand grabs one of her limbs while the damaged one flails at her face. Blood from the open wound smears her coarse wrinkled skin, but her grip does not loosen.

She emits a rising *wheening* sound, as if gathering her strength. Then, with a quick jerk of her limbs, she snaps his neck.

His head twists with such force that his face is turned to look behind him, bones crunched to fragments. A jagged-edged collarbone punches through the skin of one shoulder.

His chin drops lifelessly to rest on the top of his spine, and Mother releases him, watching carelessly as his body falls in a heap to the smoking floor.

9

Henry pushes himself back against the wall, eyes wide in horror from watching the creature shed its outer shell, reveal the strange body beneath. He feels disgust as it kills Jim with quick, savage brutality.

When she turns her yellow eyes up toward him, two blazing lights amid the dense cloud of smoke and fire, he decides that it's time to move on, to find a way out. He doesn't want to see anything more.

Coughing, he starts to his left, sees nothing but a wall of black smoke flickering with watchful slivers of scarlet flame. Confused, he spins the other way, thinking he must have gotten turned around somehow—

It was clear. Just a second ago it was clear.

He takes a step in the opposite direction when a thunderous crash shakes the room, the floor buckling beneath his feet. The burning stairway collapses. The wood screams and snaps as that side of Henry's world tumbles away amid a roar of shooting flames, the volcanic eruption of a million dancing sparks.

Beginning to panic, Henry doesn't know which way to go. He can no longer see in front of him to even find the railing and he's too afraid to grope for it for fear he'll topple downward to his death.

Cursing himself for waiting too long, he drops to hands and knees. The floor beneath him is hot and growing hotter; orange and yellow eyes stare at him greedily between the cracks. The smoke is thick and low. His eyes burn and every time he inhales it's like swallowing fire. Not knowing what else to do, scared to die, he begins crawling forward in a direction he hopes leads to safety.

Until he can go no more. The way ahead is blocked by flames, the way behind a broiling wall of death.

Smoke fills his lungs, his vision goes dark, and the world is hell.

Leaping towers of flame and scorching heat surround him, ready to pounce, to eat him alive. Hacking and crying, he collapses flat to the floorboards, his bare stomach pressed against burning wood.

He cannot see, cannot breathe, and is unaware when Mother takes three steps through the fire and leaps high into the air, through the mountainous cloud of smoke and over the tall trees of hungry flame, straight toward him.

10

Incredibly, it is Dave who sees the smoke first. The HRT members have all but vanished into the trees ahead, their stealth and dark green camo blending seamlessly into the army of tall firs and branching oak trees that make up the majority of the mixed coniferous forest. Sali watches his feet as they push through coffeeberry shrub and clinging whitethorn, eyes wary for the flat red of poison oak—not that it matters in his cargo-style pants, neatly tucked into tough hiking boots.

Long as he doesn't decide to squat on one, he'll be all right, Dave had been thinking when he just happened to glance up and see an open V of deep blue sky between two green spirals of fir.

It was the moment he saw the long wavy line of gray smoke cutting a vertical fissure through the clean blue, like the trail from the tip of the world's biggest cigarette.

"Sali!" he yells, so loudly that one of the nearby HRT guys snaps his head around to scowl at him.

Dave knows they are close. They've been walking almost an hour through the woods, and were given instruction to be extra quiet for the last quarter-mile, as if stepping too hard on a branch might alert Henry's captors that there is a killing machine moving stealthily toward them.

"Dave, you gotta be—" Sali starts, then sees Dave's stricken face and extended arm, his pointing finger aimed upward.

Sali looks to the sky, the smoke, and presses a black button attached to a thin wire near his throat. All the members of the HRT are equipped with the same earbud speakers and throat mic radios to keep communication silent, and Sali has been given the rare privilege of being distributed the same gear, even though the only person on his channel is Parker, who has open channels to both him and the SWAT leader, as well as the members of his team.

"Parker, you seeing that smoke to the north?" Sali says, and releases the button.

Dave watches Sali's expression closely, as if it might hold clues to how Parker is responding. Sali senses this and looks to Dave, hesitates, then nods. He depresses the button once more to send back a quick "copy that."

"Okay, Dave . . . don't freak out."

Dave's blood turns to ice, but he waits for Sali to continue.

"They have the house in sight, and they're moving into position, creating a perimeter. It's—" Sali hesitates, then continues in an efficient, emotionless tone.

"Dave, it's on fire. The house is burning."

Dave stares hard into Sali's eyes, his own eyes blazing.

"Dave," Sali begins.

Dave distractedly pats the black armored vest strapped to Sali's chest, turns in the direction of the growing pillar of smoke, and without bothering to reply or ask permission takes off at a run.

II

Liam tried twice to pull the axe free from his stomach. Once after he heard the first gunshot from inside the house, and again when he saw the black smoke seeping through siding seams and broken windows. But the pain was too great, and he was too weak. Just gripping the handle had taken more effort than remained in his dying body. Moving it—even a centimeter—shot hot snakes of pain into his stomach, back, chest, and legs. Trying to slide his body toward the house—as if he could somehow push himself twenty yards, up a porch, and through a closed front door with an axe handle jutting from his guts, and somehow be of some *help* to the boy—is laughable. And besides, it isn't happening. He's made it all of three feet and sweat runs off him in rivers, as if his molecules are breaking down into water, preparing his soul to sink through the soil and drip down into hell.

So instead he lies as still as he can, stares at the blue sky, breathes in and out, slow and steady, bleeding into the grass, waiting to die.

When he hears the explosion, it is dampened, but violent. The concussion, more tactile than the sound, is audible. He realizes that at some point he'd blacked out, and when he opens his eyes again it's like looking through a thin veil that someone has laid gently over his face like a death shroud. He turns his head toward the house, wills his vision to clear. The smoke billows up in great gray cotton balls of soot. Flames climb out the windows and up the walls, leak through the shingles of the rooftop.

He focuses on the open, broken-out window of the room that was Henry's prison, sees the fingers of dense smoke curl out from the under the sill and stretch up to the sky, where they dissipate and twist in the soft flows of air, the flexing currents invisible but physical, strong enough to pull the thick, gray billows into transparent ribbons, and carry them away.

As he stares, there's a loud *crack*, like the house itself has split in two.

A long, dark shape leaps through the thickening cloud that curtains Henry's window before landing with an audible thump on the burning roof.

It takes Liam a few muddled moments to decipher what he's looking at.

A skinny but powerful-looking black creature, tall as a man, cradles Henry in its arms—the number of which it appears to have in excess. He counts four wrapped around the boy and two serving as legs, bent as if at the knees, readying for another leap.

Liam is momentarily distracted when the front door of the farmhouse blows open and a belch of flame bursts onto the porch like a bull made of fire, before beginning to chew at the paint and wood of the house's charred face. A jarring motion brings his attention back to the creature, who glides through the air, Henry still in its arms, heading straight toward him.

It lands on three limbs, but Henry, whose lids are half-closed, hardly jostles within its tight grip. Liam notices Henry is bare-chested and covered in soot. His fingers, dangling from between two of the creature's smooth limbs, are badly blistered. He coughs, apparently alive. Liam thinks this creature must be the one they had called Mother, but isn't certain.

It's taller, lankier, and has two more arms than he'd seen previously, even while watching it crawl over the surface of the now-blazing farmhouse. The flexible, rounded shell that had covered parts of its body is gone, revealing a body as disturbing as it is terrifying. Liam feels like he's looking at a seven-foot-tall madwoman with six arms and black skin, strong as a hairless gorilla.

But those eyes are the same, that's for damn sure. Those awful, godless eyes.

Mother sets Henry gently on the ground only inches from Liam. Henry stirs and his eyes open. He coughs again, turns his head, and looks into Liam's drained, blood-spattered face. Henry winces at the sight, which brings a small smile to Liam's pale lips.

"Hey there, kid," he croaks.

Henry turns his attention back to Mother, tries to sit up. She scuttles toward him on all eight limbs, like a spider moving to secure a fly caught in its sticky web, with such speed and aggressiveness that he shrinks back, frightened.

Strange sounds come from her mouth—a keening, desperate whine mixed with a rapid, guttural clicking Liam thinks comes from deep within her throat. One claw rises from the earth and presses against Henry's head, stroking at first, then butting against him, as if she's trying to bring his attention to a matter of great importance.

"Hey!" Liam says too loudly, and feels a tightening in his chest so painful and sudden he wonders if it's his heart finally closing up shop—locking the front door, turning the OPEN sign to CLOSED, and pulling the big blind down over the window. *That's all for today, folks, won't be seeing you tomorrow. Don't come back now, ya hear?*

Mother gives his exclamation only the most cursory attention, then focuses on Henry once again. She's growing agitated, her limbs shuffling in the dirt like an anxious animal wanting to be let out of its pen at the approach of its master, eager to be thrown scrap from a bucket, to be fed the day's meat.

"I think," Henry says shakily, addressing Liam but keeping his eyes on Mother, "she's waiting for me to talk to her. Like I could before."

"So do it," Liam whispers, unsure if the words are loud enough for Henry to hear less than a foot away.

But he does hear, because his eyes flick to Liam's, scared and bottomless. When he whispers a reply, there's fear in his voice. "I can't."

Liam wants to answer, to help, but his throat is tightening something fierce and his lungs feel like they're being squeezed between two arms of a vise slowly cranking shut, inch by inch, on the sides of his chest. Instead, he lets the handle of the worthless gun slip from his fingers and clumsily puts his hand over Henry's, squeezes his fingers as tight as he's able, which, at this point, is a pressure so slight as to be negligible.

"She's getting angry, I think," Henry says, and now he doesn't look scared—he looks terrified, like a lion tamer who's lost control of his lion and isn't sure what to do about it as the agitated, deadly beast stalks around him in the ring. "I can't talk to her anymore, I've lost . . ."

Henry trails off, and now he squeezes Liam's hand, squeezes it hard, but doesn't move otherwise, afraid of upsetting the creature any more than he has.

Meanwhile, Mother's agitated wailing sound grows more vocal—louder, more aggressive. There are elements of a growl in those sounds now, and the clicking is coming so rapidly it's like she's yelling at the boy, an angry housewife dressing down her no-good husband for running around on her.

"I think," Henry continues in that same whispered voice, "that maybe I was like Baby to her. The way we all thought together, the way I was part of them. That's gone now, and I don't think she understands it." Henry turns his wide eyes to meet Liam's once more. "I don't think she *trusts* me anymore."

Liam is about to respond when Mother stops moving and all the sounds coming from her cease, like she's been turned off with a switch. She slowly cocks her head toward the sky, her yellow eyes narrowing. Suspicious. She looks closely at Henry, and Liam sees tears tracing a line through the soot at his temple. *Kid's scared out of his mind, and there's not a damn thing I can do to help him.*

Finally, Mother seems to have made her decision. Her eyes soften and, with one smooth motion, she raises a claw to Henry's face.

"Hey!" Liam says, wanting to scream the word but knowing it's no more than a watery croak. "Get away!"

The creature ignores him, then places the tip of one long, clawed finger to Henry's forehead. It sinks into his skin as if the boy were made of butter, and Henry's eyes roll up into his head.

"God damn it!" Liam says, voice louder now, the phlegmy undertone gone, "I said LEAVE HIM ALONE!" Liam lets go of Henry's hand, grabs the barrel of his Glock, and swings the butt of it at Mother's head. The blow is weak and glancing, but she shifts her eyes to him with such hate that he feels a rush of fear, even in dying. "Well hell," he says. "Come on then."

Mother skitters, all six limbs working, off of Henry and onto Liam, pinning his arms and legs, moving her face to within an inch of his own. She growls at him, eyes blazing, fiery and mean. He recalls the aftermath of Greg's encounter with the gluey acid she must have stored up in that ugly mouth somewhere, and he reacts the only way he's able.

He headbutts her right between her hateful, golden eyes.

The claws pinning his arms lighten, and Liam takes the reprieve to dig deep within himself, to draw from the last resources available. With a grunt he lifts his arms and brings them together, closing them around her middle—which is slippery and deceptively muscular—into a tight bear hug. Her body presses into the head of the axe, and he can feel it gnawing through his insides. Miraculously the pain is distant now, almost numb. Almost.

He turns his head away from her hissing mouth, relieved to see Henry's eyes are open, aware, and watching him.

"Run!"

Then he feels the hard tips of her claws, like a 150-pound cat trapped to his chest when its only desire is to *escape*. The sharp talons dig frantically, ripping and tearing the flesh and meat of his chest, his thighs, his shoulders. Grimacing, he watches with an eerie fascination as his own flesh and blood showers upward in a dark mist, landing in warm spurts on his mouth and eyes, giving his rapidly tunneling vision a deep red hue.

Rose-colored glasses, he thinks stupidly, as Mother's claws dig deeper and deeper into his chest to reach his weakening heart . . . and shred it to pieces.

Liam does not see if Henry ran or stayed put. He hopes he ran. He hopes, unlike his own boy, that he escaped the dark hole between the rocks. The one where the monsters wait to take you away.

As his body shuts down, there's a bright light in his mind, and with a soft jolt he's removed from his body, as if someone's gently shoved him out of his flesh.

The sky is pale, and the trees here are not leafy, but bare, black, and impossibly tall.

A hand reaches for his own, warm fingertips begging to be held.

The small, soft hand nudges his own playfully, waiting.

To welcome him.

To lead him home.

With a rush of love he does not feel he deserves, he takes it.

12

Sali yells for him to stop, but Dave isn't stopping for Sali, for bullets, for fire, or for anything else until he finds Henry and gets him free of whatever danger he's in.

The HRT leader, Parker, rises from a place of concealment at the edge of a shrubby hedgerow, the last fringe of barrier between dense forest and a wide clearing, in the center of which is a crackling, smoking inferno of a two-story house.

"Mr. Thorne, stop!" Parker says, a hand thrust forward, and Dave offers him the respect of a cursory glance as he blows by him, his authoritarian voice, and his gloved outstretched hand.

He halts, however, as he enters the clearing, his mind needing a moment to take in the chaos of the scene—his eyes absorbing too many incredible things at once.

The house to his left has been stabbed at the front southeast corner by a burning car—its driver's door flapped open, engine broiling its own tiny smoke signals to mingle with those of the house. To his right stands a large old shed, squatter and smaller than a farmer's barn.

On the ground in front of it lies a white man with an axe in his stomach.

Before Dave can register anything further, he's tackled from behind and brought hard to the ground, the man on top of him as strong and impenetrable as a slab of concrete.

Parker speaks hurriedly into his ear.

"If you want your son to live, sir, you need to stand down and let my team do their job. You are not helping, sir, you are *hurting*. Your actions could kill your child before I can save him, and potentially jeopardize the safety of my men."

Dave whimpers but, with his left cheek dug into the rough grass, continues to scan—albeit at a slant—the clearing. He sees no one else: no bodies, no kidnappers, no Henry.

"I've got him, I've got him," Sali is saying, and Dave feels the pressure on his spine let up fractionally.

Sali lies down next to him, his eyes also scanning the clearing before turning to Dave. "Damn it, Dave. You're gonna get that boy killed."

Dave goes numb at that, wonders if it's true, if he's done something horrible. "The fire," is all he can manage to say in return. "What if he's in there?"

Sali grimaces, turns his eyes up to Parker. "Let him go."

Parker's weight disappears. Dave and Sali lie there, half-in, half-out of the clearing, obvious to anyone who might have been looking that way. From what possible vantage point, Dave has no idea. Certainly not from the house.

"Dave," Sali begins, and then they both hear a loud *thump*.

Without moving anything more than their heads, both men turn to stare. On the first-story roof, the one that juts out from the eastern side, stands a tall, black . . . *thing*. Dave's mind flips through words and a lifetime of image associations trying like hell to determine what to call it, to *name* it.

It appears part-human, part-insect. Tall and narrow—too many limbs, the body lithe and powerful. But more than anything else: *terrifying*.

Henry lies in its black arms, unmoving.

"Oh dear God," Parker whispers. "Agent Espinoza?" he says, as if this is all a setup, a goofball surprise, a joke, and those nutcrackers at the local San Diego chapter of the FBI are putting a pretty good one over on the HRT.

Sali doesn't have time to answer, because the creature takes three long strides, then leaps off the edge of the rooftop, flies nearly twenty feet through the air and lands with precision right in front of the shed. Right next to the man with an axe in his guts.

They all watch in mute fascination as the creature lays Henry gently down on the ground, hovers over him as if checking for vitals.

Despite the strangeness, Dave notices Henry move, sees him talk to the man lying next to him, and relief floods his heart like the most godly, joyous light he's ever felt. Distantly, he hears Parker talking into his throat mic so quietly that even from two feet away it's almost completely inaudible. Even so, Dave catches a few words, one of which is "steady," and then a couple phrases of great import to Dave's mind: "I have no fucking idea" and "No one fires until I say."

As the men lie there watching, trying to decide what to do, there's a soft *crunch* followed by an eardrum-pounding *WHUMP* as the house caves in on itself, pieces of flaming debris snagging a ride on the east-bearing wind, carrying loose embers of fire through the air toward where Henry lies, toward the horrible creature and the dying man.

Toward the shed.

"Oh shit," Sali says, and when Dave looks at him the agent points toward the roof of the shed which, to Dave's growing dismay, has caught fire.

"What's that thing doing?" Parker asks. They watch as the creature pokes at Henry's forehead. The guy next to Henry, apparently angry, picks up what looks like a gun and swings it at the creature.

"What the hell is happening?" Dave pleads. "What is that thing?"

Parker interjects, sensing a now critical threat. "Agent, I have two guns on that . . . on the target. Say the word, sir, and we take it out."

"No," Dave whispers harshly. "Henry's right there! Right beneath it."

Parker ignores Dave, and simply repeats his intention.

"Just say the word, sir. The target is clear."

"Sali, no, wait," Dave whispers, panicked and frightened. "He's too close."

"Dave, you shouldn't be here," Sali says. "Parker, light that thing up."

"What? NO!" Dave says, his voice strained with desperation, not giving a shit about their cover or the safety of the HRT men. They can't fire bullets at his boy!

Dave's blood pounds in his ears like bass drums. The tension is too much.

Sali's right, I shouldn't have come, I shouldn't be here.

Parker taps his mic. "Mason. You got it? Okay . . . wait . . . Jesus . . . hold that order."

"Henry! Run!" someone yells. Dave thinks it must be the guy with the axe in his guts, because no one else is there. Dave focuses on the scene only twenty yards away and knows why Parker held the order. The creature—whatever it is—has leapt onto the dying man and they appear to be struggling, the creature clawing and tearing at him, the man's arms somehow wrapped around its thin but powerful body.

In pure-white horror Dave sees little Henry stand up. He's crying, shirtless, and running from the struggle, toward the trees.

Toward Dave.

"Fuck you guys," Dave says. As if hearing the crack of a starter pistol, he bolts from his stomach to his feet, shooting forward at a dead sprint, screaming as loud as he can: "Henry! Henry!"

Henry's wide, frightened eyes find his. There's a brief look of confusion, of disbelief, that passes over his features, but it's quickly wiped away by mad, uncontainable *JOY.*

"Dave!" he cries, pumping his arms even harder as they run to meet each other.

Closer . . . closer . . .

Beyond Henry, Dave notices the strange creature rise up on its legs, bloody and—to Dave's mind, anyway—extremely pissed off.

The man on the ground is still.

The creature bends its legs, preparing to make another insane leap toward Henry, and Dave's about to cry a warning when two shots ring out—*CRACK-CRACK*—and the creature is thrown backward as if tugged by an invisible rope, landing hard on the ground in a sloppy heap of black limbs with a terrible, screeching cry, a sound Dave will hear in nightmares for years to come.

Three seconds later, Dave catches Henry in his arms and they collapse into the grass, holding each other tightly, Henry crying and screaming in relief, in happiness, in hysteria.

Dave holds him tight, rocking him, saying the same thing over and over again in a rush of ecstatic relief: "I got you. I got you. I got you. I got you."

13

When Mother touched him, Henry felt the world fall away, felt himself rising up and up through the air at incredible velocity; erratic visions filling his mind with such speed, with such awesome scale and vivid detail, it was as if he were being shown whole worlds.

And maybe he was.

Massive caverns, indescribable, miles beneath the world he knew. Thousands of creatures like Mother, like Baby, and countless variations thereof. Henry didn't know if he was seeing the present, the future, or a distant past. What is a prophecy? A temporary gift of seeing through another's eyes.

Or was it a memory?

When the prick of her finger tapped into his forehead, sinking deep, something inside his mind *unbuckled*, floated loose, then expanded. It was unlike any experience he'd ever had—not at all like the familiar black eye that had shown him thoughts and colors, but something altogether different; more primal, more powerful.

She was showing him more than images, or visions. It was a whole new way of *seeing*. A brand-new sense, an evolution of what humans were capable of. Or, more accurately, what they'd been given.

Mother opened herself to him, rolled the stone away from the mouth of that familiar tunnel so he could step inside and pass through, a hardwired channel to connect them. Possibly forever.

As he soared through the scenes, drifted closer to the swirling colors of the tunnel that was Mother's mind, Henry hesitated. Pulled back. He sensed her agitation at his unwillingness to go further, but he was scared. This was different than what he'd experienced before—more physical, more real. More *powerful*.

Before he could decide whether to go forward or go back, the connection slammed closed, as if a steel door had been dropped over the threshold, the power source abruptly switched *OFF.*

Then he was falling backward and down—through whatever psychic cloud he had risen—back to earth, back to hard, cold reality. To being human.

When he wakes, she is no longer on top of him and Liam is being torn apart, screaming at him to *run!*

So Henry runs—as fast as he can. To his shock, he sees his father, bursting from the trees like an illusion, running toward him with wide arms, frightened eyes.

And then a cloud of smoke passes through Jack Thorne and his father blows away and disappears.

Another man takes his place, running just as fast as his daddy.

"Dave!" Henry cries joyously, and when he leaps, it's this man who catches him in his arms and holds on tight. Who says, over and over, "I got you."

14

"Dave! Stay down! Both of you, stay on the ground!" Sali yells, then spins to Parker. "Kill that fucking thing!"

Parker taps the mic calmly. "Fire when ready."

Two hard coughs pop from nearby cover and the creature is thrown backward to the ground. Sali leaps to his feet as the creature starts crawling, obviously wounded but still moving with decent speed, toward the open doors of the burning shed.

And it *is* burning. The roof has caught fire. Rolling clouds of smoke from the house gust eastward, carrying shards of burning debris to the smaller structure in an angry wind of soot and fire.

Through the heavy veil of smoke, Sali sees both shed doors being pulled closed, retreating black fingers disappearing inside.

He turns once more to Parker. "You have multiple eyes on that shed, yeah? Without risk of crossfire?"

"Yes sir," Parker says with a slight frown at the suggestion that his men, or the SWAT team, would put themselves in such an idiotic position that they could risk shooting one another. But he knows what's coming, and waits for the order.

Sali checks to make sure Dave and Henry haven't moved, lets out a large breath, then nods at Parker.

"Fire at will."

"Hit that shed, boys," Parker says calmly.

Shots slam out from up and down the tree line—a random, cacophonous symphony of bullets and death. Chunks of shed spatter and blow out with each blast as the blazing hut is quickly dotted with fist-sized holes. There's an ear-piercing SCRREEEECH! from inside. Sali keeps an eye on Dave and Henry, makes sure they're not dumb enough to move, then gives his attention to the shed again. He stands, allows about a hundred rounds of ammunition to tear apart the dying structure and whatever it harbors inside, then taps Parker on the shoulder. "Okay."

"Hold fire, hold fire," Parker says, and the guns stop.

Quiet rolls over the clearing like the echo of dying thunder, the ashen wind blowing away the last sounds of the assault.

Sali jogs cautiously toward Dave and Henry, gun up and searching for targets, trained eyes on the lookout for possible spots where bad guys with guns might still be hiding, hoping to put a slug through the FBI stitching of his baseball cap.

He reaches Dave and kneels. He immediately checks him for injury, but he appears unharmed. The small, shirtless boy next to him is red-eyed, ashen, badly burned, and breathing irregularly. There are cuts all over his small body, including a nasty one on his forehead where the strange creature had sliced him. *This poor kid needs a hospital, and he needs it now.*

"So you're Henry," he says, trying to smile at the small boy, keep his adrenaline-fueled voice steady, offer what reassurance he can that he's safe. That it's over.

Henry starts to reply when, less than ten yards away, the right side of the shed collapses, followed immediately by the *WHOOMP-BLAM!* of an air-shattering explosion, the blast blowing flaming chunks of wood fifty feet through the air.

"SHIT!" Sali screams and throws his body over Dave and Henry, crosses his hands over the back of his head.

Huffing, Parker slides to the ground beside him, rifle up and aimed at what's left of the shed. Two other HRT members surround them, on a knee, guns targeting to kill anything and everything that might want to do the FBI agent, or the two civilians, any harm.

"Parker," Sali says, breathing heavily. "We need medical evac. Can your guy land that Huey in here?"

Parker doesn't bother to acknowledge the question but speaks quickly under his breath into the throat mic, eyes never leaving the shed.

"I'm guessing there was another car in there?" Sali says to Henry, who nods in return. Sali smiles. "Let's make that the last surprise of the day, huh?"

Henry smiles weakly, then his lips tremble and curl downward.

He buries his face in Dave's chest and cries.

Five minutes later sirens wail in the distance. Sali wonders absently how the firetrucks are gonna get in here before recognizing that the fire department is more than capable of figuring out how to combat the flames spreading to the trees, and the hundreds of thousands of acres of surrounding forest.

There is the heavy *whoop-whoop-whoop* of a chopper above, the spinning rotors cycling the smoke into gray spirals as it lowers into a safe portion of the clearing, away from the still-burning house and the ashen debris of the blown-out shed. Two medics, red crosses blazoned on their chests, leap from its steel belly before it fully touches down.

The next few minutes are filled with the confusion of people yelling and worrying over the child. Sali steps aside to let the medics do their work but Dave stays close to the boy; although not close enough to interfere, he never lets go of Henry's hand. *Anyone trying to pry that man from the kid is gonna end up on the ground, I think. And that includes me.*

Soon, the Thornes are in the chopper and being lifted up and away. Within fifteen minutes Henry will be getting top-notch care at US-Naval Medical Center, and Dave can call his wife and tell her the good news: Henry is alive. Henry is safe.

HRT continues to sweep the area for living hostiles, primarily focusing on the barn and the thing that harbored inside of it when the shit hit the fan.

In the short time they had together, Sali was able to ask a few more questions of the boy, who assured him that anyone involved with the kidnapping was very much dead. He didn't get into details, he was too tired and hurt for that, but still made it clear that whoever was involved in this barbecue had met violent, horrific ends.

And that included Jim Cady.

Sali understands that he'll find what's left of Cady inside the burning house—once they are able to get to it, that is.

So it will have to wait, and that's okay.

He has time. Now, he has time.

Parker and four other men circle the remains of the shed, keeping a healthy distance from the dying embers but with guns poised and ready to fire if it—whatever the hell *it* was—pops its head out for one last hurrah. Even from a distance, Sali can make out the charred corpse of what he assumes to be the green Pinto wagon the Lanigan siblings had been spotted in while getting gasoline.

The rest of the shed interior, although covered in blackened planks of the collapsed ceiling and walls, appears empty.

At least, nothing is moving.

And that's okay, too.

PART ELEVEN: AFTER

1

For the second time in his young but troubled life, Henry wakes up in a hospital bed. He has an IV tube in his arm, which he hates, but otherwise feels surprisingly good. Even better, he can't help noticing how clean and fresh—if slightly bleachy (but isn't that wonderful?)—both he and his bedding feel and smell.

They must have given me a sponge bath while I was asleep, he thinks, and tests his strength by flexing his fingers and toes. All the digits check out with flying colors, but as he shifts his head on the soft pillow, something feels different. He brings his fingertips to his scalp and realizes his hair is gone. Shaved away. Despite himself, he giggles at this, finding it oddly hilarious.

He figures if he feels good enough to giggle at a bald head, he must not be too badly hurt. *Not like last time, oh please God no, not like that.*

The door to the room opens and Uncle Dave walks in. He looks tired, and skinnier than Henry remembers, but happy. His face is bright and smiling.

Behind him is Aunt Mary, who all but pushes Dave out of the way running to Henry's bed. She cradles his head into her bosom and rocks him. Henry loves it. She smells nice, and she's soft, and her blouse is silky and warm. He's suddenly overwhelmed with exhaustion, wanting to simply fall asleep again, this time in his aunt's strong, loving arms.

"Hi, Mary," he says, his voice muffled by her embrace.

He can hear her crying, her sniffles as she says his name over and over again. "Oh, Henry. My dear Henry. Henry, I love you."

A strong hand takes his own from the opposite side of the bed. Henry pulls away from Mary gently, and she reluctantly lowers his head to the pillow once more.

"No bad news, okay?" Henry says to Dave, who looks down at him with utter serenity, a man at peace after much trial.

"No bad news, son," he says. "You're a little malnourished, some tiny cuts and bruises, some minor burns from the fire. Your shoulder was sprained but the doctor says it's not too bad. They cleaned you up real nice, and when you want it, they'd like you to eat some solid food. Just a little. Right now, they're doing everything with this here," he says, tapping the clear tube of the IV drip.

"I could eat right now," Henry says, and means it. His stomach pinches and gurgles at the thought, and his mouth floods with saliva.

"I'll go find a nurse," Mary says, sniffling. "Get you some food, baby."

Mary hustles away and Dave lets go of Henry's hand, pulls a plastic chair over to the bed, and sits down. "After a while, maybe today or maybe tomorrow, the police want to talk to you. They want to talk about . . . well, they want to talk about a lot of things. Would that be okay? I'll be here the whole time, and so will Sali."

Henry's brow furrows. "Who's Sali?"

Dave's eyebrows go up in surprise, then realization. He laughs and shakes his head. "My gosh, of course you don't know. I guess I'm still a bit tired. He's the man who helped us find you, son. He's with the FBI. He's a good man."

"Oh, cool," Henry says, not sure what else to say, or think. He's becoming more tired by the second, which is frustrating because he only just now woke up, and is excited to eat whatever Mary is able to bring back. But he can't keep his eyes open, so he sinks back into the pillow and lets himself drift.

"You rest, Henry," Dave says, and in his drowsy state, Henry thinks it's his father talking to him from his bedside, and not Uncle Dave. A part of him knows this isn't reality, that his father is gone—gone forever now—but he lets the idea linger another moment, because it feels *good* to think his father is still with him, even if it's nothing but a lie he's telling himself.

Then again, he thinks, before succumbing to unconsciousness, the healing sleep his body desperately needs, *I suppose it doesn't matter if it's Dad or Uncle Dave, because it's somebody, someone that loves me, and that's enough.*

This thought makes Henry smile, and he drifts off without even smelling the plate of chicken and rice that Mary brings in and sets on a nearby table, where it cools.

2

Sali sits at his desk stoically, silent shoes propped up high on one corner, his chair reclined so far back it pushes against the floor-to-ceiling windows of his small office. As he does at the conclusion of any case, he replays the entire thing, beginning to end, in his mind. After he makes his report, his *official* report, he likes to spend a few days thinking about things he could have done differently; done better, perhaps. He also likes to double-check all the conclusions, feel confident in their accuracy.

"We can always do better" is his tagline at the end of every case when debriefing the office bigwigs, sometimes said with earnestness, when a case goes badly, or, when it ends up okay, with a sardonic joviality, a levity that belies the truth behind it. The latter is the tone he uses for the Henry Thorne case. Levity, but with truth as well.

Once the farmhouse fire had been put out and the surrounding forest deemed safe, teams of agents from different branches of the FBI and local law enforcement had gone about the methodical business of sorting out exactly what had happened in the days Henry Thorne was held captive. There were some *nutty* conclusions, that was for sure.

Regardless, bodies were found and identified.

Pete Scalera. Jenny Lanigan. Greg Lanigan. Liam Jones. Jim Cady. All found dead and, with the exception of Jones, burned down to teeth and bone, nothing left to show for their criminal machinations other than loose bones and charred skulls with blackened, forever-grinning teeth. Cause of death had been tricky and hard to pinpoint, given what they had to work with. None of them had been shot, or bludgeoned, or otherwise damaged in a way that would be easily traceable given what remained of their corporeal forms.

All the other skeletal remains found in the burned-up house were identified as animal, and dismissed.

Of course, that was all the sideshow. The real attraction—and what was fueling the gossip in the hallways and break rooms—was what the hell happened to the *creature*.

The debris of the shed had been cleared away, carefully and with many armed weapons at the ready in case whatever had crawled in there—supposedly to die—decided to make a horror movie last-gasp appearance right when they least expected it. When they were damn sure it was dead.

Anyway—*surprise surprise*—no creature. And that made for some interesting discussion. Stories were choreographed with the members of HRT, stories that said nothing of a bizarre seven-foot, uncategorizable creature, which had leapt from the burning house with the Thorne kid in its arms, clawed the body of Liam Jones to ribbons, taken two slugs from a high-powered sniper's rifle, and still scurried (on eight limbs, don't you know!) into a shed to hide and, supposedly, die.

No mention of why they had opened fire with over a hundred rounds on what reports were saying was nothing but an empty, burning shack.

No mention of the hole in the ground, freshly dug and nearly two feet in diameter. The hole that led down, down, down, and then stopped, having curved slightly off toward the forest before it ended abruptly with an impassible clog of hard-packed dirt.

That little factoid stayed out of all the *official* reports, including Sali's. If asked, the HRT guys would say they were laying down suppression fire while the kid beat it to his uncle, making sure the poor asshole with a bellyful of axe didn't suddenly leap up and run after him.

As if.

It was on the advice of counsel that Sali filed his report as-is, without any "ambivalent suggestions" of what he, the HRT and SWAT teams, or Henry Thorne himself might or might not have seen given the chaos of the assault.

So Sali let it go, and frankly? He was okay with that. He wasn't a guy who needed the truth to be told, as long as the people who needed to live lived, and the ones who deserved to die, who deserved justice, got properly served.

Check and check.

No, what bothered Sali, what *gnawed* at the toes of his shiny black shoes, was Henry.

Sali thought for sure the kid would be talking up and down about the strange woman-like, six-limbed monstrosity, offering hysterical detail that would have been easily dismissed as the imagination of a traumatized child.

But he didn't.

When he gave his statement, he made no mention of the humanoid who had, by the look of things as Sali saw them, saved his life.

Instead, Henry had talked through the details of his captivity in a vague, almost bored recounting. He'd been locked in his room most of the time. No, he didn't know how they all died, with the exception of Liam who had been given the axe—*hardy-har-har*—by Cady. A lot of it was *fuzzy*, he'd said.

Sali had been sitting right next to the kid the whole time, and didn't believe him for a second. Still, it made things easier. No testimony to explain away. No contradictions to keep the paperwork piling up. Neat and tidy.

Case closed.

And so Sali sits and thinks over all the things that occurred. Overall, he feels okay with leaving the blind spots where they were. Justice, etc.

There was one problem, of course. The one big detail that would keep him up many nights for the foreseeable future, eventually leading to night-mares, dreams he would wake up from, screaming and sweating:

What had he seen?

A psychiatrist would eventually get involved, and a couple years down the road, Sali would find himself on mental health leave for large chunks of the year, relegated to paperwork and fact-checking, kept out of the field. It would be justified to him as being best for "everyone involved."

And he would talk to his shoes a lot more than he ever had, something he kept to himself, thanks very much. That was a quirk he certainly didn't need mucking up the works in what would become, eventually, a tenuous relationship with his superiors at the Federal Bureau of Investigation.

But those days were further down the road. Far away from the here and now.

What eventually became of Agent Salvador Espinoza at the end of that distant trail is something not worth discussion, and certainly not worth thinking about.

Not right now.

Right now, he's just glad the good guys won.

That Henry is safe.

Case closed.

3

Dave has fallen asleep on the sofa again. Something he'd been doing more and more the last few weeks, since they'd brought Henry home from the hospital, since things had gotten back to normal.

Well, almost normal.

Dave couldn't totally shake the exhaustion of that week that Henry was taken. No matter how much he slept, how many pills he took, how much exercise or big meals or moonlight-lit walks they all took on cool winter nights, he was still *tired*.

Not sleepy, just . . . tired.

His eyes were heavy and his body felt weak. He went to his doctor for a full exam, to be sure nothing was Up, as they say. Make sure, for example, cancer wasn't *Up*, or diabetes wasn't *Up*, or any of those other ailments that plague those who have passed the sign on the highway that reads MIDDLE-AGED. Passed it and gone right on toward the next sign, and the next.

The doctor found nothing wrong. Perfect health. "Give yourself time, David," he'd said. Mary had told him the same, as did his partners at the firm.

Give it time.

Dave agreed that he would. Agreed he would stay home for a while, take care of Mary, enjoy spending time with Henry, back home and safe.

And while giving himself the much-needed time, Dave implemented a few other, minor, changes.

A new security system, for one. Motion detectors outside and inside their home, activated at night, when they were all asleep, and helpless.

He had also purchased a gun, something he never thought he would do. Not in a million years. He'd called Sali about a week after Henry came back, asked if he'd be willing to help him get the right weapon, train him in all the safety basics, teach him how to fire the damn thing if needed, and preferably not at his own toes.

Sali had obliged. No questions, no judgment.

They'd had a beer or two since then, just the two of them. At first, Dave thought they'd be busting to talk to each other about what they'd seen out there in the woods, in the clearing of the old, abandoned house. To his surprise, they talked about everything but. Sports. How Henry was doing. Bullshit.

Dave realized, after their second or third bull session, that neither one of them wanted to give voice to what they'd seen. As if that might make it *real*, and thereby make each of them mad as hatters—an uncomfortable feeling Dave realized would never go away. It was one of those things a man just had to live with.

And that . . . was that.

Now, Dave gets up slowly, picks up the empty bottle of Coors Light from the coffee table, shuts off the static of the television that has run out of stories for the day, of bad news to tell.

He turns off the kitchen light and begins shuffling down the hall toward the bedroom. As he always does, or at least most nights, he pauses next to Henry's closed door. It seems strange to Dave that Henry had asked for his door to be closed at night. He'd always liked it open, liked the glow from the little nightlight in the hall, and after what had happened, after being locked up like that . . .

But if that was what the child wanted, it's what he got. Whatever made him feel safe, and comfortable, was what they did. No questions asked.

As Dave suspected, Henry is talking to himself again. In his sleep, most likely. That hasn't changed, despite everything.

No . . . no, I like them . . . uh-uh . . . I don't want to leave . . . you don't understand, they're not like that . . . you mean Mary?

Dave grabs the knob, hesitates a second, then pushes the door open a crack.

The room is dark but for the usual rectangle of moonlight coming through the lone window at the foot of Henry's bed.

Dave feels a cold breeze and shivers. Goosebumps rise on his bare arms.

The window is open. Wide.

"Henry?" Dave whispers. But Henry is a dark lump beneath the covers, breathing steady, lost in sleep.

Dave walks to the window, puts his hand on the bottom of the frame to pull it shut, and hesitates.

Screen's missing, he thinks, bemused. *I'll have to fix that this weekend. Boy must have—*

"Will you leave it open?"

Dave freezes and turns. Henry is sitting up. A small body in the dark.

"It's cold, son."

"I know," he says. "But I'd prefer it open. I like the fresh air."

Dave says nothing more about it. He leaves the window alone, walks to the bed and sits next to Henry, who lies back down, settling into his pillow. Dave puts a hand on the boy's shoulder, thinking absently that the room smells funny. Like burnt leaves.

Must be coming in from outside, he thinks, and strokes Henry's shoulder and head. His hair is growing back, and he's put on a few pounds. Mary thinks he's even grown an inch, but it might be wishful thinking. Still, the boy looks good. Looks healthy.

"I love you, Henry," Dave says, and he can see in the soft light that Henry is smiling.

"You, too," he says, then yawns.

"You talking to your daddy?"

"No, Dad's gone," Henry says tiredly, drifting. "Uncle Dave?"

"Yeah?"

"Mary's not gonna get sick, right? Like my mom did?"

Dave feels a chill at these words that has nothing to do with the nighttime air coming through the window, and he gives Henry a kiss on the head.

"No, Henry. Me and Mary aren't going anywhere. I promise."

Henry, seemingly satisfied, nods.

Dave asks no more questions, but waits a few moments until Henry is breathing easily and steadily, then gets up and crosses the room. At the door, he gives a last look back toward the child's bed, toward the open window.

A powerful feeling comes over him. One that makes him want to run across the room and slam the window shut. Secure the lock and activate the alarm.

Nerves, he reasons.

Afraid for the boy, afraid something's gonna snatch him in the night. Can't worry like that, got to be reasonable. Let the boy live a normal life now. It's important he feel normal, that things are safe.

Let him forget about monsters for a while.

Ignoring his nervous impulse, Dave shuts the bedroom door and waits a few moments, head cocked, expecting to hear Henry chatting again.

But there's only silence.

Henry waits until he senses Dave is gone, back in his bedroom, lying down next to Mary, wrapped in milky grays, worrying about things like he always does.

He sits back up, looks sleepily toward the dark specter lurking at the foot of his bed. Its eyes glisten in the dark, like stars.

"I know," he says quietly. "Me, too."

Henry can't look at the shadow for too long.

The colors are blinding.

ACKNOWLEDGMENTS

There's a friend of mine who refers to *A Child Alone with Strangers* as my "cursed book." The reasoning being that during the two-to-three years (approx. 2016–19) I was writing and selling the novel you're holding right now, a lot of awful stuff happened in my writing life. Multiple agents came and went, the book itself was hot potato'd to more editors and publishers than I care to remember, and my other books at the time were entangled in all sorts of messy, stressful, publishing upheaval. Rough waters, to say the least.

So, suffice to say that it is with much joy (and relief) that the novel is now safe and sound in your hands; free of the tumultuous, stormy weather of my early career, and *finally* in a state where it can be enjoyed.

The curse, I'm confident, has been lifted.

There are many folks who were part of *Child*'s journey, and if you don't mind, I'd like to quickly thank them for their support, dedication, and expertise.

I would first like to say "thank you" to my early readers (as this was my first genre novel, there were many, and they all gave excellent notes that made the book better): Thomas Joyce, Kelly Young, Alan Baxter, Antoni Centofanti, Eileen Simard, Jordan Smith, and Jake Marley. My apologies if there's anyone I missed (it's been a minute, guys), and please let me know so I can thank you in the next one.

I want to give a special thanks to John Osa for patiently answering all of my (many) questions via email and over the phone regarding police and FBI tactics. John is a retired Special Agent of the FBI who served for more than twenty-five years in the San Antonio, Miami, and Chicago Field Offices, and has overseen a variety of national and international criminal cases. He was also incredibly kind and generous with his time toward an (at the time) unpublished novelist. As with most writers in this situation, I must wholeheartedly caveat this "thank you" by saying any errors, or liberties taken, are entirely on me.

I'd like to give a quick shout-out to Donna Fracassi, for helping me with some of the medical details, and Rod Fracassi, for answering my questions about legal technicalities.

I want to thank Oren Eades, the editor who acquired this book for Skyhorse/Talos Press, and editor Jason Katzman, who was handed the wheel and got us across the finish line.

This novel is special to me for many reasons, one of which being it was the book that landed me my amazing literary agent, Elizabeth Copps. Thank you for believing in this book, and in me. You're the best, E.

Lastly, and most importantly, infinite thanks to my amazing family, who supported me during the most tumultuous professional period of my life, and whose unfailing love and patience lifted any and all curses that may have been lingering. Mom and Dad, love you. Thanks, Dominic, for being an amazing young man, and for listening to all your dad's crazy ideas at the dinner table.

And to my wife, Stephanie, thank you for . . . well, everything, but especially for your infinite patience and love, and for keeping me in one piece. Love you so much.

And to you—yes, *you*, dear reader—thank you for reading. I hope to see you on the next one.

Don't be scared.

PF
Los Angeles, CA
April 2022